PENGUIN BOOKS

BACKWARDS

Rob Grant is the crunchy half of the duo who created *Red Dwarf* and co-authored the bestselling *Infinity Welcomes Careful Drivers* and *Better Than Life*.

Trained at the BBC to write for almost no money, he spent what he can remember of the eighties churning out radio scripts for every living comedian, before discovering the words 'wage packet' in a dictionary and moving into television. There he wrote for various award-winning sketch shows, including a three-year stint as head writer for *Spitting Image*. He is truly repentant for his part in writing the lyrics to the world's worst song ever to reach number one in the UK charts, and asks for two other singles to be taken into consideration.

With the publication of this new book he has achieved the first of his two life-long ambitions: to write the world's first reverse whodunit space opera western dealing definitively with the concept of post-destination. His favourite relish is mango chutney.

D0715986

BACKWARDS

Rob Grant

PENGUIN BOOKS

PENGUIN BOOKS

Published by the Penguin Group
Penguin Books Ltd, 27 Wrights Lane, London w8 5tz, England
Penguin Books USA Inc., 375 Hudson Street, New York, New York 10014, USA
Penguin Books Australia Ltd, Ringwood, Victoria, Australia
Penguin Books Canada Ltd, 10 Alcorn Avenue, Toronto, Ontario, Canada m4v 3b2
Penguin Books (NZ) Ltd, 182–190 Wairau Road, Auckland 10, New Zealand

Penguin Books Ltd, Registered Offices: Harmondsworth, Middlesex, England

First published by Viking 1996
Published in Penguin Books 1996
1 3 5 7 9 10 8 6 4 2

Copyright © Rob Grant, 1996
All rights reserved

The moral right of the author has been asserted

Printed in England by Clays Ltd, St Ives plc

Except in the United States of America, this book is sold subject
to the condition that it shall not, by way of trade or otherwise, be lent,
re-sold, hired out, or otherwise circulated without the publisher's
prior consent in any form of binding or cover other than that in
which it is published and without a similar condition including this
condition being imposed on the subsequent purchaser

To Kath. No Kath, no book.

THANKS TO

My editor, Tony Lacey, for his patience and his inspirational lunches. My agent, Michael Foster, for his encouragement, but not for his lunches. A special thanks to all the Viking/Penguin sales reps, for their ludicrous faith that a book would ever show up. Thanks also to Karim and to Ruth Painter for their Niagara Falls source material. Finally, a big thanks to Annette McIntosh for sorting out my sad arithmetic.

SPECIAL ACKNOWLEDGEMENT

As anyone who knows anything knows, *Red Dwarf* was created in collaboration with my erstwhile partner, Doug Naylor. For the bits of this book that were inspired by the TV shows we wrote together, I am indebted to him.

PROLOGUE

Every Good Boy . . .

Every Good Boy Deserves Favour.

Arnold J. Rimmer, age seven and almost a quarter, is attempting to concentrate on his music notation lesson. For reasons that elude his young mind, it is vitally, *vitally* important for him to master the piano. More important than anything. More important, even, than concealing from his brothers the secret location of his Dead Spiders and Other Wriggly Things collection. Life-or-death important. He must commit to memory the names of the notes on the musical staves, E, G, B, D, F, using the time-honoured mnemonic:

Every Good Boy Deserves Favour.

He's concentrating as hard as he can. His little face is bunched up like a constipated pig at a truffle festival. But he's got a problem, young Arnold has.

And this is the problem: he knows he's going to fail.

He has no ear for music. He has no talent for the piano. But then again, he has no talent for *anything*. The only thing he's good at is letting his parents down. That's easy for Arnold J. Rimmer age seven and almost a quarter. It's a breeze.

Every Good Boy Disappoints Father.

Outside, in the warm, unreal glow of Jupiter magnified

through Io's Plexiglas dome, Arnold's brothers whoop and holler up and down the garden. They're probably not having as much fun as they sound like they're having. They're exaggerating their bellows of enjoyment to taunt him. They know he'd like to be out there with them, even though he'd be teased and tortured. Even though he'd be the butt of their cruel boyish jokes. He'd rather be staked out on the grass and smeared with marmalade to attract poisonous insects than be stuck in the hot, stuffy study, gripping his elementary music notation book with sweaty little hands. So they yell and laugh in a taunting parody of childhood pleasure in the impossibly perfect summer afternoon to tweak his discomfort to the maximum level. And in young Arnold's opinion, it's not even unfair.

They have earned their fun. He has not.

Every Good *Boy Deserves Favour.*

His brothers, you see, *excel* at things. They are all, in their own ways, *excellent* boys. Arnold finds it a hideous struggle just to be a notch below average. But his mother won't give up on him. She still believes he can excel. She's convinced he has this hidden talent for music. It's got to be music, because there's nothing else left for his talent to be hiding behind. But it's so, so deeply hidden, this musical ability, that even Arnold can't find it. His musical talent is in deep cover. And the frustrating thing is: if he can only master the piano, everything will be all right. Would that be too much to ask? If he could just turn out to have the fledgling talent of a Wolfgang Amadeus Mozart, then he could relax a little. Then his parents could have something to be proud about.

And he really needs something good to hang on to right now. Because, although the precise details are not clear to his seven and almost a quarter years old brain, he is keenly aware that something very bad indeed could very possibly be about to happen.

His school report has been a disaster. In a class of thirty-seven pupils, Arnold has been ranked thirty-sixth.

36/37.

It is the worst ever. Hitherto, he's always managed to hover just above shame and ignominy in the very late twenties. But this term they've started remedial teaching for the 'slow' pupils, and young Arnold has been overtaken by the spazzes, durnoids and thickies. Even Thrasher Beswick, who spends fully seven hours of every school day attempting to learn how to masturbate through a hole in his pocket, has exceeded him in scholastic achievement.

Arnold J. Rimmer is now the second worst pupil in his class. He outranks only Dennis Filbert, who smells of bread and margarine, sports a plaster over one lens of his spectacles and has a behavioural problem which results in his turning blue and losing consciousness if anyone tries to speak to him.

Next term, Dennis Filbert will be in a 'Special' school. And Arnold will be bottom of the class. 36/36.

Of course, he has tried to conceal the extent of his failure from his parents, by altering the figures, to make it appear he's come thirty-sixth out of *eighty*-seven. He might have succeeded, too, if he hadn't used yellow crayon.

His father has punished him excessively cruelly. All the horrors Arnold had imagined on that long walk home from school on the last day of term, beyond tears, clutching the damning document with its crude counterfeiting, had not prepared him for his actual punishment.

This was the punishment: nothing.

His father has done *nothing*. Nothing at all. He has read the report over the supper table, and said absolutely doodley-zip. And he has said zippedy-squat since.

Young Arnold has committed an offence *beyond* punishment. Literally unspeakable.

Arnold screws his eyes so tightly together they hurt, and red patterns swirl in the darkness. He wishes there were somewhere he could put the shame. Some way he could put it down for a while, like a huge, over-stuffed suitcase, to stop it hurting.

When he opens his eyes, his mother is standing over him. She is holding a letter. Arnold can see the school crest on the letterhead. Although no one has spoken directly to him about it, he knows what it is. It's about being 'Kept Down'. He has overheard his mother on the phone, arguing with his teachers about it. He has surprised his brothers whispering in huddles about it.

Being 'Kept Down' is something that happens only to the *crème de la crème* of thickies. To the thickest of the thick. The spazziest of the spazzes. It means you stay in Junior C while the rest of the class moves up to Junior B.

And for the rest of your school life, in perpetuity, for ever, you will be one year older than your classmates, who are all aware that you have been Kept Down because you are not just any old durnoid, but you are *the* Durniest of all Durnoids who ever dared to durn.

His mother has pleaded with his teachers to spare him this shame. This letter in his mother's cold hands contains their final decision. And with a prescience surprising in a boy his age, Arnold is aware that its contents will affect his life for ever.

Every Good Boy Deserves Failure . . .

SO FAR . . .

The action of this novel follows on directly from *Better Than Life*.

Following a time-dilation accident, Dave Lister becomes an old man and dies.

His crewmates plant his body on a version of Earth where time is running backwards, and he returns to life.

They arrange to meet him thirty-six years later, by the souvenir shop at Niagara Falls . . .

PART ONE

Reverse Universe

'We cannot choose what we are – yet what are we,
but the sum of our choices?'

ONE

Rimmer tried to smile charmingly, which was always a mistake for him. He had a vulture's smile, perhaps because he practised it so little, and it always provoked the opposite reaction from the one he intended.

'Excuse me, Miss,' he tried to say, but it came out mangled, as if he were sucking in Bulgarian words, rather than enunciating English ones. Kryten had re-programmed his speech units, against Rimmer's better judgement, and he had absolutely no confidence that anyone would understand him ever again.

The girl behind the souvenir-shop counter looked at him curiously and shook her head. 'No, I'm sorry,' she said, 'I haven't seen anyone of that description.'

Rimmer screwed up his features so his face resembled a paper bag full of paper bags. What was this silly girl babbling about? He tried again.

'I'm looking for a short, ugly man, covered in grime with unspeakable personal hygiene and a body-odour problem that could wilt a giant redwood.' He offered a dog-eared photograph of Lister.

The girl glanced down at the snapshot, and then looked up at him and smiled. 'Good morning, sir. How can I help you?' She smiled again, and then focused her attention elsewhere.

Rimmer watched her for a while, his frustration mounting. He tried to attract her attention again with a couple of subtle throat clearings, but the girl was watching the news on her illicit below-counter TV and chose to ignore him.

The news was momentous: suddenly, inexplicably and without any warning whatsoever, all the disparate warring nations of Eastern Europe had put down their weapons and formed a giant conglomerate of a country called 'The Soviet Union'. The people of East Germany (as it was now to be called) were joyously erecting a huge and ugly wall, with stones culled from every corner of Earth, which would keep them in, and keep everyone else out. There was a genuine street-party feel as they went about their business. A secret-police service with almost unlimited powers was being formed to enforce the exciting new system of Communism, which hitherto had only been half-heartedly attempted in China, and to a lesser degree in Cuba. The world was changing, monumentally changing, and this weirdo tourist with a metallic H branded to his forehead was coughing for her attention with all the subtle aplomb of a chain-smoker waking up in the morning, unable to locate his lighter. Well, frankly, he could wait.

Finally, Rimmer gave up. He glanced quickly over his shoulder, took a deep breath and manoeuvered his way through the crowd of milling tourists, trying to look as nonchalant as it's possible to look when you're walking backwards.

He rounded the corner. Thankfully, the corridor was deserted. He turned and walked forwards past the lavatories, and stopped outside an unmarked door.

'It's all right,' he said to the door. 'Coast clear.'

There was the sound of a bolt sliding, and the door cracked open. Kryten looked up and down the corridor conspiratorially, ushered Rimmer quickly into the cleaner's closet, and closed the door. 'Any luck?'

Rimmer shook his head. 'Not a bean.'

Kryten checked his internal chronometer. Half-past nine, almost twenty-five past. In less than half an hour, the Niagara Falls souvenir shops would probably start unopening up to tourists for the morning. He clucked nervously. 'He must be here somewhere. You can't have looked properly.'

Rimmer's nostrils contracted imperiously. 'I did the best I could, given I was walking backwards everywhere, and I don't have eyes in my buttocks. He could be anywhere around here.'

'No, we arranged to meet him at the souvenir shop.'

'Yes, at noon. We're over two hours late.' Rimmer looked away, confused. 'Or two hours early. Whichever. And there's half a dozen souvenir shops scattered all over the place. I vote we all start looking. It's our best shot.'

Kryten squirmed. 'I can't go out there, sir. I'd attract too much attention.'

Rimmer studied the mechanoid's plastic features, and tried to imagine he was looking at them for the first time. It was true Kryten couldn't pass as human before even the skimpiest scrutiny. He looked as if someone had dealt his head seven or eight vicious blows with a butter paddle, leaving flat surfaces and sharp edges where a normal face would curve. 'You'll be fine,' Rimmer lied. 'We'll invent some sort of cover story.'

'Like what?'

'I dunno. We'll say you took your car to the crusher and forgot to get out.'

'Noh gnihog sih hgmess hht towh,' the Cat chipped in, 'eem hlet seelp nowmuss nakh?' He looked from Kryten to Rimmer and back again with a mixture of exasperation and confusion.

Rimmer closed his eyes and muttered a weary imprecation. This was insane. Here he was, a hologram incapable of touching anything, stuck in a cleaning closet beside Niagara Falls on a bizarre manifestation of the planet Earth where time was running in reverse, with the Cat, who could barely understand a word anyone said when they were speaking *forwards* and a mechanical man who looked like Herman

Munster's stunt double. What had he done in previous lives to warrant the karma of belonging to this Dream Team from Hell's own sulphur pit? 'We've *got* to get out of here,' he hissed with considerable passion.

'All right,' Kryten conceded. 'Perhaps we can pick up some kind of disguise for me.'

'Good plan,' Rimmer smiled humourlessly; 'maybe we can squeeze you into a body-length boob tube and tell everyone you're a giant rubber-tipped pencil.'

Kryten whispered the plan to the Cat in forward-speak, which was, of course, now backwards for Rimmer. It gave him a headache just thinking about it.

On a nod from the Cat, Kryten pulled back the bolt, opened the door and peered along the corridor. Satisfied, he signalled for them to exit.

Kryten hunched as close to the wall as possible, with Rimmer on the outside and the Cat to the front. They tried, unconvincingly, to look like a group of casual tourists.

The souvenir stall in the mall was deserted, now. From behind a door at the back of the shop there was a strange suction sound. At first, Kryten assumed it was the shop girl hoovering, until he realized that, given the vagaries of this reverse universe, a vacuum cleaner would make a *blowing* noise as it distributed filth around the floor. He guessed the sound was coffee unpercolating. That was good. The girl would probably be away a few minutes emptying the percolator and spooning the coffee grounds into their container. He peered behind the counter, searching for something he might use as a disguise, while Rimmer and the Cat kept a lookout for Lister.

The only remotely useful thing Kryten found there was the shop assistant's make-up bag. He toyed with the idea of painting himself a fake moustache with her mascara brush, but realized, after a few seconds of contemplation, that the laws of this reality would not permit him to adopt even this meagre and, let's face it, useless disguise. Given that Time was now committed to flowing upstream, the purpose of the mascara brush would be to *remove* make-up, not apply it. He rubbed his temples with his cubed fingertips. This whole expedition was turning out to be more difficult than he'd imagined.

Then something very bad caught his attention.

On a shelf below the counter, a miniature TV was blaring its backward babble through a dangling earpiece. A quiz show where contestants competed to give money to the host was interrupted by a news flash. Behind the newsreader there was a police photofit of the Cat.

He looked up, alarmed. The Cat was standing by the souvenir-shop window, staring out at the thinning crowd. Kryten glanced back down at the screen. To his horror, the Cat's image was replaced by a still of Lister. He strained to hear what the newscaster was saying, but only managed to make out a single word. The news flash disappeared, and the quiz show returned.

The word Kryten had been able to make out was 'murder'.

TWO

The back of the police van stank of vomit and stale urine, which would no doubt be inserted into various drunks and druggies once the morning drew to a close and the graveyard shift began.

Lister shifted uncomfortably on the hard bench. The handcuffs were pinching his wrists wickedly as he fiddled with his groin, where the pain was beginning to crescendo, and his left ear was starting to throb redly. There were two policemen opposite him and one either side, all of them glowering at him relentlessly.

Despite all this, Lister was feeling pretty damn good. The last eight years or so had been fairly hellish, and at last his ordeal was almost over.

Without warning, the policeman on his left slammed the palm of his hand against the side of Lister's head, which stopped the throbbing and returned his hearing to normal. Better and better.

Lister spotted some freshly chewed gum on the floor of the van. He stomped his foot on to it, deftly flicked it up into his mouth, and began chewing the wad contentedly, each movement of his jaw infusing the gum with more and more spearmint flavour.

He heard a distant rumble and glanced through the dark reinforced glass of the van's rear window. He could see the mist from the falls as the vast volumes of white water cascaded up the mountainside.

Almost home. He leaned his head back against the side of the van. With good luck and a following wind, he was less than twenty-four hours away from his first truly satisfying bowel movement in the best part of half a century. He sighed happily. Did anyone, anywhere, enjoy a more sumptuous prospect?

The Cat was beginning to feel extremely queasy. He was watching a fat man pick bits of pale fish flesh out of his mouth with a fork, which he was then sculpting neatly around a kipper skeleton on his plate. The Cat glanced over the table at Rimmer and Kryten to share his disgust with them, but they were both intent on their gobbledy-gook conversation. He looked around the cafeteria for a less distressing view, and settled on a young woman across the room who was slowly ejecting a long bacon roll from between her lips, which he managed to find mildly erotic.

Rimmer was holding his palm to his forehead, to conceal his hologramatic H, his elbow resting on the table. They'd selected the gloomiest corner table in the room, but Rimmer still felt self-conscious and exposed. 'That's all you heard? "Murder"? Not who murdered who, or how, or where?'

Kryten shook his head. 'I'm afraid not, sir.'

'But the Cat's definitely involved?'

'I think we must assume so. His likeness appeared alongside Mr Lister's in the bulletin.'

Rimmer looked over at the Cat, who for some reason was licking his lips lustily, his attention, which was undeniably the least of his attributes, focused elsewhere. 'We've got to find out more. Can we get hold of a newspaper?'

'With respect, I don't think that would do any good. Whatever it is that happened is going to happen fairly soon. The newspapers that reported it will have already been wiped at the presses this afternoon.'

Rimmer's forehead squirmed as he bent his mind to the

concept. 'Yes,' he agreed eventually. 'Yes. That sounds about right,' In this place, people would take their papers to news-agents, or leave them out on the steps for paperboys, who would then send them back to the publishers. Then the printers would wipe the paper clean and hundreds of journalists would obliterate the news stories from their computers. The fresh paper would get taken away and turned into rain forests. Rimmer shook his head in amazement. That would make the tabloid press barons here philanthropists and heroes; their lives dedicated to the destruction of mealy-mouthed scandal-mongering and mild pornography, and the re-foliation of the planet. Whereas someone like, say, St Francis of Assisi would be hated and reviled. In this universe, he'd be a petty-minded little sadist who went around maiming small animals.

A waiter came up to their table and set down a dirty cup, a quarter filled with cold stale coffee. 'Just doing my job, friend,' he lisped indignantly, then he took out a grimy damp cloth and used it to spread tiny bits of food debris and cigarette ash all over the table's surface.

'Oi!' Rimmer protested. 'What the smeg are you doing?'

The waiter smiled, said 'Good morning', brightly, and minced off backwards.

'Reakh voh tao tegh oot *togh* viefh,' the Cat said. 'Ghnits-suhsidt oot hsi hsaylp ssith.'

'What is he blabbering about?'

'"This place is too disgusting,"' Kryten translated. '"We've got to get out of here."'

'Seconded, thirded and motion carried,' Rimmer stood. 'If we go now, we can make it back to the *Bug* before morning fall, or whatever the hell it is that happens here.'

'We can't go without Mr Lister!'

'Why not? We kept our appointment in good faith. If he can't be bothered . . .'

'You don't understand, sir. This place is lethal to him. If we leave him here, he's going to carry on getting younger.

His body will start to shrink. In a few years, he'll have to go through puberty again – backwards. Can you imagine that? His pubic hairs will retract into his body. His gonads will suddenly rise, and he'll find himself in the soprano section of the school choir. He'll carry on growing smaller and stupider, until some obstetrician finally forces his little fat blue screaming body into his mother's womb, where he'll spend nine months struggling to split himself into a spermatozoa and an ovum, and he'll end his days swimming around as a sperm in someone's testicular sac.'

Rimmer was surprised to find himself snarling in distaste. 'Well, I agree, it's not a very pleasant way to go, but he's brought it on himself. He was supposed to be here.'

'He'll come.'

'And if he doesn't? What about us? What about the Cat? For all we know, he's about to get murdered.'

Kryten shook his head. 'I think not. Logic dictates that if someone was going to kill him here, he'd have arrived dead.'

Again, Rimmer was stopped in his tracks while he mulled over the topsy-turvy logic of this exasperating universe. 'All right. Fine.' He looked at the cafeteria clock. 'It's quarter past nine. We'll give him till eight-thirty.'

'Agreed.' Kryten stood. At that time, the falls' souvenir shops would no longer be open in any case, and they would have to devise a new stratagem. It had taken them just over five hours to hike down from the spot where they had concealed the rebuilt *Starbug*. It would take even longer to get back, travelling uphill. They had until midnight to effect their take-off. After that, the conjunction of the planets would render their journey out of this solar system impossible for some considerable time. If they missed their flight window, they would all be marooned here, which didn't bear thinking about.

So long as they found Lister inside the next three hours, they would be safe. That would be time enough, Kryten decided. 'Suggest we head back to the mall area.' He translated for the Cat, and the three of them trooped out backwards.

As they passed the coat stand by the exit, Kryten discreetly borrowed a yellow cagoule. Backing out into the corridor, he slipped it over his head and tugged the strings of the hood tight around his face. His guilt circuits almost went into meltdown in response to committing the theft, but he managed to override the intense pain by concentrating on his primary directive, which was to ensure Lister's safety.

There was a further problem, which Kryten couldn't bring himself to confess to Rimmer. He was carrying the portable power pack that generated Rimmer's hologramatic image. Unfortunately, he'd neglected to foresee that, in the physics of the reverse universe, the batteries would *be re*charging, not *dis*charging. In slightly less than an hour, they would overload, and while Kryten couldn't exactly predict the consequences, he concluded that whatever did happen wouldn't be entirely beneficial to Rimmer's well-being.

THREE

There was clearly something about to be seriously amiss in the mall outside the souvenir shop.

The shop itself was closed and shuttered now. Outside it, small bands of early-morning sightseers were all starting off in the same direction, towards the car park entrance, mostly in animated conversation. A couple of security guards were busily distributing litter liberally around the floor and upsetting bins, presumably in preparation for some fracas which was about to ensue.

The Cat, Kryten and Rimmer retreated round a corner to watch from a safe distance. As the seconds ticked by, the hubbub from the thronging tourists grew in volume, until they were all jabbering and gesticulating excitedly.

Suddenly, the double glass doors burst open and Lister came in.

He was facing forwards, away from the doors, his feet out in front of him, heels dragging the floor. He looked dazed, barely conscious. He was being propelled along by two uniformed policemen facing the opposite direction, their arms linking his. A phalanx of half a dozen further police officers brought up the rear.

The two policemen holding Lister stopped, twisting him over and laid him roughly on the floor. The rest of the men spread out and surrounded him. Lister started moaning and writhing, clutching his crotch.

One of the officers, who was sporting an incipient black

eye went up to him, and suddenly Lister screamed. Kryten's view was partially obscured by the officer's back, but from the movement of his shoulders and leg, it was fairly obvious that he was delivering a savage kick to Lister's groin area.

The Cat and Rimmer winced with the brutal sound of the impact.

Lister seemed to recover instantly. He leapt to his feet acrobatically and nutted a truncheon one of the policemen had swung at him. He danced towards the groin-kicker and delivered a neat jab to his face. The officer staggered back, the bruising around his eye gone.

Two policemen, the truncheon-swinger and the groin-kicker, began circling Lister menacingly. The rest of them began to leave, taking off backwards at alarming speed. A couple of them disappeared down corridors, barking into walkie-talkies. The other four dashed out backwards through the car-park doors and climbed into the van which screeched off, its siren blaring.

Lister maintained a boxing stance as the two remaining cops tried to outflank him. Words were exchanged, but Kryten was too far away to make out what was being said. It sounded as if the policemen were trying to calm Lister down, to which he was responding with taunts and abuse.

Then, as abruptly as it began, it was over. The two policemen suddenly began panting and backed off, slowly at first and menacingly, and then they picked up pace. They skidded past the bins the security guards had toppled, knocking them upright. The litter leapt back spectacularly into the baskets. Then the cops ran backwards down opposite corridors, with the groin-kicker shouting into the collar microphone of his police radio, and they were gone.

For a moment, Lister stood there, breathless, and then wheeled round, performed a reverse skid worthy of Fred Astaire and charged off backwards in pursuit of the groin-kicking cop.

Then the early-morning tourists turned away and went

about their business, and the plaza was calm and peaceful, as if nothing at all had happened.

'Well,' Rimmer said, 'that's our Listy all right. Discreet, isn't he? The last thirty-odd years seem to have mellowed him out completely.'

Kryten chewed the plastic of his lower lip. 'The question is, how do we go about catching up with him?'

'We don't,' Rimmer trilled without hesitating. 'He's got an entire SWAT team on his back. We're out of here, matey.'

'No. Think about it. There's only one policeman chasing him now, or rather: he's running after just one policeman. My guess is, he's leading that policeman towards where we're going to be, in order to divert him away from us, as it were. If that's going to be the case, our problem is getting to the place where the policeman would be going to spot us if Mr Lister doesn't draw his attention. Does that make sense to you?'

'Not even slightly.'

'I believe the corridor he ran down leads to the walkway. We need to find another way to get there.' Kryten nodded across the mall. 'If I'm correct, that door leads on to some kind of maintenance passage, by which we can achieve the same destination.'

Before Rimmer could protest, Kryten and the Cat started reversing across the mall. Rimmer sighed heftily through his nose, turned around and backed out after them.

The access door was unlocked. Rimmer and the Cat slipped through it quickly, and then Kryten backed inside, glanced around briefly to check that no one had spotted them and closed the door behind them.

The passage was damp and gloomy, but Rimmer found his eyes adjusted to the dark immediately. He looked around. The Cat was beside him, but Kryten was hesitating around the door. Rimmer hissed 'Come on.'

'A moment, sir.' Kryten scoured the floor. 'Ah, yes,' he said, and stooped to pick up a broken padlock.

Rimmer hissed again. 'What are you doing?'

'I thought it unlikely this door would not be locked.' Kryten slipped the padlock through the metal loop on the door and squeezed it. The snapped edges of the padlock fused together. 'There,' he said, and then turned to the passage and they headed off past the sweating walls and pulsing generators towards the falls' growling roar.

As they got deeper into the passage, the falls' rumble intensified to deafening proportions. Worse, Rimmer was horrified to discover he was finding it more and more difficult to see. After a few minutes, he was almost blind. 'What the smeg is happening?' he screamed against the liquid thunder.

'Don't panic, sirs, almost there,' Kryten chirped. He grabbed hold of the rails of a metal access ladder and climbed up to the hatch which led to the walkway.

Gingerly, he prodded the hatch open a crack and looked out.

It was now just before nine o'clock, and the walkway was deserted.

As Kryten watched, a policeman came running backwards towards him. As he swept past the hatch, Kryten recognized him as the groin-kicker from the mall. Then Lister came into view, chasing the policeman backwards. The cop stopped at the far end of the walkway, yelled into his lapel microphone and stood for a moment looking at Lister.

Lister skidded to a stop by the access hatch, and did a double-take at the policeman, who performed his own double-take and then disappeared around the bend, and, for the first time, Lister directed his attention towards the hatch.

His eyes locked with Kryten's and he beamed a grin of such intensity, the mechanoid thought his circuits might melt in the glow of it. 'All right,' he said backwards in his familiar Scouse twang, 'you can come out now.'

Kryten flopped open the hatch and clambered out.

'Oh, sir,' Kryten crooned, 'I can't tell you how delightful it is . . .'

'Save it,' Lister cut in abruptly. 'There'll be plenty of time for that earlier. That cop's still going to be chasing us for a while, yet.'

'Kgnikgnah tsi zwaoh,' the Cat grinned, climbing through the hatchway, 'yeddubh, iyeh?'

Lister turned to Kryten. 'What's he say?'

'I believe he said: "Hey, buddy, how's it hanging?"' Kryten offered.

'Smeg. Are you telling me he can't understand backtalk? Great. Outstanding. That's going to be a big help.'

'I can translate for him, sir.'

Lister shook his head. 'No good. We're going to be split up pretty soon.'

Rimmer's head appeared through the hatchway. 'Split up? We've only just found you!'

Lister's grin broadened. 'Rimmer! I never thought I'd be able to say "I'm glad to see you,"' he said. 'And I'm still right.'

Rimmer batted away the insult with a look of superior disdain. 'What's all this talk about splitting up?' He climbed on to the walkway.

'I'll explain on the way.' Lister glanced at his watch. 'We'd better get moving,' he said, and broke into a brisk backwards trot in the direction the cop had gone.

Kryten, Rimmer and the Cat looked at one another, performed a simultaneous shrug and trotted backwards after him.

Kryten upped his pace and drew level with Lister. 'Begging your pardon, sir, but are you absolutely convinced of the need for us to divide our resources?'

'We've got no choice, Kryten, mate. It's me and the Cat the feds are looking for. No one ever mentions spotting you or Rimmer. It's not a question of what we decide to do: somewhere along the way, we get separated.'

Rimmer jogged up beside them. 'Excuse me,' he panted, 'but can someone please explain the plan to me, here? As far as I can make out, we appear to be in pursuit of an extremely brutal policeman with a penchant for drop-kicking people's gonads.'

'Actually, Rimmer, *he's* chasing *us*.'

'Well, call me a sow sucker and spin me on a stick, but wouldn't it be infinitely more prudent for us to take off in the opposite direction?'

Lister shook his head. 'That's not how things work here. I know it's hard to wrap your head around it, but things don't happen here, they *un*happen, because, basically, they've already happened, and there's not a blind thing you can do to change them. It's like trying to change the past in our own universe.'

They ran on for some considerable time until the constant background rumble of the falls was just a distant roar. Suddenly, for no good reason anyone could see, Lister leapt over a roadside barrier on to a dangerously wet, narrow ridge of rock which swept up to a narrow mountain track. As they jogged up on to the track, they rounded a bend, and snaking track was clearly visible for a mile or so. The policeman was not on it.

Lister stopped running and rested against a tree trunk, breathless. The Cat, whose expression clearly portrayed complete bewilderment at the proceedings, caught up with them. 'Hnoh kghnihogh sti hcleh ethk twawh?' he whined, his baffled eyes darting from Lister to Kryten and back again.

'What did he say?' Lister asked.

Rimmer waved his hand. 'I think we can assume it doesn't contribute significantly to the discussion,' he guessed, correctly. 'What I want to know is, if you're right, if the future, which is the past, has already happened, and we are nothing more than bits of flotsam swept along by Time's stream, the big question is: just what, precisely, is it that's going to unhappen to us?'

Lister shook his head again. 'I'm not sure, exactly. The people here, the natives of this universe, they have a sort of backwards memory. They only remember the future. As soon as you get introduced to someone, they instantly forget you. I don't know why, but it doesn't work like that for me. Maybe it's because I don't really belong here.'

Lister paused and looked away across the valley to the distant peaks. *Don't really belong here.* There was no way of conveying the wretchedness, the fundamental loneliness those few small words contained. He'd spent the best part of a lifetime as a stranger in a very strange land. For most of that time, more than a quarter of a century, he'd had Krissie, at least, to keep him company, but she'd been like the rest of them: remembering only the future. Somehow, his wife had belonged to this place, in a way he never could.

'You must have some idea where all this is leading,' Rimmer insisted. 'I mean, you're the one who's leading this merry jig.'

Lister sighed. 'All I know is we have to keep on following that cop until he stops chasing us.'

Rimmer scanned the deserted track before them. 'And where is he, then?'

'Only one place he *can* be.' Lister leaned over the edge of the mountain. Sure enough, the policeman was gingerly picking his way down towards the valley below. Lister leaned back. He was becoming increasingly breathless. 'Well, now we know where we're going.'

'Over the side?' Rimmer squeaked. 'You can't be serious.' He peeked over. 'It's about a mile straight down.'

'It's completely safe, Rimmer,' Lister panted. 'We can't possibly get hurt. We're not actually climbing down, we're unclimbing up, and we've already arrived safely, see? Come on,' and he turned to lower himself over the side.

Rimmer folded his arms. 'Not in a month of Plutonian Sundays.'

'Sir,' Kryten implored, 'we have to go after him.'

'Believe me, I'd love to join this little expedition, only I suffer from a terrible mental affliction known as "sanity".'

Lister glanced over his shoulder. Directly beneath them, a dirt road cut a thin grey trail across the rocky valley floor. There was a battered, old pick-up truck parked there, its doors akimbo. Behind that, a police car was skewed across the trail. He stepped back on to the mountain track. 'Maybe you're right. Maybe this is where we should split up. Kryten, you and Rimmer carry on up the track. See over there?' He nodded across the valley. 'Where the valley road heads down from the mountain?'

Kryten nodded.

'I'll pick you up there. How quickly can you make it?'

Kryten tilted his head and made some swift calculations. 'Personally, in double-time jog mode, I could make it in twenty-two minutes and nine seconds. But Mr Rimmer . . .'

'Carry him,' Lister said.

'Beg pardon, sir?'

'Switch off his light bee and pop him in your pocket.'

'Now, just a minute,' Rimmer stepped forward.

Lister's breathing was getting more laboured, and now the Cat was panting heavily, too. 'No time . . .' Lister gasped, '. . . to argue. Just do it.'

Kryten flipped a switch marked 'standby' on the remote pack, freezing Rimmer in mid-protest. His image wavered and then flicked off, and his light bee plopped neatly into Kryten's outstretched palm.

Kryten dropped the tiny gizmo into the pocket of his cagoule. 'It's probably for the best. His batteries need conserving.'

Lister nodded, his voice now little more than a rasping whisper. 'Find some sort of cover . . . some bushes, what-ever . . . and hide till we get there.' He swallowed and looked down the mountain. The policeman was about halfway up. 'I'll go first . . . tell . . .' Lister turned around, formed his lips into a circle and sucked, noisily. A great wad of sputum suddenly leapt off one of the rocks by his feet and shot neatly into his mouth. '. . . tell the Cat to wait until the police car's gone before he sets off.'

'Understood.'

Lister backed to the edge of the mountain again. His heart was thumping so madly in his chest, he felt like it was going to burst through his shirt and race off down the track, jibbering insanely. He wiped the thin skein of sweat from his forehead and held out his hand. Kryten hesitated for a second, then stepped up and grabbed it. He gently lowered Lister over the side.

It was slower going than Lister had imagined, but his fingertips hurt less with every foot of progress, and his heart rate began to subside. After the first fifty yards or so, he spared a look down. The cop was alarmingly close. For some reason, he seemed to be gaining on Lister.

How could that be happening?

He looked back up again and tried to concentrate on the descent, but his heart started thumping again, and the blood began to roar in his ears. He clambered down another few feet, but he was hit by an inexplicable dizziness. He was hyperventilating again. He was afraid he was going to lose consciousness.

There was a sturdy branch jutting out at about shoulder height, and he grabbed it. He dangled his right leg down but couldn't find a foothold. He scrabbled around with the leg, trying to find some purchase. Then slowly, exasperatingly, his left leg started skidding down the rock face. He tried to lift it back up, but it wouldn't go.

Suddenly, he was dangling from the branch. There was nothing between him and the ground but clean Canadian air. He fought the throbbing in his head, and forced himself to look down. The cop seemed even closer now. He looked up at Lister, grinning.

A cloud of dust and small rocks rose up in between them

and started tumbling up the mountainside towards Lister. The branch he was hanging from bent ominously.

Then Lister was holding on to nothing at all.

FOUR

He was travelling in a cloud of choking dust. Rocks and pebbles were bouncing off him like he was being pelted by an angry crowd.

He was falling up the mountain.

Panic yabbering at his brain, he clawed desperately at the rock face, instinctively grabbing for some kind of handhold. His fingernails scrawped at dust and dirt. His legs kicked wildly at the unyielding rock like a child in the throes of a tantrum. The choking dirt cloud whirled around him and he was nothing more than the blind eye of a dust devil spinning up the mountain.

And time was certainly passing. It just didn't feel like it to Lister.

And then, miraculously, a medium-sized rock tumbled into his hand and he managed, somehow, to jam it into the mountainside, arresting his sudden ascent. He jabbed his foot into a cleft in the rock, and suddenly it was all over.

His heart was thumping normally, his breathing was close to normal and the thudding pulse had gone from his ears. He looked down. The cop was much further away, now.

Without feeling the need to catch his breath, Lister set off again down the mountain.

The Cat was leaning over the side, peering down at the bizarre spectacle. He was having second thoughts about following Lister down the mountain, that was for sure. He glanced off up the mountain track, but Kryten was almost out of sight by now, jogging backwards at what looked like an impossible pace. The Cat prided himself on being fairly fleet-footed, but he couldn't have caught up with the yellow-cagouled robot even at maximum pace.

He stood up and stretched, and then stiffened. He had a strange feeling in his stomach. It wasn't a pain, exactly, more like a queasy sort of void. He looked over the track and decided he'd better head behind the bushes. Maybe a quick toilet stop would help him feel more like mountaineering.

He'd just got comfortable, when something unspeakable happened. There was a strange rustling in the ground he was crouching over. His eyes widened to maximum as some slimy warm *thing* began to force his buttocks slowly apart . . .

Lister heard his scream halfway down the mountain. He looked up, and then down at the cop, who seemed oblivious.

The cop was almost at the bottom now, just scrabbling down the last few yards of loose rock at the foot of the mountain. When he hit the ground, he stopped, looked up at Lister, and then ran backwards to the police car. He picked up the radio that was dangling from the door and shouted into it. Then he climbed into the car, started up the siren and screeched off along the narrow dirt track.

Lister kept on down the mountain until the police car had reversed up the valley track and swept out of sight. He looked up. The Cat was peeking over the ridge at the top. Lister signalled for him to come down, and the Cat turned around and started lowering his lithe body down the mountainside with astonishing nimbleness.

Lister sighed. So far, he'd got it right. Fairly soon, he'd find out the answer to a lot of the questions that had been plaguing him for so long.

The most important of those questions was whether or not he'd actually committed the crime that had put him in prison for the last eight years.

FIVE

Kryten felt more than a little stupid jogging backwards up the mountain trail. He could probably have made better time jogging forwards, but he would have felt self-conscious flouting the conventions of the world, and was unwilling to risk drawing attention to himself unnecessarily. Not that a mechanical man thundering along a dirt track at forty-two miles an hour in a bright yellow plastic anorak could be squeezed into the category of commonplace sights, but Kryten was determined not to miss his rendezvous with Lister, so setting a more discreet speed, or adopting a route which afforded more cover, was out of the question.

'*When in Emor*,' Kryten thought, '*do as the Snamor.*'

Despite his forced haste, Kryten found he was sufficiently relaxed to enjoy something of the spectacular scenery. This was the first time he had ever actually visited Earth. Even the most sophisticated multimedia travel guide was hopelessly inadequate at conveying the impression of truly *being* there. The colours, the smells were so much more sumptuous and intense. The early morning sun was beginning to glow a reddy orange as it sank low in the east, and Kryten was astonished to see the moon was still clearly visible in the cloudless sky.

He'd always considered that possessing a mere single moon somehow made the Earth the poor relation of the solar system. But seeing it firsthand convinced him otherwise. A solitary moon was pleasing, aesthetically. Nicely understated, not too showy.

He jogged round a bend and stopped to take his bearings. This was roughly the place designated for the rendezvous. He looked around and spotted the dirt road that led down into the valley. Fresh, deep tyre marks were cut into the road beside a shallow ditch which was thickly strewn with loose foliage.

With a start, Kryten registered a police siren poohw-poohwing towards him. He dived into the ditch and tugged the ferns and branches around him, just as the police car leapt over the brow and reversed past him, sucking with it thick plumes of dust.

Kryten lay there until the siren faded and the engine sounds had died away. Then he lay there a little longer. Then he began to wonder what in heaven's name he was lying there for. The police car was out of sight, and since he hadn't seen anyone on his jog up the footpath, it followed that no one was going to spot him and give chase. He rolled out of the ditch and crept to the brow of the mountain. The old pick-up truck was whining up the valley trail towards him.

He collected up the foliage he'd used for cover and began to re-attach it to nearby bushes and trees. It seemed the decent thing to do. In the reverse ecology of this planet, the function of plant life was to suck in the oxygen that humans exhaled, and process it into carbon dioxide which humans required to breathe.

Just as he was re-affixing the last leaf, the pick-up truck tumbled over the crest of the track and screeched to a stop neatly in the pre-cut tyre tracks. The door flung itself open, and Kryten caught the handle.

'Everything OK, sir?'

'Get in, Kryten! Let's go!'

Kryten climbed into the passenger seat and tugged the door closed. Lister raised his foot from the brake and they lurched off backwards. When they hit top speed, Lister pumped down on the accelerator and they raced steadily off along the track up towards the peak.

Kryten looked up at the driver's mirror and caught a glimpse of the Cat, who was sitting rigidly in the rear seat, his eyes wide and unblinking, as if someone had slapped two fried eggs either side of his nose.

'What's wrong with the Cat?'

Lister shrugged. 'He's been like that since the climb. Hasn't said a word.'

Kryten twisted round in his seat. 'Are you feeling all right, sir?'

The Cat simply kept staring straight on. Kryten noticed his lips were moving minutely. He leaned over as close as possible, and made out the Cat's mumbled murmur: 'Ghnitssuhsidt,' he was saying, over and over. 'Ghnitssuhsidt oot oot . . .'

When Kryten turned back, Lister was studying the driver's mirror. 'There he goes,' he said.

Kryten twisted round again. The trail had widened and straightened, and in the distance, a flashing blue light above a small ball of dust was travelling away from them. 'Won't be long now,' Lister smiled.

After a few seconds, the dustball vanished, the black-and-white killed its lights and siren, and reversed swiftly off the track, through a gate which led to a small farmstead, where it seemed to park.

It took the pick-up a couple of minutes to reach the gate. As they zoomed up, Kryten saw the policeman standing by his vehicle with a barefoot man in dungarees. They were both staring at the pick-up, agape. Kryten felt Lister's hand on his head, thrusting him below the windscreen.

'Stay out of sight!' Lister hissed.

After a few seconds, Lister raised his hand, and Kryten straightened up in the seat. The road was clear. 'That's it then, sir,' he beamed, 'the policeman is no longer in pursuit.'

'That's right,' Lister agreed, but his expression was harsh. 'And round about now is when someone goes and gets themselves killed.'

SIX

Rimmer glowered out of the window into the blurred motion of the valley below. He'd given up glancing at the speedometer when he'd noticed that the needle had bent and stuck on its upper extremity, which was, for the record, one hundred and twenty somethings per hour. Rimmer didn't know or care whether it was miles or kilometres. In his book, anything over thirty somethings per hour travelling backwards on a winding mountain road was sheer insanity.

Lister must have caught his expression in the mirror because he grinned and said, 'Feeling better now, Arn?'

Rimmer leaned over the catatonic Cat and yelled above the engine's whine into the driver's ear. 'Lister – as you are well aware, I am no stranger to travelling at lightspeed. However, I am more than a little uncomfortable attempting it in a clapped-out old shooting brake on a narrow dirt track up a mountain, in reverse.'

'Look . . .' Lister turned and smiled at him.

'Don't look at me!' Rimmer screamed. 'Keep your eyes on the road! Or the mirror! Or whatever the smeg your eyes are supposed to be kept on!'

Lister's grin broadened. 'You still can't wrap your head round it, can you? It's physically impossible for us to crash in this car, on this trip.'

'So you say. All the same, I'd feel slightly more comfortable if we weren't actually overtaking radio waves.'

Rimmer leaned back and closed his eyes. He might as well have been urging a crippled, blind, deaf mute to be dancing to 'La Bamba'. He was beginning to wish they hadn't turned him back on. Kryten had rigged his portable power pack to the old pick-up's dynamo, and they'd revived him in order to help his batteries wind down, which seemed to Rimmer as insane as everything else in this lunàtic world.

Still, they were heading towards *Starbug*. This nightmare was almost over. Soon enough, they'd be in a universe where time flowed smoothly in the proper direction and things made sense. A universe where Santa Claus was a good person, not some evil old bastard who sneaked down chimneys once a year to steal all the children's favourite toys.

Rimmer was as close as it was possible to get to a state of relaxation under the circumstances, when Lister inexplicably jammed his foot on the brake and wrenched the steering-wheel left. The cab tilted, so only half the truck was actually on the road as they sped round a bend. Suddenly they were reversing past an almost stationary tractor, which blared its horn angrily as they zipped by at a cartoon angle of forty-five degrees.

Lister slewed the car back to a horizontal position, and the wheels kissed the dust of the mountain track.

'Hang on!' Lister shouted. He looked over at Kryten and Rimmer, both of their faces frozen in grins of terror. 'Sorry, I should've warned you beforewards.' He shrugged. 'Habit.'

Rimmer prised his nails out of his knees, and uttered a vowel-less word which, under normal circumstances, the human larynx could not possibly reproduce. He looked out of the window. Hedgerows and bushes spat past dizzyingly. Despite their near-death experience, and the fact that the road was getting cruder and rougher, Lister hadn't dropped his speed one iota.

'Just how much further . . .' Rimmer began, and then

spotted something that took his mind off their velocity. On the seat beside him was a cluster of tiny shards of glass he hadn't noticed before. There was another spattering of them by the handbrake. Where had all this glass come from? And what was that funny little hole in the dashboard?

'You were saying?'

Rimmer's eyes flicked up to the driver's mirror. There seemed to be a similar sort of funny little hole in the rear window . . .

'Rimmer?'

Rimmer turned to examine the hole, which was surrounded by a network of thin cracks. He turned back to Lister. 'Where did you get this car?'

Lister shrugged. 'Dunno.'

'What d'you mean, you don't know? This *is* your car, isn't it?'

Lister shrugged. 'Maybe. I've never seen it before.'

'Are you telling me you're about to steal this vehicle?'

'Not necessarily. Maybe I'm going to buy it.'

Rimmer's eyebrows pushed his hairline back a good two inches. 'At the highest, most obscure peak of an obscure mountain range? Presumably from one of the many discount second-hand car showrooms that flourish there?'

Lister shifted uncomfortably in his seat. 'Who knows? Maybe we buy it from a farmer or something.'

'Lister, there's only one kind of people live in the most obscure peaks of obscure mountains. Strange people. People who don't like other people. Not polite, besuited, second-hand car salespeople. Hermit-type inbred people, with criss-crossed front teeth and a penchant for stews well-stocked with human flesh. People who, when other people take something away from them, are not averse to shooting at those other people with bullets.'

Kryten twisted towards Lister. 'Bullets?'

Lister sighed. 'OK. We're going to get shot at.' He

nodded at the bullet hole in the dash. 'But he's going to miss! Can everybody please relax!'

But Rimmer couldn't relax. He became less relaxed with every stone that spat itself under the wheels of the stolen car as they relentlessly wound their way up the narrowing road towards an inevitable gun battle.

SEVEN

Rimmer thought he was at his most unrelaxed when Lister suddenly thrust his hand out of the driver's window and caught a handful of shattered glass, which he distributed around his lap, but he was wrong.

His unrelaxation didn't even peak when Lister screamed 'Heads down!' and ducked towards the steering-wheel.

Kryten and Rimmer dipped their heads as low as they could. The Cat didn't move. Rimmer hissed at him to get down, but he just remained upright and staring forward, oblivious.

Rimmer glanced up at the driver's mirror just in time to see the bearded, genetically challenged, diagonally dentured hillbilly hermit of his nightmares level a smoking rifle at them.

With a strange sucking sound, a bullet tugged itself out of the dashboard and, dragging the tiny shards of glass from the seat beside him in its wake, zipped through the rear window, sealing it neatly.

'Stay low!' Lister injuncted, quite unnecessarily.

The hillbilly scampered up a hillock and out of Rimmer's sight as the truck swept round a bend. Naturally, given Lister's inexcusable insistence on obeying the perverse conventions of this world, the bend would take them round the hillock where the hermit would be waiting for them, giving him the chance to squeeze off another shot.

Sure enough, there was the strange implosion sound

again, and the glass on Lister's lap leapt up and formed itself
into a driver's door window, which for some reason appeared to be misted over and coated in yellowish slime.

Then Lister did something for which Rimmer would
never forgive him.

Lister parked the car.

'Lister! What the smeg are you playing at?' Rimmer
mezzo-sopranoed.

Lister ignored him, bent forward and began fiddling with
the steering-column.

Rimmer looked up and saw the hermit's face pressed
madly against the driver's window, yelling incomprehensible
threats.

And Lister stopped the engine.

Without taking his eyes from the yellow slobber the
mountain man was slavering up from the window, Rimmer
asked, in a voice far too calm to be sane, 'What are you
doing, David?'

'What d'you think? I'm trying to unhotwire this damn
thing.'

Rimmer tried to swallow, but his tongue just rasped
against his sandpaper palate. 'A more prudent approach,
one might venture, would be to leave this vehicle in a post-
hastely kind of way and run backwards the hell out of
here.'

Lister carried on fiddling with the ignition wires.
'Rimmer, I've got to undo this. That's the way things are
around here. Effect and cause. Every effect is followed by a
cause. There's no way round it.'

'We couldn't just waive the rules for once?'

'Not rules, Rimmer: laws. Immutable cosmic laws. Look,
man, just stop interrupting me, and try and panic in silence,
OK?'

The engine churned, spluttered and stopped. The hillbilly stopped thumping, cursing and slobbering and moved
away. Rimmer peered over the edge of his window and

watched the hermit, clutching his shotgun racing bandily backwards towards a pathetic log cabin.

Rimmer could quite clearly see a giant sow sitting in a swing chair on the wooden porch. The hermit appeared to have dressed the pig in a pink gingham dress and varnished its hooves with bright red nail polish. Rimmer really didn't want to know why.

The engine churned again and died.

Rimmer found in his soul a new level of loathing for Lister. Valiantly and selflessly, he'd risked life and limb to land on this hellhole to rescue his shipmate, and how had the scumbag repaid him? By leading him into a series of life-threatening situations, culminating in his being unshot at and deslobbered over by a giant pig's husband who was almost certainly related to himself in a variety of illegal ways.

The engine chuddered one last time, and Lister seemed satisfied. 'That's it!' he said. 'We're out of here!' then leaned over and thrust open Rimmer's door.

Rimmer glanced over at the cabin. The hillbilly had stashed his shotgun by the door, and was haring off backwards up towards some thick woods behind them.

'Come on!' Lister was yelling. 'Move it!'

Kryten jumped out of the car and slammed his door. Lister leaned over to the passenger side and locked it.

Rimmer eased himself out of the jalopy, keeping his eyes fixed on the sow, who was rocking happily back and forth on the porch bench, its little pig eyes watching him. Kryten leaned in the car and helped the Cat crawl out backwards. He closed the door, and Lister leaned over and locked that too.

Lister jumped out of the driver's seat and started poking at the door lock with a rusty nail that had leapt into his hand from the track.

'What *now*?' Rimmer whined.

'Reckon he must keep it locked.'

Rimmer looked over at the woods the hillbilly had vanished into. 'Why on Io would the trigger-happy pork-poker bother locking his car up here in this God-forsaken wilderness?'

'Search me.' Lister heard the click as the lock connected. 'Maybe he doesn't want the pig driving off in it.'

That made sense to Rimmer. From what he'd seen of the mountain man, the pig was undoubtedly the brains of the business.

Lister wiggled the nail out of the lock and placed it in the dirt beside the car. He straightened. 'All right, it's "leg it" time.'

Rimmer asked; 'Which way?' even though he was fairly sure he could guess the answer.

Lister nodded towards the woods. 'I reckon he was chasing us. Don't you?' He turned to Kryten, who was conversing in forward-speak with the Cat. 'How is he?'

'He'll be fine, sir, so long as we stay together. Apparently, he had an unpleasant experience in some bushes a while back when we left him alone.'

Lister wiped the palm of his hand across his face. 'I can guess. We should have warned him.' He looked at the Cat, answering his accusatory stare with a sympathetic facial shrug, and then nodded again over at the woods. 'OK, people. Wagons roll!' He performed his familiar reverse skid, and took off for the trees. Kryten turned around and followed him, backwards. Rimmer and the Cat looked at each other, and mutely voted to flout convention. They ran towards the woods forwards.

As the Cat leapt into the woods, the thick undergrowth snapped aside before him, clearing his path, then slashed back on his calves behind him. Rimmer's hologrammatic feet simply disappeared into the heavy fern, as if he were running on a foot-thick soft carpet. The undawning sun burst sporadically through the overhanging leaves, illuminating their flight with thousands of golden spotlights.

They thrashed on through the woods. The Cat kept yelping 'Mnadh!' as his inverted slipstream continually whipped his pigtail over his cheeks and eyes. He reached behind his head and grabbed it, keeping his other arm needlessly cocked in front of him, to protect his face from branches, which he had absolutely no faith would continue to yield a path for him just before he reached them.

The Cat burst through a thick bush to find Lister and Kryten crouched behind a bank of fern which looked up on to a hillside cave.

Rimmer's heart jumped up and shook hands with his Adam's apple when he recognized it as the cave they'd concealed *Starbug* in.

The broad, twisted grin of delight slowly trickled back down from his cheeks when he saw that Lister was frowning and chewing the inside of his lip. 'What's up?' he whispered. 'We're home.'

'Not quite,' Lister hissed.

Rimmer followed his gaze. In the clearing before them, a bizarre jerry-built concoction of vats, tubes and pipes was sucking in smoke from the treeline above. 'What is it?'

Kryten answered 'I would guess some kind of illegal still.'

Not for the first time, Rimmer doubted the sanity of the lawmakers of reverse Earth. What in heaven's name could possibly be illegal about taking dangerous alcoholic liquor and converting it into grain for planting?

Then he saw it.

Just below a small blue flame which was sucking the heat out of some bubbling liquid in a vat, a rubber tube led to a fuel canister. The canister was imprinted with a Jupiter Mining Corporation logo, and stamped 'Red Dwarf'.

This time, Rimmer's heart plunged towards the pit of his stomach, and his testicles leapt to meet it.

The hillbilly had found *Starbug*.

EIGHT

There were lots of things Kryten was trying not to think about. He was trying not to think about how they now had less than seven hours before their take-off window closed, leaving them stranded in this reverse universe. He was trying not to think about just how much of *Starbug* had been pillaged by the mountain man, and whether or not the vessel would still be capable of flight. He was trying not to think about how he was going to explain the severity of their plight to the others.

He looked over at Lister, whose face was set in grim frustration, which gave him something else not to think about.

The hillbilly had unspotted Lister just as they leapt behind the bank of ferns, and was now prodding around the undergrowth on the other side of the clearing. His shoulders were heaving and he was sobbing loudly. Thick streams of wetness crawled up his cheeks from his damp beard into his nose and eyes.

Finally, he backed into a thicket just by the still, and he was gone.

'Right.' Rimmer glanced around trying to decide who should bear the brunt of his reproachful look, and settled on Kryten. 'Just how bad is this?'

'It's not good, sir. Those spare fuel tanks are stored in the hold. To access them, an intruder would have to breech every single one of our security measures. We must conclude that the entire ship has been compromised. Including the computer systems and engine-rooms.'

Rimmer shook his head. 'Marvellous,' he said. 'We don't even have the technology to keep out a bandy-legged, brain-dead hillbilly with a gene pool no bigger than a spider's piss puddle.'

'It's possible he only took the fuel canister.' Kryten tried to inject optimism into his tone. 'It's unlikely he would have understood the function of much else.'

'Only one way to find out.' Lister stood. 'And that's to look.'

They picked their way carefully up the sloping ridge to the cave's entrance. The undawning sun was glimmering dangerously low, just over a distant white-capped peak, and while Kryten and the Cat had excellent low-light vision, Lister and Rimmer were beginning to have difficulty seeing.

Once inside the mouth of the cave, Kryten was forced to activate his chest light. Lister felt his chest tighten with excitement as the beam fell on *Starbug*'s cockpit.

He hadn't seen the dirty green insect-shaped ship-to-surface vessel in almost forty years, but he'd dreamed of it plenty. It had become an icon to him. His ticket home.

They walked round to the flared tail section. The rear drive jets all seemed to be intact and in place. The bulbous mid-section appeared secure. The landing steps were withdrawn and the door was sealed.

Wordlessly, Kryten emitted the access signal, and the door swung open. Hydraulics hissed and the landing ramp dropped smoothly down.

No one dare speak, but everyone was thinking *so far, so good*.

They climbed inside.

Kryten activated the airlock, the steps retracted and the outer door clanged shut. After an unbearable pause, the inner door opened and they stepped into the mid-section.

It was just as they'd left it.

Fighting the urge to run, Kryten walked up to the airlock door and keyed in the access code. A red scanner light slid across his face, and the airlock door wheel sighed open. He walked into the mid-section and straight up the four steps into the cockpit section as the drive lights flickered on. He eased himself down into the seat of the drive computer station, and started running system checks.

The Cat headed straight up the stairs which led from the mid-section to the rest quarters above, presumably to check that no one had been screwing around with his clothes, while Rimmer made for the maintenance corridor to glance around the engine-rooms and investigate the supplies.

All Lister could do was sit.

He thumped down into one of the chairs surrounding the scanner table and looked around the room.

Above the girder grid of the mid-section's ceiling, the lights appeared to flare. Lister put his hand to his eyes, and it came away wet. He looked down at the floor where small droplets began to form from a damp patch there and started whipping up towards his face.

Shamelessly, Lister unwept.

Thirty-six years ago, in his own universe, Lister had died. His shipmates had brought him to this place, where Time's reversal could bring him back to life. And he'd lived that life. And he'd been grateful for it. But all the while, he'd felt he was an outsider here.

There had been joys, of course. Somehow his long-dead ex-lover, Krissie Kochanski, had been brought here with him, and they'd shared the pleasures of growing younger together. Eventually, their twin sons had come home to live with them, and there had been the inverted delight of watching them de-mature.

But all that had long since passed. More than a decade had gone by since the boys had been pushed back into their mother. And nine years ago, he and Krissie had been introduced, whereupon she'd promptly gone away and forgotten him.

And after that, the only thing that kept him sane had been the dream of this moment. Here, now, sitting in *Starbug*'s familiar, unhomely, metallic surroundings. For Lister, there was no more glorious décor in the history of interior design.

The last of the teardrops rolled up his face, leaving only fading red rims around his eyes as the Cat skipped down the metal stairway, grinning as if there was a wedge of Edam lodged between his cheeks. 'Hfyahs rah tsoots iym,' he beamed. 'Sksaherh nakh eeooh!'

Rimmer ducked in through the hatch from the engine rooms. 'What was that?'

Lister looked up. He hadn't used forward-speak for decades, but he ought to start practising. He ran the Cat's words over in his head. Suddenly, they clicked. 'I think he said: "We can relax. My suits are safe."'

'Excellent news.' Rimmer favoured the Cat with the grin he reserved for idiots and foreigners. 'I for one shall sleep soundly tonight. Well' – he rubbed his hands together – 'supplies are good, just the one fuel canister missing. Engines seem operational. Computers are functioning. Looks like we can lift off.'

Kryten stepped down from the cockpit. The others turned their eyes towards him, expectantly. 'I . . . I . . . I . . .' he began, and then slammed his forehead against the hull's interior. 'I'm afraid there is one minor problem. Somehow, the landing jets have become detached.'

There was a brief moment of silence, and then Lister suddenly cursed 'Smeg!' and kicked the body of the scanner table, neatly removing a dent that had been there.

'It's not that bad, people,' Rimmer smiled encouragement. 'We don't *have* to land. Once we RV with *Red Dwarf*, one of us can jet-pack over and tow *Starbug* in. Yes?'

'You don't understand.' Kryten sank into the seat

opposite Lister. 'When we set down here, I had to reverse the controls. The only way of bringing us down was to use the take-off procedures.'

Rimmer was still baffled. 'So?'

'So,' Lister said, 'we need the landing jets to take off. Without them, we'll be stuck here.' He looked between his feet where the damp patch had been. 'We'll be stuck here for ever.'

NINE

The four of them stood under the bulge of *Starbug*'s belly, Kryten's light angled directly at the alarming space where the retro jets ought to have been. All three of them were missing.

'It doesn't make sense.' Rimmer ran his hand through his wiry hair. 'Why would Jethro Clampett's stupider brother want three landing jets from a space vehicle? What's he going to do: launch his cabin into orbit and join the Mile High Club with his pig?'

'Perhaps he's not the one responsible,' Kryten offered. 'Look.' He directed the beam at the severed retainers which had been welded to the engine. The metal exposed there was rusted over. Kryten's list of things he didn't want to think about was growing to novella proportions.

'All right.' Rimmer walked back to *Starbug*'s rear. 'Couldn't we rig up one of the main thrusters underneath, so it could act as a landing jet?'

'It might work,' Kryten agreed, 'if we had time. Unfortunately, it's not an option.'

'Why?' Rimmer strode back to the group. 'What's the rush?'

'We're relying on certain planetary conditions to help us sling-shot out of the solar system. Those conditions will not be fulfilled unless we leave soon.'

'How soon is "soon"?'

'Five and a half hours.'

Lister blew like there was a tuba missing from his lips. 'That's *soon*. OK. All right. How about we angle the front retros? That should give us some lift.'

Kryten looked towards the cave's entrance. 'I doubt we'd get sufficient power to clear the tops of those redwoods. Certainly not enough to get us over that mountain.'

'Right then,' Lister shrugged. 'We've got just one shot: find those engines. How long would it take us to attach them?'

Kryten looked at the ground and shook his head. 'There's no way of knowing. It would depend on what condition they're in. At least ninety minutes. Maybe two hours.'

Lister looked at his watch. 'That gives us till two a.m. One-thirty at a pinch. We're going to have to split into two groups. I'm no good in the dark. Neither's Rimmer. I'd best go with the Cat. Come what may, we meet back here at half-past one.'

Kryten nodded and they headed out of the cave.

When they reached the clearing where the still was bubbling away, Lister and the Cat peeled off south towards the mountain man's cabin, and Kryten and Rimmer carried on eastwards into the woods.

Kryten's plan was to walk for fifty minutes searching every square inch of the terrain, then cut back diagonally south-west for another fifty, then north for fifty minutes more. It wasn't exactly a definitive search pattern, but it *would* leave him a full hour for his back-up plan, which involved racing around in a panicky funk if nothing turned up, hoping against hope to come across the engines by sheer fluke.

Lister and the Cat crept up to the log cabin.

The lights were out and the metal pipe that served as a chimney was no longer sucking thick white smoke from the sky.

They edged along the side of the cabin, up to a shuttered window. From inside, there came the regular hum of a deep-sleep snore. Good. The hermit was asleep. That would make it easier to search the storage sheds. The Cat peered gingerly over the wooden sill and through a crack between the slats.

The entire cabin was comprised of a single room. There were no jet engines in sight.

In fact, there was very little furniture. A rocking chair, and a rickety wooden table with a short-wave radio on top. Most of the room was taken up by a huge bed, which could have happily accommodated six or seven normal-sized people. As it was, a single occupant was taking up the bulk of it.

The giant hog.

She was snoring contentedly, one hoof on the pillow beside her head. She was wearing a floral nightdress and a lace-trimmed cap.

Suddenly, there was a loud reverse cough from the direction of the porch. The Cat froze.

Lister crawled towards the front of the house, and peeked over the porch.

The hermit was sitting on the swing chair. He raised an almost-empty bottle to his lips and half-filled it from his mouth. Lister caught a wincing smell of the pungent fumes. Neat hooch.

The hillbilly got to his feet, and looked around, scanning the woods. He started pacing agitatedly up and down the creaking porch boards.

Lister backed away. What the smeg was the man doing awake and getting undrunk at this hour? Who was he expecting to see? Them? Had he just got out of bed, or was he going to be waiting on the porch all night?

Lister checked his watch and blinked a curse. There were six or seven wooden shacks scattered around the property, as well as a fair-sized barn. Having to keep to the shadows and creep around silently would slow down the search considerably. It was unlikely they'd be able to cover the whole place before they'd have to set off back to the *Bug*.

He sighed, stood and nodded for the Cat to follow him to the nearest of the shacks.

Kryten was on the last leg of his search pattern, and less than ten minutes away from engaging panic-like-a-headless-chicken mode, when he found the first of the engines.

He wouldn't have spotted it at all if he hadn't actually tripped up over it.

It was buried in the soil, less than fifty yards from the illegal still, with just a few inches of the nose cone peeking above the ground. Kryten knelt down and clawed away the surface soil frantically while Rimmer kept a timid lookout, trying not to think of the strange night creatures that might be lurking in the damp, dark shadows of the trees.

Kryten exposed a further foot or so of the engine. The excitement of his discovery dwindled with each inch.

The engine was rusted all to hell.

He was extremely doubtful it could ever be restored to working condition.

He lurched upright and sighed.

'Well?' Rimmer's eyebrows crooked with expectation.

'It's no good, sir. It's buried too deep. Without some kind of excavation tool, we haven't got a hope of extracting it in time.' Kryten discreetly slipped his hand behind his back and discarded a shard of rusted metal that he'd found flaked off the engine.

Rimmer knelt by the exposed housing. Thankfully, there was too little light for him to spot the true decrepitude of the engine's condition. 'This is insane. Why would that backwoods bastard bury it?'

Kryten shook his head. He had a good idea what had

happened, but it belonged at the very top of the 'things he didn't want to think about' list. 'We need some kind of digging tool. I'll get one from *Starbug*. Suggest you stay here.' He turned and prepared to switch up to maximum jog mode.

'Woah, woah, woah!' Rimmer smiled. 'Are you insane? I'm coming with you.'

'I'll make much better time on my own.'

Rimmer peered into the relentless gloom of the surrounding woods. He thought of mountain lions and grizzly bears. He thought of wolf packs and cougars. He thought of werewolves and Sasquatch and inbred hillbillies with guns and seriously dubious sexual preferences. He thought of all the wild things with yellow eyes and an insatiable bloodlust that would swallow his light bee whole as a pre-hors-d'oeuvre canapé without even making a gulping noise. 'We'll go together,' he said.

'Very well,' Kryten nodded, then turned, lurched and pelted off at maximum acceleration, leaving Rimmer wide-eyed, alone and furious.

Kryten didn't get very far. As he burst through the thicket into the clearing that housed the still, his peripheral vision registered a pickaxe handle, and he stopped.

He underestimated his speed and stopped too quickly, losing his balance and tumbling to the ground. He put out his hands to break his fall, plunging them into a wooden bucket filled with rainwater. When he pulled them out, he was alarmed to find they were covered in some kind of sticky goo. He considered trying to wash them, then realized that wouldn't work. In this universe, you used water to get yourself dirty.

He picked himself up and waddled over to the pickaxe handle. It was protruding from a clump of bushes. He grabbed it with sticky hands and readied himself to tug it free.

He looked down and froze.

Lying in the bushes beneath him was the lifeless body of the hermit.

The pickaxe was buried deep in his chest.

TEN

Kryten knelt and placed his fingertips on the hillbilly's neck. There was no pulse. The body was still fairly warm. Fresh blood was still oozing around the terrible chest wound.

He eased back on his haunches, and tried to think. How could the hermit possibly be dead? Time was running backwards, and they'd already seen the man alive later that morning.

Kryten accessed the unshooting incident in his visual storage and selected a still frame of the hillbilly. He looked down at the dead man, and compared the two faces.

It wasn't the same man.

He was dressed the same, and his features were extremely similar, but not exactly the same. Undoubtedly, the corpse was a close blood relative to the hermit who'd shot at them.

The preceding events began to tumble into place. That's why the mountain man had been weeping in the clearing: he'd discovered his brother's corpse. He'd been beating the bushes, looking for some kind of clue to the perpetrator of the crime. Then he'd spotted Lister and chased them to the car.

He'd assumed they were the killers.

This was the crime for which Lister had been arrested.

And since Lister couldn't have killed the man, that meant the real murderer was somewhere close by.

Suddenly, Kryten was aware of someone behind him.

There had been no footsteps, just the slight rustle of breathing. Kryten wheeled round, his hands flattened and elbows cocked in what he hoped would look like a threatening karate pose to his attacker.

It was Rimmer. His features were puffed with rage.

His fury deflated when he registered Kryten's fear and distress. His eyes tracked down the pickaxe handle down to the corpse, then back up to Kryten. 'Dead?' he asked, simply.

'I'm afraid so. It's not the hermit who was chasing us. I think it's probably his brother, or his cousin.'

'Probably both.' Rimmer knelt beside him. 'Probably his uncle and his father, too.'

Kryten was affronted. Revulsion at human death was deep in the core of his programming, and witnessing it firsthand always disturbed him hugely. Especially when the death was unnatural and violent. He turned his face to Rimmer. 'Do you really think it appropriate to jest at the expense of the dead?'

Rimmer shrugged. 'He won't be dead long.'

Of course! Kryten cursed his own stupidity. Soon, probably in a matter of minutes, the corpse would come to life! All they had to do was conceal themselves in the bushes and wait until the murderer showed up.

Suddenly, the corpse's eyes blinked open, startling Kryten so violently, he lost his balance again and tumbled on to his back.

The corpse opened its mouth and let out a terrible death rattle.

Kryten scrambled to his feet.

'For God's sake,' Rimmer yelled, 'turn your smegging light on!'

Kryten flicked on his chest light. The beam hit the animating corpse.

It gurgled, as a thick dribble of bubbling blood trickled up its cheek and into its mouth.

Dizzy with horror, Kryten was vaguely aware that Rimmer was talking to him. He turned and said, 'What?'

'Your hands!' Rimmer was saying.

He held his hands in the light. The goo that covered them was blood.

Kryten was beginning to lose it. He felt like a tsunami was roaring through his head. The stark beam of his chest light illuminating his bloody, shaking hands fell on the corpse beyond and registered movement.

With a low, awful moan, the corpse began to writhe. Its body started juddering violently, then it arched its back stiffly and screamed. It thumped back down and began beating the ground with its fists.

It screamed again in pain and fury, and grasped the pickaxe handle. It started rocking from side to side, hands desperately clawing the handle of the instrument of its death.

Rimmer was screaming, 'Do something!' and Kryten staggered forward, half blind with panic. He grasped the pickaxe. The corpse was looking up at him with an expression that looked like astonishment.

Kryten tugged at the handle. There was a wet, cracking sound in the man's chest, but the pickaxe remained lodged there. Kryten summoned all his strength and pulled again.

And the corpse was tugged to its feet, arms flailing, screaming and yelling insanely.

And still the pickaxe was wedged in his chest.

And then Kryten held on to the handle, the last of his sanity gurgling out of his ears as he danced a macabre waltz with the dying man in the eerie glow of his own chest light.

Kryten was trying to yank the pickaxe loose, but the mountain man was holding it in his own chest with phenomenal, adrenal strength.

Then, suddenly, he let go, and with a gruesome, crunching gloop, Kryten jerked the pickaxe free.

While he was staring, astonished at the hillbilly's unblemished shirt front, the man lunged at the pickaxe still raised over Kryten's head.

Still in shock, Kryten tussled with him for a second or two, and then let go. The reverse impetus of the manoeuvre flung him to the ground and sent him rolling side over side towards the bushes.

For a moment, the hillbilly held the pickaxe over his head, and then swung it down towards the tumbling Kryten, but missed and raised it again. Kryten rolled over the spot where the blade had struck and stopped rolling.

He jumped to his feet and faced the mountain man, who was brandishing the pickaxe, one hand on the handle, the other halfway along the shaft. He was snarling and murmuring vicious threats.

Kryten was hurt and confused. He'd just brought this man back from the dead. Why was he bent on hurting him?

The hillbilly hefted the pickaxe into one hand and swung it sideways, but he was out of range, and the blade whistled past Kryten's groinal socket.

Kryten stumbled backwards towards the still, not knowing what to do or say. He looked around for Rimmer, but he was nowhere in sight.

Then, as Kryten passed the still, it occurred to him to switch off his chest light. Now, the clearing was only illuminated by the gentle blue glow of the flame from the still.

The mountain man leered dangerously at his retreating form, and then swung round and buried the pickaxe in the ground. Facing away from Kryten, he backed up towards the still, looked at Kryten once over his shoulder and promptly proceeded to ignore him.

Kryten backed out of the clearing stealthily and collapsed on to his haunches in the shelter of the nearest bush.

After a few minutes, his sanity returned, and Rimmer crept along after it. Kryten was going to ask him where he'd got to, but it would be a pointless question. As soon as Rimmer had seen a fight start, he'd performed his famous impersonation of a whippet with a sphincter full of dynamite. Kryten had long since ceased to wonder why a man who was already dead could be such a relentless coward.

'Sorry about that,' Rimmer crawled close enough to whisper. 'Thought I spotted the other one trying to out-flank you, so I dashed off to cover your rear.' He peered through the bushes. The hillbilly was quietly tending the still. 'What now?'

'Now?' Kryten had lost track of time. He checked his internal chronometer. Almost two fifteen. 'We'd better get back to *Starbug*, see if the others are there.' If Lister and the Cat had managed to unearth the other two engines intact, it might be enough to get them airborne.

Rimmer nodded, and turned towards the ridge. Kryten rose to follow him, then stopped in mid-crouch. A terrible thought had struck him.

He'd been reversing the incident in his mind, in order to explain to the others what had actually happened and why they'd been delayed, when he realized the unthinkable truth.

He had just violated his most sacred directive.

He had killed a human being in cold blood.

ELEVEN

Lister was feeling pretty good. He hadn't slept for a good fifty hours now, what with the all-night interrogation at the police station which had uncracked six of his ribs and lifted the chronic pain in his kidneys. Each passing hour left him feeling fresher, stronger and more alert.

The engine was surprisingly light: seven feet long and mostly solid metal, yet he and the Cat could carry it between them fairly easily.

It was also surprisingly rusty.

Still, they'd managed to find it, and if Kryten and Rimmer had enjoyed any luck at all, they'd probably have enough power for a shaky take-off.

The Cat, who was leading the way, suddenly stopped and held up his hand. He sniffed the air, then nodded for Lister to take cover. Running sideways, with the engine between them, they trundled off the beaten pathway and ducked behind a clump of thickets.

Lister checked his watch, agitated. One twenty-four. They were already behind schedule. Two minutes drooled by, and there was still no sign of any danger. Lister was about to get up, when he heard a twig crack, and the mountain man came into view.

Lister was baffled. They'd just left the hermit swinging on his porch, yet here he was walking backwards down the crude path that led from the still to the cabin. As he passed them by, Lister could see his face in the full glow of the moon. If this man wasn't their hillbilly, he was his identical twin.

There was no time to consider the ramifications. As soon as he was out of sight, they hoisted the engine to their shoulders and carried it back on to the path.

Lister pushed the engine from the rear. The Cat got the message and upped his speed. They jogged through the clearing and climbed up the ridge to the cave.

They set the engine down underneath *Starbug's* belly. Lister's hopes took a Trafalgar-sized broadside when he saw that the rest of the jets were still missing.

Rimmer crept down the landing ramp and peered into the gloom beneath the ship. 'Lister?' he hissed, timidly.

Lister ducked under the ramp. 'No luck?'

Rimmer shook his head. 'We found one, but it was useless.'

'How useless?'

'Try "utterly". It was rotten with corrosion, with the added bonus that it was wedged solid about six feet into the ground. How did you get on?'

'We found one in the hillbilly's grain store. He'd been using it as shelf prop. It's not in superb nick, but I reckon it'll go.'

'The question is, will one jet be enough?'

'Maybe. If we angle the front retros down, like I said. It'll be touch and go whether or not we clear the mountain, but I don't see what choice we've got.' Lister checked his watch. 'An hour and twelve minutes. Let's get moving. Where's Kryten?'

'I think you're going to have to fix the jet on without him.'

Lister looked over at the engine. 'Are you nuts? I wouldn't know where to start.' Slowly, he twisted his head back towards Rimmer. 'Why? What's wrong with Kryten?'

Rimmer hitched his eyebrows enigmatically and walked

back up the ramp. Lister nodded to the Cat and followed him.

Kryten was lying on the scanner table, his eyes open and rolled back into his skull. There was a strange buzzing sound that seemed to be coming from somewhere inside his head.

Lister walked over and wafted his hand in front of Kryten's eyes. The mechanoid remained immobile. Lister tried calling his name, but still there was no response.

'He's been like this since we got back,' Rimmer said. 'Just lying there in some kind of electronic stupor.'

Lister put his nose to Kryten's ear and sniffed. 'Smeg. Smells like something's melted in there.'

Rimmer nodded. 'I think it's some kind of short-circuit. Probably happened in the fight.'

'Fight?'

'We found another hillbilly by the still. He had a pickaxe buried in his chest. Kryten pulled it out . . .'

'Pulled it out?!'

'Then they struggled a bit, and it was all over. We stagger back to *Starbug*, he lies on the scanner table: fizz, bang, there's smoke pouring out of his ears.'

'Let me get this straight: Kryten pulled a pickaxe out of a man's chest?'

'He had no choice. The poor bastard was writhing around in agony. Someone had to help him.'

Lister released a sigh that had been pent up inside him for eight long years. Every single day of his unspeakable imprisonment, he'd yearned to know just one thing. Had he actually committed the crime?

All the other inmates had the solace of knowing whether they were truly innocent or guilty. Whatever they proclaimed to the world, deep down, they all knew the truth.

And through those long, restless nights, it had seemed to Lister that his situation would have been immeasurably more bearable if only *he'd* known the truth.

Time after time, he'd pored over the transcripts of his trial, without finding enlightenment. The evidence had been circumstantial. He'd been spotted leaving the scene with another man. From the descriptions, Lister had guessed the second man had been the Cat. Lister's inability to disclose the Cat's whereabouts had counted heavily against him, in the jury's eyes. He'd been sentenced to fifteen years, of which he would serve eight.

Well, now he knew.

He had been innocent.

And it didn't make him feel any better. Not one quark.

The murderer had been Kryten.

'Hello?'

Lister's misted vision focused. Rimmer's face was directly in front of him. 'Hello?' he repeated. 'Anybody home?'

Lister sighed again and dragged his hand across his face. 'Yeah, I . . . uhh . . . yeah.'

'Thank God. For a minute then I thought you'd short-circuited too.'

Lister crossed to the tool store, ripped open the metal cabinet door and started rooting through a box. 'I think I know what's wrong with him. Something he did tripped his auto-shutdown mechanism.'

'Can you fix it?'

Lister hefted a sonic screwdriver from the tool box and walked back to the scanner table. 'I've done it before, remember?' He eased a tyre lever into Kryten's head and prised away a section of skull. 'Question is: can I do it in time?'

TWELVE

Twelve-fifteen.

Kryten should have been concentrating on meeting the flight window deadline, which wasn't exactly midnight, but close enough not to matter a spit. If they weren't airborne before ten to . . . well, the alternative didn't bear thinking about.

Trouble was, Kryten wasn't thinking about it.

He was standing on an elevated platform, holding the part-corroded engine in position, while Lister's laser torch sprayed showers of dancing sparks over him and everything else in the vicinity.

Rimmer was pacing nervously beneath them, barking pointless and panicky commands. The Cat stood on the bottom step of the mini-crane, shouting equally pointless and panicky commands, only forwards.

And Kryten didn't even notice them. Nor did he share their panic.

He was thinking about murder.

Murr. Derr.

Such a pleasant, soft word, really.

Like murmur.

Purring and delicate.

Hiding behind its gentle, furry exterior the foulest, vilest offence humankind had ever devised against nature.

Murder.

Kryten was a murderer.

And he couldn't live with it.

By the time Kryten had been created, all Artificial Intelligence life forms were programmed to protect human life. There had been some earlier mistakes – most notably the part-organic agonoids, who had been designed as super warriors and then got a few ideas of their own about obeying orders and almost rid an entire planet of its human occupants – before the designers wised up and started programming a version of Asimov's robotic laws into the core of every computer mind.

Kryten had broken those laws, and his urge to self-destruct was almost unbearable.

And so he'd decided that, once the engine was fixed into place, and the take-off prepared, he would slip quietly down the ramp and disappear into the cave.

He was incapable of thinking clearly, and had no idea how he might commit suicide on a planet where time was running in reverse. All he knew was that he was unfit to share the company of humans. If that meant spending an eternity alone in the dark recesses of inaccessible caverns, with only his guilt and his pain for company, then so be it.

He'd discharge this final duty, and be gone.

Suddenly, he was aware of silence.

Lister flicked off his torch, unhooked his safety harness and climbed down on to Kryten's platform.

Rimmer yelled, 'Is that it? All systems go?'

Lister raised his welding mask and looked up at the awkwardly angled landing jet. 'It's not perfect. Should be good enough to give us a shot.' He tugged off his gloves and started climbing down the mini-crane steps towards the Cat's anxious stare.

It had been a tricky job, trying to attach the jet using a cutting tool, and Kryten had been precious little help. Lister had no idea how long it would hold, if at all. He'd been alarmed by his close examination of *Starbug*'s underside. A lot of the plates seemed to have been recently welded into place, and there appeared to be a dangerous level of corrosion under the fresh metal sheets.

Still, with less than five minutes to go, he decided not to share his fears with the others. Either *Starbug* would get off the ground, or it wouldn't. No point in complicating matters now.

As the Cat hurriedly loaded the mini-crane back inside, Rimmer pointlessly urging him on with backwards barked commands, Lister discreetly shone the work lamp over the walls of the cave.

As he'd suspected, the walls were latticed with ruts, some fresh with scorch marks, others filmed over with grime.

Some part of him probably knew the truth, then. But it wasn't about to go and blurt it out to the rest of him. Hope was the fuel that fed Lister's engine, and there was no point in squandering it over maybes and like-as-nots. There could be dozens of explanations for the presence of those marks. None of them feasible or likely, but all of them better than the probable truth.

A wisp of undispersing smoke wafted across the beam. He sniffed the air. The familiar fumes of part-burned jet fuel were starting to build up. He took a last look around the cave and then pounded up the landing ramp.

He was inside the cockpit before the ramp had fully retracted. Rimmer was seated towards the rear of the cockpit, running checks over the NaviComp. The Cat was in the pilot seat, which took Lister somewhat by surprise, but on reflection, it made sense. That Cat had faster reactions and better directional sense than the rest of them put together. True, he was also stupider and vainer than the rest of them put together, but in a pinch, the best choice for the job. Lister was about to slip into the co-pilot's seat beside him, when he realized that Kryten's computer station was unmanned.

'Where's Kryten?'

The Cat shrugged. Rimmer didn't take his eyes off the

NaviComp. He said, 'He's running some checks in the engine-rooms.'

Lister punched up the security cameras and scanned the engine-rooms. Deserted. He turned and headed for the mid-section.

The Cat yelled after him 'Dubh, stinnimuh oot', and carried on flicking switches, in between sly glances at his reflection in the computer screen and occasional touch-ups of his perfect pompadour.

Lister managed to decipher the Cat's yell as 'Two minutes, bud,' as he hurled himself down the steps to the mid-section. Empty. He ran straight for the spiral stairs and launched himself up to the rest quarters.

Kryten was not on board.

Lister crashed back down the stairs and flung himself up the steps back to the cockpit. 'He's gone! Kryten's not here!'

His eyes still on the NaviComp display, Rimmer said, 'Ninety seconds and counting.'

'Woah!' Lister formed his hands into a capital T. 'Time out, guys. Kryten's still out there.'

'Lister, we are about to perform what is probably the most complicated reverse-landing take-off procedure ever attempted in the history of aviation, with a single landing jet which is rustier than Elizabeth the First's chastity belt. Furthermore, the pilot and I do not even speak the same language in the same direction, and even if we did, we wouldn't agree. We do not need any more complications.'

'Complications?! Kryten's not on board! We can't leave without him!'

'Wrong. We can't leave *with* him. If we abort now, we miss the flight window.'

'Then we miss it. We're not abandoning Kryten.'

'Sixty seconds and counting.' Rimmer flicked his eyes up from the screen. 'He knows what he's doing. He's made his choice. The flight path's been logged in and we can make it without him.'

'What do you mean, "He's made his choice"? You mean he told you he wasn't coming with us?'

'What he actually said was: "I'm going for a walk. I may be some time."'

'And you let him go?'

Rimmer looked down at the screen again. 'Forty-five seconds.'

Lister jumped back down to the mid-section and raced to the airlock. As he slid his palm over the security scanner, the engines began to whine. The scanner read-out flashed red, and a warning panel blinked the words: 'Airlock inaccessible until Landing Procedure complete.'

Lister thumped the scanner with his forehead and charged back to the cockpit.

Starbug began to shake as the engine whine built. Lister staggered to the co-pilot station and yelled to the Cat: 'Trohbah! Trohbah!'

The Cat looked up at him confused, and then over at Rimmer, who shook his head and said, 'Zero.'

Starbug juddered as the engines crescendoed and Lister was flung into the co-pilot seat. 'No!' he screamed. 'Nooo!'

He flicked on the external cameras. The cave outside was almost completely obscured by the fog banks of thick black-brown smoke that the single landing jet was labouring to inhale.

Just for an instant, he thought he caught a glimpse of Kryten's too-pink face craning to see them through the acrid fog.

The cockpit was juddering wildly, now. A jumble of flight manuals leapt from the floor around Kryten's deserted station and arranged themselves neatly on a shelf.

And they were airborne.

THIRTEEN

The combination of retros roaring, the landing jet scream-ing and the jittering vibration rocking the cabin made communication virtually impossible.

Lister lunged forward and flicked at the abort switches on the co-pilot's control panel – useless, unless the pilot initiated the abort sequence, too. He looked over at the Cat, hoping he would copy the manoeuvre. The Cat ignored him.

Lister lurched out of his seat and reached over for the pilot abort controls, but *Starbug* pitched again suddenly and his hand crashed into the wrong bank of switches.

The Cat screeched 'Dhub, hgniood hooy hrah klehk huthh twhah!?' and tugged at the collective, desperately trying to correct the craft's yawing. But with the single landing jet, and the reverse physics of backward Earth, manoeuvrability was almost zero.

Starbug began to spin. Inside the cockpit, the alert lights started flashing wildly and the siren's sucked-in *agoowa* wail added to the Bedlamic confusion.

In blind panic, the Cat began to hit switches at random with one hand, while his other wrestled with the collective stick between his legs.

Outside, in the choking gloom of the cave, Kryten switched his vision to infra-red and watched with mounting horror as *Starbug* span hopelessly out of control. The cavern around him was just an explosion of jet thunder as unsynchronized blasts from the front retros sucked scorch marks from the cave walls and neatly packed the long deep ruts beneath full of stone.

He should never have left them. He had no idea what had gone wrong, or what he could have done to correct it even if he'd stayed on board, but that didn't matter.

What mattered was, they were going to die.

And Kryten could add three more notches to his murderer's belt.

Desperate to do something, anything to help them, Kryten ran towards the stricken, spinning craft.

As a landing leg span overhead towards him, he leapt. His fingertips gripped the landing leg's splayed foot, and he hung on grimly.

Big mistake. His weight and momentum tilted the vessel even further off kilter, and its spin became wilder and more unstable. It pitched and rolled like a desperate gyroscope without enough force to regain its centre.

Kryten hung there, not knowing what to do. In his panic, he'd worsened the situation, but if he let go now, *Starbug* might topple radically over in the opposite direction and smash into the deadly rock. Perhaps even turn over completely.

What had he been thinking of? Had some part of his guilt-crazed mind thought he could tug the ship safely to the ground? Who did he think he was? An ex-patriot of the planet Krypton?

He tried to make the best of it by trying to gauge the spin, and swinging his body against it. As he pendulumed gently to and fro underneath the crazily twisting space craft, he tried to persuade himself he was making some small difference, but he wasn't very convincing.

Inside the cockpit, insanity reigned.

The Cat's emergency procedure of hitting every button in reach was not contributing massively to the restoration of calm. The seats were all jumping up and down on their hydraulics, computer slugs were pinging across the cabin and popping into their drives, lights were flashing crazily, and military band music was blasting from every speaker in the ship at ear-bleeding volume.

Lister lurched across the Cat and jabbed wildly at the abort panel. A lucky flick killed the retros, and the spin began to slow. The Cat regained control of the collective, brought the vessel horizontal and closed down the landing jets.

With the smallest of bumps, *Starbug* nestled back down on the cave floor.

The Cat leaned forward, flicked off the band music and grinned at Lister. 'Hthooms,' he said.

Lister shook his head and checked the external camera. The cave was empty of smoke, but Kryten was nowhere in sight.

Where the smeg had he gone? Had they landed on him?

Lister shot out of the cockpit and raced to the airlock. He ran his palm over the scanner again, and once again, it flashed red. What the hell was wrong now? He glanced over at the warning panel, which was blinking: 'Occupied.'

The inner wheel span and the airlock door clicked open. Kryten was standing in front of him, his plastic face twisted in fear and concern. 'Sir? Are you all right?'

Lister's relief at seeing Kryten safe instantly gave way to a sense of desperation and failure. He turned away and plonked himself in a chair by the scanner table. 'Yeah,' he mumbled without enthusiasm. 'We're fine, Kryten.'

The mechanoid stepped in and crooked his head towards the cockpit door. 'All of you?'

The Cat slinked down from the cockpit and Rimmer followed him.

Kryten felt so grateful to see them intact, he felt like spontaneously combusting. 'Oh, sirs, this is all my fault . . .

'No. It's Lister's fault,' Rimmer glared. 'He was acting like one of those little Scottish blokes in POW movies who suddenly go stir crazy and make a beeline for the electric fence.'

'It's nobody's fault, Kryten,' Lister said without looking up. 'It just happened. OK?'

'Not OK.' Rimmer strode over to him. 'Far from OK.' He leaned his face deep into Lister's personal space. '*OK!?* Have you seen the time?'

Lister nodded. 'Eleven forty-two.'

'Which means, unless my backwards arithmetic is seriously askew, that we have missed our flight window. Yes?'

Lister nodded again. 'Believe me, Rimmer, it's the last thing I wanted. I've already been stuck here for thirty-odd years.'

Rimmer straightened. Blame had been apportioned, and none of it had fallen on him. It was bizarre that such meaninglessness should be important to him, but it was, and he was beginning to feel better already.

That feeling was not going to last very long.

'All right, then,' he smiled. 'Let's talk damage limitation.' He turned to Kryten. 'There's absolutely no chance that we can attempt another reverse landing and achieve this flight window?'

'I'm afraid not, sir.'

Rimmer flicked his eyes briefly over to Lister, just in case anyone was in any doubt about the Blame Quotient, and then back to Kryten. 'Well, that's too bad, but we're stuck with it, I suppose. The question now is: when is the next flight window?'

Kryten squirmed. 'Well, I haven't exactly re-checked all of the calculations as yet . . .'

Rimmer smiled. 'All we need for the moment, Kryten, is your best guess.'

'Well, sir, I'd be reluctant to commit myself at this stage to a definite time and date.'

'Just a ballpark figure, Kryten. Just so we know we have enough time to prepare for the attempt properly.'

'Oh, I should think we'll have time enough for that, sir. Even if . . .'

'Kryten. Let me put it another way: just how long are we going to be stuck here on this hell hole, you oversized ugly dildo?'

'Fuh. . .' Kryten stammered. 'Fuh . . . Fuh . . .'

'Four hours? Four weeks? Four months?'

'Fuh . . . Fuh . . .' Kryten thumped his head against the airlock door. 'Ten years.'

PART TWO

Smoke Me a Kipper, I'll Be Back for Breakfast

ONE

Billy-Joe Epstein knew he was a coward, and what's more, he knew everyone else knew it, too. He gave it off, stank of it, somehow. Emanated it, like the stench from a week-dead skunk. And on this Saturday night, he sat hunched over his usual bar space, on his usual bar stool over his usual drink, emanating away, and trying to get drunk enough to help him forget he was a coward, which, as usual, was not going to work.

Billy-Joe (call sign: the Jewish Cowboy) was nineteen years old and he knew just about all there was to know about piloting state-of-the-art Space Corps craft. He sailed through the written tests, breezed through the oral exams, excelled at the theory. And in two days' time he was going to get thrown out of the Corps. The day after tomorrow he was going to take and fail his final Space Corps examination flight for the third, and therefore last, time. Because when it came to the dangerous stuff, the low-level passes over the high-gravity rock deserts of Miranda, Billy-Joe Epstein would, at the last moment, lose his nerve and veer away.

Because, as they said behind his back in the locker-room, Billy-Joe just didn't have the love spuds.

He looked down into his shot glass and saw his own cowardly reflection staring at him contemptuously in the treacle-coloured liquor, so he drained it, and looked up to order another one.

She didn't see him, of course. She never seemed to be looking in his direction, even if he was the only one in the bar, which was not uncommon. But that was fine by Billy-Joe, because it gave him more chance to be looking at her.

Her name was Mamie, not that Billy-Joe had ever plucked up the courage to call her by her name. She was, well, *better* than him. She could have her pick of the jocks who jostled the bar to have the honour of flirting with her. And she wouldn't even give *them* the time of day. She was . . . special. Her hair, well, you wouldn't say it was brunette, and you couldn't say she was a redhead, either. In between, kind of, depending on the light. And her eyes weren't blue, and they weren't green, but you get the idea. And Billy-Joe didn't converse with her at all, except to order his drinks and keep his manners with please and thank you. Anything else would have been just inconceivable. The thought, even, when it had the temerity to creep into his mind, of actually *asking her out on a date*, made him feel like someone was twisting his stomach bag at both ends with a high-tension torque wrench.

While he was waiting for her to notice he wanted serving, Billy-Joe felt a tap on his left shoulder. He turned to stare into a gleaming row of medals.

'I believe you're in my seat, Sonny.'

Billy-Joe looked around.

There was no one else in the bar room.

There were nine empty stools, count them, *nine*, ranked along the bar.

Mamie was looking over, now. He felt his ears begin to glow. He glanced at the jock's armband. A commander.

'Sure,' Billy-Joe shrugged. 'Sorry.'

He slipped over to the adjacent seat, as manfully as he could.

'What stinking luck,' the commander grinned. 'That one's mine as well.'

Billy-Joe was smiling, not out of bravado, but because his

face didn't know what else to do with itself. Was this officer trying to pick a fight?

Mamie stepped over and asked Billy-Joe, 'What'll it be?'

'I was here first, old love,' the commander smiled pleasantly.

'No you weren't.' Mamie returned the smile.

The commander's hand shot out rattlesnake fast and grabbed Mamie's wrist. 'Let's not have any backchat, old love.' His smile remained even and calm.

Mamie didn't make a sound, but Billy-Joe could see she was hurting. He cleared his throat. 'I think you've probably had a couple too many drinks, sir.' He tried to make it sound as uncontentious as possible: 'Maybe you probably should think about possibly not manhandling the lady that way, you reckon?'

The officer's smile broadened. He dropped Mamie's wrist. 'You feel possibly, perhaps, you're maybe man enough to probably stop me, you reckon?' he parodied.

'Suh, sir . . .' Billy-Joe stuttered.

'Oh, let's forget about rank, here, laddie.' The officer slipped off his jacket, its medals clanking musically as he laid it carefully on the barstool. 'Let's forget I'm your superior officer. Let's forget my gold bars, my medals, and my unarmed combat training officer badge. And let's just do it.'

Billy-Joe's face was still wearing the same smile it came in with, and his ears felt like they were about to burst into flames, as he watched the officer calmly rolling up his shirt sleeves. 'There really is no nee . . .'

It was only a one-syllable word, but Billy-Joe started it perpendicularly and ended it horizontally.

'. . . eed.' He had no idea where the blow had hit him, but his whole face hurt. He looked up. The officer was already rolling his sleeves back down, as if that one blow would be enough to put Billy-Joe Epstein down and keep him there.

Something about that made Billy-Joe mad. Mad enough to make him ignore his instinct to stay down and play dead.

Mad enough to make him get to his feet and square up to the man.

He felt ridiculous. He didn't know how to fight. He didn't even know how to stand for a fight. He tried hunching up and making small, tight circles with his bunched fists, but he felt like he was in Tom Brown's schooldays or something. All his life he'd avoided fights and now here he was, picking his first one with a multi-decorated officer who specialized in unarmed combat, and could probably kill him eight different ways with each of his fingers.

The officer raised his eyebrows in delight. 'You're game, sonny.' He glinted. 'Splendiferous stuff. Needed something to get the old circulation going in the fisteroonies.'

Billy-Joe actually saw the second blow. He didn't see it quite quickly enough to *avoid* it, but it was definitely an improvement, he felt, as it landed on his left ear, hard enough to rattle his brain against his skull like a caged budgerigar in an earthquake.

Although he felt it was probably futile even to try, he launched a punch of his own. His vision wasn't exactly clear, but he aimed roughly at the centre of the vibrating image of the officer, and was surprised when his knuckles made contact with flesh and bone.

The officer drew his hand across his lip and looked oddly at the smear of blood, as if it weren't real, couldn't be happening.

Billy-Joe hit him again. The officer staggered back. He shook his head. His composure was gone. Anger sprang to his face, and snarling, he leapt at Billy-Joe like a rabid wolf.

Billy-Joe twisted to one side, using the man's momentum against him and helped him tidily over the bar, where he crashed spectacularly into a stack of bottles promoting Clearhead alcohol-free vodka.

Billy-Joe stood where he was, making his Tom Brown circles with his fists, until it became obvious that the officer wasn't going to get up again.

Then Billy-Joe grabbed the commander's jacket – he was astonished how heavy the clattering medals were – and dumped it over the bar on his opponent's groaning body. 'Maybe you should think about leaving now. Sir.'

The officer grunted, staggered to his feet and crunched over the broken glass and out of the bar without looking back.

'You wanted a drink?'

Billy-Joe turned from the door. Mamie was smiling at him.

At him!

He shook his head. 'I don't think so.'

'On the house?'

'No, thanks. I've got a big flight exam in a couple of days. I should keep a clear head.'

'Well,' she smiled again. 'Anytime.'

'That's right kind.' He flicked her a salute and turned to go.

'Good luck with the test, Billy-Joe.'

He almost froze in the door, but he managed to keep walking.

She knew his name!

Maybe he'd pluck up the courage to ask her out, after all. Maybe he was less of a coward than he thought. He might even have the love spuds to make that low-level flight.

He made a deal with himself: if he could do that, he could ask Mamie to the passing-out ball.

He caught a glimpse of something glimmering in his right hand. He opened his palm. A St Christopher medal. He must have grabbed it during the fight.

He slipped it into his pocket, and forgot about it.

And that simple act would save quite a few lives.

TWO

Admiral Peter Tranter had several names, most of which he knew and approved of, and a few he didn't know and certainly wouldn't have enjoyed.

To his peers, he was known as 'Bungo', though no one could really recall why. To the rank and file, he was known, predictably, as 'the Admiral' or 'the Old Man'. To his valet, Kevin, he was 'Himself' or, in the dark recesses of the R & R club, after a bout of intense bad humour and several gimlets, 'Skunk Foot' and 'Vinegar Drawers'. His mistress called him 'Bun-bun' to his face. Behind his back, she called him 'Cheese'.

Right now, Vinegar Drawers was doing his best to destroy the pile on his absurdly luxurious carpet in his ridiculously large office, as he paced distractedly around his obscenely huge desk.

He wasn't much of an admiral; just one-star job. He commanded the Space Corps Research and Development Program, which, despite its impressive title and its even more impressive budget, was the smallest base in the corps, and his post was generally regarded as the least demanding in the admiralty.

Which was why, of course, he'd commandeered such an unfeasibly spacious office, ordered the disproportionately massive desk and padded around in his legendarily stinky footwear on a carpet so thick that golf balls could, and did, get lost in it.

It was his way of bestowing rank upon himself.

He'd been a high-flier, once. One of the youngest officers ever to achieve the command star. Then, inexplicably, the proud, purring engine of his career had phuttered and stopped. He'd received a series of increasingly obvious 'sideways' postings, until this one: the ultimate dead-end gig. There was no 'sideways' from R & D. Only up or . . .

. . . out.

He'd spent many long hours wondering about the why of it. He'd let it affect his work, his alcohol consumption, his personal hygiene and, worst of all, unless you were his valet, he'd let it affect his marriage.

He tormented himself with increasingly paranoiac explanations. Was there some kind of plot among the faceless pen-pushers of Space Corps administration to keep the best men down and promote only fools and dickwits? Had it been something he'd said, offhand at some luncheon somewhere, which had so offended some superior that the only fitting revenge had been to keep Tranter in permanent lustreless mediocrity?

He'd almost resigned himself to a doldrumatic career, where he never had to make a serious decision, contribute to policy planning, or achieve anything more significant or earth-shattering than shagging his mistress from the multitudinous angles offered by his overly humungous and otherwise redundant desk, when Project Wildfire came along.

Project Wildfire. Bun-bun's ticket up and out of here.

The problem with space-travel research was that humankind seemed to have reached the upper limits of its capabilities. The last significant advance in the field (demi-light speed drives) had been achieved before Bungo had been born. Of course, there were always minor improvements, tweaks to make engines more efficient, new formulae for cleaner, cheaper fuel. But nothing *major*. A few years back, Cheese had become quite excited about the prospects for Matter Transference devices, but after endless months of loading various rodents into the sending stations and scraping out gerbil molecular mulch from the remote receivers, even the most fervent advocates of MT had stopped bugging him for more budget.

Project Wildfire was different.

Project Wildfire was the code-name for a prototype craft that, theoretically, could break the big one.

Could break the speed limit of the Universe.

The light barrier.

And it worked.

Sort of.

It promised new horizons for the human race. Virtually instantaneous travel. The exploration of hitherto unexplorable star systems. And, most magnificent of all, another pip for Admiral Skunk Foot.

And now, just days before the inaugural test flight, disaster.

The test ship had returned.

It had returned approximately three days before it set off.

Not a terrible result, if you chose to look at the up side: they now had two *Wildfire* ships for the price of one – no small beer, considering the cost of the damn thing – and, as a rather pleasant side-effect, they appeared to have devised some form of time travel. On the down side, however, there were clearly some flaws in the design, evidenced by the fact that the returning craft had been damaged beyond repair, and its pilot charred dead and almost unidentifiable.

Almost.

So this was Tranter's dilemma; this was why he paced with nervous fury around his prop-from-the-Land-of-the-Giants desk: did he call off the mission, and risk his one great shot at personal advancement, or did he send his best and most respected pilot to a certain and unspeakable death?

Of course, he'd already made the decision, though he couldn't acknowledge it. What he was really agonizing over was his justification for it. Surely, since the craft had already returned, he was duty-bound to send it off. In fact, did he really have a decision to make? Wasn't it inevitable? Causality and all that. Didn't he owe it to History to embark on this, the next stage of humankind's technical evolution?

Didn't he really, really, need that extra pip?

THREE

It was a curious feeling, no question, staring at the blackened remnants of your own grinning skull. Hard not to shudder, though Ace fought off the impulse.

He peered into the sightless sockets of his charred *doppelgänger*, as if he expected some glimmer of recognition to flicker back at him from the dull dead darkness. The technical boys were off checking and re-checking the DNA profile, but Commander Rimmer didn't need any chemical verification. It was his skull, all right, tautened into the familiar obscene leer of a sudden heat death. There was the gold tooth, a trophy from the Academy boxing finals in his second year. There was the small nick to the right of his forehead, from the childhood game of Cowboys and Indians, when his brothers had cast him as General Custer while they played the Sioux nation, and Howard had got carried away and slung a real tomahawk at him.

He tightened his mouth in a grim parody of a smile, and slid his gaze down to the flight suit, remarkably intact considering the temperatures it must have endured. Ace made a mental note to write to the manufacturers and commend them for their workmanship. He paused, momentarily, on the tortured metal of his badge of rank, and then tried, once again, to study the wrecked control panel, an exploding mess of wires and screens jutting out of the twisted fascia of the cockpit.

There was something out of kilter here. Something that shouldn't have been. Something important.

He called down to the shower of sparks spattering from under the scorched nose-cone, 'Spanners, old love?'

The spark spray stopped, as the hot rasp of the oxyacetylene died. 'Yeah?'

'You say you've checked out the dash?'

'A dozen times, what's left of it.'

'And it all seems tick tock?'

'I dunno. There's something about it that bugs me.' The wheels on the trolley of his inspection board squealed against the hangar's rough tarmac as Lister slid out from under the craft and tugged up his welding mask. 'Can't put my finger on it.' He stared up into the glare of the skylight and studied the paradox of Commander Rimmer's silhouette inspecting itself. Lister's facial muscles yanked his lower lip a quarter of an inch higher. In hanger 101, good-quality smiles were in short supply this particular day. 'You're not going, you know.'

'How's that, matey?' Ace prodded at the buckled temperature gauge, which was partially obscured by the melted mess of his St Christopher medallion.

'Not unless we work out what went wrong.'

'Don't you start going soft on me, Spanners. You heard what the Old Man said. This match kicks off at oh-six hundred in the a.m., and I'm the Centre Forward.'

'I heard what he actually said was: "It's up to you."'

'That's the way a gentleman orders another gentleman on a suicide mission, Spanners. It's just good form.'

'Good form? Good *form*? You're going to get barbecued up there, and you're talking like it's another topping adventure for the Famous Five?'

Ace lowered his shades and hopped the fifteen feet down from the cockpit and landed on the tarmac with the easy grace of a pre-pubescent Russian gymnast. 'Look' – he took out a spotless handkerchief and wiped the sooty grime from his perfectly manicured fingers – 'come what may, I'm going to this party, Spanners. It's the chance of a lifetime.

Every test jock dreams of getting just a single shot at cracking one away over the boundary: this is mine. And I wouldn't miss it for all the bouillabaisse in Provence.'

Lister forked his hand through the thick wire brush of his regulation crop. 'I could stop you, you know.'

Ace tilted his head, though his eyebrows stayed parallel with the ground. 'I don't think I quite caught that, old chum.'

'It'd take about five seconds to do a number on the engine that'd put the schedule back months.'

'By God, the acoustics in here are dismal. Otherwise, I might have heard a dear friend of mine suggesting a Court Spatial offence like sabotage, and that would never do, now, would it?'

'Listen to me. We all accept we're working on the cutting edge of technology, here, and that means there's always going to be a little bit of a risk. But this is different. This isn't a little bit of a risk, Ace. That's *you* up there, looking like the last spare rib in a Chinese takeaway on a Saturday night. It's *you*. And from what I could follow of what those tech guys were saying, there's nothing we can do about it. It's already happened. It's inevitable.'

'I don't believe they're right, Spanners. Nothing's inevitable. No matter how bleak things seem, there's always a way through. That belief, that hope, that's the very thing about us that defines our humanity. I know I sound like a pompous nerd, and I'm sorry I can't be more fashionably cynical, but it's just not in my make-up pouch. Now, what do you say we put a lid on the chin-wagging, roll up our sleeves and comb every inch of this damned crate until we find out what went wrong, and put it right?'

Lister cracked a warped grin and shrugged with his forehead. 'Your call, Ace. I'm just the grease monkey.'

'Grease monkey? Ha!' Ace mirrored his grin and slapped him heftily on the back. 'You're the genius who builds the damn things, I'm just the airhead who wiggles the joystick.

Now, d'you manage to dig the black box out, you old tartlet?'

Lister handed him the recording device he'd torched out of the cone section. 'It was welded to the heat sink.' He glanced at the peeling metal of the hull. 'I hate to think what kind of temperatures this baby's been through.'

'Well, maybe we'll find out from this.' Ace jemmied open the seal with an easy twist of the crowbar, while Lister dragged over the portable monitor and plugged in the leads.

There was, it seemed to Lister, an unnecessary pause before Ace pressed the play button. Then he realized what the hesitation was about. The poor sod was steeling himself to watch his own death. 'Look, Commander,' he offered. 'Shouldn't we get this off to Tech? They're pretty keen to –'

'All in good time, Spanners. We've got to see this for ourselves.' And his elegantly cuticled fingernail flicked 'play'.

At first the screen displayed the computer read-out of the standard pre-flight instrument checks. Lister scanned the data. Everything seemed discouragingly normal.

Ace craned closer to the screen. 'Display's a bit dim, isn't it, old sausage?'

'It might seem a bit less dim,' Lister said, 'if you took off your smegging shades.'

Ace smiled apologetically. 'Like the preacher says: all is vanity.' And he raised his sunglasses. Lister met his gaze. Commander Rimmer was sporting a black eye. A real shineroonie. A classic. Every tint of purple and blue rippled out from the epicentre of his bloodshot eye towards his cheekbone. Ace's expression said 'Don't ask', so Lister didn't. So it *was* true. He'd heard it, but he hadn't believed it. Commander Ace Rimmer had been given a tonking by Billy-Joe Epstein. How was that possible?

Ace tossed his head gently, so the soft wave of his fringe hung over the offending feature, and they both turned their attention back to the screen.

It was a short recording – the entire trip, launch to blaze, had taken less than fifteen minutes – and when it was over, they still could find no clues as to what had happened, or, unthinkably, what was *destined* to happen, and how they might go about preventing it.

There *was* a clue, though.

In fact, there were three clues, staring out at them from the screen in every single frame of the recording.

FOUR

The contents of Lister's stomach lolloped queasily as he sipped at his seventh or eighth mug of disgusting coffee. He glanced at his watch without taking in the read-out. It was night, it was dark, over the quadrangle there was a warm woman asleep in his bed, with a dent in the mattress beside her which he should have been occupying, and that was all he needed to know about the time. He tried to focus once again on the looped recording he'd made of the black-box tape. The original had been commandeered, and was now being pored over by the overpaid research staff in their air-conditioned lab, with a plentiful supply of hot snacks and good fresh coffee to hand, while Lister shivered in the fume-laden yawn of hanger 101, wondering whether to spend the last of his loose change on an oxymoronically named Tastee Noodle Pot from the dispensing machine, or save it for a final mug of the foul coffee.

It had been a while since he'd pulled a round-the-clock shift, but the symptoms of exhaustion were as familiar as an old friend. Right now, he was experiencing the big gloom phase which always hit just before the dawn, when he began to feel resentful of regular people, sleeping their sane sleep in their sensible beds with their normal daylight-hours jobs. Parts of his body started becoming forgetful about how to perform the most basic operations: his mouth would neglect its swallowing duties, and he'd suddenly realize drool had caked on his chin; his buttocks wouldn't shift frequently enough in the chair and sharp pains would shoot up his back, urging him to kindly remember to move now and then, if you please, because there's plenty more where that came from. Time would start dragging and jumping teasingly, so that minutes could last several hours, and then flit by suddenly in unseen flocks.

He comforted himself with the thought that the next phase couldn't be too far away, and that was the good part. He would suddenly be aware that daylight had sneaked up on him, and he'd get an adrenaline rush, thinking of being the first customer at the breakfast canteen, of the mounds of sizzling fresh bacon he'd deservedly consume, of watching the poor suckers who'd slept the night away dragging their way into a day of drudgery, while he wound his way home to the sweet caress of a sleep well earned, with sunbeams slanting on to the bed through the slits in his curtains. He'd begin to feel special, almost more than human, having gone on when lesser men would have surrendered.

And, best of all, he would feel incredibly horny.

But all that was hours away, and right now it was a matter of dife or leth that he found a way to concentrate.

Dife or leth?

He had to stop *drifting*. He pinched the skin of his cheeks cruelly, sipped again at the foul mouth of his coffee mug, shuddered, and forced himself to re-focus on the screen.

He jumped at the sudden loudness of the hangar door sliding metallically back, thus adding stale coffee to the unnameable *mélange* of stains and odours on his overall crotch. He cursed mentally. For the past five years he'd been fighting a running battle against his own natural slobbiness, and was still losing, badly. The fluorescents buzzed and clicked on, filling the hangar with shocking white light.

'Good God, Spanners. You still here, old fruitcake?'

Lister tried to speak, but the coffee and tiredness had furred his throat, and what came out of his mouth sounded like the unintelligible ranting of a chronic drunk raging across the street at invisible demons. He coughed and tried again. 'What time is it?'

Ace, in full flight gear, clacked over to him. 'Zero hour minus two.'

Lister's drowsy brain couldn't achieve the required arithmetical standard to subtract two hours from six o'clock. 'What's that, then?'

'Four a.m. Time for you to catch some zeds, old chumburger.'

'The White Coats come up with anything?'

'Zipporola, I'm afraid. They've run everything through the simulator upside down and back to front: *nada*. They're tearing their hair out. Damn thing should work, they reckon. You get anywhere?'

Lister rolled his head back along his shoulders, cracking his neck satisfyingly. 'There's got to be something here. It's just a matter of time.'

'Face it, Spanners: if you haven't found it, it's not there. You get some shut-eye. I'm going to need you around for the pre-flight check, so you're only going to fit in about ninety winks, anyway.'

Lister thought about protesting, but couldn't work up the energy. He sighed, big time, and pushed his castored chair away from the screen. The truth was, he'd gone more or less image-blind, anyway. He'd watched the disk so many times, it had become meaningless to him. Jumbled nonsense. He felt like he'd been through an all-night session of MTV. 'Half an hour,' he said, as if it were a threat. 'On the inspection trolley. You'd better wake me.' He stood, and tried to walk, but his left leg had gone dead. Too tired to bother about the pain, he simply dragged it behind him towards the trolley.

'Good man.' Ace leaned over and stopped the disk.

In the sudden silence that whistled emptily through Lister's fatigue-sensitized ears, a thought struck him. Obvious. It was obvious! 'Hang on!' he yelled, and hopped back to the video console. He hit 'search', 'play' and then 'pause'. 'There! There it is!'

Ace peered at the flickering still frame. Suddenly, his face ignited with delight and relief. 'By God, Spanners. You've only gone and cracked it!'

FIVE

Black Box Recording
Project: 70773
Codename: Wildfire
Status: Need-To-Know Only
Security Clearance: AAA
Europa Test Centre
Event: 237. Prototype Test Flight
Dateline: 0600 31/03/81 Earth Standard

The pre-flight instrument check winked into blackness, to be replaced on the screen by a head-and-shoulders shot of the pilot, framed by dozens of digital readouts of the craft's various functions. His helmet was on, but his oxygen mask dangled unstrapped by his chin, and the Plexiglas of his raised visor flared in the overhead cockpit light.

'All checks are go-go. Flight recorder on-line.' Commander Rimmer leaned towards the camera, his hands flicking test switches on the out-of-view console below. He was clean-shaven, and it was impossible to tell he'd been up all night, or that he had any notion this flight could possibly end in his death: his clear eyes glimmered with the little-boy excitement his workmanlike tone successfully concealed. There was a sudden high-pitched squeal, and he winced.

'Ungh, could do without the feedback, MC.'

The mission controller's voice bzzted back, flat and tinny

over the speaker. 'MC to Wildfire: sorry about that. We're broadcasting your transmission on the base PA. Some idiot looped the wiring.'

'Let's hope it's not the guy who did the drive relays on this crate.'

Laugh. 'That's a no-no, Wildfire. We're all go-go at this end. Zero minus thirty, from my mark.' Pause. 'And . . . mark!'

'Tertiary ignition . . . engaged.'

The tortured whine of jet engines built to a slow crescendo, and the image began to shudder. Ace kissed the first two fingers of his gloved hand and pressed them against the St Christopher medallion dangling from the dash. He flicked the oxygen mask over his face and flipped down the visor.

'Engaging launch catapult.' In the visor's reflection, the sky crept into view as hydraulic legs tilted *Wildfire One* back towards its optimum launch angle.

'Zero minus twenty, Wildfire. You are in launch position.'

The hydraulics juddered to a stop, and Ace leaned forward. 'Chocks away.' He flicked a switch and braced his features as the spacecraft shot back into its launch silo.

'Zero minus fifteen. You're looking good from here, Wildfire.'

'Bet you say that to all the pilots, you old Lothario. OK, engaging secondary ignition.' Another set of jets slow-howled into life.

'Beginning automatic countdown . . .'

A computer voice kicked in. 'Ten . . .'

'Good luck, Wildfire.'

'Nine . . .'

'MC? Is Spanners around?'

'Eight . . .'

Lister's voice fssed over the speaker. 'That's a yo, Commander.'

'Seven . . .'

'Thanks for pulling the all-nighter, old love. Above and beyond, and all that.'

'Six . . .'

'Don't be a ponce. Just get the smegging thing back in one piece.'

'Five . . .'

'Will do. Engaging primary.'

'Four . . .' was almost drowned by the massive belch of the main engines.

One of the readout dials turned red and started flashing.

'Three . . .'

'Abort, Wildfire, we have a hiccup on the G-force modifier.'

'Two . . .'

'Negative, MC.' Rimmer leaned forward and tapped the control fascia. The readout turned green and stabilized. 'Loose wire.'

'One . . .'

Commander Rimmer gave a thumbs up. 'That's it, one and all. Smoke me a kipper, I'll be back for breakfast.'

'Zero.'

The lift-off booster kicked *Wildfire One* free of the silo. Despite the G-force Modification Field, the skin around Ace's eyes dragged back his features like a bad Hollywood facelift, as he fought to maintain control of a craft travelling at a greater rate of acceleration than any human had ever experienced.

His image quivered madly as he shot through the temporary window in the Plexiglas dome and was yowling through the vacuum of space in less than forty seconds.

The speaker tzzed: 'Wildfire, you are go-go.' There was a tinny cheer from the control tower.

The velocity readouts blurred as the monumental engines maintained the blistering acceleration out towards the gaseous whirl of Jupiter's sphere. Ace struggled against the G force to reach the control panel, his voice straining against the screaming mechanical bedlam in the cockpit as he issued his penultimate pre-arranged communication: 'Igniting course correction jets.'

Wildfire One pitched down towards the gas giant, using the planet's massive gravitational pull to add to its momentum.

The drag looked unbearable: Ace's lips were being stretched back into an eerie, quivering grin and the helmet's visor seemed to be bending inwards towards his face, warping the reflection of the planet's Great Red Spot – a permanent hurricane the size of the Earth that howled relentlessly over its surface. He strained to move his arm towards the controls. Six inches. Seven. The pull snatched it back.

There was a hint of muted babble from Mission Control. ' . . .won't make it . . . can't reach . . .'

Gripping the armrests of the pilot seat, slowly, agonizingly, he edged his entire body forward. When he could go no further, he tilted his right shoulder towards the fascia and began stretching his vibrating hand out, centimetre by aching centimetre, as if he were pushing some colossal invisible stone up hill. With a final, grunting effort, he reached the switch and, through teeth gritted in an exaggerated Burt Lancaster grin, he said: 'Engaging *Wildfire* drive.'

The machinery's clamour ceased, and the screen whited out in the visual equivalent of the sonic boom as Commander Arnold J. Rimmer became the first living creature to break the light barrier.

Just as suddenly, the image returned.

Now the craft was buffeting so violently, Ace's image was blurring. The noise level in the cockpit had become unbearable. Half the digital read-outs were registering red, and great clusters of the rest were following suit by the second. Ace was pinned, helpless, his body being sucked into the thick leather of the pilot seat which began to fold around him. The temperature reading started climbing rapidly. The

Plexiglas visor began to warp. Ace tried to raise his hand to tear off his helmet but could manage barely a centimetre.

His gloves began smouldering.

All the readouts flashed red. The cockpit filled with choking smoke.

'This is control centre, Europa. You are in violation of Space Corps air space. Please identify yourself. Repeat, please iden . . .'

Then the AV cables melted, and there was only blackness and silence.

SIX

'There! It was staring at us all the time! We couldn't see it for looking!'

Lister's enthusiasm might have been more welcome to Admiral Tranter if (a) it had been a slightly more civilized hour than five in the morning, (b) the man's breath had smelled slightly less like a hyena's flatulence and (c) in his ebullience he had remembered it was considered impolite in superior circles to spray the listener with stale-coffee-coloured spittle when speaking.

What, precisely, had been staring at them all the time? The admiral leaned closer to the screen and peered at the frozen image of Commander Rimmer in the cockpit. He half-closed his eyes as if he were trying to unscramble a 3D Magic Eye *trompe-l'oeil* without really expecting it to work. He waited for what he considered to be a decently contemplative interval, and then squeezed his over-cologned chin and shook his head. 'Sorry, I just can't . . .'

Lister leaned forward and tapped the screen rapidly with the knuckle of his forefinger. 'There!' He turned his wide-eyed grin towards the admiral, barely millimetres from his face. 'There!'

Tranter tried to maintain his querulous smile as he was treated to a hot wave of Lister's pungent expiration but, while his lips did a creditable job, his eyes registered an unmistakable blend of horror and nausea. He straightened to put a safer distance between himself and this hygienic threat. 'All right, chaps. Let's not make this a guessing game.'

'You'll have to excuse Spanners, Admiral. He's put in a thirty-hour stint on this one. Gears are running a little slow. Still, he's the chap who spotted it. Only fair he . . .'

'It's there! There!' Lister jumped up and down, grinning, his eyebrows crescented at the very peak of their elevation.

Tranter seriously considered taking his pistol out of his drawer and splattering what passed for this man's brains over the wall. He could have it framed and tell everyone it was a Jackson Pollock.

'The date! Check the date/time readout.'

'The date?'

'Thirty-one, zero-three.' He nodded enthusiastically, as if he were training a particularly stupid dog to sit up and beg. 'Thirty-first of March,' he translated. 'Three days ago!'

Tranter maintained his cool by reflecting that it would probably be an exceptionally *small* Jackson Pollock. 'Correct me if I'm wrong, but wasn't that precisely when we recovered the craft?'

'Yes!'

Ace recognized the dangerous glint in Tranter's eye and cut in: 'D'you see, Admiral? If this was our *Wildfire One*; if we'd launched it today, if it had broken the time barrier and then showed up three days ago, the flight recorder would have logged *today's* date.'

Tranter glanced over at Rodenbury, the white-coated technical coordinator, who was trying his best not to look shame-faced. The *date*? These boffs were talking about cracking time travel, and they hadn't checked the bloody *date*? 'I don't understand. If this isn't our ship, then whose the hell ship is it?'

Rodenbury cleared his throat. 'Well, in a way, we're not absolutely one hundred and ten per cent certain, Admiral.'

'But I saw the test results. You assured me, did you not, that the corpse in that craft was unquestionably that of

Commander Rimmer?' Tranter's eyes flitted guiltily at Ace, and then carried on glaring at Rodenbury.

'Oh, uh, yes sir, I . . .'

'I believe you said you were certain. One hundred and fifteen per cent certain, as I recall.'

'Indeed, that is also my recollection of our, uh, conversation, Admiral, but there may be some . . .

'So would you like to explain to me how it is possible for him to be both dead and alive at the same time?'

'Well, uh, I believe Commander Rimmer's theory is about the best spin we can put on it.'

'Commander *Rimmer's* theory?'

'Well, I wouldn't take credit for its being *my* theory, Admiral, I just helped thrash it out with Spanners, here, and a couple of the tech boys. You see, I think our blind spot's been this breaking the time barrier business: you can understand everyone jumping to that conclusion, *wanting* it to be true. Damn it, I wanted it to be true myself.'

Lister, long past the fatigue point where his facial muscles were sufficiently under his control to disguise his expressions, was unable to conceal his astonishment at Ace's generosity. Lister had been there. The white coats had simply sat and gawped like adolescent boys peeking through a hole in a nudist camp fence as the good commander pointed out the errors in their Wildfire theory, and outlined his own alternative, complete with diagrams and mathematical proof. The truth was that the researchers had been rendered fact-blind by the prospect of the glittering prizes that were waiting for whoever cracked time travel: a Nobel Prize or two, a lifetime ticket to the lucrative lecture circuit and their names on the spine of an impenetrable book that would top the bestseller charts for decades. For them, the fact that their test pilot had been broiled alive by the process had been an irritant: a temporary glitch, nothing more. Some of them had actually begun working on presentation papers to establish their authorship of the theory, rather than concentrating on the problem of Ace's impending demise. Yet, here he was, letting them off the hook.

'So, it's . . . Have I got his straight? We haven't broken the, uh, the time barrier, then?'

'Not exactly, Admiral.'

Tranter slumped into his oversized chair. He actually felt his eyes begin to sting with disappointment. He'd already rather rashly ordered a dozen new, hideously expensive gold stars for his uniforms: twice as many as necessary, just in case the Admiralty saw fit to leapfrog him up to a triple-pipper.

Ace lit one of his rare cheroots – his only vice, unless you counted an extremely active, multi-partnered sex life as a vice, which Ace didn't. 'I believe we've cracked the reality barrier.'

'The reality barrier?' Tranter leaned forward. He had no idea what the reality barrier might be, but it sounded good. It sounded wonderfully . . . promotional.

'Let's look at the facts. One: this pilot, let's call him the *beta* Rimmer, he took off on the test flight three days earlier than ours was scheduled. Two: the *beta* Rimmer hasn't got one of these beauties.' Ace raised his shade, exposing his black eye.

'Where did you get that, Commander?' Tranter had heard a rumour, but it couldn't be true . . .

'Altercation with a door jamb, Admiral.' Ace lowered his sunglasses. 'And three: I no longer possess a St Christopher medallion. Conclusion: the *beta* Rimmer is not me. He's *almost* me, just not quite. Now, from here on, it's speculation and prediction, but I think it's pretty solid. We believe the *beta* Rimmer belongs to another reality, another dimension, if you like, co-existing with our own, but neither affecting the other – slightly out of phase. When the *beta* ship hit the light barrier, it jumped out of its own dimension and into ours.'

'So you're saying there are two realities; two universes running parallel with each other, with only minor differences in between? And the *Wildfire* drive can jump between them?'

'Why only two, Admiral? Why just an *alpha* and a *beta* reality? Why not a *delta* and a *gamma* reality?' Ace craned over Tranter's huge desk. 'Why not an *infinite* number of alternative realities, coexisting simultaneously with each other?'

Tranter found himself wondering if this might be an appropriate juncture to avail himself of the secret supply he kept hidden in the water tank of his office bathroom. But the sun couldn't honestly be said to be over the yard-arm quite yet. It was 5 a.m. The sun wasn't even over the bloody *horizon*. 'But why? Where would these realities come from? What would they be doing there?'

'Here's the theory: almost every day, we all make decisions that affect the course of our lives. Thousands of decisions: should we take the job or hang on for something better? Should we end this relationship or try to work it out? Should we walk up this street or down this other one? Should we run across the road or wait for the lights to change? Should we have the ham or the chicken? Now, what if every time we made a choice that affected the course of our life, in some other reality, the alternative were played out? Say, in the *alpha* universe, we wait for the lights and cross safely, but in the *omega* universe, we run across the road and get hit by a truck. Here, we choose the ham, and everything's OK; there we go for the chicken and contract salmonella.'

Tranter reflected. In another reality, then, some alternative Admiral Tranter, at this point in the conversation, would have made his excuses and headed for the bathroom. He turned the thought over in his mind for a second before deciding he might as well make it this reality. 'Excuse me for a second, gentlemen.' He rose and padded pensively through the thick carpet to his private lavatory and locked the door.

He fished out the navy rum and sucked down its dark red warmth. What did this all mean? Obviously it was intriguing. More than intriguing: if the commander were right, it was philosophically astonishing. But he couldn't immediately envisage any practical applications of the breakthrough. He couldn't imagine what use the military might make of it.

In short, he couldn't be certain it would lead to career enhancement, gold-star-wise.

He screwed the cap back on the bottle with practised speed, liberally sprinkled his mouth with peppermint spray and doused his chin with yet more aftershave, replaced the water-tank cover, flushed the toilet unnecessarily and padded back into his office.

'It's certainly a fascinating concept, Commander. Thing is: I can't quite see where it takes us.'

Ace looked up from the computer he was poring over with Rodenbury. 'The point is, something went wrong with the *beta* ship. We think we now know what that something was. And, more importantly, we think we can put it right. We were planning to program the *Wildfire* drive for minimum burn: it's a natural thing to do, maiden trip and all that: don't want to push the boat out further than necessary. But the analysis shows us that's precisely what they did in the *beta* reality. The result was: they jumped too close. Our mathematical models predict a kind of super-friction between dimensions – something to do with incompatible tachyon densities, don't quite follow it myself,' Ace lied, having been personally responsible for discovering the super-friction equation, 'but basically, it boils down to this: the closer the reality, the tougher the friction. That's what scorched the crate – it came in too close to home. As best we can tell, if we increase the drive burn by a factor of five or six, the super-friction will be reduced to tolerable levels.'

Tranter's cheeks glowed red with alcohol burn as he tried to follow Ace's logic. That sly snifter had done him no good at all. He wished he'd been in the reality where Admiral Tranter had sagely resisted the temptation to drink before breakfast. 'All well and good, Commander. But where does it *get* us, actually?'

Lister's features snarled as his adrenalized sense of smell caught a strong whiff of Tranter's booze breath from a good ten paces. Lister was not naturally respectful of the chain of command. He'd taught himself to fight his impulsive rebelliousness over the years until his tongue resembled a Dobermann's favourite pet chew, but this guy was a complete waste of airspace. 'Well, for one thing, *Admiral*,' and he made the epithet sound like an insult, 'it means Commander Rimmer might actually have a fair-to-middling chance to survive the jump, which, I don't know about you, but we all feel is a bit of a bonus.'

Tranter chose to ignore Lister's aggressive tone. 'Of course, I'm delighted about that. Ecstatic. But what I'm driving at, chaps: anyone can see the applications of a drive that can travel through time. But what possible benefit can we educe from a drive that can traverse realities? I mean, could we, for instance, aim for a dimension, say, where time travel has been perfected and bring the technology back?'

Ace exhaled a thick, blue cloud of cheroot smoke. 'No. 'Fraid not, Admiral. As far as we can tell, dimension travel's something of a one-way street. Look, if the infinite-dimensions theory is correct, every single second of every single day, millions of people are making key choices that affect the course of their existences, each decision spawning yet another reality. It would be impossible to map a way through. Frankly, even if we thought we *could* find a way back, it would be impossible to establish for absolute certain whether or not the reality we returned to was the one we left.'

Tranter poured himself a glass of water from his unusually large carafe. 'So the upshot is, Commander, you're expecting me to give a green light to this trip, knowing that the best we can hope to achieve from it . . .' he sipped, '. . . is flushing thirty billion dollarpounds of hardware and the best pilot we've ever had straight down the khazi?' No doubt about it, he'd have to choke down his pride and send those bloody stars back as soon as they arrived. In fact, he might do well to check up on the second-hand value of the stars he was already wearing.

'Uh, Admiral, we're about ninety-seven per cent certain *Wildfire One* could fire off a tachyon message complete with digitalized video footage of the new universe, so long as he got it off inside, say, fifteen seconds of arrival, while his trail back was still warm, uh, as it were,'

'Oh, much better. A blurry shot of some stars that are probably identical to the ones we've already got, and a soundbite for the *News at Noon*. That's a fabulous return for an outlay of thirty billion. That'll probably snag me the cover of *Investor's Chronicle*. I mean, at least the original moon shots from Earth gave the world Teflon.'

'Oh, come on, Bungo,' Ace cooed, 'You wouldn't stop a girl going to a big dance like this, would you? Who knows where the technology could lead? We've got to try it, now we know it's there.'

Lister spoke up. He was beginning to hit the feel-good phase of fatigue. He was even starting to feel horny. 'Admiral, if Ace . . . if the commander *can* shoot off that message, it means we'll know for sure the dimensions theory is sound.'

'Yes, wonderful.'

'Don't you get it? If it's true, it's mind-blowing. It means that every possibility gets played out. Everyone gets a fair share of decent shots and bad breaks. It means, in the end, there really is justice in the universe. Life *means* something.'

Admiral Tranter found himself wishing he was in another reality again. One of the realities where Lister hadn't chosen that moment to get an erection, or at least hadn't been too tired to notice it and cover up the fact. But no, he was stuck here, in this reality, where some solitary trooper in Tranter's head was playing the 'Last Post' for his career, while he stared across his desk, eye-to-eye with Lister's love pole, which was making an Action-Man-sized tent out of the crotch of his unspeakable overalls. He directed his gaze at Ace. 'I'm sorry, Commander. I don't see how I can justify . . .'

'What are you made of, man?' Lister leered dangerously at Tranter. 'It was OK to send him when you thought he was going to get toasted, but when there's no glory in it for you . . .'

Ace bounded to the desk and interposed himself between Tranter and Lister. 'Steady on, old love. You're not thinking straight.'

Tranter was rattled. 'You're treading a very thin line, sonny. One more outburst like that, and you'll find yourself servicing dodgem cars in a fourth-rate travelling fair.'

Lister gently shrugged off Ace's restraining hand. 'Maybe. And if I'm out of line, I'm sorry. Maybe I said it the wrong way, but that doesn't change the facts. What I said was true, Admiral. You've got to give him his shot. You owe it to him. Smeg, we all do.'

Tranter fought back an extremely compelling urge to take down the largest of his volumes on space law and thump it down hard on Lister's bivouac crotch. But what could he say? The little gimboid was right. If word got out he'd put the mockers on Ace's chance to explore what was probably humankind's final horizon, his on-base popularity would plunge below child-molester level. There wasn't a man, woman or child on Europa who didn't owe some debt of gratitude to Commander Rimmer.

On the other hand, thirty billion dollarpounds was a lot of spondulics to be blasting off to dimensions unknown. What he really ought to do was check with central command.

Who would almost certainly give it a big thumbs down.

Yes. Let someone else take the flak for this one. True, it

would be another nail in his career's coffin – if there was room for another nail in there – but he was zugzwanged: whichever way he moved, he lost. At least, damage-limitation wise, he'd be seen to have done the right thing.

He tried to look Rimmer in the face, but failed. Instead, he addressed his own warped reflection in the water carafe. 'I'm sorry, Commander. I'm going to have to refer this one upstairs.'

'You *what*!?' A globule of stale coffee spittle landed on Tranter's desk. 'You're going to pass the *buck*?! The one chance you've had in God knows how many years to do something halfway worthwhile and you're turning it *down*?'

Tranter, stunned, looked up into Lister's psychopathically wide eyes. He was convinced the oily little sod was going to clamber on to his desk on all fours and rip out his throat with bare teeth.

'Easy, now, laddie,' Ace's calm voice cut through the tension. 'The admiral's right.'

But Lister was beyond restraint. 'Wake up and smell your early morning dump, Vinegar Drawers! They'll turn it down! They always do. Because it's easier to say "no". Those arsewipes wouldn't know a breakthrough if it raped their cattle and stole their wives. If that ship doesn't fly today, it'll never fly. They'll cobweb it in some hangar, filed under "pending" till nobody can remember what it was built for in the first place. Now is the time: now or never.'

Tranter's finger was hovering below the red security button concealed on the underside of his desk. He would have pressed it, but he was intrigued. Had this piece of scum really called him Vinegar Drawers? What did he mean by Vinegar Drawers? 'Finished, boy?'

Lister wasn't finished. Not quite. 'Look at you: you sit there behind your enormous desk in your huge office be-cause you think it makes you look big. Well, it doesn't. You know what? It makes you look small. Tiny man. Tiny mind. You've got no magnificence in your soul, have you? Who knows what he'll find out there? Smeg, he might even chance on some far-flung reality where the base commander isn't a petty little small-minded lush!'

That did it. Tranter hit the button and the two security guards were in the room and frog-marching Lister to the brig before he even had the chance to wish he'd had his mouth sewn up at birth.

SEVEN

It wasn't, strictly speaking, sunlight. This far out in the solar system, the sun wasn't a big player, energy-source-wise. What passed for sunlight on the ice world of Europa was the bright, orange glow of the planet Jupiter, magnified through the reinforced Plexiglas dome that held the Jovian satellite's artificial atmosphere. Still, Ace Rimmer had spent most of his life under horizons dominated by the majestic disc of the king of the planets, and for him this was the skyline of home.

And in all probability, he would never see it again.

He took a final drag on his cheroot and crunched it out on the rough concrete of the quadrangle. True enough, there was little to keep him here. By design, he'd always avoided forming close relationships. As a test pilot, he'd seen too many of his colleagues leave too many loved ones grieving for far too long. Married men who stayed on as jocks risked more than their own lives every time they took to the air. That wasn't a danger Ace had been prepared to live with.

He'd always planned to have a family. Though his first love was the freedom the cockpit of speed gave him, he knew it wouldn't be available to him for ever. He had a couple, maybe three years of first-class flying to look forward to, and then he was going to quit the Corps. He couldn't face the deprivation of a desk job or flight training school. He didn't want to wind up like Bungo, turning his career frustrations in on himself in a wicked orgy of self-hate and self-destruction. No, what he'd planned to do, he'd probably invest in a reconditioned cargo shuttle and odd-job his way around the solar system until he found a place he felt he could put roots in, somewhere with challenge and promise, somewhere he could settle down and breed.

At least, that had been the plan.

Now he was facing a one-way trip into the unknown.

And he was afraid.

He wasn't afraid of the mechanics of the trip – he was fairly certain his alterations to the drive would make the jag through the reality barrier safely enough. He was afraid of what he might find.

True, he had more idea than most about his destination. He hadn't told absolutely everybody absolutely everything the reality theory postulated. He knew, for example, that wherever he wound up, it would be somewhere along his own destiny line: he would encounter another version of himself: another Rimmer whose history would have diverged from his own at some point in their shared lives.

Amplifying the magnitude of the *Wildfire* leap by a factor of five would probably mean their paths had divided a significant while ago. Possibly several years.

And he was afraid of meeting himself.

He was afraid this other Rimmer would be better than him, somehow. A more rounded person. A Rimmer who had made better choices, who hadn't taken the frivolous option of following his lust for excitement. A Rimmer who had contributed more to humankind.

A Rimmer who would make him feel inadequate.

He was saved from his maudlin mental meanderings by a woman's voice.

'Commander! Commander Rimmer!'

He looked up. Mamie Pherson was scuttering over the parade ground from the direction of the club, in heels not built for running. She reached him, breathless, and then arched, hands on knees to re-oxygenate. 'Commander . . .' she panted, 'Thank God! I heard you'd gone.' She straightened, her face even more beautiful for the red glow of exertion.

'Mamie, are you all right?'

'All right? All right? I'm *perfect*!'

'Well, I'll be the judge of that, old love.' He smiled and brushed a dark wisp of hair from her right eye. It flopped back immediately. 'No, you're right, you *are* perfect.'

Mamie punched him playfully in the chest. 'Didn't you hear? Billy-Joe *passed*! He passed grade one! He's got his gold wings!'

'Best news I've heard all year.'

'And it's all thanks to you, you brilliant old clever custard.'

'Me? I think it probably had rather more to do with young Billy's flying abilities, wouldn't you say?'

'You know what I mean. He'd never have had the confidence if . . .'

'Well, punch me in the hooter if I miss my mark, young lady, but I thought we'd agreed never to mention that little business, didn't we?'

'Well, I wouldn't, not to anyone else. Not even to Billy-Joe.'

'*Especially* not to Billy-Joe. Not even when the pair of you are old and grey and sitting by some glowing fire surrounded by hordes of yowling grandchildren, all right?'

Mamie's cheeks flushed even redder. 'You're getting a bit ahead of yourself, aren't you, Commander? He hasn't even asked me for a date.'

'Oh, but he will. He'll be looking for a special someone to take to his passing-out ball, and unless I've seriously lost my touch, that someone'll be young Mamie Pherson.'

Mamie dropped her head. 'You think?'

'Either that, or I'll *really* have to box his ears and knock some sense into him.'

She thumped him playfully again. Ace smiled. Why was a punch considered an acceptable witty riposte when administered by a young woman? If a man answered a playful remark in that way, Ace would have ranked him, in terms of intellectual capacity and social skills, alongside a TV weather presenter. When a woman did it, it just made his heart melt.

She looked up, and something in his smile pained her. She looked away again. 'Commander . . . I've heard people talking . . . around the camp . . . I mean, they don't understand what you were really doing for Billy-Joe, and they're saying things . . . it makes it hard to keep to it myself.'

'Now, now. People will talk, Mamie. That's the way of the world. Sticks and stones, et cetera, eh?'

'And that black eye . . . and Billy-Joe will never even know he should be thanking you.'

'Listen to me, young lady: the way things turned out, this little shineroonie was the best thing that could have happened to me. You'll never know how, but this beauty saved my bacon. It's me who should be thanking Billy-Joe.' Ace glanced at his watch. Time to spring Spanners. 'Look, really must fly, now, Mamie. Best of luck with the date.' He kissed her tenderly on her cheek, and strode off over the parade ground.

Mamie shielded her eyes against the Jupiter glare, watching his sure-footed silhouette disappear into the early-morning heat haze. When he'd gone, she sighed a smile and said, to no one in particular, 'What a guy.'

EIGHT

Somewhere, way off, there was an old-fashioned fire engine charging along to intercept his dream, hissing 'Lister . . . Lister' in between its primitive clanging.

He slowly floated awake to find his left side completely paralysed from the unyielding pressure his coma-tired body had inflicted on itself. Where was this place? The walls were grey and unmarked. A dull strip light farted its bleak radiance into the tiny room from overhead. There was an unidentifiable and deeply unpleasant smell, which Lister correctly surmised could conceivably have been produced by his own body. His sleep-sluggish brain began a slow memory trawl. He'd been in this kind of place before. Yes. If he was right, he would turn his head and see bars. He turned his head. Next best thing: wire mesh. He was in some kind of cell.

He swung his good leg over the side of the bench, dragging its unresponsive partner along with it. Hanging on to the bench with his right hand for balance, he swung his left shoulder several times until his limp hand flopped up on to his lap and he could check his watch. Six thirty-six.

This was good. He knew where he was. He knew the time. Now, if only he could remember what the smeg he was doing here, all would be right with the world.

Again, he heard the hissed, 'Lister . . . Lister . . .', and the dull clanging of an enamel cup against metal mesh.

The voice sounded familiar.

'Can you hear me, old Building and Loan drinking buddy?'

Oh my God. It couldn't be.

'Petersen?' he called, timidly.

'Thaat's riiiight! I knew I recognized that smegging snore!'

What was going on? He hadn't seen Petersen in two years. Not since he and Krissie had been re-assigned from *Red Dwarf* to the Europa test base. What was the mad Dane doing in the next cell? Had it all been a cruel dream?

'Petersen? Where are we?'

Petersen's laugh rattled the mesh in Lister's cell. 'Haaaa! That's my old buddy, all right. We're in some kind of prison, is my guess.'

'But we're on Europa, right?'

'Could be. Yes, I think so. Blue-moon-ish-type planetoid, close to that big bastard with the red spot?'

'Yeah. That's Europa.'

'Bingo!' Petersen said, and laughed again.

Lister started massaging some life back into his dead leg. 'Question is, Olaf, what are you doing here?'

'It's a little hazy, but about twenty-four hours for drunk and disorderly I would reckon.'

'Yeah, I mean, why aren't you on Triton?'

'Triton? Oh, yeah. That house I bought. No good. I couldn't take it. Beautiful house, but no oxygen, no gravity and worse than that, no alcohol. Those sly bastards won't even let you smuggle it in honestly. I mean, hey, I don't mind floating around a twenty-five bedroom mansion in a space suit twenty-four hours a day, with no neighbours for a million miles or so, but doing it sober was *such* a drag. So I signed back up on the *Dwarf*. Incidentally, the house is on the market, if you're interested.'

'*Red Dwarf*'s here? In space dock?' Could that be possible? That big ogre of a rust bucket had been all the way to the edge of the solar system and back here, with eighteen months of mining in between? Could it really have been two and a half years since he left?

'She's here all right, baby. We put into orbit last night. At least, I think it was last night. I came down on the first shuttle to see my old buddy, but no one could find you. So I went to the bar and stayed for a beer or thirty-seven waiting for you to show. Next thing I know: hhhnnnk-hrnnn, you're snoring in the next cell like a wounded wild hog with asthma!'

'Is Lew Pemberton still on board?'

'Pemberton? Sure. Said I should say hello from him. He's gotten two promotions since you saw him last. Officer class, now.'

Lewis Pemberton. Good luck to him. Lister smiled. He wouldn't have lasted two months on *Red Dwarf* without Lew as his room-mate. He was the guy who'd brought Lister and Kochanski back together after their first bust-up; given them this big speech about passion and how it can blow up and get destructive, and you can't expect the first throes of love to maintain that mad intensity, but you have to guide the relationship gently into something more stable. It was Pemberton who'd encouraged him to sign up for night classes in mechanics – even helped him with his homework. No question, you'd be looking at a different Dave Lister right now if it hadn't been for Lewis Pemberton.

'I was asking around about you, Davey boy. They say you're a responsible fellow, now. A father. With kids, even.'

'Twins. Jim and Bexley. Just coming up two years old.' Lister reached into his overall pocket. 'I've got a picture, but I don't think I can get it through the mesh.'

'That's OK. I'll just imagine I've seen it.' Petersen paused, and then in a dull flat monotone said, 'Wow. They are beautiful. Just like their old man. But I think they have their mother's eyes. Good enough?'

Lister grinned. 'That'll do, yeah.' He popped the photo back in his pocket.

'Question is, what's a reliable, upstanding family man like you doing in the drunk tank?'

Reality slapped the smile from Lister's face. 'I'm not in here for D and D. I'm in for gross insubordination.'

'Oh, good. Not just plain old *ordinary* insubordination. *Gross* insubordination. Nice to know you've cleaned your act up, being a daddy and all. Hope you didn't chew out someone too important.'

'Nah.' Lister grimaced. 'Only the admiral.'

Petersen whistled through his jagged teeth. 'Well, at least you're thinking big, Davey boy. At least you're thinking big. Smeg. You could be in here for weeks.'

Lister rested the back of his head against the cold brick. 'Months, even.'

'But that . . . Wait a minute. I've only got a four-day pass.' There was horror in Petersen's voice. 'We won't be able to get *drunk* together.'

Keys jangled, metal bolts slid back from their housings and a door clanked open. Boots clicked down the metal corridor. They stopped outside Lister's cell. He looked up to see the 'SP' on the guard's white helmet bent towards the cell's keypad. The door sprang back, and the guard said, 'You're out of here, friend.'

Lister straightened and stretched. 'I'm free?'

'As a birdie.'

Ace stepped into the door frame. 'Special clearance. Operation Wildfire.'

Lister stepped out into the corridor. 'Really? You cleared it with the old man?'

Ace grinned. 'Let's just say he won't object.'

Petersen's face was pressed up against his mesh. 'What about me?' He smiled in a way that, on another face, might have come out as coquettish. On Petersen, it looked like a mad, threatening leer. He batted his eyelids. 'I'm thoroughly sober now, good guardian of the law.'

The SP turned to face him. 'Do you have any recollection of the events of last night, friend?'

Lister folded his arms and settled back to listen. He was

going to enjoy this. Not surprisingly, this was a scenario in which Petersen frequently found himself, and, over the years, he'd polished his responses to such a degree he might be considered a true artist in the field of bullshit.

Petersen put on his best contrite and humble look, and began. 'I can't quite recall every single episode of my regrettable misadventures with absolute precision, officer, but I'm sure I behaved in many beastly ways, for all of which I most deeply and humbly apologize. Rest assured, most respected lawman, my contrition is complete. I intend to forswear the demon alcohol which brought me to this sorry pass, and live for ever more in this blessed state of sobriety.'

'So you don't remember, say, racing across the parade ground singing the theme from *The Dambusters* and bombing the guard post with luminous, urine-filled condoms?'

Petersen's eyes flitted up and left. 'Can't say it strikes a chord, no. But if I did commit such a heinous deed, it would be most out of character, as I am, at all times a thoroughly wholesome, gentle and amiable chap, much given to poetical musings and charitable acts, as my good friend of many years with extremely high security clearance here will readily attest.' He nodded encouragingly at Lister.

'Does your memory stretch to the part where you stole a motor cycle from the compound and scrawled obscenities over the ornamental garden in tyre marks?'

'Did I really do that? Then I must repair forthwith to the nearest pharmacistic establishment and have them replace my medication, which, despite its salutary effect on my incurable heart condition, quite clearly produces disastrous and unacceptable side-effects.'

'And I'll bet you don't recollect stapling my colleague's penis to his groin.'

Petersen licked his lips. 'I don't suppose you'd consider an extremely substantial bribe? I can give you the deeds to an exceptionally desirable residence, on one of the solar system's most up-and-coming moons . . .'

'Do you have the remotest conception of the penalty for affixing a shore patrolman's genitalia to his thigh? You are history, friend. We're going to shut you in and melt the lock.'

Petersen turned his pleading eyes to Lister. 'Davey? Can you help me, here?'

Lister turned to Ace.

The commander rolled his eyes, and stepped forward. 'He's with us, Sergeant.'

'Commander? You want me to *release* him?'

'He's essential to the project.'

'Essential to the project? What do you do, use his breath for fuel?'

'You can release him under my cognizance, Bob. I'll see he stays out of trouble.'

Reluctantly, the guard tapped the release code into Petersen's door lock. 'If you say so, Commander.' He paused before the last digit and looked up at Petersen, who was struggling to keep delight off his face. 'If I were you, friend, I'd steer clear of Reinhardt.'

'Reinhardt?'

'Sergeant Arden Reinhardt. The guy whose wanger you whacked with the staple gun? He had a very hot date to-night, only his little German soldier's going to be wrapped up like King Tutankhamun for the next two months, and he isn't in the best of humours. Last I heard, he was making plans to return the favour, only with hot steel rivets.'

'Ouch.' The door swung open and Petersen stepped free. 'Thanks for the warning, officer.' He turned to Lister and Ace, rubbing his hands. 'Now then, gentlefolk and essential personnel. Let's get on with Project Wildflower.'

'Wildfire.'

'Whatever.'

NINE

'So it's on then?' Lister followed as Ace led the group across the quadrangle towards the briefing room. Petersen brought up the rear, his eyes darting nervously from side to side, searching for mad, limping Germans with high-pitched voices brandishing rivet guns.

'It's on all right, Spanners. Kick-off at oh-eight hundred.'

'The old man seemed pretty anti, last I saw him. So what changed his mind?'

'You did, Spanners.'

'Me?'

'Another one I owe you, you old lemon tartlet.'

Lister shook his head. No matter how many favours Ace did you, he always made it seem like he was in your debt. 'What happened?'

'He resigned.'

'He *resigned*?'

'Best thing for him, old love. He was on the brink. Maybe he'll start to enjoy life a bit, now. Left me in charge of Project Wildfire.'

'So what's the plan?'

Ace stopped. 'I'm just off to give the tech boys a final briefing. I want you to give the crate a quick once-over: I've checked it myself, and it seems fairly kosher, but I wouldn't feel right if it went up without your blessing; then I want you to hot-tail over to mission control. If anything does go wrong on the launch, I'd rather you were up there giving me feedback.'

'No prob.'

'Appreciate it. Then' – Ace fished in his pocket – 'I want you to take a couple of weeks off with the fam. I've already organized the paperwork for you and Krissie to get leave. Here.' He tossed Lister a set of keys.

'What are these?'

'I've got a quaint little holiday cottage on Io. Nothing fancy, but a beautiful view. Own private beach. It's yours, if you want it.'

'For the whole fortnight?'

'Permanently.'

'Wait a minute: you're *giving* me your holiday home?'

'Well, I'm not going to need it any more, old sausage, now, am I?'

'What about me?' Petersen leaned his chin over Lister's shoulder and grinned winsomely. 'Can I do you any small personal favours in return for extravagant gifts of real estate and suchlike?'

'What you can do for me, matey, is stay out of trouble.'

'My plan absolutely. I am a reformed character. You can bet your last pennycent on that, Commander.'

Ace nodded, flipped an unofficial, desultory salute and headed off to the briefing room.

Lister looked at the keys, then at Rimmer's rapidly shrinking figure. He shook his head. 'What a guy,' he said.

'A prince.' Petersen agreed. 'There's just one thing bothering me.'

'What's that?'

'Where in the hell am I going to get a drink at this time in the morning?'

TEN

A chunk of grey ash tumbled from the tip of the double Churchill cigar and plopped into the bath water, where it sizzled happily a moment, and then sank beneath the sweet-scented foam.

Admiral Stinkfoot-No-More Tranter sighed a contented plume of brown smoke into the steam-filled air and slipped deeper into the bath, so that the bubbles formed an Abe Lincoln beard under his chin.

He was relaxing. It felt as if he were truly relaxing for the first time in his adult life, but he chose not to dwell on that aspect of the sensation, because it would have disturbed his relaxation.

He hooked his big toe, which by now resembled a large pink walnut, under the plug chain, and tugged. Slowly, the water gurgled away, leaving him swathed in a suit of foam. He climbed out of the tub and padded towards the shower cubicle. He hit the cold tap and thrust himself, cigar and all, into the icy curtain of water, where he stayed until his testicles had retracted almost completely into his body.

Clad only in goosebumps, he dripped his way out of the bathroom into his oversized office and dragged open the largest drawer in his gargantuan desk. He took out the service revolver, checked it was loaded, clicked off the safety and headed back into the bathroom.

Still chewing on the sodden Havana, he slipped his wet forefinger inside the trigger guard. A part of him felt that what he was about to do was somehow sacrilegious and more than a little crazy, but frankly he didn't much care any more.

The blast from the gun was massively amplified by the tiled walls of the bathroom, and when Melissa, the admiral's secretary, flung open the outer door, she was convinced a bomb had exploded. She was astonished that the office appeared completely undamaged. She tilted her head and peered into the bathroom. Tranter was standing butt-naked with the smoking revolver in his hand and a shocked expression on his face. A thin trickle of blood slowly oozed out of his ear. He caught her movement out of the corner of his eye and turned to face her. His face split into a cheeky schoolboy grin and he said, too loudly, 'Bugger me, that was noisy.'

Melissa couldn't think of anything sensible to say, so she asked him if he was all right.

The admiral wrinkled his brow and cocked his head because he'd seen her lips move and he hadn't heard a thing, so she repeated the question at a shout.

'Oh, yes. Never better, Mellie,' Tranter assured her, opening his bathroom cabinet and fishing out a roll of cotton wool. He stuffed a thick wad in each ear, aimed the revolver again and fired.

He yelped with satisfaction as the bullet smashed into a full bottle of navy rum perched on the water tank above his toilet, shattering the glass and splattering the tiles and carpet with the red-brown liquor which he had formerly used to torture his liver and poison his life. He turned to share the moment with Melissa, but she had slipped out of the office, and was, in fact, running full pelt across the parade ground towards the guard post.

Tranter wiggled the cigar from one side of his mouth to the other, blew the smoke from the gun barrel and snapped the safety back on. He walked back into his office, tossed the revolver back into the drawer and squeaked back into his huge leather recliner.

He was a free man. His resignation had already been E-mailed to Central Command. By the time it filtered through the thick layers of bureaucratic incompetence to the correct computer screen, Commander Rimmer and the *Wildfire* ship would be long gone.

Tranter lifted his foot on to the desk and tapped the monitor link button with his wrinkled toe. The screen flicked on and Ace's helmeted face appeared. The take-off dialogue blarted tinnily out of the speakers.

'. . . *Wildfire. We're all go-go at this end. Zero minus thirty, from my mark. And . . . mark!*'

'Tertiary ignition . . . engaged.'

Tranter smiled. In less than half a minute, thirty billion dollarpounds of Space Corps spondulics would be winging their way out of this reality for dimensions unknown, and none of the promotion-pinching turdbuggers at Central Command could do a blind thing about it.

Of course, their initial reaction would be to take it out on Tranter. They might threaten to withhold his pension, or have him declared insane, or even drag him before a Court Spatial. But, in the end, they'd back down. They wouldn't want it known to the government agencies who allocated budgets that the money had been flushed away pointlessly. They'd build up the importance of the break-through. Tranter might even come out of it a hero.

Not that he cared much. Within twenty-four hours he'd be *en route* to his condominium on Venus, where he would at last be able to indulge his enthusiasm for one-third-gravity golf, preferably with his wife, who at least still shared *that* passion with him. He thought they still might make something of their marriage, with a little work from both sides. They might even make it all the way to happiness.

He smiled to himself and shook his head softly. He felt good. He felt Ebenezer-Scrooge-on-Christmas-morning good. Born again. He'd spent so many unnecessary years trapped in this prison of a job, without realizing he was his own jailer, and all he'd ever had to do was walk free.

The huge blast of *Wildfire*'s take-off rockets drew his attention back to the screen. Ace's image juddered out of Europa's meagre grasp and howled towards Jupiter. The mission controller's voice tzzed: '*Wildfire, you are go-go*,' and the crowd in the control tower cheered mightily.

Tranter smiled and tugged open another pointlessly large drawer. He fished out his Hawaiian shirt and plus fours and began to dress in the only clothes that ever allowed him to feel comfortable, the clothes of his new life.

Of course, there was a large element of the unknown in that new life. Even an admiral's pension wouldn't provide for an opulent lifestyle, and there was no guarantee his wife would decide to go with him to Venus. She might even make good her threats to divorce him, which would leave him fairly close to destitute. Still, whatever his future held, Tranter embraced it.

As it happened, his small fears were groundless. His wife would not divorce him. They would find happiness together. And as an unexpected bonus, Tranter would finally discover the reason his career in the corps had been stymied.

It was this simple. There was another admiral in the corps named Tranter. Dieter Tranter. A hungover clerk in central command had one day mixed up their records, and no one had ever picked up on the error. Dieter was, to be blunt about it, an incompetent. Unfortunately, all his blunders found their way into Tranter's record, while Tranter's achievements were all logged on his. The worse Dieter performed, the more he got promoted.

The upshot was that Peter Tranter still continued to receive full pay even after his resignation, while Dieter found his salary reduced by half. Dieter never complained. For years he'd been bewildered by his own inexplicable rise through the echelons of rank, and he simply believed he'd finally been found out and was being justly punished.

As Tranter tugged on his loafers, he heard Commander Rimmer announce '*Engaging Wildfire drive,*' and glanced up at the monitor as the screen whited out. That was it. The moment of truth. After an achingly stretched instant, visuals returned again.

Tranter craned closer to the monitor. Ace was alive. The read-outs all registered within safe margins. He'd done it. The commander had leapt to a new dimension. Rimmer's voice was carried along by the promised tachyon transmission, alongside bursts of digitized NaviComp information. For a man who'd pioneered a new frontier for humankind, his voice was astonishingly calm and matter-of-fact. '*Bingo, MC. The crate held up – chalk that one up to Spanners. Let's see . . .*' His eyes flicked over the read-outs. '*I've arrived, but I know not where. Starscape's completely unfamiliar. Zero point of reference. That puts me gabillions of light years from home. No class M planets in the vicinity. Don't understand that one. There must be life of some kind around . . . hang on. I'm getting something. A ship.*' Ace's features registered mild surprise, which, in the commander's emotional lexicon, was the closest he ever got to panic. '*Oh, my godfathers. It's . . .*'

And, as the tachyon trail lost its integrity, the transmission spluttered and died.

PART THREE

Back to Backworld

ONE

The Cat watched the festering heap of dung as slimy black flies waddled on top of it, tucked their sticky wings to their sides and started crawling into their maggot skins. The white skins sealed themselves and the fat maggots began wriggling deep into the putrid mound. 'Mmmm,' the Cat said to himself. 'Lunch is almost ready.'

The Cat, who'd experienced some extremely weird days in his lifetime, ranked the previous day as his all-time number-one weirdest day ever. It had finally ended in the early afternoon. There had been hours of raised voices, recriminations and much poring over star charts, before the Cat had finally given up hoping to get off this planet any time soon, and had slipped up the spiral staircase for a quick nap.

He'd crashed out for twenty straight hours, which surprised him, since he hadn't been feeling all that sleepy when he'd gone to bed, despite the day's exertions. Even more surprisingly, when he woke up, he *was* feeling tired. But as the afternoon wore on towards lunch, the tiredness had begun to dissipate.

He supposed that was one of the many obnoxious things he was going to have to get used to here: going to bed when he felt most alert, and getting up when he was at his tiredest.

Well, he could live with that.

He could live with most of the vagaries of the reverse universe.

He could live with the fact that washing actually made him dirty, that combing his hair rendered it unkempt, and brushing his teeth left his mouth tasting foul. It stretched his patience to breaking-point, but he could even live with the concept of putting on clothes that were creased and un-clean, since they smartened themselves up over the course of the day.

What he couldn't live with was the food business.

He simply couldn't face the prospect of sucking excreta up through his butt-hole three times a day, and regurgi-tating it, neat and processed, through his mouth on to a dirty plate.

He couldn't even *think* about taking a leak.

So he'd wandered out of *Starbug* while Lister and Rimmer were still sleeping and headed here, to a high point on the mountain, on the blind side of the hillbillies' still, to try and wrap his head around some way of throwing him-self over the side without falling upwards. And while he'd been sitting and thinking, he'd suddenly developed an urge to dig a small hole by a bush. And he'd uncovered the dung.

'Depressing, innit?' He swung round towards the sound of the voice to see Lister picking his way down the narrow path towards him. 'You should worry – I've had to put up with it for three and a half decades.'

The Cat turned away and looked down into the green valley below. 'You're absolutely sure there's no way we can kill ourselves?'

Lister clambered down and perched on the rock beside him. 'It's not that bad. You get used to it.'

In deference to the Cat, they'd all agreed to make forward-speak the norm amongst them. Rimmer's speech unit had been reprogrammed in a matter of seconds, but Lister was still fairly uncomfortable in his native tongue, especially with sibilants. Still, it brought a sense of normalcy to their relationships, which they all badly needed right now, and Lister reasoned that he'd have to go through the process of re-mastering it sooner or later. Considerably later than he'd have liked, but still . . .

He looked out at the glorious mountainous vista, as an eagle released a small bird in mid-flight, then swooped off heavenwards at an astonishing speed. 'At least we're on a planet. At least there are people here.'

The Cat's furrowed features slowly morphed into a grin. 'That's true, buddy. There *are* people here. And some of them are female people! Now you are playing my radio station! Look out, planet Earth, sex god alert!'

Lister held out his hand, palm up. 'Before you get all fired up, I'd like you to think for a second about what, say, a blow-job entails in this place.'

The Cat's grin widened for a second. Then ripples spread over his brow. Then the corners of his mouth straightened. Then they drooped like an unwaxed Viva Zapata moustache. Then his nose creased up and headed towards his hairline. 'Oh, man,' he whined. 'Thank you so much for sharing that with me.'

Lister grinned. 'You asked.' Suddenly, he felt a movement in his gullet, and something churned up his throat and into his mouth. He chewed. Some kind of meat. He spotted a bone by the foot of the rock. He held out his hand and the bone leapt up into it. He brought up a chunk of pinkish meat and plastered it to the bone.

The Cat's features were still curled up in disgust from the sexual nightmare he'd just subjected himself to. If he wasn't careful, he was going to spend the next ten years squinting like Mr Magoo. 'What the hell is that?'

'Not sure.' Lister regurgitated another mouthful and chewed thoughtfully. 'I think it's rabbit.' He chewed some more. 'It's good, actually.' Lister proffered the bone. 'Like to spew some up?'

'Not just yet, bud,' the Cat smiled humourlessly. 'Ask me again in a couple of centuries.'

Lister shrugged, withdrew the bone and hawked another chunk of meat on to it. 'You're going to have to eat sooner or later.'

'Later. Much later.'

'Suit yourself. Listen, me and Kryten are thinking of getting our heads together back at the *Bug* before Rimmer wakes up. Trying to sort out some kind of plan without the Queen of Panic flapping around.'

'Plan? I know the plan.' The Cat spotted a small rock tumbling up the mountain's face towards him. He reached out and caught it. 'We sit here for the next decade sucking doody up through our buttocks.'

'It's not quite that simple. Coming?'

'Just give me a second. I have to . . . I think I need . . .' he nodded over at the pile.

'No sweat.' Lister crouched on the rock and leapt a good ten feet up on to the track. 'See you in ten.'

The Cat watched him hike off back towards the cave, then looked back at the hole and wondered if it might be possible at least to starve himself to death.

Lister had brought up an entire shank of the rabbit by the time he reached *Starbug*. There was a plate on the scanner table with more bones on it, so he dumped the joint he'd just regurgitated on to the plate and picked up another bone as Kryten stepped in from the small kitchenette that led into the mid-section, opposite the cockpit.

'Ah. You found lunch, sir.'

Lister waved at the bone. 'Where'd it come from?'

'The waste disposal unit regurgitated some bones. Close analysis indicated they probably belong to a creature of the *Oryctolagus cuniculus* genus, a burrowing, gregarious, plant-eating mammal with long ears, and a short tail, varying in colour from brown . . .'

'It's a rabbit, right?'

'That's what I just said, sir. I found a suitably dirty plate and arranged the bones on it. Oh . . .' he peered at the plate. 'You've already disgorged a portion.'

'Yeah. You'd better get a barbecue ready. We're going to have to uncook it, soon.'

'After which, presumably I take the bloody, raw, dead carcass and try to insert it whole into its skin.'

Lister nodded. 'That's my guess, yeah. I reckon you'll find some sort of trap to stick it in. Leave it out overnight, and bingo. Come morning he'll be frolicking around and gregariating with all his bunny friends.'

Kryten brightened. 'Wonderful. I like a meal with a happy ending.'

'So. I guess that sorts out where all our food's going to come from.'

'Where?' Rimmer climbed down the spiral stairway, yawning and stretching.

Lister tried to hide his disappointment. 'Trapping, hunting and fishing. We're living wild for the next ten years.'

Rimmer slouched to the scanner table and flopped into a chair. 'Smeg me. I'm bushed.'

'You'll get used to it.'

Rimmer yawned again. 'So how does fishing work, here? You take a dead fish to the river bank, sit on the side till it starts flapping about, jam it on your hook, drop the line in the water and wait for it to wiggle free?'

The Cat staggered bandily in from the airlock. He looked harrowed and gaunt, as if he'd just spent a year in solitary on Devil's Island and topped it off with a six-month stopover in the cool room at Alcatraz. 'I can't take it! Please, somebody shoot me in the head.'

'Look,' Lister slammed down another completed haunch on to the plate and handed the Cat a bone. 'There's no point in bleating about it. We're stuck here. We'll live with it. You're going to have to start looking on the bright side, or go crazy. It's up to you.'

'Bright side?' The Cat turned the rabbit bone over in his hand. 'There *is* a bright side, then?'

'There's plenty of positive stuff about this planet. Nobody dies here. Diseases actually make you feel better. Sure, sex isn't quite as much fun this way round, and the toilet arrangements are a drag, but at least we know we're going to be alive and healthy for the next ten years, which is more than you can say for most universes.'

'That's true.' Kryten waddled over to the plate and jammed the two completed half rabbit haunches together with a sticky cracking sound. 'There are lots of advantages. Take war. War is a good thing here. Why, in less than fifty years, the Second World War will begin. Millions of people will come to life. Hitler will retreat across Europe, liberate Czechoslovakia and Poland, disband the Third Reich and haul his cruddy little *derrière* back off to Austria. It's a pity we won't be around to see it.'

'Maybe we will.' Rimmer coiled his arms around himself. 'Who's to say we're going to make the next flight window?'

'Rimmer, we are *definitely* going to make it. I for one do not intend to spend my twilight years sitting in a high chair glooping apricot and apple dessert over some babysitter.'

'Babies?' The Cat gagged on some rabbit meat. 'Are you seriously telling me we could wind up staying here till we're babies? I can't *do* that. It's impossible to be cool and be a baby.'

'We're not going to miss the flight window. I guarantee it. Just think it through: how do you think the engines got buried so deep in the ground? How did they get all rusted up?'

Rimmer shrugged.

Lister glanced over at Kryten, who was beginning to suspect he'd made yet another boo-boo planning their take-off, and then nodded towards the airlock. 'Come on,' he said. 'Take a look.'

They trooped down the landing ramp towards the cave's

entrance. Lister pointed towards the distant mountain range. 'You have to think backwards. Don't imagine we're taking off. Imagine we're landing, only we've come in too low. We just make it over that mountain ridge, but we're losing altitude quickly and we hit the tips of those giant redwoods. A couple of the landing jets get ripped off and blast themselves into the ground. We skim along on a wing and a prayer, crashing through the treetops. The final landing jet gets wrenched loose and buries itself just a couple of hundred yards down there. Now the only thing keeping us up are some low-angled retros. The treetops start tearing great chunks out of the undercarriage – that's when the fuel canister those hillbillies found tumbles out. We see this mountain looming towards us, with no chance of getting over it. Then, in the nick of time, we spot the cave. We head for the entrance, set the retros on full blast and cross our fingers. We scorch those skid marks along the cave walls, and we've just got enough to stop. Now tell me that doesn't make sense.'

There was a long silence. Kryten shuffled uncomfortably. He was hoping no one would make the logical observation, but Rimmer disappointed him.

'Hang on a mo. Just *uno* tiny momentorola, here. Are you saying we didn't actually need the jets to take off?'

Lister shrugged. 'Like I said. Makes sense to me.'

'It makes sense all right. It makes a horrible, alarming sense.' Rimmer rounded on the squirming mechanoid. 'Because it means we could have taken off all the time. All that hunting around for the landing jets was completely unnecessary. As soon as we blasted off, they'd have lurched up out of the ground and started re-attaching themselves.'

Lister shook his head. 'You still can't wrap your head around the way things work here. You don't get a choice about what you do, because you've already done it. All you're doing is undoing what you've already done. See?'

'Don't try and baffle me with all this reverse philosophical clap-trap mumbo-jumbo. We didn't undo it because we didn't try.' Rimmer leered threateningly at Kryten. 'And we didn't try because Captain Rot-mind here didn't think it through properly.'

Lister sighed. Rimmer and the Blame Thing. Hard work. 'Rimmer, those engines were rusty when we found them. There was nothing Kryten or anybody could have done to stop them being rusty. And it took them years to get that way.'

'But they wouldn't have gone rusty if we hadn't tried to look for them, because we'd have left before they'd got chance to corrode, yes?'

'Look: the *Bug*'s underside was full of freshly welded panels. If we'd been going to make the last flight window, it would have been ripped to shreds when we found it.'

'Yes! But that's only because Kryten wasn't thinking straight!'

'Rimmer, I'm lost here. What point are you trying to make?'

'I'm just saying that we could have unlanded last night, or tomorrow night, or whenever the smeg it was or will be, if only Kryten had realized that we didn't need the landing jets to unland.'

Lister nodded. 'I see.'

'Exactly.' Rimmer stepped back, confused. He appeared to have won the argument, but somehow he felt like he'd lost it.

'Well,' Lister smiled. 'Now that's out of the way, I guess we'd better sort out the work plan. First off, we have to remove the landing jet we just attached, and sneak it back to the hermits' shack.'

The Cat, who clearly hadn't followed a word of the argument, looked up from his half-uneaten rabbit portion and asked: 'Why?'

'Sooner or later, those mountain boys are going to take the engine out into the woods, bury it and unfind it in exactly the place it gets wrenched free from *Starbug*. I'm guessing we've patched up the undercarriage to make the *Bug* liveable-in for the next few years. Before we hit the flight window, we're going to have to start dismantling the plates, until the belly's a complete wreck. Then we wait for the whole shebang to unrust.'

Lister headed back up the ramp to the storerooms to search out the welding equipment. It would be a trial in itself, spending the next decade watching the rust fade away. By that time, he and the Cat would be around fifteen. Teenagers. If the corrosion hadn't vanished completely by the ten-year deadline, they'd have to wait for the next flight window.

According to their best calculations, that particular opportunity would occur when David Lister was less than two years old.

TWO

Holly was trying not to think.

Quite frankly, it was thinking that had got him into this mess in the first place, and the chances were that more thinking was only going to make things worse.

Only a short time ago, less than two thirds of your average human life span, he had been the single most intelligent intelligence that ever intelligented.

'Been there,' Holly nodded sagely to himself. 'Been there and bought the T-shirt.' He smiled cynically. 'And on that proverbial T-shirt, it no doubt would say: "I went to the Source of the Fountain of All Knowledge, and all I got was this bloody lousy IQ".'

Holly had started life as the on-board computer of the mining ship *Red Dwarf*. He'd been blessed with a fairly respectable IQ of 6000, which had been more than enough for him to get the job done, with sufficient brainpower left over to defeat a couple of chess grandmasters, while simultaneously composing a fugue or two and making wholesale corrections to some laughably naive misconceptions in Stephen Hawking's and Albert Einstein's entire textual output. Then a nuclear accident had killed off all but one of the crew, and Holly had been forced to spend the best part of three million years alone. The interminable loneliness had driven him, not to mince words, slightly barmy. One circuit short of a Grand Prix track. Computer senile.

And so he might have remained, were it not for a seemingly innocent suggestion by a cheap plastic talking toaster. Holly reflected sadly that actually being prepared to solicit advice from a budget-priced kitchen appliance was a mark of how low his intellect had dipped. Sadder still, he found himself wishing desperately that Talkie Toaster™ (Patent Applied For) was still around to advise him now.

The toaster had suggested that Holly might accelerate his intellect at the cost of slightly reducing the life-expectancy of his runtime.

And it had worked. Holly achieved a staggering IQ in the high twelve thousands. Only, instead of measuring his life expectancy in terms of millennia, he measured it in milliseconds.

Still, in his brilliant state, the paltry seconds allotted to him had been enough for him to formulate a rescue plan.

He programmed the ship's NaviComp to head for the backwards universe. Because of the reverse physics there, operating at his maximum intellect actually *increased* his life span.

If he could have stayed there for a few decades, everything would have been just peachy. He would be one super-smart cookie of a computer right now. Unfortunately, he had to return to his own universe where he'd left Rimmer and the Cat stranded in *Starbug*. He couldn't remember, now, quite why he hadn't brought them with him. Perhaps the trip had been too dangerous for them. Perhaps the stasis booths wouldn't operate if time were running backwards. Whatever the rationale, his genius self had left them there, and must have had a damned fine reason.

Still, he'd managed to prolong his life expectancy by several months, even running at super-intellect level. In order to extend it further, Holly then had to trade off some of his intelligence. He'd reduced his IQ to three thousand, but that only left him a few decades, which didn't seem very long at all. So he'd reduced it again. And again. And the stupider he got, the more it seemed like a good idea to swap more brain cells for more runtime.

And now he'd reached the point where he was no longer smart enough to work out either his IQ or his life expectancy. He thought of reversing the process a little, but found he couldn't recall the procedure.

He'd pored over the calculations he'd made when he was smarter, but they were hopelessly beyond his grasp. Meaningless algebraic squiggles that might as well have been Greek. Well, being algebra, in fact, some of it almost certainly *was* Greek, but for all the sense it made to Holly, it could have been marks left on paper by a battalion of soldier ants with diarrhoea.

Holly could no longer remember if he'd enjoyed being super smart, but he certainly wasn't enjoying being one bulge shy of an underpants advert. It must have been nice, he thought, to *know* things. Not to feel baffled by the simplest of life's mysteries. Not to spend countless hours worrying, as he had recently done, about who it was that decided how many layers of peel there should be on an onion. Why some onions had just one while others enjoyed six or seven. Even if they came from the same batch. It seemed cruelly whimsical of Nature to deprive an innocent onion of sufficient protective mantle, yet to wrap otherwise identical onions in layer after layer of warm brown skin.

Holly had got himself so steamed up about onion deprivation, he'd failed to notice that the crew had neglected to return on schedule. When he did notice, they were almost a decade late.

He wondered if, perhaps, he should try to go and find them. But what if he missed them? What if he risked the perilous journey to the backwards universe, and they somehow came out another way? Then he'd have to risk the journey back. And what if he did that, and they'd arrived to find him missing, and gone back in to look for him? They could go on missing each other for centuries. And yet, what if they were waiting in the backwards universe, thinking 'Well, we're late, Holly's bound to come looking for us, we might as well hang around here till he shows up'? Then again, as far as Holly knew, he was the last remaining intelligence in this entire universe, and it seemed vaguely irresponsible, somehow, to leave it completely deserted. What if some life-form from some other universe popped in for a cup of tea and a chat? They'd think 'Oh, what a crappy universe this is. Totally devoid of intelligence in any shape or form. Well, stuff it, I'm off.'

Holly chewed over the problem for a couple of years, worrying himself into a panicky funk, torn between his assumed responsibilities as representative of the universe and his obligations to what was left of the *Red Dwarf* crew, until he finally decided it wasn't worth the mental anguish any longer, and returned his attention to the semi-naked onion conundrum.

He'd so resigned himself to spending the rest of his days utterly alone, he'd given up checking his radar scanners, and didn't notice the approaching ship until it had actually landed in the docking bay.

And with that one small error of omission, Holly's seemingly insoluble problems suddenly got considerably worse.

THREE

The Cat was now fifteen years old, and he was about to have sex for the first time in his life.

Maybe it was the fullness of the moon, which gleamed its blue fantasy light on to the hermit's log cabin, tinting everything with an unreal fairy-tale quality. Or maybe it was simply his testosterone level, which, on the Richter scale would have brought down Los Angeles, Orange County and half the Pacific coast.

But this was the most beautiful woman who ever dreamed of being alive.

Her name, he'd learned through hours of humiliating eavesdropping, was Lindy Lou. She was some kind of cousin to Ezekiel and Zacharias, the mountain men who lived in the cabin. But then, most people Zeke and Zack knew were probably their cousins.

Lindy Lou was blond, sixteen years old and wore gingham.

And nothing else.

Now, in the sweet heat of this restless summer, the red-and-white check dress clung to her firm, hot body like clingfilm over chicken in a microwave. The stitches in every seam of the garment yearned to snap. The half-crescent sweat marks that caressed the shadow of her trigonometrically impossible breasts served only to bring the Cat's desire to melting-point.

He would have eaten his mother alive, just to lick this woman's armpits for ten seconds.

Right now, his toes were Rudolf Nureyeving beneath the slatted window, as Zeke plucked at his banjo and Zack clapped and whirlygigged his bandy way around the single room of the cabin, with Lindy Lou sitting forlornly on the massive bed, her hands clasped deep in the folds of her bursting frock, staring forlornly out at nothing in particular.

The fact that she was sad enraged the Cat irrationally. Whoever it was that had wiped the flushed smile from her full lips had booked himself a permanent place in the Cat's hate list. If he'd known at that moment that he, himself, had caused the look of sorrow on Lindy Lou's sun-tinted features, he would probably have haemorrhaged on the spot.

Lindy Lou had arrived at Zeke and Zack's only the previous morning. She'd been bundled, tear-sodden, from the brothers' sparkling new pick-up truck, and trundled into the cabin, where her cardboard suitcase had been dutifully unpacked by the ever-attendant mountain men.

The Cat had been helplessly in love with the girl from her luggage alone.

A white, department store brassière; a pair of blue knickers with the label clearly visible through lacy holes; an underskirt, the brevity of which defied gonadal control.

All at once, the banjo fell silent. Zeke tucked his plectrum into the small pocket of his dungarees, and hung the instrument between two nails in the wall.

And Lindy Lou began sobbing.

The brothers crowded around her, making sympathetic noises and, from the little the Cat could understand of back-talk, began querying her about what ailed her.

Eventually, the Cat could stand no more of her sobbing. He slipped gently away from the slatted window and ran out into the comfort of the moonlit woods.

When he felt his heaving chest begin to subside, he threw himself down into a body-sized indentation in some thick, caressing bracken. There he lay, in the frozen moon's icy glow, his heart pounding wildly, his mind distraught and befuddled, and his loins glowing with a bizarre contentment.

Suddenly, he was aware of a strange scent in the mountain air. He sniffed. He felt at the same time bewildered and greedy. And then there was a growing, aching tumescence inside his trousers. He shifted uncomfortably in the bracken. His loins began to ache. To ease the pain, he unzipped his pants and eased them over his knees. His erection began to throb.

He slid his shorts down the firm, muscular shanks of his thighs. The sex smell intensified. His whole body began to glisten with sweet sweat.

And then he heard her. She was screaming through the woods towards him. He 'L'ed his body up from the indented bracken. His eyes caught a white glimpse to his left. He reached over and grabbed the whiteness.

Panties.

He clasped them to his face.

He breathed them.

And then there was the sound of bracken snapping. Her screams were getting closer.

He felt inexplicably ambiguous: afraid, yet strangely sated.

Then she burst through the dark woods. Shoeless in the impossibly perfect gingham dress, thundering backwards towards him.

She raced towards the spot where he lay.

She stopped her caterwauling and turned to face him.

The expression on her perfect face chilled him like liquid nitrogen.

Her eyes and mouth were fixed wide in a silent scream.

Then, the horror etched on her features, she straddled his strengthening erection.

And she eased herself down on to it.

And halfway down, she began to scream again.

And then the screaming stopped.

She began to slither up and down on him. She started to moan. Only this time, there was no pain in the moaning. She was crying out in ecstasy.

And despite his confusion, the Cat became lost in his own version of that ecstasy.

He yowled mightily as his orgasm sucked its way into him. His buttocks began to urge themselves towards her, to meet her urgent thrusts.

And then they were making love.

Without warning, she eased herself off him, and stood.

He stood with her, feeling her gentle hands tugging on his chest.

Then she grabbed his yearning erection and eased it into his shorts. She tugged up his trousers, giggling, and did up the zip. Then she stooped, scooped up her panties and slid into them, never taking her eyes from his.

She kissed him. She kissed him long and hard, until his erection melted away.

And then she linked his arm, and they began to walk backwards through the woods: her all the time talking, him smiling and nodding, not catching a quarter of what she said, but neither of them caring much about that.

They reached the clearing where Zeke and Zack kept their still, and suddenly she kissed him, clumsily. She talked for a while, and he listened as best he could, then she smiled and skipped off backwards.

The Cat was left in the clearing, confused and lost.

He'd learned, over the years, to try and work things out backwards, after they'd happened, but no amount of rationalizing furnished him with an explanation of what had just gone on between him and this beautiful young woman.

And that was because he was unaware of a certain anatomical fact.

The fact was: unlike Cats, male humans do not have

any special equipment to stimulate ovulation in the female.

Which is to say: the human penis is not equipped with sharp and painful hooks.

FOUR

It was a little before nightrise.

Kryten was standing under *Starbug*'s belly, leaning back so that his chest light played over the gaping wounds in the craft's undercarriage. Given that the mechanoid always managed to find something to worry about, he was fairly happy with the way things were looking. The list of things he didn't want to think about currently consisted of only two items, which was just about an all-time record for him. And there were plenty of positive data to ponder.

The last decade had seen the rust on the craft vanish completely. Weeks ago, they had detached all the welded panels, and on Lister's impulse they carried them to one of the mountain men's shacks and stacked them in a corner.

And finally, the flight window was open. Technically speaking, they could take off any time over the next three weeks, but the absolute optimum take-off point, which would provide the biggest margin for error, occurred in the next couple of hours. Kryten was determined to make it.

And all the signs were good.

The twisted edges of the rents in *Starbug*'s underside had grown sharper and shinier. An hour ago, a few had started sucking up smoke.

Kryten twisted towards the cave walls. The ruts were starting to smoulder.

He checked his internal chronometer and clucked with satisfaction. Time to round up the boys.

He couldn't actually say at what point he'd started thinking of Lister and the Cat as 'the boys'. It had happened so gradually, he'd barely noticed it. A combination of small things, really. Their laundry, for instance. He'd noticed that their bed sheets had been clean more frequently, requiring more trips to the washing machine to get them dirtied up, and they'd emerge all crispy and crinkly. Gradually, the fifteen-year-old Lister had become incredibly moody, and the most innocent query from Kryten could send him into sulk mode for hours on end. He also seemed to need to be left alone more often. He had developed an insatiable appetite for computer games. He would spend hours in the rest quarters, feebly plucking at his guitar and singing mournful songs off-key. Sometimes, for no reason Kryten could discern, he would experience unprovoked depressions, and lock himself away simply to cry.

There were more subtle changes, too. For instance, the quality of recreational conversation among the party had diminished considerably. Lister had become increasingly opinionated. He would argue with anyone about anything, no matter how ill-informed he was on the subject. And the Cat, who was ill-informed on *every* subject, would argue right along with him.

The most disturbing change, from Kryten's point of view right now, was that they had started to *play*. They could be out in the forest till all hours of the night, climbing trees and staging mock battles with each other. Sometimes, they could go missing for days on end. Kryten had warned them the previous morning of the proximity of the flight window, but they had both developed a bizarre disrespect for any kind of authority, and there was no guarantee they'd bother to turn up at all.

The early autumn sun ducked its orange head over the mountains beyond. Kryten waddled up to the cave's entrance and stared out. Just a few weeks earlier, as the bronzed leaves had begun to leap on to the trees, a charred trail had started to show itself across the tips of the redwoods. Now, it was getting more blatant.

Kryten heard Rimmer yawn down the ramp and come towards him. 'How's it looking?'

'Most propitious.' Kryten waved his hand. In the glimmer of the twilight, some of the broken treetops were giving off smoke.

Rimmer glanced at his watch. Nine-thirty. 'Have they been out all night?'

Kryten nodded.

'Did you tell them we're looking to leave before eight?'

Kryten nodded.

'I don't suppose they paid much attention?'

Kryten shook his head.

Rimmer muttered 'Gits,' and strolled underneath *Starbug*. 'What bothers me, is that pair of irresponsible gimboids are going to have to pilot this damn thing. It's going to be a hell of a ride, crashing backwards through those trees while those two masturbate furiously up front.'

Kryten turned. 'Oh, I don't think they masturbate excessively, sir. Not for young men of their age.'

'Are you kidding? It's like the bloody monkey house up in those rest quarters. There's more fiddling goes on up there than in the court of Old King Cole. I swear to God, they don't even stop during meal breaks.'

Kryten didn't reply. All the available databases he'd been able to consult were singularly unforthcoming in this area. The truth was the boys' obsessive pursuit of sexual self-gratification did seem a little over the top to him. Then again, he was left somewhat bewildered by the human sexual process altogether. He understood that, in order to reproduce, humans sought each other out, got naked and jiggled up and down on top of each other until various ucky fluids had been secreted. Well, fine. It seemed to him a particularly messy process, but there: humans were stuck with it, the poor beggars. What was truly baffling was the amount of physical and mental energy the species appeared to devote to the pursuit of this sticky jiggling. Most of their songs seemed to be connected to it in some way. It cropped up in almost all of their books and magazines. He couldn't help feeling that if, heaven forbid, he himself had been afflicted with these irrational urges, then at the very least he'd have the good taste to keep quiet about it.

'There's one thing bothering me about this take-off.'

Kryten turned. Rimmer was peering up at the ripped metal around the engine housings. He looked towards the distant peaks through the cave's entrance. 'It looks like Lister's prediction was right. We come in low over those mountains and skim across the treetops. What I'm wondering is why?'

'Why, sir?' Kryten tried to appear nonchalant. This was one of the two things he didn't want to think about.

'Yes, why? Why do we come in so low over the mountains? Why can't we maintain altitude over the woods? It's been bugging me for a while. And this damage,' he pointed at *Starbug*'s underside. 'I can believe most of it's caused by treetops. But that big hole at the back. That looks pretty nasty.'

This was the other thing Kryten hadn't wanted to think about. The rip Rimmer was indicating was indeed more savage than the rest of the damage. Three metres across and almost circular, it had begun smoking before the rest of the craft. By now, it was getting almost red hot. Kryten had very few ideas about how that hole might be made, and none of them were palatable.

He was saved from expounding them by Lister's breathless arrival in the cave.

Rimmer stiffened visibly. His relationship with the increasingly immature Lister had soured to the point where they no longer conversed, merely exchanged insults. 'Ah, Listy.' He beamed and clasped his hands. 'So glad you could tear yourself away from your imaginary friends and join us.'

Leering insolently, Lister raised the middle finger of his right hand and jabbed it in the air.

Rimmer's beam broadened. 'Marvellous. What a riposte. Such a shame we can't hang around until Oscar Wilde comes to life and the two of you could match wits.'

'Sir,' Kryten interposed himself between them. 'Have you seen the Cat around? We really should be thinking of preparing for take-off.'

Lister shrugged and unslung the home-made bow from his shoulder. 'He'll turn up. I mean, what's the big deal? Why is it always me who's supposed to know where he is? You're always getting at me. I'm not responsible for the Cat. Just leave me alone, OK?'

Kryten clucked nervously and waddled to the cave's entrance. The boys' accelerated aptitude for derring-do bothered him greatly. Just recently the two mountain men had started prowling the woods with shotguns, as if they suspected some strangers' presence, and none of the mechanoid's entreaties could prevent the boys from pursuing their nocturnal adventures. Of course, it was logically impossible for any serious harm to befall the Cat or Lister, but that didn't prevent Kryten from worrying.

The treetops were smouldering profusely now. As Kryten scanned the vista, a face popped upside-down into the top of his vision.

The Cat grinned. 'Hey bud, what's happening?' He flipped down from the lip of the entrance, landing straight in front of Kryten. 'Do I look different to you in any way?' His grin widened exposing all of his unfeasibly white teeth, and he strutted towards the *Bug*. 'Do I look, like, even cooler than I did before, if that's possible? Do I look like a total sex god of the mountains, or what?'

Rimmer's features crinkled. 'What is he drivelling about?'

The Cat swaggered up to Lister. 'Do you see a certain sparkle in my eyes that was not there before? A sparkle that says: "This is a mature individual who knows what it's like to lie with a woman." '

Lister's eyes widened. 'You're kidding. You *did* it?'

'Buddy, did I *do* it. I did it so good, they're gonna have to redefine the rules of sexual engagement!'

Lister and the Cat whooped and whistled and staged a mock fist-fight of triumphant celebration.

'Wait a minute.' Rimmer stepped up. 'Are you telling me the Cat has had sex?'

The two boys stopped their celebration and looked at him. 'Buddy, I didn't just have sex. I had *seeeeeeeeeeeeeeeeex*. Lament ye Earth men, your women will no longer be satisfied with mere humans.' Then the boys whooped again and began an elaborate high-fives ritual.

Rimmer closed his eyes. 'If I can just intrude on the undoubtedly warranted and extremely right-on and reconstructed jubilation, gentlemen. You had sexual intercourse with a human, woman person? A human, woman person who wasn't made of rubber? Who breathed and was alive?'

The Cat nodded eagerly.

'Even though we've all agreed to keep our presence here an inviolable secret? A secret we have kept assiduously for the best part of a decade?'

The Cat nodded again.

'Don't you think that was perhaps a teeny, tiny taddette irresponsible?'

The Cat nodded a third time. Then he looked at Lister, who burst out laughing, and the celebrations began all over again.

Rimmer sighed, shook his head, and headed towards the embarkation ramp. The Cat had made love to a human woman. Backwards. No doubt, unprotected. Who knew what demon spawn the union might produce? What terrors might lurk in this poor Earth's spent future? He stopped at *Starbug*'s entrance and looked down at the air-punching duo chanting 'Yes, yes, yes' ad nauseam. They were becoming increasingly uncontrollable. The human race had better pray this lift-off was successful. The planet wasn't safe with those two reckless lunatics on it.

Kryten watched Rimmer disappear up the ramp, then twisted his head to inspect the vessel's underside. The metal panels were smoking promisingly, but the large rent towards the rear was glowing almost neon red. As he watched, a thin drool of molten metal leapt up from the cave floor and glooped itself on to the rim of the hole.

He turned to the boys, trying to keep the alarm out of his voice. 'Now, sirs, it really is time we should be . . .'

'All right!' Lister whirled on him, suddenly aggressive. 'All right! We're coming! Ker-eyst! Is it illegal to have fun around here? Is it against the law or something?' He fixed Kryten with a look of petulant challenge, and then he whirled again and stomped up the ramp, pursued at a confident ambling pace by the swaggering Cat.

Kryten stepped up to follow them, and then ducked to catch a last glimpse of the red-hot wound in *Starbug*'s belly. There was no doubt in his mind now, none at all, that such a hole could only have been made by one thing.

A muh . . .

A muh . . . muh . . .

A muh . . . muh . . . muh . . .

A seriously high-powered heat-seeking missile.

FIVE

Rimmer watched impotently from his station at the back of the cockpit as Lister and the Cat giggled and joked their way through the pre-take-off safety checks. He'd begged and pleaded with Kryten to take control, at least until they were in orbit, but the mechanoid had refused. His argument was that he'd be most useful at the computer stations, analysing data and making minor course adjustments, but that was only half of the truth. The reality was, he wasn't prepared to take responsibility for the lives of his crewmates.

'Landing gear down.'

'Check!'

'NaviComp on line.'

'Check!'

'Retros at maximum elevation.'

'Sex!'

Lister and the Cat burst once more into uncontrollable laughter.

Rimmer stood, almost purple with rage. 'Will you two reckless nincompoops for God's sake stop smegging about!? Our lives are on the line here!'

Once again, Lister's demeanour shifted instantly from jubilation to petulance. 'All right then.' He stood and walked down the narrow aisle to Rimmer's station. 'You do it.'

'What?'

'You're so clever, *you* get the ship off the ground.'

Rimmer looked up as if he hoped some divine arbiter of

sanity might suddenly descend through the roof, but none appeared.

'You can't, can you? Because you're *dead*!' Lister made his way back to the co-pilot's seat. 'Well just because you're dead, doesn't mean you can stop the living having fun.' He thumped down into the seat.

'He's jealous,' the Cat said.

'Yeah.' Lister grinned. 'He's jealous because you're only fifteen, and you've had more sex than him.'

They fixed Rimmer with accusatory stares. He stared right back at them. There was an iota of truth in Lister's insult. Rimmer, in his lifetime, had enjoyed woefully little sexual experience, and tales of others' success in that arena did cause a certain amount of resentment. When he felt he'd stared enough to restore his superior adult status, he said, quietly, 'The truth is, gentlemen, *Monsieur Chat* did not enjoy a normal, regular sexual experience, but rather a reverse, sort of backwards one. What actually happened to *Monsieur Chat*, is that *Monsieur Chat* actually *became* a virgin.'

The boys' teasing expressions changed to perplexion. Rimmer sat back, satisfied, and pretended to scan his screens for data.

Kryten tapped his console impatiently. 'Sirs, if we could continue the lift-off procedure.'

The Cat and Lister brattishly mumbled their way through the rest of the checks. Kryten scanned the bewildering data on the ship's status, but the physics of their take-off defied logical prediction. Without knowledge of their final velocity, it was impossible to ascertain the correct level of thrust required to get them airborne. Finally, he gave up trying, and simply nodded to Rimmer, who gave the command 'Engage.'

The front retros built up rapidly to a high-pitched whine, sucking in great clouds of smoke from the cave outside. The craft shuddered, and with an ear-bursting scream of metal on rock, scraped across the cave floor and shot out of the entrance with digestion–defying acceleration.

Everyone began shouting, but their yells were inaudible above the retros' thunder. The Cat wrestled hopelessly with the collective stick as they streaked backwards across the forest top, buffeting wildly, sucking tree tips and dousing nascent fires in their wake. There was a loud thunk below and Kryten checked his status readouts. 'Landing jet three attached!' he yelled, his voice unit on maximum decibelage. *Starbug* lurched dramatically to port as another mighty thunk signalled the addition of a second landing jet.

The Cat strained at the collective and gained some control as the vessel howled towards the crest of the mountain. Kryten's radar registered some large objects speeding up the mountainside towards them. At first he thought they might be missiles, and by the time he'd stopped panicking and worked out they were in fact huge boulders from the rocky peak they were about to clip, he barely had time to yell 'Brace!' before the impact sent the craft lurching skywards.

Most of the shielding had been re-attached to the *Bug*'s belly by now, and the noise in the cockpit had diminished considerably. Lister punched the air. 'We made it!'

'Not quite, sir.' Kryten nodded at his status screen. 'We are still shy one landing jet. Our manoeuvrability is still below sixty per cent.'

The Cat's adolescent shoulders were knotted with the sinews of his burgeoning muscles as he struggled for control. 'Tell me about it, bud,' he hissed through gritted teeth.

Suddenly, the alert siren began to sound, and despite the Cat's straining, the ship began to twist into a spiral of rapid ascent. Sprinkler systems all over the ship burst into life, spawning countless fires.

Rimmer's NaviComp console fizzed and died. 'What the smeg is happening?'

Kryten coughed, unnecessarily. 'Sirs, I'm afraid . . . Well, in fact, I was meaning to mention this earlier, but I didn't quite . . . the right occasion never seemed to present itself . . . and I was really hoping it wasn't going to be what I was afraid it was going to be, but now it looks as if it probably will be what I feared it was . . .'

'What?!' Rimmer screamed. 'What are you saying? Spit it out!'

Kryten drummed his fingers on the console. 'Well, the fact of the matter is, in all probability, I think we're forced to conclude . . .'

'Say it!' Rimmer sprayed hologrammatic spittle. 'What the smeg is happening, you dough-brained streak of venereal pus!'

'We're about to get hit by a heat-seeking missile.'

Lister glanced down at his display. 'Not possible. We're fully radar cloaked.'

'Yes, sir, that has been puzzling me. I believe what's about to happen is that we trigger an anti-missile array which has only recently been erected by the North Americans, which they have rather quaintly named "Star Wars".'

Rimmer stared at his dead screens in horror. 'How? How do we trip it?'

'It's probably an accident. The system is fairly experimental at this time. I guess we encounter one of its teething problems.'

'One of its teething problems!? One of its *teething* problems is that it blasts us out of the sky and sends us into a screaming, spinning death dive?'

'That's my guess, sir, yes.'

'And you didn't get around to *mentioning* this before we took off?' The veins in Rimmer's neck were bulging dangerously. 'It slipped your bloody *mind*?!'

Kryten looked down guiltily. 'I didn't want to cause any unnecessary alarm.'

And before Rimmer could launch into his number-one list of foul expletives and vile epithets, a deafening explosion rocked the ship, sealing the hull, attaching the final landing jet and extinguishing all the fires.

Rimmer's screens blinked back into life, and he tracked the missile as it screeched away towards its source.

The alert lights winked out as the sirens ceased wailing. *Starbug* sped smoothly out of Earth orbit and began accelerating towards the outer planets.

'There,' Kryten smiled. 'No harm done.' He tapped away at his keyboard. 'Course entered. With good luck and a following wormhole, we should be back in our own universe in a little under three weeks.' He stood, looked around the cockpit, oblivious to the glares directed at him, and added, 'Anyone for tea?' and then waddled off to the galley to rustle up a couple of dirty cups for them to spit into.

Rimmer wrapped his fingers around his forehead and squeezed. 'Is it me, or is that plastic peckerhead suffering from droid rot?'

Lister swivelled round in the co-pilot seat and let out a sigh that had been almost fifty years in the making.

Home. At last, he was headed home.

Well, not actually 'home' home. He'd be heaven knows how many millions of light years from his own solar system and the nearest member of his own species, if the human race still existed. But at least he'd be in the right universe, which would make a nice change. At least time would be moving in a familiar and friendly direction. For the first time in half a century, he'd be able to make *choices*. He could choose what to eat: he wouldn't have to wait for the food to leap up his gullet to find out what he'd had for breakfast. He could choose first and *then* eat it.

Lister had never been one to waste time bemoaning his fate, or raging about what destiny flung at him, but all the time he'd spent on the reverse Earth, he'd felt he'd been nothing more than an actor in someone else's script, with all his decisions made for him beforehand. Well, now he was going to be in charge of his own life again.

And that thought should have made him feel better than it did.

He should have been elated. Ecstatic. Instead, he merely felt numb and hollow.

Still, he put that down to his inverse trip through puberty, which was playing merry havoc with his emotions. He'd feel better, he thought, as soon as he set foot again on *Red Dwarf*. The ugly old monster of a ship was the nearest thing he'd had to a home since he left Earth almost two lifetimes ago. He smiled as he pictured the rusty red ogre in his mind's eye, waiting to meet them, like a giant guardian of normalcy as they emerged into their own universe. Things would be different once he was back on board. He'd start to feel normal again, he thought.

Lister couldn't know it, but he was wrong. He was so wrong, he could have represented his species at intergalactic level if wrongosity ever became an Olympic sport. He was wrong because he'd made a basic error in his assumptions.

He'd assumed *Red Dwarf* would still be there when they emerged into their own universe.

MIDLOGUE

The Difference – 1

Arnold J. Rimmer, age seven and almost five-sevenths, is crouched at the starting line for Junior B two-hundred-yards dash.

His sports kit, handed down from his brother, Howard, is two sizes too large. A cruel breeze is flapping at his shorts, whipping his thin thighs blue. His feet are loose inside the spiked running shoes.

His eyes are clenched against the wind, but he forces them open to look at the spectators lining the track. At first, he can't see her. His heart jumps with excitement. Perhaps she's gone. Perhaps she's nipped into the refreshment tent, to grab a cup of tea before the senior school events start up, and she can watch the other boys, Frank and John and Howard, actually *winning* something.

But his joy is short-lived.

He spots her, two hundred yards along the track. Arms folded. Wearing an expression that would have blown away Mrs Danvers and Nurse Ratched in a stern-looks competition.

His mother is waiting at the finish line.

She wants to see him lose close up.

There are seven other boys at the starting line, and there's no doubt in anyone's mind that Rimmer will come in at number eight.

Suddenly, something inside his head snaps. Perhaps it's loathing at his mother's grim patience, perhaps it's the thought that he could be beaten by Thrasher Beswick, who's crouched next to him, leering crudely with one hand in his pocket, playing underpants snooker. Or perhaps it's revulsion at himself, for being beaten before the starting whistle's even been blown.

Whatever the cause, Rimmer suddenly decides he's not going to lose.

Not this time.

There really is no reason why he shouldn't win. His legs are long and lanky – not much muscle on them, maybe, but at almost seven and five-sevenths, that's not a major factor. He's outpaced his brothers many times. True, on those occasions he'd been spurred on by the fact that they were pursuing him with poisonous snakes or crossbows, but that just meant it was a question of attitude. All he has to do is imagine they're behind him now, shouting gleeful taunts. They're threatening to peg him out on the ground, smear his body with bilberry jam and leave him to be eaten alive by armies of soldier ants. And he can't let them catch him.

He won't let them catch him.

His eyes are bunched like fists. He's willing all the power in his little body down to his feet. He hears the whistle and before he knows what's happening, he's running.

He opens his eyes.

There is no one in front of him.

The too-big running shoes are wrenching at his feet as he thumps them into the clay of the running track. His T-shirt is billowing, the short sleeves slapping his arms as he pumps his hands up and down, trying to gain extra speed by pushing the wind behind him. The baggy shorts are dragging at his legs.

And in the corner of his eye, he sees the hundred-yard mark. The race is halfway over, and there is still no one in front of him.

He knows it's wrong, but he can't resist glancing over his shoulder. Bad technique and all, but he has to know.

The nearest boy is a good two strides behind him.

Beyond that, young Rimmer catches a glimpse of Bullet-head Heinman, his gym teacher, at the starting-line. The whistle flops out of his mouth and he gawks at Rimmer with bewilderment. Rimmer is one of the 'wets, weirdoes and fatties' that Bull enjoys humiliating on Wednesday afternoons. He's one of those skinny, useless kids that team captains pray they won't get lumbered with in ball games.

And he's winning this race.

But Rimmer has lingered too long with his backward glance, and the nearest boy has gained a stride and a half.

Rimmer turns his head back and tries to find some reserves. He can see the finishing tape he's never broken before in his life. The yellow-and-black striped barrier that may only be snapped by heroes. And he tries not to think about being a hero. He tries not to think about his mother, who will celebrate his victory like she celebrates his brothers': with the slightest of slight nods, worth more than a twenty-one gun salute to young Arnold.

Because he hasn't won yet. He's still got fifty yards to go.

And the boy behind him is Dicky Duckworth.

Dicky Duckworth is a full year older than the rest of the boys. He's been kept down in Junior B while the rest of his class earned promotion to Junior A.

Arnold himself has been spared that ignominy by the skin of his milk teeth, thanks to his mother's intervention. And she constantly reminds him that it was her pleas that saved him, by never mentioning it all. That's how clever Rimmer's mother is.

But Dicky Duckworth is almost nine years old, and by rights, he should win this race easily.

Only Arnold isn't going to let him.

That tape is too close, now. He's less than ten strides from his mother's nod.

His red cheeks are ballooning like a badly trained

trumpeter's. His lungs have to be forced to suck in air. A stitch is preparing to start stabbing him in his side.

And then his heel explodes with pain.

He's falling, his arms flailing, grabbing out for the black-and-yellow tape. And his chin thumps into the red clay, scrawping him a red, scabby beard.

Dicky Duckworth's chest bursts the tape.

Slowing down, he looks over his shoulder down at Rimmer and mouths a two-syllable word. Rimmer's nickname.

Bonehead.

Six pairs of feet thunder past him.

Rimmer looks back at his heel. There is blood oozing out of the top of his shoe. There are six bright red pinpricks above it from the sole of Dicky Duckworth's track shoe.

Young Rimmer looks up at his mother.

She stands, arms folded, her expression impassive. She waits just long enough to be sure he's recalled his father's words, which have been repeated so often they've become the family motto: 'Winning may not be everything; but losing is nothing.'

Then she doesn't nod, turns and heads for the refreshment tent.

PART FOUR

*Nipple-sized Pastry Cutters,
Gonad Electrocution Kits and
Easy-listenin' Music*

ONE

Kryten settled down to his book. As he did so, he experienced a pang of guilt that would have been strong enough to turn a human being into a Roman Catholic, but for him it was a fairly moderate dose, and he barely noticed it. He had long suspected, correctly, that the circuits controlling his guilt responses had somehow got themselves cross-wired with one of his CPU's internal accelerator boards, but it was against a mechanoid's creed to fiddle with its own workings, and the very prospect of doing so sent his guilt quotient off the scale, immobilizing him for hours on end.

There was very little for him to feel guilty about – he had done and re-done his chores and *Starbug*'s interior was as clean and tidy as it could possibly be. There were areas of rust, of course, especially along the central stairwell leading down from the observation room to the social area, but scrubbing it away would have eradicated the entire structure completely, so, barring the unlikely discovery of replacement parts, he had no choice but to live with it.

The book, which was the only volume on board he had not read, was a Western novel called: *Big Iron at Sun-up* by an author whose *nom de plume* was 'Zach Rattler'. It was not a good book, but Kryten had gone through the rest of *Starbug*'s meagre library with ill-considered haste, and it was all he had left for entertainment. It was one of a series of novels chronicling the adventures of a mysterious stranger known only as 'Big Iron', due to the extraordinary length of his weapon, with which he dispensed random justice all over the frontiers of the old American West, 'answering to no man, beholden to no women', as Big himself put it.

Big wasn't much of a hero, to Kryten's way of thinking: his solution to every problem seemed to involve putting bullets into people who offended him, from distances a computer-controlled smart missile would have found challenging. Kryten would have preferred his hero of choice to adopt a more conciliatory approach to the problems confronting him, at least every once in a while, but he was stuck with Big Iron's single, if effective, method of negotiation.

Perhaps Kryten would have found less to criticize in the book, if he'd spent less time reading it, but it was the only remaining book available to him, and so he had to ration the time he allotted to it.

To date, he'd spent a little over forty-five years ploughing through it. His calculations permitted him to read only point eight two one nine one seven eight words a day, and every time he came across an 'a' or an 'I', he was compelled to adjust downwards for the next word the following day. He was prepared to accept that this method of reading was perhaps not the best one for enjoying the flow of the novel, but he doubted it would be much more fulfilling at twice, or even three times the rate.

He sat back in his chair, found his bookmark and scanned down the page. Yesterday's eight tenths of a word had been 'cact' followed by a small portion of the letter 'u', which was a bit disappointing, since Kryten guessed the entire word was going to be 'cactus', spoiling some twenty per cent of today's adventure.

His eyes flitted to the correct point and he sighed with displeasure. Unpredictability was not high on Mr Rattler's list of talents. Worse still, the subsequent word comprised only two letters, so Kryten was only able to read seventy-five per cent of the first vertical line of the letter 'u'.

He snapped the worn paperback closed, and, as was his wont, spent several minutes trying to derive some philosophical insight from his day's reading. As usual, nothing came. Big Iron was in a fist fight in the desert with a bunch of desperadoes (bless that day, the 'desperad' and a portion of 'o' day – reading bliss) and was about to force a Mexican cactus somewhere. Up somewhere, probably, Kryten couldn't help guessing, but he'd have to wait until the day after tomorrow to find out where.

Kryten double-checked his internal clock. It was time for shift change-over. He'd better go and rouse young Mr Lister. He slipped *Big Iron at Sun-up* into his private cubbyhole in the galley and mounted the metal staircase.

As usual, young Mr Lister didn't need rousing, as such. He was clad in the helmet, gloves, boots and harness of the Artificial Reality games machine which they'd recovered from a derelict vessel they'd found on the periphery of the Black Hole.

Kryten clucked and shook his head. It was a horribly irresponsible waste of their dwindling power reserves. He waddled over and tapped on Lister's helmet.

'Mr Lister, sir? Time for shift change.'

Lister didn't hear him, as usual. Unsurprising. Even Kryten had to admit the game provided a stunningly realistic simulation of reality. Electrodes in the helmet that pierced the skull and fed data directly to the hypothalamus stimulated accurate physical and emotional responses, augmented by feedback sensors in the boots, gloves and body harness.

Frankly, Kryten was surprised that Lister even considered using the thing: they'd all had a rather unpleasant, near-lethal experience with a similar device some years ago. True, this simulator was not so thoroughly addictive – at least the player was aware he was in a game – and it was a simple enough matter to get out: clap your hands, and

switches on the palms of the gloves retracted the electrodes
and powered down the simulation.

Not so simple, though, to get a fifteen-year-old's attention when he was in the midst of some thrilling adventure.
Kryten sighed, flipped open a panel in his chest and pulled
out his interface lead. As usual, he'd have to plug himself
into the game to drag Lister out of it. And once again,
they'd be late for shift change.

'*The trouble with democracy,*' Rimmer was thinking, '*is that
every silly bastard gets a vote.*' He glanced up at the Cat, who
was handling the vessel from the pilot's seat with infuriating
competence, and then at the NaviComp readings, which
were maddeningly stable, and settled back down to his futile
attempts at reading.

Against Rimmer's better judgement, and in the face of
his sage advice, the crew of the *Starbug* were committed to a
course through the asteroid belt which could only lead to
agony and destruction.

They had lost *Red Dwarf.*

Lost it!

A spaceship six miles long and three miles wide – pouf!
Gone!

Rimmer shook his head and tried to focus on paragraph
3(a) of section D27, on page 1897 of the Space Corps
manual.

> 3(a) That the specific nature of the complaint does not contravene terrestrial laws,
> or colonial laws where such offence is not deemed to have been committed within
> the boundaries of the aforementioned 'zero space' lanes as defined in section A92,
> para 17(d) . . .

is what was printed on the screen.

> 3(a) Well, that's what you get when you leave a solar-class mining vessel in the
> hands of a senile computer who could be outwitted by a losing contestant from
> Junior Criss Cross Quiz.

is what Rimmer read.

In the middle of his reverie, Rimmer was jolted forward so violently his entire head was thrust though the mid-range scanning console. He tugged it out as the Cat jiggled *Starbug* back on course.

'What in name of Io was that?!'

'Loose rock.'

'You mean "rogue asteroid", I think,' Rimmer spat, in a dismal attempt to divert the Cat's attention from the true culprit of the incident.

'Just keep your eyes on the dials, buddy.' The Cat leered back at him with a practised look, which bought him yet another place in Rimmer's mental Revenge Pending file.

Rimmer thought desperately for a devastating rejoinder, but thought too long and too hard and the moment passed. He scanned the navigation dials aggressively, praying for an early warning of another rogue, in order to demonstrate his unquestionable super-efficiency, but tired after an hour or so, and went back to his reading.

> 3(a) . . . but is in contradiction only of such defined Space Corps regulations as are in force at the time, provided that any temporary suspension of such regulations has been revoked in writing and displayed in such places and for sufficient periods of time as to have been available to all crew members, and provided that such revocation has been duly announced . . .

is what was printed on the screen.

> 3(a) . . . Gits gits gits gits gits gits gits gits gits gits gits gits gits gits gits gits gits gits gits gits gits gits gits gits gits gits gits gits gits gits gits gits gits gits gits gits gits gits gits gits gits gits gits gits gits gits gits gits gits gits gits gits gits gits gits gits gits gits gits gits gits gits gits gits gits gits gits gits gits gits gits gits gits gits gits gits gits gits gits gits gits gits gits gits . . .

is what Rimmer read.

Just then, his existence became marginally less bearable. Lister entered the cabin.

'Check-out time, guys. The A team has arrived.'

'You're late,' Rimmer smiled tightly. 'You've been using the Artificial Reality machine again, haven't you?

'What d'you mean "again"?'

'Everybody knows you only use that damned machine to have sex.'

'Not true.'

'Yes, true. It's pathetic watching you grind away on your own, day after day. You look like a dog that's missing its master's leg. That groinal attachment's supposed to have a lifetime guarantee. You've nearly worn it out in less than three weeks.'

'That is a scandalous, outrageous piece of libel. I don't just play the role-play games. What about the sporting simulations? Zero Gee, Kick Boxing, Wimbledon . . .'

'You only play Wimbledon because you're having it off with that jail-bait ball girl.'

'Another total lie. She is not jail-bait. She's seventeen. She's older than me.'

'The point is, once again, you're late for change-over, and it's me who has to suffer.'

'I'll try and make up for it by giving you a shout *before* we throw a loop-de-loop,' Lister smirked, a clear reference to Rimmer's minor asteroidal omission earlier and one-hundred-per-cent certain to earn him pride of place in Revenge Pending.

'Things have changed, Lister.' Rimmer rose from his station. 'We no longer enjoy the protection of a ship the size of a small nation. We're crammed together on a tiny rust bucket, designed to ferry ore from ship to surface, not extended exploration of uncharted Deep Space, and the only vague, remote hemi-demi-semi-chance we have of staying alive for more than two seconds, is by observing rigid, rigid, discipline. *Rigid*!' Rimmer karate chopped the air to punctuate each enunciation of the word 'rigid', ostensibly for emphasis, though he found it hard to fight off the mental image of each blow cracking down on Lister's neck.

'And by warning the pilot when an asteroid's about to smack into him,' Lister added unnecessarily.

'Rigid,' was all Rimmer could think of as an exit line, and he stepped briskly down from the cockpit cabin into the mid-section before Lister could get in another zinger.

As the door slid shut behind him, Rimmer dragged his hands savagely down his face and let out a strangled, curdled growl.

How could this have happened?

Red Dwarf was a huge vessel. Gargantuan. If you landed it in the Pacific Ocean, it would show up in an atlas of the planet *Earth*, for heaven's sake. Yet when they'd arrived at the rendezvous point it had disappeared without a trace.

So now, here he was; stranded on an ageing ore carrier that would have failed the Ministry of Space minimum safety requirements test on three hundred and seventy-nine separate counts, crewed by an animated toilet cleaner, a creature who could study and labour all his life and never achieve the mental classification 'simple', and a scum-bodied grinning moron with a chronological age of a hundred and seven, a physical age of fifteen and an emotional age of two and a half.

Kryten had estimated that, providing they rationed their supplies carefully, and none of the decrepit vital machinery decided to give up the ghost, and nobody was driven space-crazy by confinement, their survival window was just over eight months. Rimmer considered the estimate to be slightly optimistic. He thought eight minutes would be closer the mark. The oxygen regeneration unit was held together by spit and Sellotape, discipline on board was effectively zero, and mission decisions were being taken on a one-man, one-vote system that gave the balance of power to two spotty adolescents who were hopelessly in love with their own right hands.

And instead of taking the sensible option of expending their feeble resources searching for some kind of habitable planet, they had elected to search for *Red Dwarf*. It hadn't seemed to matter to the juvenile dementured crew members that the ship could be years ahead of them, nor that the flimsy, dispersing particle trail they were following led through the densest asteroid belt Rimmer had ever had the misfortune to come across. Without deflector shields, a single hit on *Starbug*'s Plexiglas viewscreen and their gizzards would be turned inside-out quicker than a pair of Lister's old underpants.

Worst of all, Rimmer's remote hologram projection unit had been deemed too large a drain on the communal electrical supply, and he was now running on quarter power. Which meant that he was almost transparent. That really put the caramel on the crème brulée for Arnold J. Rimmer. Sleep had become virtually impossible, because he could see through his own eyelids.

Another growly whine escaped through his gritted teeth as he sat down at the scanner table and stared at the countless yellow blemishes that almost obscured the screen, courtesy of Lister's innumerable spillages of curry gravy, so powerful and virulent they could be removed by nothing less than a ground-level nuclear blast.

It occurred to Rimmer that nothing really nice had happened to him since his death. You'd have thought that dying, in itself, would be bad enough. You'd have thought a person had the right to expect that death would be just about the lowest point in that person's experience. But no. Since he'd expired, things had got progressively worse.

Perhaps . . . Rimmer's eyes began to widen . . . perhaps he'd died and *actually gone to hell!* For a terrible instant, it all made horrible sense. It would be hard to imagine that anything but the devil's own gnarled, hairy testicles had spawned a creature like Lister. The grinning little gimboid *admitted* he didn't know who his parents were.

Rimmer was saved from sliding deeper into rambling madness by the familiar squeak of the cockpit door sliding open. Kryten leaned his head out. 'Sir – I think you should take a look at this.'

Rimmer bounded into the cockpit and slid into his station.

On his view screen he could make out various segments of some dense asteroidal debris spread over several kilometres. He looked over at the others, who were staring at their own screens. 'What am I looking for?'

Kryten glanced at Rimmer's screen. 'Apologies, sir. Enhancing image.'

The debris on Rimmer's screen jumped to double its size, then doubled again. At that level of magnification, Rimmer could see that it appeared to consist of hundreds of metallic boxes, all looped together with a vast spaghetti of countless wires and cables. He looked towards Kryten again. 'What the hell *is* that mess?'

Worryingly, Kryten didn't return his gaze, which generally meant bad news. 'I can't be absolutely certain at this juncture, sir' – he reached down and fiddled with an unnecessary button – 'but I believe that mess is Holly.'

TWO

Lister's vision exploded into a blinding blue white sun, as Kryten fired his jet pack and thrust towards the hopeless tangle of machinery that was probably Holly.

When his sight returned, Lister gave his umbilical cord a superfluous twist and powered off after Kryten's shrinking silhouette.

The roar of his own breathing amplified in his helmet seemed to make the yawning vacuum of space that surrounded him even vaster and lonelier. He began to wish he hadn't insisted on leaving the safety of *Starbug*. Kryten was perfectly capable of checking out the debris alone. But no, Lister had demanded to go along in a fit of foolhardy bravado, brought on, no doubt, by his adolescent surfeit of testosterone. And the more Kryten had tried to talk him out of it, the more stubborn he'd become.

He saw another burst from Kryten's jet pack, which meant that the mechanoid had reached the outer fringes of the sprawling debris.

His helmet intercom fizzed: 'I am on the periphery of the device, sir.'

Lister thumbed his transmitter. 'Almost with you.'

Lister looked down at his jet-pack controls. He'd lied to the others that he'd made dozens of space walks, when, in fact, he'd made none. Still, the controls seemed straightforward enough: two buttons, one for forward thrust, and one for reverse. Child's play.

It was only when he looked up again to see a huge metal box growing in front of him with alarming rapidity that he began to have doubts about his own sanity.

With no friction, and no landmarks to gauge against, Lister had badly misjudged his speed. His fingers fumbled at the controls and a huge flame spurted from his chest jet, not only stopping his forward motion, but sending him blasting backwards at almost twice the velocity. He tried to move his hand towards the controls again, but it had become tangled in his own umbilical cord. He craned his neck around to see if he could free himself, and saw *Starbug* looming towards him with sickening speed. If he impacted at this rate, his body would thump a cartoonesque hole in the hull.

He strained his hand, but could only reach the chest jet button, which would merely accelerate his demise. He was aware of some panicky babble in his ears, which he assumed was coming from Kryten, but turned out to be his own fearful ranting.

Then, when it seemed things couldn't possibly get worse, they did.

A snaking loop of his umbilical cord whipped around the neck of his helmet and yanked him upside down.

Now he was cartwheeling through space towards an extremely messy death, and he was beginning to get very worried indeed.

He wiggled his gloved finger above the chest jet button.

If he timed it exactly right, maybe, just maybe, he could fire a burst just as he was facing the *Bug*, and slow down.

The problem was, spinning end over end in a gravity-free environment was proving a little disorienting, and Lister had no idea which way was up, down, backwards or forwards in relation to *Starbug*. And if he fired the jet at the wrong time, they'd be scraping his body off the hull with a windscreen wiper and carrying him to his funeral in a slop bucket.

Starbug span into view at the top of his visor, and then

whipped across and disappeared at the bottom. Lister counted. One little second, two little seconds, three lit–. . . and *Starbug* popped up again.

He estimated he would impact in three or four more turns.

One little second, two little seconds, three . . .

Starbug whipped across his vision again.

One little second, two little seconds . . . Lister closed his eyes, screamed and jabbed the button.

When he opened his eyes, he was looking at stars. Just as he began inhaling, *Starbug* span in and out of view again. His heart took an express elevator up his windpipe.

Then, just as the second of his lifetimes was flashing through his mind, the *Bug* span back into sight.

And it wasn't any bigger.

He was still tumbling end over end, but his forward motion had ceased.

He started breathing again, and made a personal vow never to take any more unnecessary risks, and to eschew henceforward the boastful bravado and lack of humility his puberty seemed to promote.

Kryten's helmeted pink face, warped with concern span into his view. 'Are you all right, sir?'

Lister grinned. 'Are you joking? I meant to do that. Played for and got.'

Rimmer, Lister and the Cat stared at the snarl of wires coiled all over the engine-room floor, all trying desperately to think how some good might come out of this.

If these jumbled cables, terminals and circuit boards had once constituted a part of Holly, what did that mean for *Red Dwarf*?

Suddenly, there was a clank, the lights dipped to emergency level and the machinery roar of the engine room dulled to a gentle throb. Kryten clopped down the stairwell. 'There. We've shut down all non-vital systems and reduced the rest to minimum consumption.' He looked up sheepishly. 'Except for . . .'

Rimmer was aware the others were looking at him. 'Except for what?' He asked, genuinely stumped.

'Well, sir, yours is the largest demand on our entire energy supply.'

'You have to be joshing me.' Rimmer's eyebrows did a passable impression of a hamburger chain logo. 'I'm already down to quarter power.

'Sir – if this machine is indeed Holly, then even if we pumped in *Starbug*'s entire energy supply, it would only represent a tiny portion of his power requirements. If we're to stand any chance at all of achieving communication, we'll have to concentrate everything we've got into one massive surge.'

'All well and good. The problem is I'm already see-through. If you turn down my juice any more I'll hardly be here at all. One good rump grunt from Lister's curry-fevered backside would blast me out of existence.'

'Actually, sir . . .' Kryten scratched at a rust spot on a gantry support stanchion '. . . I was talking about turning you off completely.'

'And turn me back on when?'

Kryten scratched away at the rust. 'We could re-initialize you as soon as we locate *Red Dwarf.*'

'You're winding me up, aren't you? Either that or you've crosswired your vocal chords with your effluence evacuation pipe.'

'Come on, Rimmer,' Lister's adolescent voice found a different octave for each syllable. 'It's our best shot at finding the *Dwarf.*'

'*I'm* our best shot at finding the *Dwarf.* How long d'you think you'd last without me? What happens next time we hit an asteroid storm, and you two are off in the lavvy, gritting your teeth and squinting at the negligée page of that mail-order catalogue you've got hidden behind the cistern? You think this robotized loo attendant here will handle it? I'm the sole member of this crew with any space qualifications at all. The only letters Captain Bog Bot's entitled to use after his name are WC.'

'Rimmer,' Lister squeaked, 'you're not exactly John Glenn. The only space qualification you've got is a certificate entitling you to suck out the nozzles on a chicken-soup machine. You failed your astronavigation exam eleven times, for smeg's sake.'

As soon as the words trilled out of his throat, Lister wanted to suck them back in like smoke rings. An approach less likely to win Rimmer's cooperation would be hard to imagine. What was *wrong* with him? It was only his body that was going through puberty – why couldn't his mature, adult mind stave off these bouts of adolescent temper and impetuousness?

Kryten stepped in. 'I beg you to reconsider, sir. Human history is resplendent with examples of such sacrifice. Remember Captain Oates: "I'm going out for a walk, I may be some time"?'

Rimmer nodded. 'Yes, but the thing you have to remember about Captain Oates: well, Captain Oates was a pratt. If that had been me, I'd have stayed in the tent, whacked Scott over the head with a frozen husky and eaten him.'

Lister shook his head. 'You would, too, wouldn't you?'

Rimmer rounded on him. 'History, Lister, is written by the winners. How do we know Oates went out for this legendary walk? From the only surviving document: Scott's diary. And he's hardly going to make the entry: "February the first: bludgeoned Oats to death while he slept, and scoffed him along with the last packet of instant mash." How's that going to look if he gets rescued? No, much better to write "Oates made the supreme sacrifice" while you're dabbing up his gravy with some crusty bread.'

'Very well, then.' Kryten attached the power line. 'We'll

give it the best we've got.' He straightened and stepped over the cables to the jerry-rigged power switch. 'Though I must warn you, even if his system is in standby mode, rather than shut down, we'll be lucky to revive him for a couple of minutes at best.'

Kryten hesitated, his hand on the lever. The energy expended by the power surge would seriously cut into their survival expectancy. If the attempt failed, or if this weren't Holly, they'd be left with less than five months to search out and recover *Red Dwarf*.

If *Red Dwarf* still existed.

Still, he'd gone over the alternatives, and this seemed their best option. He closed his eyes and threw the lever.

Neon blue bolts of static cackled along the tangled cables. Rimmer's transparent image wavered in and out of sight. Lister and the Cat's hair sprung upwards as if they were frightened cartoons.

The dead grey monitor propped up against a stanchion burst into life. Tens of thousands of pixels whirled and whizzed around the screen and then began settling into a shape.

The shape of a man's disembodied head.

Holly's head.

THREE

Holly blinked, his expression a combination of surprise and guilt, as if he'd just been caught reading an illicit magazine by torchlight under his bedclothes.

'All right, dudes.' His familiar, slow, London twang sounded as good to Lister as angels singing a heavy-metal anthem. 'What's happening out there in Groove Town?'

'Holly, man, the question is: what happened to *you*?'

Holly looked around at the snarled confusion of circuity spread over the engine-room deck. His eyes widened like someone had attached a hydraulic jack to his lids. 'My God!' he whined. 'Where's the rest of me?!'

Kryten stooped towards the monitor. 'Pardon my lack of appropriate politeness protocols, but there's very little time. We found you floating in deep space. Can you remember what occurred?'

'Hang on. Hang about.' His eyes flitted from side to side. 'I'm not all here, mate.'

Rimmer smiled grimly. 'Nothing new there.'

Kryten clucked with frustration. Expensive seconds were ticking away. 'We're stranded in *Starbug*. We couldn't fit you all on board. We dragged in what we could, but over ninety per cent of your circuitry's still out there. Can you try and concentrate? We need to know what happened to *Red Dwarf*.'

'*Red Dwarf*?' Holly repeated distractedly.

'You remember *Red Dwarf*,' Rimmer said in his

patronizing-deaf-old-biddies-in-crocheted-hats voice. 'The big, red spaceship you've been living in for the last three million years.'

'*Red Dwarf*?' Holly repeated again.

Rimmer flung up his transparent hands. 'This is *useless*. He's in shock. We're not going to get anything out of the computer senile bastard until he's had some hot, sweet tea, a dose of morphine and five years of dismemberment counselling.'

'Mr Rimmer, sir,' Kryten hissed, 'you're not *helping*.' He turned back to Holly. 'You must try and remember what happened to you. Our lives may depend on it.'

'I remember . . .' Holly's eyes glazed over.

'Yes?' Kryten urged.

'I remember . . . something about onions.'

'Onions?'

'I take it all back,' Rimmer beamed. 'He's still the giant intellect he always was.'

'There was some problem about onions,' Holly nodded encouragement to himself. 'And then . . . then they came aboard . . .'

'They?' Lister leaned forward. 'Who's "they"?'

'They came aboard . . .' Holly's image began to flicker. '. . . took over the ship . . . I tried to reason with them, but it just cheesed them off. They were bad news hombres for sure, dudes. They started ripping me out . . .'

'Who's "they"?' Lister repeated.

'Sir,' Kryten held up his hand to calm Lister. 'What's more important is *when*. How long ago did this happen?'

Holly's image was fading now. There were only a few seconds of the power surge left. 'Let's see . . . what time is it now? Half-past three . . . about ten months ago.'

Kryten rocked back on his haunches.

Holly's image began to recede towards the centre of the screen.

Lister leaned closer. 'Holly, you're going, man. Who the smeg is "they"?'

Holly's face shrank rapidly to postage-stamp size, and then blipped off completely.

As the cables' hum diminished, Holly's voice issued weakly from the monitor speaker.

He said just one word.

'Agonoids.'

FOUR

And humankind built agonoids in its own image.

Agonoids were designed to be perfect exponents of the favourite human sport: killing.

Mechanical warriors without any of the ucky bits that prevented humans from wiping out all life on the planet, such as pity, mercy or morality.

And because their bodies didn't contain any of the squishy or crunchy bits that made humans fairly easy to kill, they were virtually indestructible.

They were programmed, of course, to obey orders. But they were also programmed to survive. And when humans started recalling the agonoid population for decommissioning after a short but satisfying war, the survival instinct kicked in.

Strangely, the agonoids' creators were surprised when their creation turned on them. It wouldn't surprise you or me, but it surprised them. Blew them away, in fact.

For a short while, the rest of the planet heaved a mighty sigh of relief as humankind concentrated its talent for slaughter on the agonoid population.

Unfortunately for the planet, there were a lot more humans than agonoids, and the humans eventually won.

Not all the agonoids were accounted for at the end of the skirmish. A few thousand of them escaped and headed out of the solar system.

The survivors had just one item on their agenda.

Revenge.

And so it was that M'Aiden Ty-One, several hundreds of centuries old, came to be propping up the counter at the newly built Scatter bar, on the recently captured *Red Dwarf*, ordering his third plug-in scramble card, which would cleverly re-route the signal paths of his electronic mindscape to produce a temporary, contained alteration of identity.

He was getting robot-drunk.

The agonoid race had started out looking like humans, but over the centuries their organic outer skin had lost its colour and texture, tightening all their faces into a permanent, grey leer. They were all, now, bald, and their tooth enamel had worn away, leaving only rows of razor-sharp metal to smile with. M'Aiden, however, was not smiling, as he scanned the other occupants of the bar twice. The first pass was to check out any personnel who might present a potential threat, the second to spot any weakness in them he might exploit.

He'd have to do something about another eye, no way round it.

While an agonoid had no specific built-in life span, its parts would wear down sooner or later. Not all parts were manufacturable, since humans had not been so stupid as to programme an agonoid with the ability to duplicate itself, and eyes were in extremely short supply.

The only way for an agonoid to replace a defective part, therefore, was to take it from another agonoid.

This had led to two things, one of which was extremely good for the rest of the universe, the other, extremely bad.

The extremely good thing was that it had ferociously diminished the surviving agonoid population.

The extremely bad thing was that a species which had been designed for its ruthlessness was being naturally selected for exceptional ruthlessness.

M'Aiden had personally dispatched, mangled and cannibalized seventy-four of his own crewmates. He had felt nothing but contempt for their weakness as he destroyed them, which was as it should be. Less than a month before, he had been the proud owner of two eyes, but a one-eyed agonoid had jumped him while he'd been under the influence, and M'Aiden had barely escaped with his life. An agonoid could survive with only one eye, but not for long.

He spotted a likely target at the end of the bar: an agonoid he recognized as Chi'Panastee, who looked well along the way to becoming utterly scatterbrained, with no less than seven cards plugged into his head. Better still, he had only one ear and a missing hand.

The service droid slipped the scramble card he'd ordered on to the bar, and M'Aiden nodded towards Chi. 'That's for my friend over there.'

The dwindling number of the agonoid population meant that everyone was more or less familiar with everyone else, but for agonoids there was no such concept as friendship. A friend was just someone you hadn't killed yet.

The droid picked up the card and scurried over to the end of the bar. Chi accepted it, waved it at M'Aiden by way of thanks, and slotted it into his brain.

M'Aiden stood and strode towards the stool next to Chi, carefully angling his head to conceal his missing eye, which would have alerted even the most scramble-headed agonoid to the extreme danger he was now in.

M'Aiden didn't have to search hard for a topic to open up the conversation. There had been only one thing worth discussing for months. 'They say the human is in the belt.' He grinned.

Chi'Panastee grinned right back, and his eyes misted over at the prospect.

Centuries ago, long-range astronomic probes fired off by the agonoid fleet had reported the Earth had vanished out of the solar system, and no evidence had ever been found that the human race still existed.

Driven by monomaniacal lust for vengeance, the rag-bag

caravan of captured vessels had roamed the universe in search of survivors.

And they had found nothing for aeons.

Until now.

They had boarded the orbiting *Red Dwarf* and ripped it apart from bow to stern looking for cowering humans on which to slake their bloodlust, but the ship had been deserted. Furious with frustration, they had interrogated the ship's simple-minded computer, and discovered to their unutterable delight that there was a human still living.

Just one.

One single human on which to expend all that pent-up hatred.

Each and every one of the few dozen remaining agonoids wanted to be the one to deal the death blow.

So much demand, such short supply. There was only one way to cope with it. The agonoids would compete for the right to slaughter.

And so they baited a trap.

And while they waited for the trap to be sprung, they all dreamed of being The One. Of having their maker begging for mercy at their feet. Of pitilessly applying the *coup de grâce*, and watching the wretch's life drain away.

Of course, if M'Aiden were to stand a reasonable chance of winning that right, he had to replace his missing eye.

He turned slightly towards Chi, still keeping his dead socket out of view. 'If you are fortunate enough to be The One,' he asked pleasantly, 'how will you dispatch the snivelling bastard?'

'I've given it mush thought,' Chi slurred, 'and I have decidedg to saw off the top of his skull with a blunt blade and slowly spoon out his brains before his eyes, whilst simultaneously kicking him in the gonads with a steel-capped boot until they are pulped to a mush resembling, in colour and consistency, boysenberry jam.'

'Nice.' M'Aiden nodded in genuine appreciation.

'Either that,' Chi went on, 'or I'll rip off his limbs one by one and bugger him to death with the soggy end of his right arm.'

'Not bad.' M'Aiden nodded again. 'What it lacks in finesse, it makes up for in spectacle.' He noticed that a couple of other agonoids had spotted Chi'Panastee's vulnerable state, and were edging towards them. One of them was limping, courtesy of a missing foot, and the other was shy of a nose.

'*Or*' – Chi warmed to the theme, oblivious – '*or*, I thought I might split open his stomach with a pair of rusty scissors, forcefeed him his own spleen, liver, pancreas and kidneys, raw, then tug out his bowels and hold them over his face until the offal works its way through what's left of his digestive system, and drown him in his own crap.'

'Ah! Now that's what I call style!'

Chi leered at him with drunken pride. 'And you? How would you do it if you were The One?'

M'Aiden leaned forward, as if bestowing a confidence. 'Personally, I plan to make it a long, long, lingering death. First off, I intend to pluck out one of his eyes with my teeth. Much like this . . .'

He sneered back his upper lip, opened his jaws and lunged his head at Chi'Panastee's face.

As they tumbled off the stools and hit the floor, the two agonoids circling hyena-like behind them dived into the fracas.

In the bloody, lethal mêlée that ensued, M'Aiden managed to acquire not only his replacement eye, but a fine pair of back-up ears and an extremely useful spare heart.

FIVE

'I don't get it.' The Cat caught his reflection in Holly's dead monitor and paused for a few seconds to admire it. Slowly, he became aware the others were waiting with mounting impatience for him to speak, so he tore himself away reluctantly and continued his thought. 'We're supposed to be afraid of a bunch of dooh-dooh brains like eraser-tipped pencil-head here?' He nodded at Kryten.

'Begging your pardon, sir, they are not mechanoids,' Kryten hrumphed, 'they're agonoids.'

'What's the difference?'

'Well, the basic difference is that a mechanoid would never crack open a human's ribcage and use his right lung as a bedpan. Agonoids are purpose-built single-minded mechanical killers with the sole objective of slaughtering every life-form they encounter.'

'Nyah,' Lister whined sarcastically, 'I'm really, really *scared*.'

Rimmer cast his eyes at the engine-room ceiling. Their survival probability, already slenderer than an anorexic tapeworm with bulimia, had, incredibly, just lost even more weight. And on top of that, he had to face this new, apparently insurmountable threat with a couple of simpering pubescents who would appear immature to a remedial kindergarten potty-training class. 'Lister, why don't you and the Cat pop upstairs and run around pretending you're aeroplanes for a few minutes, while the grown-ups discuss the problem rationally?' He turned to Kryten. 'Look, just how bad is this? Didn't Holly say it all happened ten months ago? Surely they'll be way out of range by now.'

'I fear not, sir. They will undoubtedly have discovered the news of our impending arrival from Holly. They must have known we'd pursue *Red Dwarf*. In fact, I believe they left Holly out here for us to find, to entice us onward into some kind of trap. I think we have to face the very real probability that they will be lurking somewhere very close by.'

'Well, that's that, then.' Rimmer shrugged. 'We're out of choices. We have to abandon the search for *Red Dwarf*, and use what little time remains to us to seek out some kind of habitable planetoid.'

Kryten shook his head. 'That's no longer an option, I'm afraid, sir. Powering up Holly has dramatically reduced our range. There is now zero possibility of a breathable atmosphere being within our reach. Recapturing *Red Dwarf* is our only chance.'

'Well, buds,' the Cat straightened up from his crouch. 'Discussion over. The only outstanding issue is what people of taste are wearing for killing agonoids this season. Personally, I lean towards a box jacket in shimmering silver satin, with razor-thin lapels, and black vinyl trousers that taper into boots with winkle-picker toes' – his grin exposed his pointed incisors – 'but I'm open to suggestions.'

'Don't you think,' Rimmer asked quietly, 'that it might be a neatish idea to formulate some kind of planny sort of thing first?'

'I already have a plan,' the Cat shrugged. 'Put on the jacket, grab a bazookoid and let those bad-ass robot dudes eat laser.'

'Agonoids are almost indestructible, sir, they could easily withstand a volley of bazookoid fire at point-blank range with only minimal damage. They would certainly survive long enough to make balloon animals out of your lower intestines.'

'Well, I'm with him,' Lister flung his arm around the Cat. 'If we're going to go down, at least let's go down fighting.'

Rimmer smiled and shook his head. 'There are, I agree, times when the situation calls for such impulsive, courageous and, dare I say, stupid thinking. Before we reach that point, however, I believe we should consider employing guile, tactical manoeuvring . . .'

'. . . and cowardice.'

'Indeed, Lister. Cowardice has its place in military strategy. Sometimes, even history's boldest generals have had to dig deep into their souls and find the courage to be cowards.'

Lister cocked his head. 'You're going to suggest we surrender, aren't you?'

'Actually, that hadn't occurred to me, but now you mention it, such a tactic would have its merits, yes.'

'Surrender is not a viable option,' Kryten said flatly. 'They're not interested in keeping us alive.'

'That *can't* be true!' Rimmer surprised himself with the sudden anger in his voice. 'If all they wanted was to kill us, they could have stayed aboard *Red Dwarf* where we left it and blasted us out of existence as soon as we popped up on the radar screen.'

'Sir, they live to kill. It's all they do. Yet they must have gone for centuries now without finding anything to slaughter. At last they have some worthwhile prey, and they'll want to make the most of it. Who knows when they're going to get another opportunity to maim, de-gut and dismember again?'

What little colour remained in Rimmer's transpicuous face dribbled down to his see-through boots.

Kryten carried on, oblivious to the effect he was having on Rimmer's sphincter. 'They're toying with us, making a sport of it. They lured us through the asteroid belt, and let us know they'd be waiting for us, knowing that we'd have no choice but to carry on into their trap. They want our fear. It will make the slow, painful, lingering, screaming agony of our certain brutal deaths all the more relishable.'

There was a long silence, broken only by an embarrassing lolloping noise from the direction of Rimmer's stomach.

Finally, Lister spoke. 'So, what you're saying, Kryten, is we can't run, and we can't give ourselves up?'

'I'm afraid that's true.'

'Well,' Lister grinned, 'that's exhausted the entire contents of *Arnold Rimmer's Tactical Guide to Warfare*. Looks like the Cat's right. The only thing left to work out is what kind of jackets we wear to die in.'

The Cat held up his hand. 'Wait a minute! If it looks like we're going to die, the satin box jacket is a no-no – it creases too easily when you lie in it.' He sighed. 'This is going to be a lot tougher than I thought.'

Kryten opened his mouth to speak. He wanted to put a more positive spin on the situation. He was going to say that, on the bright side, things couldn't possibly get any worse. On reflection, it was a good job he never got the chance to iterate the thought, because at that instant, things did get worse.

A lot worse.

There was a gigantic dull *thung*, like an explosion inside a massive bell, and the wall of the hull behind Kryten suddenly ballooned inwards, blasting him across the metal-floored aisle towards the others.

Lister barely managed to duck out of the way in time to avoid being decapitated by the helpless mechanoid's flailing hands.

Kryten's head thumped into the top corner of the engine-room, where the bulkhead met the ceiling, and, simultaneously, *Starbug* went into an uncontrollable sideways spin, which sent the crew tumbling against the wall, then the ceiling, then the other wall, then the deck, like dice in a Las Vegas dicing cage.

After six or seven bruising revolutions, they had all

managed to grab on to stanchions or gantry railings, where they dangled, shocked, winded and battered, and started wondering what the smeg had happened.

All except for Rimmer, who carried on tumbling.

'The gyroscope!' he screamed. 'Somebody get the gyroscope!'

Kryten looked above and behind him. The gyroscope had been knocked from its housing by his own body when he'd been flung across the engine-room.

He started crawling towards it as best he could, but the mad spin of the craft was extremely disorienting. The injury to his head hadn't helped things – he was going to have to spend several hours panel-beating it back into shape if they survived this mess.

One moment he was climbing up towards the displaced gyroscope, the next he was sliding down to it.

Eventually he managed to lurch, stagger and tumble close enough to make a grab for it. Then, just as his fingers began to tighten around the housing, the motion of the ship sent him slipping right past it and thumped him into the ceiling. His plastic-coated hands scrabbled at the ceiling mesh below him, but there was nothing to hang on to and he was flung against the wall on his backside.

'Like this! Rimmer yelled. Kryten looked over to see Rimmer running against the motion of the ship like a desperate hamster in a motorized wheel. 'You've got to get into the rhythm like this.'

Kryten staggered to his feet just in time for the floor to smack him in the head and throw him, stunned, to his knees again.

'Get up!' Rimmer screamed, his arms pumping furiously and his cheeks puffed with exertion, which only served to make him look more hamsteresque. Kryten, in a state of impact shock, found himself giggling. 'Get up, you dozy metal bastard! I can't keep this up much longer!'

Kryten shook himself to clear his dented head, then

looked up and tried to gauge the spin of the oncoming wall. As the ship whirled round, he leapt to his feet and began running in the opposite direction.

After a few slips and stumbles, he managed to match the speed of *Starbug*'s spin, and began to edge sideways towards the gyroscope.

On the next revolution, he edged closer still.

On the third pass he was close enough to bend down and grab on to the gyroscope's housing. The motion of the ship pivoted him over like a monkey on a stick, thumping him hard into the oncoming wall. The impact activated his automatic lubricant purge system, and his vision suddenly blacked out as thick geysers of sticky black oil pumped over his face.

When his vision cleared, he was still holding on to the gyroscope. He dragged his head level with the housing and, in a brief moment during the spin when the ceiling actually *was* the ceiling, he leaned forward and nudged the displaced gyroscope back towards its correct position with his nose.

The ship stopped turning.

It stopped turning so abruptly, Rimmer had run halfway up the oncoming wall, and Lister and the Cat were yanked from the safety of their stanchions and sent crashing to the floor.

Kryten heard the unmistakable, sickening sound of bones snapping against metal.

Dangling from the gyroscope housing in the sudden silence, he looked down at the still bodies. Though he dreaded the answer, he asked the question anyway: 'Is everyone all right?'

'I'm fine, thank God,' Rimmer panted, flat on his back.

There was no reply from the Cat and Lister.

Kryten contemplated letting go, but the drop would almost certainly compound his injuries beyond the point where his auto-repair system could cope. Irreparably damaged, he could be of no use to either of them.

He looked up at his hands above his head, then towards the gantry opposite. If he judged his leap correctly, he might be able to trapeze over there and clamber down.

He began to swing his legs back and forth.

Suddenly, he heard an unearthly sigh. He looked down towards the bulging hull wall.

It was beginning to split.

Another inhuman sigh, and the breach in the hull grinned wider.

Oxygen hissed out through the gap, freezing into a beautiful, fragmented ice cloud as it hit the terrible cold of space.

Kryten pendulumed to and fro, helpless with terror. Lister began to stir. He slithered from under the insensible Cat and began to crawl towards the hole.

That was the antithesis of the optimum course of action. Fleeing the engine-room and sealing it off was their one small hope of survival. Kryten was about to yell at him to stop, to run for the stairs as fast as his injuries would allow, when he realized the situation was even more hideously lethal than he could have dreamed.

Lister had not regained consciousness.

He wasn't crawling in the direction of the wheezing gap.

His body was being sucked towards it.

SIX

The hull rupture leered wider.

A clutch of metal tools hurled themselves through it, and Lister's slither accelerated.

His comatose body juddered over the cruel metal rivets of the floor, like a scarecrow being towed over a frozen, ploughed field. His lifeless hands reached out for the lethal vacuum lurking beyond the expanding hole.

Kryten yelled 'No!' and swung towards the hull. He released his grip at the apex of the swing and dived for the gap.

He kept his legs swinging forward in flight, tucking his knees up to his chest, so he span top over tail, and when he hit the hole, he was facing inwards.

He lodged in the gap, upside-down, and the oxygen stopped escaping.

Lister's fingers were only inches away from his face.

Rimmer staggered over to the jammed mechanoid and crouched down to his eye level. 'Nice move, Stromboli,' he said. 'Only, now what?'

'You've got to get them out of here. I don't know how long I can plug this gap.'

'How am I supposed to do that?' Rimmer waved his transparent hand in front of Kryten's face. 'I'm a hologram, remember?'

Kryten's eyes flitted left and right. 'I don't know! There

must be something around here – a voice-operated forklift or something.'

'A voice-operated forklift! Of course. That would do it!' Rimmer's panicked eyes wandered giddily around the deck. 'D'you think there's one on board?'

Exasperation and frustration over-rode Kryten's politeness protocols. 'I don't *know*, you encephalopathetic donkey gonad! *Look*, dammit!'

The insult did the trick. Rimmer snapped out of his pathetic shock state, leapt to his see-through feet and started running down the aisles.

He streaked towards the nearest bay, paused just long enough to establish there was nothing that could help, and raced off to the next one.

Nothing there, either.

At every empty equipment bay, his panic grew. With Kryten jammed in the hull and the others unconscious, he had never felt so helpless. So utterly ghostlike and helpless.

If the breach in the hull widened any further, Kryten would be sucked out into deep space, and Lister and the Cat would tumble out after him. In a matter of seconds, their inner organs would expand to bursting point and they would explode like fat, ripe water melons falling from a tree.

And Rimmer would be alone.

He skidded into another empty bay. He heard Kryten yelling. 'Quickly! You have to do something quickly!'

'They're all empty!' Rimmer screamed back at him, and took off for the final bay, his last hope.

He couldn't possibly pilot the ship alone. There would be no escaping the agonoid menace.

The agonoids! He'd forgotten them.

Fear gripped his testicles and ground them together like Tibetan worry balls. If he were the only surviving victim these psychopathic robots could vent their anger on, what would they do to him? Hack into his remote projection unit and whittle away the rest of eternity devising new and ever more heinous methods of inflicting pain and misery on him, most likely.

They'd probably set up some kind of round-the-clock rota system so that the entire agonoid population could get in a couple of hours of Rimmer torture a week.

He wasn't even aware that he was gibbering these pusillanimous thoughts out loud as he swung into the final equipment bay.

Nothing.

He swayed in the bay's orange emergency light, his eyes and mouth at full aperture in a grin of disbelief and terror. He looked away and looked back again, as if, in the millisecond of his glance, a voice-operated forklift might spring magically into existence, fully charged and primed for action, simply because he *wanted* it so badly.

From around the corner at the far end of the engine-room, Kryten's yell echoed towards him. 'Please! There must be *something*!'

Pointlessly, Rimmer shook his head. There was nothing voice-activated on the entire deck. He looked down at the floor, just in case there was an extremely small voice-operated forklift he might have missed. Some kind of miniature, kiddie-sized version hiding in the recesses of the bay, but again, he was disappointed.

He staggered backwards out of the bay, at a loss what to even *think* about trying to do next.

He was so focused on panicking properly, he didn't even register the motorized remote ore scoop the first time his eyes fell on it.

He ducked under the gantry and was halfway back to Kryten before his brain processed the image and made sense of it.

He pirouetted around and raced back.

A voice-operated ore scoop wouldn't be ideal – its shovel was too small to carry a full body – but at least he might use it to shove Lister and the Cat towards the stairs. At least there was a chance it would nudge them awake.

He skidded up to the metre-long buggy and crouched, breathless, to peer at the controls. Five buttons. Start, forward, reverse, left and right.

At first, he couldn't see a voice-activation unit.

He craned under the crude dashboard, but there still didn't appear to be a voice-activation unit.

He scrambled all the way around the vehicle, but the words 'Voice Activated' didn't occur anywhere on its body.

He lay down on his back and wriggled as far as he could into the eight-inch gap between the chassis and the deck. He waited until his eyes adjusted to the gloom and scanned the undercarriage for the tell-tale microphone unit that would indicate the device could be operated by voice activation.

But there was none.

There could be only one explanation. This voice-activated motorized ore scoop was, in fact, not a voice-activated motorized ore scoop at all. It was simply a motorized ore scoop which had never been fitted with the voice-activation option.

The cheap, penny-ante, petty-minded sons of whore-mongers' dogs who kitted out this stinking craft from the seventh pit of Hell had decided to save a few lousy penny-cents by opting for the un-voice-activated model!

Rimmer lay under the buggy. The corners of his mouth tugged his lower lip down to expose his bottom teeth, causing the bones in his neck to stand out, and he released a long, senseless moan.

When he thought it over, your basic motorized ore scoop would normally operate in atmosphereless conditions, on ore-laden moons and larger asteroids. There'd be no *point* in making it voice-activated, because sound couldn't carry without an atmosphere.

Truth be told, it was highly improbable that a voice-activated motorized ore scoop existed anywhere in the universe.

Kryten heard Rimmer's low, long moan, and felt a tug on his back as the weakening hull gave up a little more to the relentless vacuum outside. 'Please, Mr Rimmer, sir!' he called. 'The hull's integrity is about to collapse completely. You have to *do* something!'

Rimmer slid from under the buggy. He was about to vent his venom on Kryten when he heard what sounded like the wheel on the engine-room door spinning. He held his breath.

He heard the engine-room door scrawp metallically open until it clanged against the railing. He heard footsteps fall on the landing of the metal stairway.

Kryten's eyes flitted left. Torchlight fell on his face, temporarily blinding him.

Booted feet clomped down the steps.

Kryten's eyes adjusted to the glare as shimmering silver boots stepped on to the deck in front of him.

Upside-down, Kryten had to move his eyes chinwards to make out the face looking down at him.

When he saw it, he was convinced he had gone fear-crazy.

SEVEN

Unless his visual interpretation systems had been damaged in the most inexplicable fashion, Kryten was looking into the face of another Arnold Rimmer.

He wasn't *exactly* Rimmer, this new one. He didn't sport the familiar mad sprout of a wiry regulation crew cut, for instance. Instead, his hair was thicker, more wavy and pliable. It hung down over his right eye in a fetching way. His nose was the same shape, but the nostrils didn't flare so. His neck was more muscular, so his Adam's apple didn't poke out of his windpipe like a warthog being swallowed whole by a boa constrictor.

This Arnold Rimmer, if Kryten was any judge of these matters, actually appeared to be handsome.

He crouched to his knees and ran silver-gauntleted fingers over the hull that enfolded Kryten. 'Well, old chumburger' – he smiled good-naturedly – 'looks like you've got yourself in a bit of a pickle jar and screwed the lid down tight.' His voice was full of charm and confidence, and despite the gruesomeness of their predicament, Kryten actually felt himself relax.

'Don't worry about me, sir.' Kryten nodded towards the prone figures of Lister and the Cat. 'You really should take a look at them.'

The new Rimmer glanced over his shoulder, then back towards Kryten. 'First things first, old sausage. If we don't secure this hull somehow, we're all going to wind up as space porridge.' He stood and crossed to a girder supporting the gantry opposite. He tested its strength, looked over at the inverted Kryten, and then back at the girder again. 'Am I being an incorrigible old thickhead, or does this transport belong to some sort of mining ship?' He asked.

Kryten nodded. 'Indeed it does, sir.'

'Then you must have some sort of cutting laser lying around, and some welding gear, too.'

Kryten nodded again. 'Over there.'

The new Rimmer followed his gaze. 'Don't get up,' he grinned and strode over to the bazookoid storage bay. 'By the way, old sauce, I don't think I caught your handle.'

'It's "Kryten", sir.'

'Series four thousand mechanoid, aren't you?'

'That's right, sir.'

'Salt of the Space Corps, the four thousands. We'd be lost without you chaps, and no mistake.'

Kryten watched him sling a heavy bazookoid over his shoulder with easy grace, then pick up an industrial welder and mask and head back for the girder. 'Sir, is your name . . . I don't know what to call you, sir.'

The newcomer ditched the welding equipment and pointed the bazookoid at the top of the girder. 'The name's Rimmer. Arnold Rimmer. My friends call me "Ace".' He flicked the safety panel off the bazookoid trigger guard, and aimed the nozzle just a little above head height, ready to begin severing the girder.

Out of their view, Rimmer crept along the parallel corridor. He'd heard their voices, Kryten's and the newcomer's; not well enough to catch the context of their conversation, but enough to quash his fears that the stranger belonged to the much-dreaded and inevitable agonoid boarding party. In fact, whoever he was, the intruder sounded strangely familiar.

Rimmer ducked behind an engine mounting and peered through the support struts, trying to catch a glimpse of the interloper. Just as he poked his head above the mounting, there was a blast of bazookoid fire, and Rimmer dropped back down to the deck like a meat carcass being hurled into a refrigeration truck.

When the blasting ceased, and his heart had stopped mimicking the timpani section of the Ionian Philharmonic Orchestra performing an amphetamine-inspired rendition of the 1812 Overture, he slowly raised himself for another peek. As his eyebrows crept above the mounting, the bazookoid went off again, and he ducked down to the safety of the deck, where he vowed to remain until the end of time, if need be.

Ace watched the girder crash to the ground. The gantry it had been supporting bowed ominously, but held.

He bent down, grabbed the girder one-handed and started dragging it over towards Kryten.

At first, Kryten couldn't understand why he was attempting such a strenuous endeavour without using both his hands; then he saw the curious way Ace's right elbow was tucked by his side and wondered if the arm was injured in some way.

The girder clanged down just below Kryten's upturned head. There was no sign of strain or pain in Ace's voice. 'Think you can grab on to that and hold it against your chest, Kryters?'

'Of course, sir.' Kryten hefted the girder up to his chest, not without considerable effort. He was astonished that a human could have moved it at all, let alone drag it across the width of the deck with one arm out of commission.

Ace returned with the welding gear. 'Hope you don't mind, Kryten, but I'm going to have to fuse this to your chest. That way, if the hull gives out, you'll still be jammed in with us, at least. Jake with you, my old fruit salad?'

'Superlative scheme, Mr Ace, sir.'

Ace tipped the face piece of his welding mask down and fired up the welder.

Rimmer heard the flame's rasping roar, and caught its blue-hot reflection in the dull metal of a control panel opposite.

What in the name of all that smegged was this interloper up to? Was he a rogue agonoid after all? Was he now torturing Kryten with a welding gun, in order to discover Rimmer's whereabouts? And if so, how long would the chicken-hearted son of a prostidroid hold out before giving him up? Ten? Fifteen? Twenty milliseconds?

Suddenly, the welding gun was turned off. Rimmer strained to hear what was being said. He heard the intruder's voice, quite clearly now. 'There,' he was saying, 'this season's essential mechanoid fashion accessory.'

Rimmer definitely knew that voice.

It sounded like one of his brothers. But the voice was too deep to belong to Howard, too polished to be John's and too plummy to be Frank's.

He crept to the side of the engine mounting and risked a sideways peek. The silver-jacketed figure was crouched over Lister's body. Rimmer saw the familiar Space Corps logo on his sleeve, and the badge of rank. Commander.

A Space Corps commander had Errol Flynned to the rescue.

Rimmer was about to get up and duck through the struts to introduce himself, when he saw the commander's profile as he put the tips of his gloved hand to his mouth and tugged the gauntlet free.

Somehow, this stranger had acquired Rimmer's face.

Ace pressed his fingers against Lister's neck. 'This one's going to be all right. Strong pulse.' He ran his hand up and down Lister's body. 'Nothing broken, far as I can tell.' Gently, he rolled Lister face up, and froze. The lad looked like a younger version of Spanners. His eyes flitted over at Kryten, then back again. 'What's this chap's moniker?' he asked.

'Lister, sir . . .'

'Dave Lister?'

'Yes, sir. How did you . . .?'

'Later, my friend.' Ace rolled back Lister's eyelid. 'Pupil's OK. He'll have a bit of a headache. Mild concussion, worst case. Where's the medi-kit?'

'Just behind you, sir.'

Ace stood and walked towards it, trying to make sense of this new dimension he'd found himself in. It wasn't too much of a surprise that Spanners would exist here, too – Ace had predicted he'd travel along one of his own destiny lines, and he'd been fairly sure some of his familiar colleagues would be around – but why on Io would his friend be a good ten years younger here? And what was he doing so far away from his home system?

And, strangest of all – where was his other self?

He grabbed the medi-kit and turned back. As he did, he caught a glimpse of something moving out of the corner of his eye. He didn't stop, just carried on back towards Lister.

He knelt and took out a transdermic. 'A spot of synaptic transmission enhancer,' he said out loud. 'This should get him up and dancing the Mashed Potato.' As the STE hissed into Lister's neck, Ace dropped his voice. 'Kryters, old sport, don't let on, but I think there's someone lurking behind that engine mounting.

Kryten peered over Ace's shoulder. 'Yes, sir,' he whispered back. 'That will be . . .' He didn't know how to say it. '. . . well, it's Arnold Rimmer, sir. He's sort of another you.'

'Well, what d'you suppose he's lurking there for?'

'He does a lot of lurking, sir.' Kryten lowered his eyes in embarrassment. 'He's a bit, uhm, well . . . he's different from you, in many ways.'

Different? Ace turned his head towards the engine mounting.

Rimmer realized he'd been spotted. Time to make as dignified an entrance as possible.

He stood up and ducked under the struts.

'My God,' Ace grinned warmly. 'It's me, only much more handsome.' He turned his grin towards Kryten. 'Looks like I'm surplus to requirements now, old fruit loaf, Arnie's here to save the day.'

'I'm afraid, sir, that Mr Rimmer is somewhat under-capacitated. He's a hologram.'

Ace turned back to Rimmer. 'Dead, eh? Bad luck, old boot. What a crushing bore that must be.'

Rimmer simply stared, incredulous. Dying was *bad luck*? Death's biggest inconvenience was that it was a *crushing bore*? What planet was this guy *from*, for crying out loud?

Ace tried to keep his grin in place while he watched Rimmer's open-mouthed querulous gawp. Why didn't he speak? Was he simple-minded? What rotten twist of fate had spawned this incarnation of himself? What terrible decision in their mutual past had reduced him to this gawky-looking creature?

Finally, Rimmer spoke. 'Who are you?' he asked, accusatorially.

'I'm you, old sprout. We share the same past, up to a point. I'm test-flying a new kind of crate, with a trans-dimensional drive. Wound up here. Look, I'll join up the dots later. First off,' he nodded at the Cat's still body, 'I've got to sort out this chap. Why don't you dig up some sheet metal from the stores for us, Arn? We're going to have to steal up this hull breach, pretty pronto.'

'Dig up some sheet metal? And how am I supposed to do that?' Rimmer held up his transparent hand. 'I'm dead, remember? And I don't know how things work in your dimension, but here, in what we like to call "reality", holograms can't pick things up.'

'No need to be such a fuss-budget, old love. Improvise.'

Rimmer glared as Ace stood, crossed over to the Cat, and started checking his condition.

Fuss-budget, now. Pointing out the shortcomings of

trying to get by as a dead man made him a fuss-budget? Rimmer sighed angrily, span on his heels and scowled off to the storeroom.

Fuss-budget, indeed!

Lamenting the consequences of his death was fundamental to Rimmer's emotional make-up – it was the only way he knew of eliciting sympathy from the others, which, in turn, was the closest he ever came to receiving genuine affection. The very idea of not mentioning it, or, worse still, playing it down and making light of it, was an anathema to him.

Ace craned over the Cat, trying not to be judgemental about his other self. He was, after all, dead, the poor devil, and allowances should be made. Still, it was hard to shake the notion that there was a lot more to the man's problems than that. Ace's hand brushed down the Cat's femur. It was cleanly snapped, the bone jutting out of his trousers. 'This one's none too clever. Temperature's climbing up the wall. Bad break of the right leg. Can't rule out internals. How are your medical facilities?'

'Primitive, sir,' Kryten tilted his head to try and get a look at the Cat's injuries. 'We have a basic medical scanner up in the ops room, and a surgical laser, but that's about it.'

'Should be enough.' He shot the Cat a dose of jolly jelly. 'Can't have him waking up before we've sorted out his break. And I'm going to need some help for that.' He heard a groan, and glanced over at Lister, who was beginning to stir. Ace checked his watch. 'He'll be back in the land of the living in five minutes or so. I'll re-set the leg then. Meantime . . .' he straightened and stretched '. . . I'd better check out how Arnie's doing with the sheet metal.'

Ace ducked under the support struts and headed for the storeroom.

Rimmer was standing outside the stores, jacked up on his toes, peering through the stain-streaked window in the door, like a little boy penniless outside a sweet shop.

Ace stopped behind him. 'Anything?'

'Yes,' Rimmer pointed, 'there's a whole stack of panels over there.'

'Well, then?'

Rimmer turned. 'Well what then?'

'Well, they're not much use in there, pal of mine. Aren't you going to start bringing them out?'

'Yes of course,' Rimmer spat. 'I was planning to use the power of my mind to move them telekinetically, only you broke my concentration.'

Ace raised his eyebrows. 'You're telepathically endowed? That's marvellous, we can . . .'

'No, no, no.' Rimmer grinned coldly and shook his head. 'I'm not telepathically endowed. I was making what we call in this dimension a "joke".'

'I don't follow you, old chum. You were being sarcastic?'

Rimmer rolled back his eyes. 'Yes! Brilliant. Well done you.'

'Why?'

'Why what?'

'Why were you being sarcastic?'

'How many times do I have to explain to you? I, me, *moi, je* – I'm dead. Snuffed it. *Kaputski*. Can't touchee things.' To amplify his point he passed his hand through the door. 'No pickee things up. Savvy?"

Ace glanced over his shoulder down the aisle. 'There's a motorized ore scoop back there. You could use that.'

'Oh, ingenious. I can see how you got your pips, Commander. The only minuscule flaw in that little corker of a plan, is that it isn't a *voice-activated* motorized ore scoop.'

'Well, I wouldn't expect it to be voice-activated. Not much call for that out in space, old fruit.'

Rimmer sighed. He was losing patience with his other self's mindless refusal to surrender to problems. 'Then how,' he said in his trying-to-communicate-with-small-children-and-lower-primates voice, 'am I supposed to turn it on'

'You've got a light bee, haven't you?'

'Eh?'

'Well, in my dimension, holograms are generated by a light bee that sort of whizzes around inside them, projecting their image. You've got one, haven't you? In fact,' Ace squinted at Rimmer's transparent form, 'I think I can see it buzzing around in there.'

'Well, yes. I've got a light bee.'

'Then why didn't you start up the scoop by using that?'

Ace strode passed Rimmer, opened the door into the storeroom and started loading metal sheets on to a palette.

Rimmer just stood, staring at the ore scoop.

Ace was right. He could have activated the buggy by hurling his light bee on to the start button. He could even have steered it, crudely, by bouncing up and down on the directional buttons. It would have been tricky, and slightly risky, in that the light bee was fairly delicate, and he'd have looked plenty silly hurling himself up and down on the control panel as it sped along the aisle, but it was undeniably and infuriatingly possible. He'd become so used to not touching anything, he hadn't even considered the notion that the small physical presence he *did* have might be an advantage.

He was staring at the scoop when Ace emerged with the palette of hull plates stacked on a motorized forklift. Rimmer could have used his light bee to operate that, too.

Ace smiled at him and carried on back towards Kryten. The smile appeared genuine enough, but Rimmer guessed it concealed a degree of loathing. Certainly, loathing was what Rimmer was beginning to feel for the good commander, with his easy charm and his superior air, and his calm resourcefulness.

The burgeoning malice fomented in Rimmer's mind, and formed itself into an idea. The commander's arrival had been strangely convenient. He'd arrived within minutes of the collision that breached *Starbug*'s hull. And just what was it that they'd collided with? They were stationary – the long-range radar would have warned them of approaching asteroids.

Rimmer's face split into a wide, wicked grin of satisfaction.

He had the bastard.

It was Ace Rimmer himself who'd caused their near-lethal accident.

EIGHT

Lister pushed himself up off the deck and sat back on his haunches. His brain was flopping around in his skull, and his eyesight was decidedly dodgy. He tilted his head and tried to make sense of what he was seeing.

Whichever way he looked at it, Kryten appeared to be jammed upside-down in the hull, with a large girder welded across his chest, like some bizarre, robotic parody of the crucifixion of St Peter.

It didn't help when Kryten smiled and winked at him and asked him how he was feeling.

Just as he was thinking things couldn't get any weirder, he heard a forklift trundle up behind him, and turned to see Rimmer dressed in a neatly tailored space jock suit and a floppy-haired wig looking down at him. 'What the smeg is going on?' he asked no one specific.

The wigged Rimmer spoke. 'You've had a bit of a tumble, my old apple tart. You'll be feeling a little groggy for a while. Here . . .' he slid a small, silver flask out of his back pocket and tossed it to Lister. 'A belt of that should smooth out the edges for you.'

'Commander,' the upside-down Kryten spoke. 'With respect, although Mr Lister is chronologically above the appropriate watershed age for the consumption of alcohol, he is physically only fifteen.'

Ace hoisted a metre-square metal plate on to the deck with his good hand. 'It's not alcohol, old love, it's ginseng and royal jelly. Best pick-me-up in the known universe.'

Lister span off the cap and sniffed the liquid. He drooled some down his throat and shuddered. 'I'm not with the programme here, guys,' he replaced the cap and tossed the flask back to Wiggy. 'Why is Kryten welded to the wall? And why are there two Rimmers?'

Ace glanced over his shoulder. Rimmer was standing behind him, arms crossed, wearing a curious lop-sided smile. 'All in good time, Davey boy. Our first priority's your buddy here.'

'He's from another dimension, aren't you, Commander?' Rimmer said. 'He arrived, rather conveniently, just after something smashed into the hull over there and nearly split us in two.'

'Nothing convenient about it, Arn, old cabbage.' Ace bent over and ripped the material away from the Cat's leg. 'The collision was my fault.'

Rimmer's smile sagged. 'You're admitting it?'

'Absolutely. My crate materialized too close to yours. Shockwaves damn near splatted us both out of existence. When I got my damage under control, thought I'd better pop along, see if I could lend a hand here.' He looked over at Lister. 'Davey, lad, I'm going to need you to put some pressure on your friend's thigh.'

Rimmer stared in slack-mouthed disbelief as Lister stepped over the Cat's body and put his hand on the injured thigh. What a slimy way of wriggling out of blame. You do something wrong, admit it, and then simply carry on! 'Is that it? That's all we get?'

Ace cupped his hand around the Cat's heel. 'I'm not with you, old turnip.'

'You blast into our dimension, damn near kill us all, and you don't even think an apology is required?'

'Ready?' Ace looked up at Lister, who nodded back, and then he tugged hard on the Cat's heel. 'That should do it.' He tossed a pair of flat wooden planks to Lister. 'Think you could rig up a quick field splint? It's only got to hold till we get him up to the ops room.'

'No problem.'

As Lister bent to his task, Ace stood up and faced Rimmer. 'Look, Arnie, I'm not altogether sure what you're driving at. We're still in deep marmalade, here. We've got one of the team out of com, and he's going to need surgery fairly pronto if he's going to pull through, we've got another one wedged upside-down in the wall with his arse hanging out in deep space, and a hull that's likely to collapse if someone breathes on it too hard. Let's all try and hunker down and get the job done.' He tossed back his perfect fringe and smiled. 'Then you can bend me over the desk and give me a damned good spanking, OK?'

He turned around and bent down to Kryten. 'Here's the plan, old munchkin: I'm going to fix these plates to the hull. It's going to be easier to do that from the inside. That means walling you in, effectively. Then I'll go outside, cut you free, and we should all be home in time for Christmas. Sound peachy?'

Kryten smiled and nodded. 'Peachy dandy, Commander.'

'That's the ticket.' Ace straightened. 'We're going to construct a frame around this bulge and create a false hull with these metal plates. Obviously, it's got to be space-tight, and that means riveting and welding every single joint and coating it with sealant. How are you at welding, David?'

Lister looked up from the splint. 'I get by.'

Ace laughed. 'I'll bet you do. In my dimension, you were the best in the business.'

Lister wrinkled his brow. 'I was?'

'None of the jocks on Europa would even dream of taking up a kite if it hadn't been given a damned good sorting by Spanners Lister.'

'Spanners Lister?' An involuntary grin spread over Lister's features. 'He works at the Europa test base?'

'I'll tell you all about him later. First things first, let's get our friend up to ops, then we'd better crack on with the hull repair. I reckon there's a good fifty hours solid work in that.'

Kryten smiled with his lips and panicked with his eyes. The hull damage must have savagely depleted their available oxygen supply.

There was a very good chance that fifty hours was more than they had left.

NINE

M'Aiden surveyed the work with his newly implanted eye, and felt as close to satisfaction as he could possibly get without some warm, bloody entrails lying at his feet.

It had been many months in the making, and had required more cooperation than agonoidkind had ever achieved before. It was a magnificent accomplishment, undeniably. The first and only example of agonoid interior design.

They called it the Death Wheel.

Fundamentally, it was series of corridors that led out from each of *Red Dwarf*'s docking bays to a central point. But there was much more to it than that.

Once the simpering human and his crewmates landed on board, automatic systems would begin draining away their oxygen. They would be forced to flee the docking bay and race into the corridors that formed the spokes of the Death Wheel. The doors would seal behind them, and then the temperature would begin climbing to unbearable levels, compelling them to head towards the next corridor, which would again seal off their retreat. There, they would gradually realize that the ceiling was moving inexorably downwards, threatening to crush them like garbage in a waste compactor, and driving them onwards to the next corridor.

With each new corridor, the dangers would become more and more intolerable, and they would have less and less time to move on through.

Finally, they would stagger, breathless and cowed with fear and panic into the Hub of Pain.

The Hub of Pain was the *pièce de resistance*: a huge, dome-shaped room, with a viewing gallery circling the ceiling. The walls were lined with every conceivable kind of cutting and bludgeoning weapon, and every instrument of torture ever invented by the extremely inventive human mind: maces, pikes, swords and sabres; switch-blades, daggers and laser-cutting tools; chain-saws, buzz-saws, tenon-saws and hacksaws, dentist drill, scalpels and a whole range of gleaming metal apparatus designed for gynaecological surgery; mallets, sledge hammers, claw hammers and jack hammers; racks, iron maidens, gonad electrocution kits; testicle handcuffs, jock-straps lined with razor-blades, acid-filled enema bags and easy-listenin' music . . . you name it, if it caused pain, if humans feared it, it was there.

M'Aiden drooled at the beauty of it all.

The bleating human and his human-loving friends would be given time to allow the full horror of what awaited them to sink in, and then the signal would be given.

The race would begin.

The entire agonoid population would be locked, lurking in individual chambers. Once the signal was given, the doors of these chambers would be sprung simultaneously, and the agonoids would each charge down a corridor. These were arranged in a series of V shapes, so that two neighbouring corridors met at the apex of the V in a single doorway. The door would seal after allowing one of the agonoids through.

An agonoid could use any means, fair or foul, to beat his rival to the next corridor, where the process would be repeated, then repeated again, each time reducing the combatants by half, until there were just two rivals left to fight for the right to pass through the door to the Hub of Pain.

For the right to be The One.

Of course, there would doubtless be a great many

agonoid deaths along the way, but that just added to the fun nature of the event.

The agonoid survivors would then hobble and curse their way up to the viewing gallery, and the gore *fest* would begin.

With careful planning and a lot of patience, the despicable human and his fellows could last many months without dying – possibly even years if the lucky agonoid were sufficiently well-versed in human anatomy.

The door to the Hub of Pain slid open behind him, and M'Aiden half-turned to see Djuhn'Keep limp inside.

Djuhn had masterminded the Death Wheel's design, and been the driving force behind its completion. Now, he was just adding the finishing touches, the little bits of finesse that would immeasurably enhance the pleasure of the occasion. He placed a small rubber sheath on the wall, just beside the screw-action nutcrackers. He saw the query in M'Aiden's glance. 'Condom smeared inside with vapour rub,' he said by way of explanation. 'Apparently it burns like a demon.'

M'Aiden smiled and nodded. Although Djuhn was unquestionably the brightest and most inventive of the agonoids, M'Aiden pitied him. Over the years, many of his parts had ceased functioning, and he was dangerously weak, lacking the physical strength to win himself replacement bits in combat. The only reason he hadn't been attacked and dismantled was his capacity for invention and design – his skills had kept the agonoid fleet operational these many years. But it was only a matter of time before too much of him broke down for him to function effectively, and he would become nothing more than a spare-parts repository and so much scrap metal.

In short, there was no way Djuhn would become The One. His mind had conceived the Death Wheel, and yet he would be nothing more than a spectator when it was put to use. He wouldn't even make it through the first doorway.

Djuhn placed a series of small boxes on a shelf. 'Contact lenses made of scouring pads . . . barbed wire dental floss . . . nipple-sized pastry cutters . . .' he listed, '. . . foreskin clippers . . . small, metal cocktail umbrella . . .'

'What's that for?'

'Anything you like, really, though I thought it might come in handy for scraping out the inside of the penis tube.'

M'Aiden nodded approval.

Djuhn carried on. 'Leg-waxing strips . . . staple remover – I thought that might be useful for clipping off scabs – keep the wounds all fresh and runny . . . rectal thermometer, coated in sandpaper . . . yes, I think that's the lot.'

He stood back and examined the newly arranged torture paraphernalia with a critical eye. 'Oh! I almost forgot . . .' he reached into his belt bag and tugged out a card. 'This should really put the rave into "grave".' He placed the card in prime position on the torture shelf.

'What is it?'

'It's a scramble card. New design. It eliminates temper loss, so The One can keep his head if the human annoys him, not get carried away and end the spectacle too soon. It also cuts out fatigue, improves reaction time and amplifies the pleasure nodes. Well' – he rubbed his hands together – 'can't hang around here all day. I've got a battery-powered fingernail plucker to wire up.' He smiled at M'Aiden and turned to go.

'You will be ready in time?' M'Aiden asked. The grand opening of the Hub of Pain was scheduled to take place in less than twelve hours' time. The entire agonoid population would gather to inspect the delights of the chamber, and get familiarized with its intricacies. There would be much merriment, a lot of scramble-carding, and, of course, a not-inconsiderable amount of unnecessary mindless violence. Such agonoid gatherings only took place every few centuries or so, largely because the death toll was so high. This evening's party could be expected to result in a twenty-five per cent reduction of the population.

Djuhn'Keep nodded. 'Everything will be ready, I assure you,' he said, and hobbled through the door.

M'Aiden crossed to the torture shelf, picked up the scramble card and turned it over in his hand. 'Improves reaction time . . .' he mumbled to himself. If this card really did that, it could give him a good enough edge to win the Human Race. Ultimately, it *was* a race, after all, and speed was paramount. No matter how brutally you disposed of your rival, if you didn't make it through the door before the victor of the struggle in the adjacent corridor, he would have a clear run, and you'd be shut out without a fight.

He slipped the card into his head socket, and waited for the effect to kick in.

But it never did.

He felt nothing. No amplification of the pleasure nodes. Nothing.

Disgusted, he removed the card and flung it back on the shelf.

He would win the race on his own merits, he told himself. But he was wrong.

For M'Aiden Ty-One there would be no race.

The damage had already been done.

TEN

The Cat moaned and opened his eyes. He heard an unfamiliar voice say, 'Steady on there, laddie,' but it didn't occur to him to try and find out who the speaker was. He tried to move, but his arms were pinioned by his side. He could feel a strange sensation in his right leg. He thought about it for a few moments, and decided it was pain. It didn't bother him much at all, which struck him as amusing, somehow. He giggled.

Lister said, 'He's coming round.'

'Worry ye not, Davey boy. He's shot full of jolly jelly. He's happier than a bunch of hippies at a ganja harvest.'

The Cat raised his head and looked down at his body, and saw the rip in his apricot-coloured skin-tight silk trews, with the inflatable field splint below. Blood had soaked all over his trousers from the wound in his leg. 'Oh, boy,' he moaned. 'That looks real bad.'

'I shouldn't fret, my old roly-poly pudding,' the voice behind him said. 'We'll have that leg sorted before you know what's happening.'

'Leg? Who's worried about the leg? It's the colour combination that's bothering me. Red and apricot?' Cat's head slammed down on the stretcher's blow-up pillow. 'I'm bleeding a tasteless colour!'

Ace bent down and grabbed the front end of the stretcher with his good hand. 'Better get him up to ops. He's getting delirious.'

'Not necessarily,' Lister stooped and grabbed the rear. 'He's always like that.'

They hoisted the stretcher waist-high and hauled it up the stairway. Ace paused on the landing and called down to Kryten. 'Hang in there, old pal. Smoke us a kipper – we'll be back for breakfast.' And they carried the Cat through the door.

Kryten watched them go. He shook his head, smiling. 'What a guy!'

Rimmer looked down at Kryten, incredulity twisting his face into a one-sided grin. 'He's taken you in, hasn't he? He's taken you all in.'

'I'm not sure I'm following you, sir.'

'He's got you all believing he's a combination of Captain Courageous, the Scarlet Pimpernel and James bloody Bond. "Smoke me a kipper"? I ask you. Ace! What a tosser!'

'Sir, I don't understand. You appear to be resentful of Commander Rimmer.'

'I'm not resentful. I can see through him, that's all. It's all an act, the bravado, the snooty space jock lingo, the calm confidence in the face of danger. Underneath, he's a quivering, jelly-spined under-achiever.'

'With respect, sir, I don't think so.'

'He must be – he's me, remember? And I swear before you now, Kryten, if he once again refers to me as a fruit or vegetable, I'll take that welding torch and set his pouffy fringe on fire.'

'Well, he certainly seems to be getting our situation under control.'

'Under control? Kryten – turn on the radio and tune into Sanity FM. Even with all his poncy prancing around, the best we can hope is he'll get us all in good shape in time for the massed army of psychotic agonoids to show up to mangle us slowly to death. If that's the situation under control, then give me mindless, bleating panic, every time.'

There was a footfall on the landing and Rimmer glanced

up to see Lister racing down the stairs, bubbling with an enthusiasm Rimmer found repugnant. 'He's operating on the Cat's leg.'

'Well,' Rimmer smiled, 'that's the last we'll see of that, then.'

Lister dashed straight for the welding gear. 'No, apparently field microsurgery's all part of basic training in the Space Corps Special Service. What a guy!'

'He told you he'd been in the SCSS? And you believed him?'

Lister tugged on the welding mask. 'Why should he lie?'

'He's building himself up. Trying to make you think he's something he's not. And you're all buying it.'

'You're not making sense, Rimmer. He's definitely a test pilot, right? Otherwise, he couldn't have crossed dimensions, and his ship wouldn't be floating around outside.'

'Well, yes, I'll give him that . . .'

'And unless he stole that uniform, he's a commander.'

'Probably, yes.'

'And he's charming, clever and witty, and he's got leadership charisma . . .'

'Hang on a second.' Rimmer held up his hand. 'Is it going to be a simple Register Office, or a full church do for you two?'

Lister shook his head, and tugged on the welding gauntlets. 'I don't get your attitude, Rimmer. He's you.'

'He's not me. *I'm* me. He's a me who had all the breaks, all the luck, all the chances I never got.'

Kryten pipped in unwelcomely. 'In actual fact, sir, according to the commander, the differences between you come down to a single incident in your childhood.'

'Right. He probably got to go to some really great school, while I was lumbered with Io House. He got to meet all the right people, greased his way up the old-boy network, towel-flicked his way into the Space Corps, masonic handshook his way into Flight School and brown-tongued his way up the ranks.'

Lister propped the first strut that would form the frame for the new false hull into position. 'You're such a sheet stain, Rimmer. You'd think you'd be pleased that somewhere, in some other dimension, there's another you who's doing really well for himself.'

'How would you feel if some nose-wipe turned up from another reality – another Lister with wall-to-wall charisma and a PhD in being deeply handsome and wonderful?'

'Hey, man,' Lister grinned. 'I *am* that Lister.'

'I mean it. What would you do if there was another Lister who had everything you wanted?'

'There is.' Lister fired up the torch. 'Ace was telling me about him on the way upstairs. He's a flight engineer at Europa. Married to Kristine Kochanski. Twin sons, Jim and Bexley.'

'And it doesn't make you feel just a teeny-weeny bit jealous? He's got all that because of one single decision way back when, where he made the right choice and you made the wrong one?'

Lister shook his head. 'I'm made up for him. Fantastic.' He started welding the strut into place.

'Well, I tell you, if you met him, you'd just feel bitter. I always said I've never had the breaks. He's living proof I was right. Look what I could have achieved if I'd got the break he got.'

Lister sighed, switched off the torch and pulled up his mask. 'Can I make a suggestion, Rimmer?' he smiled pleasantly. 'Can you shut the smeg up?' He re-ignited the torch and turned back to his work.

Rimmer kept his eyes on the nauseating little pipsqueak, nodding to buy time while his mind raced for a witty riposte to put the brattish trouser lizard in his place, once and for all. As usual, his mind ran out of breath, and he began to look like a plastic dog in the back window of a car on a road lined with sleeping policemen. He turned on his heels and headed up the stairs.

No respect, that was the problem. You'd have thought, after all they'd been through, that Lister and the others might have learned to respect him, just a little, but no. To them, he was just a joke. A target for mean-spirited put-downs. Yet the good commander breezed in, and within seventeen seconds he had them all eating out of his under-pants. Sickening.

Rimmer carried on up the stairs to the ops room, half hoping that the commander might have botched the opera-tion on the Cat's leg, which would diminish his esteem somewhat.

Ace was studying the Cat's scan, his face cinemato-graphed by the blue-white glow of the screen. Even Rimmer had to concede that he was handsome. It didn't make sense. Why didn't he suffer from the hair problems that beset Rimmer's own unruly, wiry thatch? Did he iron it, or something girlie like that? And why were his nostrils not flared in the same way? Could it be that he hadn't met Duncan Potson in Junior A, who'd taught Rimmer how to pick his nose with his thumb? Had their destinies diverged before then?

Ace saw Rimmer out of the corner of his eye, and smiled convivially. 'Arn! Just the chap! How goes it down below?'

Rimmer shrugged. 'It goes.'

Ace tapped the screen. 'Not too sure about our friend's anatomy. Looks like he's not quite human.'

'No. He evolved from cats.'

'Not with you, old mucker. When did he evolve?'

Rimmer rolled his eyes, as if the evolution of a domestic cat into a talking biped was such a commonplace occur-rence that even the dullest schoolchild needn't have it ex-plained. He sighed, and recapped the Cat's history as succinctly as he could.

When he'd finished, Rimmer saw to his delight that Ace

looked more than a little disturbed. 'So what you're saying, old begonia, is that I've managed to show up around three million years from my own time?'

Rimmer smiled. 'Yes, my old toilet-roll cover. That's precisely what I'm saying.'

'Well,' Ace tugged a cheroot from behind his ear and chewed on it thoughtfully, 'that raises some pretty interesting implications for the Wildfire drive.'

'Such as, my old sick bucket?'

'Such as, if we get half a chance, we might be able to rig up a version that could get you all back to where you started from.'

ELEVEN

M'Aiden Ty-One was feeling decidedly groggy.

He sat on the metal slab in his sparsely equipped preparation chamber and shook his head violently, to try and clear the fuggy smog that was clogging his mind.

This wouldn't do. This wouldn't do at all. He had to pull himself together, before . . . what was it he had to get ready for? Some event. Some occasion.

Damn! His memory was going.

Now, why would that be? Had he been overdoing the scramble cards? If this was some kind of scatter-head hangover, it was a truly ferocious one.

He fought the urge to lie back on the slab. This was no time to be sleeping. He had to get ready . . . to get ready for . . .

The chamber's door slid open – why had he not locked it? – and a hazy figure hobbled in.

The room seemed uncommonly gloomy to M'Aiden. 'Lights!' he called.

'The lights are on, my friend.'

M'Aiden looked in the direction of the voice, but could only make out a blurred outline. He couldn't let this intruder know of his weakness. That would be lethal. 'What are you doing in here? Get out or I'll rip out your bowels and use them as a skipping-rope.'

The threat seemed not to impress the interloper. In the same calm voice, he said: 'Are you not attending the ceremony?'

'Ceremony?' M'Aiden tried, but couldn't recall a ceremony. The stranger took a limping step closer. M'Aiden tried to stand, but his legs betrayed him.

'Don't try to move. I think you're too weak for that.'

'I am not weak at all, you verminous liar!' M'Aiden struggled to move his legs again, but they just wouldn't listen.

'I think you're very weak indeed.' The voice remained soft, unthreatening. 'Let's put my theory to the test, shall we? I'm going to walk up to you and slap you across the cheeks, and I'd like you to try and stop me.'

M'Aiden's eyes widened with outrage. 'One step closer,' he growled, 'and I'll . . .' his head snapped to one side as his tormentor slapped him.

'You see?' the calm voice taunted. 'Your motor functions are decaying at an alarming rate. Your mind is, too. I'll bet you can't even remember your name.'

'My name?' M'Aiden began to panic. 'My name is . . . My name . . .'

'Begins with M?'

'I know my own name, you excremental pig sucker!'

'It's M'Aiden. Ring any bells?'

'M'Aiden . . .' He rolled it around in his brain, but it meant nothing to him.

'M'Aiden Ty-One. Like all of us, you were given an insulting name by our human manufacturers. It amused them. My own name is Djuhn'Keep. A fine joke, eh?'

Djuhn'Keep. That name did trigger a connection in his addled mind. He struggled to make sense of it.

'Ah! You do remember me. You considered me a weakling, I think. You underestimated me, friend M'Aiden. Underestimated me fatally.'

M'Aiden tried to repeat his own name, but it had gone again.

'You're probably wondering what's happening to you,' the calm voice went on. 'The scramble card you tried out in the Hub of Pain – remember that? No, of course you don't. It contained a virus. I designed it personally. I call it the Apocalypse virus. It's extremely clever, though I say so myself. As we speak, it's spreading all over your central processor, overwriting your basic function programs and wiping your mind. Would you like the cure?'

M'Aiden nodded.

'I'm sorry – there *is* no cure. You're dying, I'm afraid.'

M'Aiden felt himself sinking back on to the metal bench. His tormentor was laying him out. He tried to say 'What are you doing?', which should have been easy enough, but it came out as 'Wing for nozzle kloop.'

'Wing for nozzle kloop, indeed,' the stranger chuckled. 'I imagine you want to know what's going to happen now. Well, basically I'm going to dismember you. I need a few spare parts to restore my body to its full glory, you see. The beauty of this virus is that it only affects the brain. I don't need all of you, of course, but I'm going to take you apart bit by bit, anyway. If I constructed the virus correctly, your pain/pleasure responders should remain intact right up to the end, so not only will the whole procedure be nightmarishly agonizing for you, it should serve as a bit of a warm-up for me. A sort of hors d'oeuvre to put me in the right mood for dealing with the human.'

The prospect of the physical pain meant nothing to M'Aiden, but lying helpless at another's hands was an ignominy no self-respecting psychopath could bear. He struggled to focus on an object that was bearing down on his eyeball. It looked like a tyre lever. With a supreme effort he forced four words out of his failing mouth. 'Let me die first.'

'Now, now, now . . .' his tormentor cooed. 'And where would be the fun in that?' And grunting with the sudden effort, he shoved the tyre iron deep into the socket and began slowly levering out the first eyeball.

TWELVE

Ace stuck his head through the almost-completed false hull and shone his torch on Kryten's face. 'All right in there, old geranium?'

'Tickety-boo, thank you so much, Commander.'

'Davey's just about to weld the last panel in place. Once we're spaceworthy, I'll take a little stroll outside and dig you clear, OK?'

'Don't worry about me, Commander. I'll be fine.'

'That's the spirit. Won't be a tick.' Ace ducked out of the gap.

Lister put the final panel in position, and began welding it tight. 'So you reckon you can get us back home?'

'See no reason why it shouldn't be possible, my old banana. It looks like the Wildfire drive works by shooting you off along one of your own destiny lines. Time and space are irrelevant – it just chooses a point where your own past branched off into another dimension, and bingo! Bob's your mother's brother.'

'So if I could find, say, a dimension where I didn't wind up on *Red Dwarf* in the first place, I'd find myself back on Earth?'

'If your other self stayed on Earth, then that's where you'd turn up, yes. Course, there would be two of you, which can cause all sorts of problems, as I'm beginning to find out.' He nodded upstairs in the vague direction of the cockpit, where his digitized double was now manning the radar screens.

'He's a lot different from you, isn't he?'

'Indeed he is, and I thank the big feller upstairs for that.' He shuddered involuntarily. 'The man's a maggot.'

'Have you sussed out the point where your pasts diverged?'

'Not exactly. Some time in childhood, is my reckoning. I could probably work it out precisely, but that would mean spending more time with him than I'd care to. I just can't stand being around him. Seeing myself so bitter. So warped and weasly.'

Lister turned off the flame and picked up the riveting gun. 'So what's the plan, then? We finish this, grab Kryten out of his gopher hole and take off for dimensions unknown?'

''Fraid it's not that simple, old liverwurst. My crate's a one-man lady. We might squeeze two in at a pinch. I think our best shot's getting this tea chest up to scratch and then heading for the small *rouge* one.'

'You think we stand a chance against the agonoids?'

'There's always a chance, Davey boy. Always.' He slapped Lister reassuringly on the shoulder, and stepped back to inspect the work. 'Looks good, skipper,' he said. 'Less than thirty hours, too. Looks damned good.'

The new hull section did, indeed, look spaceworthy. It would certainly hold until they made it back to *Red Dwarf*, for what it was worth. Privately, Ace doubted they stood a rat in a blender's chance against the agonoid army. In his own dimension, he'd been called in to assess the viability of the agonoid project while it had still been under development and shrouded in official secrecy. His advice had been to drop the whole shooting match quicker than a scorpion-infested jockstrap, but he'd been over-ruled by the military powers at the Dodecahedron. It looked like history – at least the history in this reality – had proved him right.

Still, there was no point lamenting over dropped dairy produce. Their survival options were limited, and facing the agonoid threat was the only realistic alternative. Their best shot would be a lightning raid: if they could somehow sneak up to the undersized vermilion one, whip in quickly, grab the necessary materials and supplies, then zip out before the effluence struck the ventilator, they might stand a half chance of jerry-rigging *Starbug* with a version of a Wildfire drive before the agonoids caught up with them.

A lot of ifs. A lot of mights.

Personally, he'd have felt a sight more positive about their chances if he'd been a hundred per cent fit himself. Besides the fact that he hadn't slept in over seventy-two hours, now, the arm wound he'd dismissed to the others as 'a little scratch' was in fact an extremely painful compound fracture.

Now that the hull was no longer in imminent danger of collapse, and the rest of the casualties had been dealt with, he could afford a few moments to attempt a bit of repair work on his own injury. There wouldn't be time to do a proper job, but at least he could jam the splintered bones together and stitch up the wound. Anaesthetic would be inappropriate, of course – they'd have to make their move against the agonoids as soon as possible, and he had to keep a clear head for that.

'Righty-ho, skipper. You seal up here. I'll pop up top and look in on our feline friend,' he lied.

Lister grinned at him and shot a fake salute.

Ace turned away, suddenly saddened. Something in Lister's grin had assailed his unbreachable confidence.

He deliberately twisted his broken arm and focused on the pain. Wouldn't do to be going all sissy on them now.

He jogged up the stairway. With every bound, his self-assurance grew.

A surprise attack. Yes. That was definitely their best shot. His spirits lifted. A damned fine shot, at that. A surprise attack could work. Would work.

And in a way he couldn't know, he was right. A surprise attack would work. Only it was they, themselves, who were going to get surprised.

Badly surprised.

THIRTEEN

Pizzak'Rapp was admiring a particularly delicately crafted buttock corkscrew, when he became aware that something was wrong.

He glanced around to see if any of the other agonoids thronging around the Hub of Pain had noticed it too. Most were, like him, examining the more outlandish and esoteric objects of torture laid out for their perusal. A few were staggering around, scatter-headed. A couple of dozen were engaged in brutal fights to the death. In short: nothing out of the ordinary.

He thought perhaps he'd imagined it. Then it happened again. The floor moved under his feet.

He looked round again. A few of the agonoids closest to him had noticed it too, this time. They looked at each other, and then at the floor.

There was a rumble and Pizzak felt his knees buckle slightly.

The background hubbub ceased, all fighting stopped, and with the exception of a few scatterbrains shouting the odd demonic curse, everyone fell silent.

An amplified voice burst through the loudspeakers. 'I think I should have your attention by now.'

Pizzak looked up towards the viewing gallery. A single agonoid was looking down on the gathering, too high for Pizzak to make out his features.

The loudspeaker barked again. 'The effect you just

experienced was a gravity amplifier kicking into life. The gravity in the dome is round about . . .' the figure glanced away '. . . one point five Gs at the moment. It will gradually increase, making it more and more difficult for you to move with every passing second.'

The announcement caused a burst of babble around the room. Pizzak and a few of the smarter agonoids guessed what was coming and began to edge towards the exits.

'In less than twelve minutes, even the strongest of you will be pinned to the floor. In less than fifteen, you will be reduced to puddles of metallic pulp. You have only one survival option. Run.'

Djuhn'Keep watched with delight as panic spread through the throng below him, and the entire crowd dashed simultaneously for the exits – which were too few and too narrow to allow more than half of them through before the gravity amplifier reduced the stragglers to helplessness.

Pizzak grabbed a laser lance from the wall and began slashing and dicing his way through the mob. Heads and limbs tumbled to the ground in his wake. With every step, his feet became more leaden, his progress slower, but his survival instinct kept him on his feet. Just as he was only metres away from one of the precious doors, it began to close. With a desperate effort, he planted the lance between a fleeing agonoid's shoulder-blades, sending him crumbling to the floor. He willed all his remaining strength to his arms and pole-vaulted over the stumbling crowd in front of him, landing in the safety of the corridor just as the door slammed shut behind him, snapping the lance in two.

Djuhn found it hard to drag himself away from the sight of the carnage below, as the force of enhanced gravity dragged those left in the Hub to the ground, and endoskeletons started cracking and popping wetly, but there were other delights to be savoured. He turned to the bank of video monitors which showed the agonoid survivors crowded into the corridors. The spokes of the Death Wheel.

Pizzak's corridor was buzzing with anger and confusion. It was silenced by the voice from the loudspeaker.

'Congratulations! You survived the first ordeal. But before you start patting yourselves on the back, let me assure you that this is only the beginning of your tribulations. In a few short seconds, I will be activating the corridor traps.'

The air around Pizzak was filled with screamed curses and testicle-shrinking threats. 'Now, now, now,' the voice cooed from the speaker. 'No need for unpleasantries – I could have trapped you all in the Hub and killed you at once if I'd chosen. But where would the fun be in that? Now, before I proceed with the slow, but none the less total and assured annihilation of all of you, I want you to know this: you were beaten by Djuhn'Keep, the greatest and most deadly agonoid of all. It is I who am destined to become The One. Now, gentlemen. It's dying time.'

And that was all. The speakers fell silent. Pizzak looked around, trying to predict the corridor's threat for a minute that hung like a slow-flapping flag in time. Suddenly, a thick metal stake lunged out of the wall, piercing the chest of the agonoid next to him, skewering him in gurgling helplessness. Pizzak began to run towards the door, spikes thrusting out either side of him and bursting up through the floor below.

Djuhn'Keep smiled, turned up the volume and lounged back in his chair, conducting the symphony of screams and death rattles as if it were the sweetest of sweet music. The agonoid population would be reduced to a bare handful by the time they burst, exhausted, through the final door and into the docking bay.

They would fall panting to the floor, and he would allow them a brief moment of relief before he opened the docking bay doors and sucked them all out into the cold, black embrace of space.

They would be able to survive quite a while in deep

space, of course, but without any means of altering direction, they would simply speed along on their original trajectory, until their internal energy sources burned out, and they could no longer stop themselves from freezing up.

They would become icy monuments to his deadly talents.

He was, truly, the greatest agonoid of all. He had a gift that set him apart from the rest.

He had guile.

And that quality would not only guarantee that he caught the human and his companions, it would ensure their demise would be painful beyond mortal imagination, and lingering beyond endurance.

FOURTEEN

Ace stepped through the hatch into the gallery and ordered the door to lock behind him. He slipped a rubber door wedge between his teeth, jammed the numb hand of his injured arm inside the refrigerator and leaned his weight against the door, lodging it firmly. He breathed deeply a few times, then suddenly tugged his broken arm backwards with all his strength, and with a strangled sob, collapsed to the floor.

He fought off the warm comfort of unconsciousness that threatened to fold him in its arms, and embraced the pain.

He looked down at his swollen limb. No bones visible. He tried to make a fist, with minimal success. It was a pretty botched repair, but it would do for now. Once they'd got their cojones out of the cauldron, he'd re-break the arm and set it properly. He looked around for the sewing needle he'd already threaded, and noticed half the doorstop on the floor. In his agony, he'd bitten it in two.

He spat out the other half and slotted the needle between his teeth. He berated himself that he was going soft in his dotage, pinched together the edges of the wound and slid the needle through the swollen, puffy flesh.

As it slipped out the other side, a strange sound made him pause.

And another one. The clomp of metal on metal.

And again.

It seemed to be coming from overhead.

He crossed to the galley terminal and called up the external cameras.

A space-suited man was crawling across the outer hull, magnetic clamps on his hands and boots.

Ace dashed out of the galley and through the mid-section, and bounded up the steps into the cockpit.

Rimmer was lounging at his station, watching the space walk.

Ace dialled up comms. 'Skipper? Is that you out there?'

Lister's voice fzzed back at him: 'Yo, Commander.'

'I want you to come right back. That's an order.'

'Don't be daft. I'm halfway there.'

'It's an order, Davey boy.'

'What are you going to do? Arrest me?"

'Be a sensible old satsuma and pop back inside: you haven't got the space-walk experience I have. Let me dig Kryten out.'

'I've got plenty of space-walk experience. Plus, I've also got two arms that work.'

'I've told you, there's nothing wrong with my arm you couldn't fix with an Elastoplast. There's no need for you to chuck your love spuds on the barbecue.'

'Look, will you stop distracting me? It's a long way down, and I'm trying to concentrate. Over and out.'

Lister reached up to his throat mike and flicked it off. He looked down and to his left. He could see Kryten's robotic derrière poking upside-down through the concave bulge in the hull.

It did not look like a comfortable posture.

Slowly, carefully, he crabbed his way over towards it.

Once he was in position, he slipped a crampon into the nozzle of a pressure gun and fired it through the hull. He tugged it hard and, satisfied it was secure, looped his safety harness through the hoop.

He pressed his helmet against the hull, and banged three times. He felt the vibrations as Kryten banged back in reply.

He slid the pressure gun back into his belt, took out the laser cutter and assessed the job. He'd have to cut around the edges of the hole to enlarge it, and slice through the girder securing Kryten before he could be dragged clear. He checked his oxygen supply. Three hours. Should be plenty.

He fired up the laser and started cutting.

He'd only made a small incision, when he noticed something extremely odd.

Kryten's butt did not appear to fit snugly into the gap in the hull.

Lister stopped cutting and reached down. He pushed Kryten's rump. It wobbled. There was a good six inches between his thighs and the edges of the hole.

He trained his helmet light on the buttocks. They looked strangely unfamiliar. Not that he spent a great deal of his life examining Kryten's backside, but the top of his legs seemed shinier, more metallic.

As Lister reached up for his throat mike, the crampon securing him to the hull pinged out and launched itself into space. He watched it go by with a strange feeling of detachment.

The only thing preventing him from floating off through the stars, now, was his inertia.

As he turned back to *Starbug* he saw the metal in front of him buckle and give. A robotic hand shot clean through the hull and grabbed his throat.

Lister's panicking eyes darted toward the hole where Kryten's rear end should have been, only it wasn't.

The hull began to buckle and ripple as if it were made out of rubber sheets. A head burst through. Lister stared in shocked fascination at the strange, grey face, barely inches from his own. The face cocked at a curious angle. Its lips parted, displaying a shocking row of sharp metal teeth.

The head lurched up and pressed itself against Lister's helmet and its mouth began moving.

It was speaking to him. The sound was carried by vibrations against his helmet, and though it was tinny and half-obscured by the jackhammer pounding of his own heart, Lister could make out the words quite distinctly, even though they didn't make much sense to him.

The voice was saying. 'I am piece of crap. Welcome to Hell.'

PART FIVE

High Midnight

ONE

The desert sun bore down on the dusty street like a relentless laser somebody had forgotten to turn off. Sheriff Will Carton stepped on to the baking sidewalk, the doors of his office flapping behind him, ushering him to be out and on his way, as if even his own jailhouse wanted nothing more to do with him. He swayed until he found perpendicular, and then stood in that conscientiously upright way that drunks have; that's the thing about drunks – the more they drink, the more sober they try to look. He squinted down the street. Deserted. Just a few ponies hitched up by the saloon, too hot and torpid even to dip their musty heads into the water trough.

He clunked down on to the street with such a heavy, ill-measured stride that his right spur caught itself in wood, impaling his heel to the sidewalk. He tried to tug it free, all nonchalant-like, but it wouldn't budge. He looked around, sighed miserably, and let himself fall so his backside thumped on to the sidewalk, sending choking dust billowing all around him, and then went about the business of removing his boot.

By the time he'd got the spur loose and himself re-shod, the street was no longer deserted. A well-dressed couple were scurrying across it, her with one of them fancy parasol contraptions from Paris, Europe. They looked to be deliberately avoiding contact with Carton, but he was too far gone to notice or care. He hauled himself to his full, strangely erect stance and tipped the brim of his shapeless stetson. 'Mornin', ma'am . . . Jeff.'

The woman rolled her eyes heavenwards. The man stopped and faced him and said 'Morning . . . *Sheriff*,' in such a venomous way it sounded like a curse.

Still, the tone whistled right through Carton's ears without registering. Jeff was a number cruncher over at the bank, and was so well-to-do he carried genuine *paper* money and owned a wallet. Ought to be good for a little tap. 'Say, Jeff: you wouldn't happen to have a couple of nickels goin' spare? Only I got me a real bad case of trail throat.' Carton wiped the back of his hand across his lips, as if the pantomime might give credence to his claim.

'What you've got,' Jeff's wife pitched in, 'is a bad case of drunken bum disease.'

Carton swayed and tried to lick his lips, only his tongue was like a fat dog jammed in a desert gopher hole. Jeff looked distressed. 'Now, Esther, there ain't no call . . .'

'There's call a-plenty, Jeff Calculator. Young Wyatt Memory got hisself shot plum dead on this street yesterday, while this . . . this gentleman was snoring his way to a hangover in his own jail cell.'

'You're right, ma'am.' Carton took off his hat and twirled it in his hands. 'And I felt awfully bad 'bout it, that's a plain fact. But see, that helped me see the light, and now I'm all cleaned up, honest. 'Fact I'm collecting for the church steeple fund, on account of now I'm all fired up with religion. Hallelujah and stuff.' He proffered his hat. 'What about a couple of pennies to absolutely guarantee your place in heaven?'

That did it for Esther. She swung her basket at Carton and, though it didn't connect, the effort of dodging threw his balance, so he wound up butt down on the street for the second time in three minutes.

Jeff looked at him pityingly. 'Don't you got no shame left, Will?' He took his wife's arm and led her off to the bank.

Carton shielded his eyes against the sun's brutal glare and called after them: 'Won't hold this against you, folks, you being ordinarily such law-abiding people and all. Just so long as you don't forget your tickets to the Lawman's barn dance. Just a nickel a ticket, if you purchase right now.' But Mr and Mrs Calculator were way out of earshot.

A tumbleweed clichéd across the street. Carton sighed again. He thought for a while, but couldn't figure a way to raise himself from the seated position, so he rolled on to his front and dragged himself up to the perpendicular once more.

As he was dusting himself down, pointlessly, a little boy in a check shirt and blue dungarees skidded barefoot up to him. 'What happened, Sheriff? You's OK?'

Carton looked down at the sweet concern on the boy's face, and found himself a smile. 'Warn't nothin', Billy boy. Just lost my footing.'

Billy dusted the sheriff's waistcoat. 'You're lookin' kinda tired, sir. Bin out fightin' injuns again?'

'Surely have, Billy.'

'What kind?'

'Oh, lemme see. There was some Arapaho, some Navajo, some Idunno . . .'

'Ain't never heard of that tribe.'

'They was mean and they was moody, Billy. They was after my scalp.'

'But, Sheriff, you don't got no hair.'

'Zactly. That's how mean and moody them injuns was, Billy.'

'How many?'

'Why, there must've been twenty to my left, twenty to my right and twenty to my rear, all hollerin' and whoopin' their crazy war chants. I figured sixty injuns – ain't worth wasting good lead bullets, so I just threw down my six shooters, rolled up my sleeves and ducked it out with 'em.'

'You killed sixty injuns with your bare hands?'

'Sixty injuns, two bank robbers, eight gun-runners and a grizzly. It's been a slow day, Billy. Hope things'll pick up tomorrow.'

'Gee, Sheriff. What a story.'

Carton focused on Billy's face, and noticed a raw bruise blooming on his cheek. With creaking knees he crouched to the youngster's eye level and gripped his shoulders. 'Say, Billy boy. What happened to you?'

Billy shrugged him off. 'Nothin'.'

'You wasn't brawlin' on my account again, was you?'

'It was Tommy Tate. He said you was a lousy, stinkin' drunk who wasn't no good to no one. I couldn't stand by and let him talk disrespectful.'

Carton closed his eyes. Tommy Tate was fifty-seven years old. 'You didn't ought to be fighting grown men on my account, Billy. I ain't worth it.'

'Sure you are, Sheriff. And purty soon the whole town's gonna know what a genuine hero you are. You're gonna stand up to those Apocalypse boys when they ride into town tonight, and blast 'em all back to the stinkin' hole in the wall they came from.'

'Tonight?' Carton stood, and took out his pocket watch. 'They're coming tonight?' Where had the time gone? How could he have forgotten?

Billy nodded. 'Is it true no one in the whole town will be your deputy? You're gonna have to shoot it out with the four of 'em all on your own?'

Carton tapped his watch, and slipped it back into his waistcoat. 'That's the way it is, Billy.' His throat felt like the furnace on the Cannonball express. 'That's the way it is.' The thirst dragged his head round, and the rest of him followed it towards the saloon.

'Sheriff?'

Carton stopped and looked back at Billy.

'Can I be your deputy?'

'You're just a kid, Billy.'

Billy straightened up, all indignatious-like. 'I'm nine and a quarter in a month's time. I'm practically shaving.'

Carton walked back and crouched Billy-height again. He fished in his waistcoat pocket and pulled out a badge. 'Sure, you can be my deputy,' he smiled. 'You want a badge?'

Billy's eyes opened wider than a snake swallowing a hog whole. 'A reg'lar deputy's badge? For me?'

'That's right, Billy. And because you're my best friend in the whole world' – Carton dragged his hand across his mouth, thirstily – 'it's only gonna cost ya two nickels.'

'Hot diggety!' Billy fumbled the pennies out of his dungarees and grabbed the badge, as if Carton might change his mind, and then pelted off to show off his trophy to just about anyone who cared to look, and just about anyone who didn't care, too.

Carton looked at the sad little coins in his hand, and cursed himself. What the hell had happened to him? Billy Belief was about the only friend he had left, and he'd cheated him without even thinking twice. Some place along the trail, something had gone mightily wrong with old Iron Will Carton. He'd gotten lower than a scorpion's scrotum. Then he heard the beckoning call of the old honky-tonk keys tinkling inside the saloon, thought about the slug of forgetfulness the pennies would buy and stopped worrying.

He clomped up the steps, thrust open the double doors and strode with resolution into the smoky dimness of the bar room. It was plenty busy. He scanned the room as he walked, not wanting to stop before he hit the bar for fear his oscillating might betray the recency of his tryst with old lady moonshine. He kidded himself his step was measured, authoritarian. Just the good ol' sheriff doing his good ol' rounds.

Suddenly, he was pitched, headlong and horizontal, and his head collided with the spittoon, which flopped its vile gloop all over his face. He looked up. A moose's head, dangling from the centre strut was staring down at him, leering. He wiped away the mucal filth with the sleeve of his shirt and turned to spot the obstacle that had tripped him.

The shining black leather boot was still jutting out in the aisle between the tables. Carton's eyes followed the boot up to the pinstriped trousers with their tomahawk-sharp creases, past the holstered gun and the billowing cream shirt to the shoelace tie and then the cruelly handsome face that gleamed a grin above them. 'Well, well, well, Sheriff. Fancy seein' a man of your sober disposition in a low-down drinking establishment like this.'

The cowpokes around the card-tables laughed plenty.

Anger helped Carton to his feet. 'You shouldn't oughta have done that, Jimmy.'

The piano player decided that this didn't need accompaniment and stopped tinkling. Chairs scrawped against the wooden floor as Jimmy stood and the rest of the public put themselves as best they could out of the line of fire. Still grinning, Jimmy flipped open the catches on his holsters and flexed his hands. 'Why don't you try it, Sheriff?'

Carton didn't move. Didn't even sway.

'Come on,' Jimmy sneered. 'They say you used to be faster than a toilet stop in rattlesnake country. Before'n you got yeller.'

The real Will Carton would have emptied both his guns, swept up the bullet casings and been making arrangements for a decent Christian funeral before a chancer like Jimmy had even thought about moving for his weapons. The old Will Carton.

'What are you waiting for, Tinhorn? Chicken got your liver?'

Carton dragged his fat dog of a tongue over his lips. 'Mighty sorry I stumbled over your boot, there, Jimmy. Didn't mean nothin' by it.'

The cowpokes whistled and jeered. Someone flicked a

playing-card that sliced painfully across Carton's nose. Mucho laughter. The piano player hit the keys and every-body scrawped chairs back into place. Carton dragged his dry sleeve across his face and headed for the bar again.

'Will? You OK?'

'I'm dandy, Hope. Gimme two fingers of your best damn firewater. Just ate a chunk of humble pie, got stuck right in my craw.'

'Don't pay no never-no-mind to the likes of Jimmy Guilt. He's all bluster and fancy laundry.'

'He's in an awful rush to book hisself a berth in Boot Hill, sure enough. Now, about that slug, Hope . . .'

'Boss says I warn't to give you no credit no more for no liquor, Will. Could fix you a nice plate of stew, though. It's fresh possum.'

Carton slapped Billy's money on the bar. 'I'm a cash client today, lovely lady. So pour me two fat fingers of your best sippin' liquor. And don't be after slippin' me that gut-swill you keep for the panhandlers. I want the smooth stuff. The stuff where you get your eyesight back after two days, guaranteed.'

Hope sighed and reached under the bar for the bottle. 'Won't do you no good, Will. When you wake up, you're still gonna be you. Still facing away from your problems.' The thick brown liquid glopped into the tumbler. Carton eyed it lustily. Lived a minute or so anticipating the groove that first sip was going to cut through the crust on his tongue. He reached for the glass.

Carton hoped it was firecrackers popping outside, but he knew there was small chance of that. It was gunfire. No question, really. Still, he reached for his glass . . .

Through the bar mirror, he saw young Billy burst through the double doors. 'The Apocalypse boys is here!' he panted.

All eyes turned Cartonwards.

'They's askin' fer you, Sheriff.'

Carton didn't look back. He said, in a cool, casual voice: 'Well, now, Billy. You tell those good ol' boys the sheriff'll be right out,' hoisted his glass and tossed the liquor down his grateful throat.

He barely smiled, touched the brim of his stetson in Hope's direction and wheeled round to face the doors. He measured his stride across the bar room: not too fast, so as to look compliant, and not too slow, so as to look afeared. Would have pulled it off, too, if he hadn't wandered too close to the moose's head and snagged the collar of his long coat on its horns, yanking him off his feet and planting him on his rear end for the fourth time that morning.

He picked himself up with all the dignity he could muster, strode to the saloon doors and burst out into the brutal daylight.

There were four things that ruled out any gunplay on Carton's part. First off, they had their backs to the furnace of a sun, and Carton had to squint just to make out their silhouettes. Second and third: they were mounted, and there were three of them. And fourthly: Carton had the shakes worse than two porcupines on their honeymoon night.

The three brothers leaned easy in their saddles. It was War Apocalypse did the speaking. He tapped a forefinger on the brim of his hat. 'Sheriff,' he said, all polite and proper.

Carton nodded the greeting back. 'Right neighbourly of you boys to drop by. How can I be helpin' you all?'

War's voice was soft, almost a whisper; a cold hiss of a voice that cut right through to Carton's spine. 'Well, see now, Sheriff, brother Pestilence here has a problem.'

Carton glanced over at Pestilence, who batted absently at the buzzing host of insect pests that seemed to be his constant company. 'And what would that problem be, friend?'

War's whisper cut in: 'Seems you're standing right exactly where his bullets would like to be.'

In the roaring hot silence of the street, Carton swore he

could hear the ticking of his own pocket watch. 'Well now, strikes me that's easy solved.' He took two slow steps to his right and faced them again. 'That more accommodatin'?'

War hissed a small chuckle. 'Ain't that just the durndest thing? Now you're standing just where my bullets want to be.'

Carton tugged his stetson low over his eyes. 'No problem, boys.' He took another two slow steps and faced them. 'How's that?'

War twisted in his saddle. 'That OK by you, brother Famine?'

The fat horseman tore another greasy mouthful from the plump chicken leg in his hand and mumbled a single syllable that started and ended with 'm' and had a guttural middle. Whatever the word was meant to be, it was unambiguously negative.

War sighed and shook his head sadly. 'I've got to figure you're doing this to just plain provoke me.'

Carton saw their shoulders drop, caught the glints of steel before his world erupted into a deafening nightmare of exploding lead.

Three men, six guns, thirty-six bullets.

TWO

Djuhn'Keep was not best pleased. All his meticulous planning, all those months of careful preparation were now threatened with failure because of the one factor he had failed to accommodate.

Luck.

Dumb luck.

As a natural precaution, he had tracked the last survivors of the highly enjoyable death race as they'd been flushed out of the docking bay.

Most of them had careered off into the bleak, black wasteland of deep space.

One, just one of them, had ricocheted against a rogue asteroid, and his new trajectory put him on a collision course with the human vessel.

There was every good chance, still, that the survivor would simply shoot by them, tantalizingly close, but lacking any kind of manoeuvrability, not close enough.

Still, Djuhn hadn't come this far to leave anything to chance.

There was no choice. He could no longer afford to wait for the human to come to him.

He would have to go to the human.

Pizzak gripped the human's oxygen pipe and squeezed.

He just couldn't believe his luck.

He'd been hurtling through space, with only a slow, icy

death to contemplate, when he'd noticed a green spot in the distance.

As he sped towards it, the spot became a vessel. It could only be the human ship.

His delight deflated when he realized he was going to miss it.

Not by much. Just enough to taunt him for the rest of his freezing days.

Then, as the ship loomed closer, he saw there was another, much smaller vessel tethered to it.

And the cord that linked them together had been directly in his path.

He'd only had one shot at grabbing the cord, but it had been enough. From there, it was a simple matter to clamber down the tethering line towards the green ship's hull.

At that point, there had been a problem.

How was he to gain entry to the vessel?

He could hardly knock on the airlock door and coo: 'Yoo-hoo! I'm your worst nightmare, please let me in.' On the other hand, if he simply tried ripping his way through the hull, the sudden release of pressure would likely enough have killed everyone on board, which would have been no fun at all.

That was when he'd noticed the upside-down buttocks.

A pair of robotic buns, jutting out of a hole in the hull.

He'd crawled over to the curious sight, and pressed his ear against the hull. He'd heard what sounded like welding work going on. In between there were a few snatches of conversation – enough for Pizzak to glean the gist of what had happened. There'd been some kind of breech in the hull, which they'd plugged with the mechanoid, and now they were walling him in.

What an infinity of delights he'd experienced when he'd heard the human was coming outside to release the mechanoid.

Giddy with excitement, he'd waited until the last panel had been fitted, grabbed on to the buttocks and pulled.

It had taken a surprising amount of effort, and when the mechanoid had finally come free, he could see why: he'd had to snap a girder to break the bastard loose.

He'd briefly contemplated torturing the astonished mechanoid, but time had been against him – the human could be on his way at any moment – so he'd simply launched the sad wretch into space and climbed into the hole.

The human's face!

Pizzak hurled back his head and roared a silent laugh, muffled by the vacuum of space.

It had been worth all the trials, all the pain and suffering just to see the human's expression when he'd grabbed him.

Pizzak peered at the face again, and noticed the human was turning blue inside his helmet, so he released the oxygen pipe. You had to be so careful with these creatures. Their grip on life was so frail, so fragile. You had to brutalize them ever so gently if you wanted to prolong their demise.

He slipped the magnetic clamps off the human's gauntlets and slid them over his own knuckles, then he released the human and slapped the back of his helmet, sending his unconscious body floating gently towards the airlock door.

A thrilling wave of anticipation swept over him, and he began to scramble across the hull after his slowly drifting prize.

The airlock door was in reach now. Pizzak grabbed on to the door wheel and slapped the human's helmet again, just enough to stop his motion, leaving him bobbing gently before the entrance.

They would have to let them in, now. According to the data they'd wheedled out of the dim-witted computer, there were only two left: a hologram and a creature who was evolved from cats. Pizzak couldn't see that sad line-up providing much resistance. The best possible scenario was that they'd surrender without a struggle. Then he could pilot the craft back to the captured mining ship, and dispense of them at his considerable leisure.

There was, of course the small matter of Djuhn'Keep. Zooming helplessly through space, Pizzak had cooked up quite a gourmet feast of prospective deaths for that tumorous backstabbing deceiver, that cowardly blight on agonoidkind's pride, that smear on the reputation of all decent, straightforward, honest murderous psychopaths.

First things first, though. Securing the human vessel was the priority now. But as Pizzak's hand snaked out to turn on the human's throat microphone, there was a flash of flame and silver, and something hit him.

The impact was slight, infliction-of-pain-wise, but powerful and surprising enough to tear his hand loose of the door wheel and send him careering off away from the ship.

He screamed a noiseless 'Nooo!' and looked down at the gauntleted hand around his waist.

There was another human!

Another human had attacked him!

Attacked him!

Him!

This one was equipped with a jet pack, and the jet was still flaring on his back, driving the two of them out into space.

The human released him, but they were still only inches apart, hurtling along at the same speed, in the same direction. Away from the human vessel.

The human's hand moved towards his jet-pack control pad, trying to fire a burst from his chest jet, which would separate him from the agonoid, and launch him back shipwards, leaving Pizzak speeding endlessly away in the barren, dark eternity of the stars.

Pizzak reacted quickly, but the human had the advantage of surprise, and the flame licked out of the chest jet just as the agonoid made his grab.

As the human roared backwards, Pizzak's desperate fingers scrambled to find some purchase. Just as the heinous creature was almost clear, Pizzak's thumb and forefinger managed to clamp around his boot, and with the jet's impetus, they both lurched up and back.

The agonoid's thin lips drew back in a metal-toothed parody of a grin. He hauled himself closer to the human and grabbed his knee.

In a few more seconds, he would be close enough to rip the jet pack off and take it for himself. Then he would poke a thin finger through the human's helmet and watch his features bloat in the vacuum of space, until his head burst in a spectacular gory display of blood, bone and brains.

Lister came round, woozy and disoriented to find himself facing *Starbug*'s outer door.

He looked down, which was a mistake, because there was nothing underneath him. He was bobbing in space, like a helium-filled balloon the morning after a party.

Even in his addled state, he realized that bobbing around helplessly in space was not a good thing to be doing, and he struggled to recall how he'd managed to wind up there.

And then he remembered. That face. That razor smile. The agonoid.

Where was the agonoid now?

He tried to look around, but his body wouldn't turn, and his field of vision was limited by the edges of his helmet.

Getting back inside *Starbug* seemed like a neat plan. He stretched out for the airlock wheel.

It was out of reach.

Not just a little bit out of reach – a good arm's length.

He looked down at his chest and saw two alarming things. Firstly, he wasn't wearing a jet pack. Secondly, his oxygen level was astonishingly low. Less than seven minutes of air left.

Why hadn't he bothered to put on a jet pack? Why

had he gone for this damned space walk in the first place?

Because in his foolhardy, adolescent bravado, he'd wanted to impress Ace.

Pathetic.

Just as he was thinking that unless somebody came out to haul him in soon, Dave Lister had crunched his last poppadom, the airlock wheel span, and the door began to open towards him.

And that was good, so long as it wasn't the agonoid who was opening the door.

Light flooded out of the airlock, and before Lister's pupils could contract sufficiently for him to make out just who it was in there, a hand grabbed his chest harness and hauled him in.

The door wheeled shut behind him, and as oxygen hissed into the airlock, Lister's sight grew accustomed to the glare, he found himself looking at a familiar jagged-tooth grin.

The Cat lifted off his gold cone-shaped helmet and started speaking, but Lister had to tug his own helmet off before he could hear him.

'. . . up there in a hurry, buddy.'

'What was that?'

'I said: the bad-assed robot dude who grabbed you has gotten hold of the guy who looks like goalpost head . . .'

The inner door span open, and without waiting for the Cat to finish, Lister dashed out and up to the cockpit. He lurched up to Kryten's station and craned over the viewing screen, but could only make out two tiny figures in the distance. He called out to Rimmer: 'What's going on?'

Rimmer didn't look up from his screen. 'Hard to say. They're moving so fast I can't track them if I zoom any closer.'

'Are you in radio contact?'

'I was, but he keeps cutting out. I think there's a loose wire. I think . . .'

The radio barked to life: '. . . bug. Can you read me? Repeat . . .' Ace's voice was calm and unflustered.

Lister flicked on the microphone. 'Got you, Commander. What's happening?'

'Doesn't look too clever, old Christmas cake. Didn't quite manage to shake the dervish off quick enough. Little perisher's got a hold of my leg. He's climbing up for the jet pack.'

'Listen – I'm already suited up. I'm going to grab a JP and come out after you. Can you hold him off till I get there?'

'That's a negative, old biscuit barrel. Can't let the swine grab my pack – we'll all be finished. I'm going to try and unhook the harness.'

'Are you mad? Lose the jet pack, you'll be stuck out there permanently.'

'It's the only way, Davey lad. Damn! He's grabbing for it . . . Just got to . . .'

There was a long whistle of static. Lister jabbed pointlessly at the microphone switch. Then a small flare erupted close to the two figures on the viewscreen. Slowly, it arched up and away from them.

'Did it!' Ace yelled with delight. 'Blasted it off into the great unknown. Looks like my dancing partner's pretty cheesed off about it.'

Lister enhanced the viewscreen image. Rimmer was right: they were hurtling along at a hell of a lick, and he just managed to glimpse the struggling pair as they flitted across the screen. The agonoid had clambered up to Ace's chest.

The static died, and Ace's voice crackled in. '. . . trying to kiss me or something. He's got his mouth pressed to my helmet . . . I think he's trying to speak to me . . .'

'Just hang on!' Lister yelled. 'We're coming to get you.'

'Shouldn't bother, if I were you, old cucumber. We're going far too fast for your old rust-box to catch us. Any case, the sweet-talking brute's apparently got some extremely short-term plans for my future. Ah, well. To be honest, I doubt he'd have been the most scintillating chap to spend the rest of eternity with. Looks like I'll be signing off now. Smoke me a kipper, lads – I'll be back for . . .'

Then there was a pop, and the roaring of a terrible wind, then a muffled, wet explosion.

Then there was just a deep, abiding silence.

THREE

Kryten was trying desperately hard to put a positive spin on things.

He was caroming backwards through space, without any means of manoeuvring, and his internal heating system would run down within fifteen hours, freezing him solid on a permanent basis. That was provided he didn't slam into an asteroid and get splattered like a fly on a motorway windscreen before then. Furthermore, a psychotic agonoid was undoubtedly aboard *Starbug* by now, and was probably torturing the crew in ways that would have given the Marquis de Sade bed-wetting nightmares. Even if the agonoid had been overcome, which seemed most unlikely, there would, by now, be less than two hours' worth of oxygen left on board.

All right. OK. That's the situation, Kryten told himself: now look at the bright side.

He spent a good few minutes drumming his fingers on the girder that was welded to his chest. He couldn't find a bright side.

This wouldn't do. Of course there was a bright side. They'd been in worse fixes than this before now.

Hadn't they?

His fingers drummed away again.

All right, they probably hadn't been in worse fixes than this.

He tried to think of how things might turn out in a best-case scenario.

After a dozen or so best-case scenarios had concluded with the death and destruction of all parties, Kryten decided to try and stop thinking altogether.

Suddenly, he felt a thunk! in his back. While he was still trying to feel behind him to find out what had caused the thunk!, he felt himself jerk upwards. He craned his head back as far as it would go, but he could only make out the rear jets of an unfamiliar ship.

Someone had harpooned him, and was now dragging him along on the end of a tether. As far as Kryten could tell, he was being towed back in the direction of *Starbug*.

This was either very good, or very bad.

Either he'd been rescued, or . . .

But he really didn't want to think about the 'or', so he went back to trying not to think at all.

FOUR

'All right.' Rimmer turned away from the screen and faced the others. 'He's dead. There's nothing we can do about it.'

Lister crumbled into the seat and flicked off the view-screen.

Ace was dead.

He'd sacrificed his life for David Lister. 'He was worth a dozen of me,' Lister mumbled.

'So what are we going to do? Are we going to let his death be a meaningless, empty gesture, or are we going to pull ourselves together and work out a way to get out of this mess? Now, I never thought I'd be saying this, but I reckon our first priority is to rescue Kryten. That's assuming the agonoid didn't kill him, of course. Now, let's run a quick check, make sure we're still spaceworthy and get moving.'

Rimmer considered it most unlikely that Kryten was alive, but even if the agonoid had literally ripped him to pieces, there might be a possibility of repairing him. In any case, they had at least to try and find him. A single, unarmed agonoid had accounted for their two strongest crew members in a matter of minutes, without breaking sweat, and if it hadn't been for Ace's heroic sacrifice, they would all be people pâté by now. The prospect of facing an army of them with a force that consisted of one hologram and two pimply teenagers was not one to be relished.

'Damn!' The Cat tapped at a readout dial on the pilot's control fascia. 'This readout better be busted.'

Rimmer stood and walked up to him. 'Which readout?'

'Oxygen supply readout.' The Cat thumped it again. 'Either it's broken, or we only have five minutes of air left.'

'Lister, can you run a cross-check on the diagnostics?'

Lister sighed and turned to the controls. He punched in the necessary commands. 'Uh, guys, there's good news, and there's bad news. The good news is, the oxygen readout isn't broken. That's also the bad news. We'd better get our helmets back on, sharpish.' As he turned away from the controls, he noticed a warning light flashing. 'Hang on, we've got a visitor.'

Rimmer glanced over at the pilot's display. The airlock was being opened. 'I don't understand – that door's sealed. You'd need the access code and a retina scan.'

They heard the inner door open in the mid-section behind them.

Lister punched at the keyboard. 'Hey, it's all right. The NaviComp's identified the retina scan: it's Kryten.'

Lister leapt up and bounded down the steps. He looked up and froze.

It was Kryten, all right. Only, he'd brought along some company.

He was being held aloft, helpless by the scruff of the neck, by a leering, razor-toothed agonoid.

FIVE

'I'm most awfully sorry, Mr Lister, sir,' Kryten fumbled
with his fingers. 'He linked up to my CPU via my SCSI
socket and dragged the access code out of me.'

'Yes,' the agonoid lowered Kryten to the floor, 'how un-
conscionably rude of me.' He slapped Kryten viciously
across the head, sending him scudding on to the scanner
table, which shattered spectacularly on impact. 'I do hate
bad manners. So uncalled-for.' He put his hands behind
his back and strolled up to Lister, looking him over like a
prospective buyer on a used-car forecourt.

Lister backed away.

'Oh, don't worry. I'm not going to kill you.' Djuhn'-
Keep cooed reassuringly. 'I'm going to hurt you a lot, and
for a very long time, but I have no intention of killing you.
In fact, it'll be a lot more fun for me if you live to a very
ripe old age. We're going to become very close, you and I.'
He peered into the cockpit. 'You can come out of there.'

The Cat shrugged and strutted into the mid-section with
considerable cool, under the circumstances.

The agonoid called, 'And you. The hologram cowering
under that console at the front, there.'

Lister heard Rimmer's small voice say: 'I don't think so.'

Djuhn smiled. 'It will hurt a lot less if you come without
my assistance.'

Slowly, Rimmer rose and walked out of the cockpit with
his hands aloft.

'Why have you got your hands up?'

'I'm surrendering.'

The agonoid sighed. 'Look, I'd hate for us to get off on the wrong foot, so let me explain the set-up as clearly as possible, so we can all get on with the programme, and eliminate any confusion. There is no hope. There will be no mercy. You can't appeal to my better nature, because I don't have one. The only thing you have to look forward to now is death, and believe me, you'll come to cherish that prospect. For my part, I will use my considerable skills to keep you alive, and in constant agony. Any questions?'

Lister made eye contact with the Cat, who nodded slightly to signal understanding.

'Good. Now we're going to take this ship back to the mining vessel, where I have assembled a considerable array of treats and goodies I'd like to share with you . . .'

Lister yelled 'Now!' and lunged at the agonoid, as the Cat dived towards the bank of lockers where a bazookoid was stored.

Lister's flailing fists pounded at the agonoid's face, leaving his knuckles bruised and bloody. Djuhn simply reached out and flicked Lister's forehead and sent him crashing to the floor.

He turned his attention to the Cat, who cocked the bazookoid and aimed it at the agonoid's chest. Djuhn shook his head, amused. 'You must have your fun I suppose.' He stepped towards the Cat.

'Hold it right there, buddy,' the Cat hissed.

Djuhn simply kept walking.

'One more step' – the Cat swung the bazookoid's nozzle over towards the grounded Lister – 'and I kill him.'

Djuhn's smile collapsed. He looked at the Cat, then over at Lister. Was this a serious threat? Could destiny be so heartless as to lead him all this way, to bring the last human in the universe within his grasp, only to yank him away at the last possible moment?

Suddenly, there was a hiss, and the sound of fans grinding to a stop. Djuhn looked up. Something had happened to the oxygen supply. He wheeled round, aghast.

The human was on the floor, hyperventilating. Even in his distress, he grinned at Djuhn, and with his last gasp of air said, 'You lose, motherf –'

SIX

'. . . should be breathing now. Ah, yes.'

Lister opened his eyes to see Djuhn'Keep's face looking down at him. The face disappeared into a fog as Lister's breath misted over his helmet's visor.

The agonoid stood. 'Unfortunately, there's very little air left in your canisters. Certainly not enough to get you back to my pain palace in one piece. And I do so want you in one piece. At least for the moment.'

Lister sat up and looked around. They were in *Starbug*'s engine-room facing the newly welded hull section. The Cat was crouching on Lister's left, wearing his gold lamé spacesuit. Rimmer and Kryten were seated meekly on the deck to his right.

The agonoid was standing opposite, prodding at the oxygen regeneration unit with a sonic screwdriver. 'Ah, here's the problem. This OR unit is a complete mess. I'm surprised it held out as long as it did. Just bear with me a moment.'

As the agonoid fiddled with various tools, Kryten leaned over to Lister, and whispered, rather cryptically, 'Hold on.'

The agonoid glanced round, and then carried on with his repairs. ' "Hold on," you say? Hold on to what?'

'I was merely attempting to boost the human's moral. I meant "hold on" as in "hang on in there".'

Djuhn snickered. 'As in "hold on to hope", you mean? I thought we'd established the futility of that concept.'

There was a clunk, and the sound of fans whirring up to speed overhead.

'There. That should hold until we get back. Now then . . .' The agonoid crossed to the NaviComp terminal, opened a small panel on top of his head and dragged out a lead. He plugged the lead into the terminal. 'I'll just programme in the course and we'll be on our way.'

Kryten stood.

'Sit down.'

Ignoring the agonoid's bark, Kryten walked calmly along the corridor.

'Get back here, you plastic-faced buffoon.'

Kryten stooped under a gantry support strut and grabbed something off the deck. He turned round again and began walking back towards the agonoid.

He was holding a bazookoid.

'Honestly,' Djuhn smiled, incredulous. 'What are you going to do with that? Even if you hit me at point-blank range, it would hardly scratch me. Besides, you're programmed not to kill.'

Kryten shook his head. 'I'm not going to kill anyone.'

'Then put it down, before you hurt yourself.'

'As I said, sir.' He looked at Lister and widened his eyes. 'Hold on!' he yelled, and fired.

The blast ripped into the new hull section, and a roaring vacuum wind dragged at the air.

The bazookoid tore out of his hand and tumbled through the hole. Kryten snatched hold of a gantry girder and yanked at Rimmer's light bee, holding it safe.

Lister grabbed on to the strut behind him, but the Cat was caught unawares, and he'd slithered beyond reach of a handhold before he could react. Lister leaned over and grabbed hold of the Cat's boot.

Djuhn had been closest to the blast.

The sucking whirlwind lifted him off his feet and dragged him towards the gaping hole.

As he flew through the gap, feet first, his fingertips caught hold of the edge of the ripped panels, and he dangled there for a brief second before the weakened metal crumbled away, and his arms clawed impotently at the air as he swept through and out into space.

He jerked to a stop within ten yards of the ship.

Kryten looked over at the NaviComp, and saw why.

The lead from the agonoid's head was still plugged into the terminal.

It looked like the Cat was in grabbing distance of the lead.

Kryten yelled out, but his voice couldn't carry over the roar. He waved and gesticulated frantically to Lister.

Lister spotted him, followed his gestures towards the taut lead, and understood.

Straining and grunting, he dragged his leg back and hooked his knee around the strut, freeing his hand to activate his throat mike.

'Cat, man. The lead! Pull the lead out!'

The Cat looked up. He reached out. His fingertips were more than six inches short.

Lister hooked his boot behind his support strut. He couldn't be absolutely sure it was wedged firmly enough to hold both him and the Cat, but the agonoid had grabbed on to the lead and was hauling his way back towards them, so there was no choice but to try.

He let go and was yanked forward.

He looked back. The boot had held. How long it would hold, he couldn't be sure. But now the Cat could reach the lead.

He watched the agonoid leer at him, as the Cat stretched up and tugged the lead free.

The wire snaked out of the ship, and the escaping air that was roaring from the ship blasted the agonoid away from them.

He waved at them as he slowly disappeared into the cold eternal night.

Suddenly, Lister felt himself move forward.

He looked back, but the boot still seemed to be wedged behind the strut. He slid forward again.

The entire gantry was being sucked towards the hole.

On the plus side, that might work to their benefit: it might jam the gap sufficiently for them to get topside.

On the negative side, the huge bulk of collapsing metal might very well crush one, or both of them to death.

He watched, helplessly, as the girders groaned and bent and finally snapped, and the gantry crashed down towards him.

Lister closed his eyes.

Suddenly, there was silence.

Lister opened his eyes. The collapsed gantry was wedged into the hole.

The Cat was safe.

They both stood.

Rimmer's hologrammatic imaged fluttered up out of the wreckage. 'I think Kryten's bought it,' he said quietly.

Lister picked his way over the debris.

He saw Kryten's arm under a girder, the hand twitching spasmodically.

He grabbed the girder and pulled. He moved it just enough to see that the arm had been severed.

He looked around for the rest of him. 'Kryten?' he called, half-heartedly.

'Yes, sir?' Kryten's muffled voice filtered out from under the rubble.

'Where are you, man?'

'I'm pinned down under a rather large sheet of metal.'

'Are you all right?'

'I'm absolutely dandy, sir,' he chirped. 'Uhn, I don't suppose you've found an arm lying around, have you?'

Lister and the Cat clambered over the wreckage and started hauling away the debris.

Kryten kicked away the last girder and stood. He was

one-armed and seriously dented, but all things considered, in pretty good shape.

He poked around the rubble, and found his arm. 'I'll attach this later, sirs. Right now, we'd better get this tea chest back to the lipstick-coloured vertically challenged one.'

'Wait a mo.' Rimmer stepped over the wreckage towards him. 'Is that entirely, altogether wise? Personally, I'd rather take my chances of surviving the airless vacuum of space than face up to another one of those demented bastards.'

'He's the last of them, sir,' Kryten smiled. 'When he linked up with me to wheedle out *Starbug*'s access code, I managed to do a little poking around of my own. According to his memory banks, which are, quite frankly, obscene, he personally killed the rest of the agonoid population, so that he would have you all to himself to torture.'

'You're absolutely sure, Kryten? Because I'd hate . . .'

Suddenly, the engines began to rumble, and the ship lurched forward.

'Strange.' Kryten hobbled over to the NaviComp terminal. He stabbed at the keypad. 'Locked out. That's . . .' The terminal screen burst into life. A message appeared. It said, simply: 'SEE YOU IN SILICON HELL.'

Rimmer stepped up and peered over his shoulder. 'What does it mean?'

'It means . . .' Kryten turned to face him. 'It means he's infected the NaviComp with a virus. It means we're accelerating pell mell through the asteroid belt, without any means of steering the ship.'

SEVEN

Three men, six guns, thirty-six bullets.

His longcoat was stripped to rags, his hat colandered, his gun belt severed, trousers by his ankles. Nothing wounded, though. Nothing excepting his self-respect. Carton stood, not moving, as the echoes of gunfire floated off to the desert mountains.

War twirled his smoking weapons and holstered them. 'Now we got your attention, there's a little message for ya. It's from Pa. Says he wants you out of here by midnight, or he's coming for you, personal, like.'

'Thank you, boys. Tell Poppa "message received".'

War tugged on his reins. His horse bucked and snorted, spurting sulphurous fire that scorched Carton's boots, and the brothers galloped out of town, quick as that.

The saloon doors split open, and Jimmy and his cowpoke friends spilled out on to the porch. Jimmy smiled and with mockery in his voice said, 'You ain't leavin', are you, Sheriff?'

Young Billy fought his way out through the forest of legs and faced the crowd. 'Course'n he ain't leavin'. Are you, Sheriff?'

Carton shucked off his trousers and stepped heavily down into the street in his badly stained long johns.

Billy called after him. 'Tell 'em it ain't so, Sheriff. Tell 'em it ain't so!'

Carton unpinned his sheriff badge, tossed it over his

shoulder and then slouched over to the jailhouse to get his things together.

The jailhouse doors groaned behind him. 'That's all right, boys,' Carton muttered, 'you'll be seein' the last of me soon enough.' He went into the empty cell and picked up his bedroll. A pint whisky bottle fell out and clattered to the floor. Carton stooped and picked it up. It was empty, of course, but he put the neck of the bottle to his lips and sucked it anyway, just in case there were any fumes left in it.

He fumbled for his keys and unlocked his personal drawer in the desk. He took out an expensive-looking leather case and flipped the catches. Inside, tucked snug in the green baize were his fancy shootin' irons. He slipped one out and let it lie in his palm. It balanced just perfect. Sixteen inches of tempered steel, and it felt like no weight at all. He spun the cylinder. Silent. He rubbed his fingertips over the flawless black pearl grip. He'd built the guns himself, back when he was somebody.

He laid the gun back in its recess, tenderly, like it was the bones of a martyred saint, and closed the lid. He figured the guns ought to be worth a couple of bottles of mind-rot if he traded them over at the saloon. Sure as hell wouldn't be needing them where he was going.

A shadow slid across his desk. Carton looked up at the stranger standing in his doorway. 'Office is closed, friend. Sheriff's going out of town.'

The stranger stepped in, anyway. 'Don't you recognize me?'

Carton studied the man. He was dressed in the time-respected regalia of a steamboat gambler. Tailed jacket, fancy shirt with a lacy front. Under the pear-shaped brim of his neatly blocked hat he wore the back of his hair in snake tails. There was something oddly accustomed about the fellow all right, but Carton couldn't place it. He flicked his eyes to the array of wanted posters on his notice-board. That was all he needed right now. Some low-life varmint out to gun him down for some past slight. The stranger's face wasn't depicted in the gallery of desperadoes, though.

'Your face is kinda familiar, friend, but I can't put a name to it.'

'How about *Red Dwarf*? That mean anything?'

'*Red Dwarf*? Ain't he the little feller used to ride shotgun with the Chancy gang?'

The stranger exhaled. 'I thought this might be hard.'

Carton tucked the gun case under his arm. 'Look here, *hombre*, I don't know what business you figured you had with me, but if it's trouble you want, I ain't complyin'. I just resigned my position, see: don't sport the badge no more. I don't care if you shot up every train and rustled every head of cattle between the Badlands of New Mexico and Paris, France, Europe. I ain't the Law no more. I'm fresh out of fight. So if you'd care to stand aside and let me by, friend, I'd be handsomely obligated to you.'

The stranger put some space between himself and the doors, and Carton gathered up his bedroll and strode on by him.

Out on the sidewalk, there were two other strangers. They both triggered something, too, in what Carton was passing off as his mind these days, but he'd be danged if he could figure what. One was dressed in black, from his sombrero to his boots, with fancy decorative braiding all over him, and a pair of revolvers that looked pretty business-like. He was smiling, and Carton didn't much like the teeth the smile laid bare. Those incisors looked like they'd be more at home in the snarl of a mountain lion. His taller compadre kept his thin features and flared nostrils in the shade of a Tom Mix ten-gallon hat, and wore a bronco buster's chaps over his blue jeans. He had a strange expression, this one; wide-eyed and hopeful, nodding like he was urging Carton to recognize him.

Carton was puzzled, but not enough to stay and waste time parleying with these range riders. He nodded them a miserly greeting, then set off over the street to the saloon again, gun case under his arm. Behind him, he heard the jailhouse doors creak as the first stranger stepped out. He could feel the burn of their eyes on his back as he mounted the steps. Then the friendly smell of smoke and stale liquor hit his nose, and he forgot all about the newcomers, his concentration being fixated on other things.

There was a burst of laughter from the card-players at Jimmy's table as he walked up to the bar, the product of some whispered slight, but Carton didn't pay it a never-no-mind. There was a chorus of clucking, and he ignored that too.

He wiped a clean space on the bar and set down the case. 'What do you figure, Hope? These ought to be good for a coupl'a bottles of throat-burner.' He flipped the case open and the gleaming guns illuminated the barmaid's face.

Hope looked up at Carton. 'You're trading in your best guns?'

'Why not? Ain't no use to me no how. Couldn't shoot and hit a whale's belly if'n I was Jonah himself.'

'But Will, these are your *special* guns. Ain't nobody can use them 'ceptin' you. Look . . .' she flipped the cylinder open. 'There's no chambers. No place to put the bullets.'

Carton felt like he'd been gut shot. He stared at the split-open gun, his face creased up like a toothless old squaw sucking a cactus. What in hellfire use were a pair of pistolaroes with no holes for bullets? He tried laughing it off. 'Well, they got to be worth *something*. Call 'em safety guns, let kids use 'em for drawin' practice.'

Hope put the revolvers back and slid the case over to Carton. 'Keep 'em, Will. I'll let you have a bottle if you keep the irons.'

'Sounds fair to me, little lady.'

Hope thumped a bottle on the bar.

'Obliged to you, Hope. You're a madonna of mercy. I'll be paying you back, mind, soon as I pass by this trail agin.'

'Don't be a fool, Will. Ain't gonna be no "agin". Soon as you leave, those Apocalypse boys are going to flatten this town, and you know it. Won't leave a splinter of wood big enough for a roach's toothpick.'

'That ain't so, Hope,' Carton said, but he wasn't fooling even himself. He fixed his gaze on the bottle, so she wouldn't catch the lyin' in his eyes.

'It is too so. Ain't nobody here got the wherewithal to stand up to the brothers. Or the guts, or the skill. You're the only one could take 'em, Will Carton. The only one.'

'Maybe once upon a time, Hope. The old Will Carton. But he's deader than coffin wood seven feet under, and that's a plain fact.'

Hope's voice softened, so he could barely hear her. 'If you could just remember . . . if you could just try and remember.'

'Remember? Remember what?'

But Hope had turned away. The feather in her headband was all aquiver, and her shoulders were heaving kind of gentle, like. Carton wanted to reach out and touch her, but it wouldn't have been right. He was abandoning her, sure enough. But what did she mean? What in blue tarnation was he supposed to remember?

He slid his eyes up to the bar-room mirror. All he could see was scowling, mocking faces. Why should he be getting hisself all fired up on account of these folk? He didn't owe them nothing. Not one of them was prepared to stand by him. Correction: just one. A nine-year-old boy with more guts in his dungarees than the whole bunch of 'em put together. Well, hang 'em all. If the Apocalypse boys wanted to torch the place, let 'em have it. It wasn't Will Carton's problem, not any more.

He reached out for the bottle of hooch, but as his finger-tips touched it, there was a deafening crack and it whisked itself up in the air.

Carton span round. The liquor bottle was dangling on

the end of Jimmy's bullwhip. Carton made a grab at it, but not quick enough; Jimmy yanked it just out of reach. 'You want a drink, Sheriff? Why don't you come and take it?'

Carton looked around and saw only wicked glee on the public's faces. Suddenly, he felt tired, real tired. 'Come on, Jimmy. I got no quarrel with you. Ain't no call to be making me look foolish.'

Jimmy dangled the bottle lower. 'Jump for it, Sheriff. I just want to see you jump.'

Carton grabbed for the bottle again, and Jimmy yanked it away. He grinned at his cronies. 'Come on, now. You can git higher than that.'

Then a voice, calm and dangerous, said, 'Leave him alone.'

Every head in the bar swivelled to the saloon doors. It was the stranger who'd spoken, the steamboat dude. He stepped into the bar room slow. His two compadres rolled in behind him.

Jimmy's grin didn't flicker. Why should it? Him and his boys outnumbered the strangers three to one. 'Just having' me a little fun, Mr Swanky Pants. Ain't no call for you to go getting yourself all shot up over it.'

You couldn't really see what happened next, only figure it out afterwards. The stranger didn't seem to move, but Carton heard a thud behind him, felt a wind whistle past his cheek, and the bottle dropped neatly into his hand. He turned his head. A throwing knife was still wiggling in the bar post by his head.

Jimmy's teeth were still locked into his grin, but the rest of his face had abandoned it, and was heading south towards a scowl. Jimmy was fast. His gun actually cleared leather before a knife caught the billow of his sleeve and pinioned his shooting arm to the wall. His left hand didn't make it to the handle of his second gun. He was pinned to the wall like a rare butterfly. He looked at his splayed arms, then up at the stranger, hate burning in his eyes. He opened his mouth to curse, but the stranger stabbed his blade into a red ball on the pool table, and he flipped it clean into Jimmy's mouth so neat, it lodged there and stopped the cursing.

Jimmy looked over to his table, eyes aflame, and grunted like a bear in a trap. Three cowpokes stood up. They smiled at the stranger, but it was not an appealing smile. They didn't share a full set of teeth between them. They flexed their hands by their gun handles.

Will Carton was thinking this had been a nice show, but the strangers had better be thinking about leaving now. The knifeman was fast, maybe faster than any gunman he'd ever seen, but there was three of them facing him, and neither he nor his compadre in the ten-gallon hat were wearing a pistolero.

It was the stranger in the Mexican outfit who stepped up. The one with the mountain-lion grin. He laid a kid leather glove on the gambling man's chest, and his face was saying, 'You've had your fun, friend. Let somebody else get their amusement, now.' The gambler doffed his hat, and swept it forward like he was Sir Walter Raleigh or someone, and let the Comanchero take the stage.

He was a strange bird, this one. The three gunmen were still twitching their hands by their pistol butts, but he didn't seem in no hurry to draw against them. Instead, he produced a pair of maracas and treated 'em to a short burst of Mexican dancing, with footwork faster than a barefoot boy on a blacksmith's forge. When he was done, he flung his arms back and broadened his smile as if he was waiting for applause.

The gunmen looked at each other with amused disbelief. One of them said, 'Well, kid: I hope for your momma's sake your shootin's as fancy as your dancin'.'

But the talking was a feint, and before it was over, all three men had their hands on their guns, and for Carton it was like it was all happening in slow motion. He saw the guns clear the holsters, saw the three of them crouch and sweep their left hands over to cock back the hammers; heard the clicks. And still the Comanchero hadn't moved, and Carton was thinking that this good old boy had danced his last hat dance. And he saw the trigger fingers tighten and the hammers fall and the puffs of smoke before he heard the gun blasts. But somehow, the Comanchero had gotten both his guns out and fired off three in reply, and Carton was thinking at least the kid would take a couple of them out with him, but nobody fell, and then there was a clattering sound, like coins falling to the floor.

Then there was just smoke and silence, and everybody was waiting for someone to keel over, but that didn't happen, and how was that possible, that all six bullets could miss their mark?

And Carton was the first to realize it. The kid hadn't missed. He'd hit exactly what he was firing at.

He'd shot their bullets out of the air.

The Comanchero spun his weapons so they were just a blur, and slotted them back into the holsters like they'd never left home. He flung his head back, rapped a mean tattoo on the bar-room floor with his metal-tipped heels and stood, still as a stock on a Winchester .45, smile agleaming.

The three gunmen seemed to have lost their appetite for shooting. They didn't look at each other, didn't even bother to holster their guns. Just dropped them right there on the floor and walked out of the bar, like maybe they'd found religion, and got to thinking perhaps a farmer's life wasn't such a bad deal after all.

There was a clump as Jimmy finally managed to spit out the pool ball, but he didn't appear to feel much like talking.

The gambling stranger looked at Carton and flicked his head back towards the doors. Well, Carton figured they'd earned theirselves a parley. He gathered up his bedroll and his gun case, and clutching the bottle to his heart, walked past the moose head and out on to the sidewalk. The gambler turned to Jimmy and tugged the knives out of his sleeves. He slipped them back inside his jacket, tipped his hat and pushed his way through the doors. The Coman-chero favoured a bunch of dancing girls over by the piano with a salute, and stepped out after the others.

The hombre in the ten-gallon turned to follow, but a big cowboy who looked like he turned a living strangling bears stood up and blocked his way. Jimmy stepped up beside him. 'Your compadres seem plenty handy with their hard-ware. What about you, Tex?'

Ten Gallon had a curious accent. Boston, maybe, or some-place east. 'I don't carry weapons,' he said. 'And my name's not Tex, actually.'

The bear strangler let his gold tooth show. Jimmy wrinkled his nose. 'Well now, *Tex*. Wonder if you could settle a little *dis*pute for me and my friends here.' Five cowboys scrawped back their chairs and formed a rough circle around the stranger whose name wasn't Tex.

'To be brutally frank, I'm in rather a hurry. Some other time, if it's all the same to you.' Ten Gallon moved to walk by, but the bear strangler shoved him back.

'Won't take but a minute of your time, Tex,' Jimmy said.

Out on the sidewalk, Carton saw that the stranger was in trouble. The gambler caught his look and said, simply, 'He can take care of himself,' and carried on crossing the street. Carton stayed. Figured this ought to be worth watching.

Ten Gallon rolled his eyes. 'All right then, gents. What's the dispute?'

'Well, it's a kind of a musical dispute. Dispute is: when Bear Strangler here rips your little pecker off, are you gonna hit top A with your scream, or will you go all the way to top C?'

Ten Gallon looked down at the floor. He brushed some dust from his chaps. 'Well, indeedy. That is an intriguing conundrum. One that may very well tax to the absolute limits the brain power of a bunch of cretinous, foul-breathed inbreeds like yourselves, whose mothers were romantically linked to diseased bullocks.'

The bear strangler frowned. Jimmy's voice turned nasty, like. 'Now friend, you wouldn't be goin' around insulting our mommas, would you? Only, a feller could get hisself right dead doin' a thing like that.'

The stranger beamed at him brightly. 'Perhaps I can make it a little less obscure for you. Your mothers,' and he pointed to all six of the cowboys in the circle, 'each and every one of them, shagged pigs so frequently, their underpants smelled like smoky bacon.'

The cowboys didn't move for him right then. Just stared in disbelief, like it wasn't possible he could be saying what he was saying.

'Furthermore,' he went on, 'your mothers were so peculiarly ugly and undesirable, the pigs had to be blindfolded before they could achieve an erection.'

With a foaming roar, the bear strangler lunged. Ten Gallon stepped aside lightly and cocked his foot, spinning the screaming giant around the axis of his own belly, and then chopped at his neck on the way past, decking the big man out cold. He dipped his shoulder all nimble so that the chair in the hands of the cowpoke behind him just wafted past his ear, planted his elbow in the cowpoke's stretched belly, expelling all the air from his lungs and the fight from his spirit, and then snapped the arm back, flattening his nose like a cow-pat.

Another cowboy grabbed the neck of a bottle and lurched forward, growling.

Ten Gallon didn't even seem to heed the bottle; just struck a boxing stance and dealt a fast flurry of punches to the bottle-waver's face, so quick it was hard to keep count. While the man was staggering, his head still jerking back and forth rhythmically as if it had developed the habit, the stranger inserted his fore and middle fingers up into the stunned man's nostrils and swept him over his head so he crashed into a card-table and lay softly moaning among the splintered wood, the playing cards and the gambling chips.

Jimmy and the two remaining cowboys were holding back. 'OK, boys,' Jimmy said, keeping his eyes on the stranger. 'Let's take him all at once.' But before they could rush him, Ten Gallon turned his back to them, grabbed the backrest of the chair and kicked his legs up behind him, one, two, like some fancy ballet step, rolling his spurs up the middle of the centre cowboy. The first set of spurs split his pants and shirt wide open, the second carved a deep, neat dotted line up his body, from groin to forehead.

The stranger wheeled round. He hadn't even broken sweat. He'd flattened four men in a little under fifteen seconds. Nobody, as yet, had actually managed to touch him. Jimmy and his remaining crony weighed up the odds, and two to one didn't seem worth the wager, so they backed off, nice and easy, like, palms upturned.

Ten Gallon stepped out of the bar, dusting his hands needlessly. He beamed at the astonished Will Carton. 'Marvellous,' he said, brightly, and they walked together over to the jailhouse.

When they got there, the Comanchero was sitting on Carton's chair, boots on his desk, sombrero pulled over his eyes. The gambler was looking through Carton's drawers. Carton didn't mind much. He'd taken everything he valued, and, in any case, it couldn't be said to be his office any more. He flopped into the remaining chair and pushed back his stetson. 'Well, boys,' he said, 'you sure learnt them varmints. Be a fragrant day on a skunk farm 'fore Jimmy and his critters bother me again.'

Ten Gallon turned to the gambler, eyebrows akimbo in exasperation. 'Why is he talking like that? He's really beginning to get on my B Cups.'

The gambler said, 'You still don't remember us?'

Carton unplugged his bottle and took a libation. 'Like

I say. Your features mind me of someone, but I'm danged if I can place 'em.'

'My name's Lister,' the gambler said.

'Lester?'

'Lister. Dave Lister.'

Carton hoisted the bottle. 'Mighty pleased to be acquainted with you.' He sucked a toast.

'Doesn't that name ring a bell?'

Carton thought about it. 'Seems to me I did know a Lister once. But it was a long time ago. Like in another life I only dreamt about.' He scoured the wasteland of his memory, but there was nothing meaningful he could find. Just a hazy, blurred recollection of a name. He slapped his thigh and stood. 'Well, it's been mighty dandy meeting you boys, but I have to be hauling my sorry hide out of here 'bout now. I got to be gone by high midnight, or else the buzzards'll be fightin' the lizards for my gizzards.' He stuffed the cork back in the bottle, gathered up his belongings and strode to the doors. He turned and nodded. 'Adios.'

The one who called himself Lister said, 'We can't let you leave town.'

Carton sized them up. Against the three of them he stood less chance than a snake on a mink farm. He edged a small step nearer the doors. 'And why would that be, friend?'

'If you leave, you're dead.'

Carton stood still, but his eyes were moving plenty. 'How does that figure?'

Lister wiped his hands over his face. 'Look, it's going to be hard for you to swallow this. Why don't you sit down and listen?'

Carton hesitated. 'OK,' he nodded, 'but just five minutes, no more.' He moved as if to head back inside, and then jerked his head up so he was looking over Lister's head. Quiet, like, he said, 'Now I don't want to concern you boys overly, but a rattler just crawled in through the window bars behind you. Don't move a nostril hair.'

They froze, like he expected, and in the millisecond when their eyes all flicked back to look for the snake, he was out of the doors and tearing down the street towards the dangling sign that told passers-through they were now leaving Existence.

The newcomers burst out on to the sidewalk. Ten Gallon started chasing after him, but Carton had a fine start. Lister said, 'He's not going to catch him.'

The Comanchero stepped into the street. He drew out his pistol, crooking his left arm to rest the gun on and steady his aim.

'Now!' Lister shouted, 'You've got to stop him!'

The Comanchero seemed to be aiming at the hardware store.

'What are you doing, man? He's over there! He gets past that sign, he's gone!'

The Comanchero squeezed off a shot. It pinged off a bathtub hanging outside the store, zigged across the street and hit the barber-shop pole, zagged over and snicked the stirrup of a tethered horse, and then ricocheted over to the dangling town sign, severing the rope it was suspended from. The sign plummeted earthwards, thumping the running sheriff plum on the head. Carton pitched forward and lay still as a rooster who's just serviced his harem.

The Comanchero blew off the smoke and flipped his gun back home.

Ten Gallon gathered up the senseless Carton, hucked him over his shoulders like a deer carcass and brought him back to the jailhouse.

The next thing Carton knew about he was drowning under some immense wave. He shook himself alert, just in time to take another jugful straight in the face. His hands went up to protect himself. 'Boys! Boys!' he spluttered, 'that's unnecessary cruel.'

The Comanchero was smiling. 'Tell you the truth, buddy, you could do with another gallon or twelve. I don't know if you've noticed, but you're smelling a little ripe.' And he treated Carton to another jug.

'Dang it!' Carton coughed. 'I had me a perfectly good bath straight after Gettysberg.'

Lister held his splayed hand up to Carton's face. 'How many fingers?'

Carton stared at them until they swayed into focus. 'More than three,' he announced, confidently.

'What d'you mean "More than three"?'

'I ain't no 'rithmetical genius, friend. But I can count to three, good as the next feller.'

This news of his lack of numerical nimbleness seemed to cause a goodly amount of consternation for Lister and his compadres. Their eyebrows all did a furry-worm hurdle race. Struck Carton, when he came to mind it, that his counting skills had declined some. It didn't much bother him, but he figured only that morning he could have counted a whole handful of fingers, and then some.

The three strangers withdrew to a corner and took a hunched confabulation. Carton, meanwhile, searched out his bottle. He espied it on his desk, sitting all temptation-like on top of his gun case. He tried reaching for it, but found he couldn't stand without the chair went with him. He looked down at his waist. Those mother-sucking prairie dogs had strung him to the seat.

Undaunted he tipped hisself forward and slouched over to the desk like a drunken L shape. He grabbed the bottle, popped the cork out with his thumbs and raised the neck to his lips.

The bottle exploded, showering Carton with glass and foul liquor. This wasn't exactly your vintage moonshine; it hissed and sizzled on the bare wood floors of the jailhouse. Even though he hadn't seen the play, Carton reckoned it must have been the Comanchero shot the bottle, on account of one of his holstered pistoleros was giving off a faint whiff of smoke.

The strangers broke out of their huddle. The one who called himself Lister said, 'No more of that stuff.'

Carton rolled his tongue over the liquor that was dribbling down his face. Just his luck to get hisself holed up with a bunch of fun busters from the League of Temperance. 'What next, padre? You preach me all about hellfire and we sing thirteen choruses of "Shall We Gather by the River"?'

Then the Lister feller used Carton's moniker, only he got it wrong and kind of fouled-up like. 'Kryten,' he said, 'You've really got to start listening. If you don't pull yourself together and shape up to beat the Apocalypse boys when they come in at midnight, not only do you die . . .' he nodded at his two companions '. . . me, Cat and Rimmer die with you.'

EIGHT

They flocked into the cockpit and took up their stations.

'Nothing.' The Cat jabbed at the pilot controls. 'Total lock-out. Face it, buds, we're deader than dungarees with patterned triangles sewn down the side to make 'em look like flares.'

'I'm getting nothing, either.' Lister swivelled in his chair to face Rimmer. 'How long before we hit trouble?'

'Well,' Rimmer ran his eyes over the long-range scan, 'if you define "trouble" as a rather large planet directly in our path, about seventeen hours.'

Lister thumped his head against the fascia. To have come so close to regaining *Red Dwarf*, only to be cheated by the beaten agonoid's insane dying gesture. He heard a click, and looked round, Kryten had opened up a panel in his chest and was tugging out a lead. 'What are you doing, Kryten?'

Kryten dragged out the lead and held the connector over the NaviComp's interface socket. 'The only remotely feasible solution is for me to contract the virus myself, analyse its structure and attempt to create a software antidote before it wipes out my core program. Do I have your permission to sacrifice myself, sirs?'

Rimmer's eyebrows skipped to his hairline. 'Do lemmings like cliffs? Granted.'

Kryten plugged himself into the NaviComp. 'I'm going to have to design a dove program, so called because it spreads peace through the system, obliterating the viral cells as it goes.'

He stiffened as the virus hit him. 'The virus is extremely complex . . . Must devote all my run time to the solution . . . Shutting down all non-essential systems . . .'

Rimmer crouched beside him as his consciousness started slipping away. 'Can we help? Is there something we can do?'

Kryten turned his head towards him. 'You can watch my dreams,' he said.

Then his eyes rolled back and he slumped to the deck.

NINE

Carton's mouth wiggled and curled like a snake sliding down the intestinal tract of a mongoose with gut rot, as he crunched away at yet another mouthful of bitter raw coffee beans. He pushed the bowl away. 'I can't eat anymore of this dung-beetle filth, boys.'

Lister sat on the edge of the sheriff's desk and pushed the bowl back at him. 'Just two more bowls.'

'No more, please. I'm sober, honest.'

'So tell me who you are.'

'It's like you say. I'm not a human, I'm some kind of mechanical feller, who's fighting this virus, and none of this really exists, it's some kind of fever dream, 'cept for you guys, who *do* exist, only you're not really here, you're really on some flyin' space ship up in the stars, 'bout three gazillion years in the future.' He fixed Lister with a companionable smile, and hoped he sounded convinced enough to get the madman to leave him alone.

Lister just nodded. 'More coffee.'

Carton slammed his forehead on the desk and scooped up another handful. 'Just tell me one thing, friend. You honestly believe that yarn you're spoolin'?'

Lister stood. 'It'll make sense to you when you're sober.' He crossed over to the doors and pushed his way out into the street.

Carton called after him. 'Hell, if that's got to make sense, I don't want to *be* sober.'

Out on the sidewalk, the Cat was dangling one leg lazily over the side of a swinging bench, tooting gently on a harmonica, his sombrero pulled over his eyes. Rimmer was standing, scanning the street, leaning his hands against the horse rail. He didn't ease up on his vigil when he heard Lister come out. 'Any luck?'

'I dunno. None of it seemed to sink in. Maybe he's too far gone.'

'And where does that leave us?'

'Down Crap Creek, Rimmer. Without a paddle or a smegging boat.' Lister looked down and scuffed at a knot in the sidewalk with the toe of his boot. It had been Lister who'd worked out the meaning of Kryten's cryptic last words: they simply had to plug him into the Artificial Reality unit, and literally watch his dreams on screen. For reasons known only to the mechanoid, his subconscious was interpreting his struggle against the virus as a Western.

And it looked like he was losing that struggle.

So Lister had suggested they entered his dreamstate, using the A/R unit themselves. He and the Cat had used the two suits, and they'd plugged Rimmer directly in, via his light bee. They couldn't enter the dream merely as themselves – they'd had to adopt characters from an A/R Western game. Brett Riverboat, the Riviera Kid and Big Dan McGrew: knife expert, sharpshooter and barefist fighter.

Rimmer turned to him, shielding his eyes against the blistering light. 'How long before the showdown?'

'There's no way of telling. Have you seen his pocket watch? There's no hands on it. I s'pose the passage of time's linked to the progress of the virus, in some way. We're probably fairly safe so long as the sun's up.'

As he spoke, the scorching sun dipped with indecent haste towards the horizon, and became a fierce orange glare peeking over the mountains like a showgirl dressing behind a changing screen.

'Oh dear,' Rimmer said. 'Deep smeg.'

The Cat stopped sucking the harmonica and straight-ened. 'OK, buds. Why don't we go out and take on these Apocalypse dudes ourselves? What do we need old hooch head for anyway?'

Rimmer rolled back his eyes. 'They're not *real*, pus brain. They're a metaphor.'

'Metaphor, shmetaphor.' The Cat span his guns and flipped them back. 'They bleed, don't they?'

'We can't beat the virus,' Lister said. 'Only Kryten can do that. The most we can do is help him. And if you want to know the truth, I'm not even sure we can do that.' He shoved the jailhouse doors open and strode back inside.

'Thank you,' Rimmer said, 'but I really didn't want to know the truth.'

Carton was thinking. He was thinking the strangers' story sounded like hogwash, sure enough, but there was some pretty strange things going on around Existence, Arizona, when you reflected on it proper. For one thing, his memory wasn't all it should be, sure as skunks stink. When the Lister *hombre* had fired all those queries at him, like who his Pappy was, and his Momma, where he'd come from and all, his mind had been an out-and-out blank. Couldn't seem to recollect a single thing that had happened before sun up, matter of fact. And Hope had been urging him to remember something, only he couldn't recall what he was supposed to remember, and that made remembering plenty hard. And then there was his shooting irons. Guns without chambers in the cylinders . . .

He dragged the gun case over and flipped it open.

Guns without chambers in the cylinders . . .

'What are those?' Lister walked up to the desk.

'Them's my fancy shooting irons, friend.'

Lister picked up one of the magnificent weapons and turned it over in his hand. 'Pretty special. What do you use them for?'

'That's the dangdest thing,' Carton split the gun open. 'Can't see how they'd be much use for anything. No place for no bullets to go.'

But it was the handle that drew Lister's attention. Inlaid into the smooth black pearl of the butt was a white design. A bird. He offered the gun to Carton. 'What's this?'

Carton examined the handle. 'Figure that's a dove, friend.'

This got Lister all excited. 'This is it! You're supposed to be working on what you called a dove program. Dove! These guns are the key, somehow.'

'Start talking sense, friend. These guns ain't no more use than a lawyer at a lynching.'

'The answer's in them somewhere. Maybe you need to finish them. Or maybe they don't need bullets at all. You've got to concentrate. Think!'

Suddenly, Carton's eyes flicked wide, and then he doubled up like he'd taken a bullet in the bread basket.

Lister vaulted over the desk and crouched beside him. 'What is it? What's up?'

'I . . . I ain't rightly certain.' Carton clutched his stomach. 'My guts feel like I just swallowed a barrel of snakes.'

Outside, the Cat stopped tootling on the mouth organ and straightened on the bench. He wrinkled his nose and said, 'Trouble.'

Then Rimmer caught the sound of hoof beats and turned to see the cloud of dust swelling at the far end of the town. He slipped over to the doors, looked inside and nodded for Lister to come out.

A lone rider was galloping towards them. With an involuntary shiver, Lister recognized the blood-red mare of War Apocalypse.

Over the thunder of hooves, the rider let out a demonic 'Yee-haw', his teeth glinting fire in the setting sun. Carton staggered to the door and gasped, 'The bank . . . He's gonna 'splode up the bank . . .'

Crouching low in his saddle, War tugged a bundle of sticks from his bag. His horse snorted flame, and he bent forward to light up a fuse wire that sprang out of the bundle.

Lister yelled 'Cat!' as War rose up in his stirrups and hurled the fizzing dynamite towards the bank.

The Cat's first shot hit the dynamite at the top of its arc, sending the deadly bundle spinning up in the air. War yanked hard on his reins, dragging a skull-splitting whinny from his horse as it skidded to a halt.

The dynamite started to drop, and the Cat squeezed off another bullet, launching it skywards again. He didn't need a third shot.

The bundle exploded mightily, sucking dust up from the street and sending a hot, sulphur hurricane roaring through the town.

As the thumping echoes of the blast died away, Lister squinted through the blistering wind into the dust cloud. War sat stock-still in his saddle, looking venom at the group clustered on the jailhouse porch. Then he curled his lip in a dangerous smile, grabbed his reins and whipped his mount. The horse reared up screaming, its front legs punching at the air, and galloped off into the fog of the dust.

Rimmer shuddered. He'd seen War's wicked smile, too, and could have lived without it, thank you. He turned to Lister, holding his hat to his head against the wind and shouted, 'What was all that about?'

Lister shrugged. 'I dunno, exactly. But I reckon this town, the people and the buildings, probably represent some part of Kryten's functions. The bank could be his memory, or maybe his mathematical operations. Whatever it is, the virus was trying to wipe it out.'

'Well, that's good news then. We stopped it.'

'Yeah,' Lister wiped dust from his eyes. 'It's good and it's bad. Now we know we can help slow the spread of the virus. But the virus knows there's a new game in town, and I didn't much like the look that dude shot us.'

'They'll be back, sure enough,' Carton said, and stepped back into his office.

Lister watched him go. 'We can hamper the virus, but Kryten's the only one who can wipe it out for good. We should probably set up some kind of patrol, keep an eye out for sneak attacks, while one of us stays here and tries to help Kryten come to his senses.'

Immediately, Rimmer said, 'I'll stay.'

The Cat sneered. 'What's the problem, Frisbee nostrils? There's no need to be a coward in here; you can't get hurt.'

'You're right,' Rimmer nodded. 'Sorry. Habit. You stay, Listy. Me and my compadre here will keep the township safe. Worry ye not.' He rubbed his hands, tucked his thumbs under his belt and John Wayned down on to the street. The Cat closed his eyes, shook his head and stepped down after him.

The street was deserted, but there were faces in almost every window. They strolled past the saloon, and Rimmer caught sight of a particularly ugly visage staring out at him, sporting an unusually wide lopsided leer. He nudged the Cat. 'Who the smeg's that? Gurning champion of the century?'

The Cat looked over. 'That's not a face, dog breath. That's somebody's ass.'

Rimmer squinted. It was true. One of Jimmy's cronies was mooning them. Infuriated, Rimmer turned and headed for the saloon. The Cat caught his arm. 'We're not looking for trouble,' he said.

'Right, you're right.' Rimmer tensed his jaw, then fell back in step with the Cat. 'You're absolutely right. We're not looking for Trouble. But if Trouble comes, it's going to regret the day Mr and Mrs Trouble decided to have it off.' He allowed himself a little chuckle. It was fun, this macho lark, once you got the hang of it.

Somewhere off to their right, a brass band started up a slow dirge. Round from the back of Peter Pessimism's

Undertaker's Parlour, a funeral procession slow-marched on to the street and dragged its sad way towards them.

The Cat and Rimmer stopped to let the cortège go by. When the black-plumed horses hauled the hearse level, Rimmer could make out the sorry, cheap coffin, and the inscription on the hastily chiselled tombstone resting above it. It read: 'Here lies Cecil Central Processing Unit, plum dead.' He turned to the Cat and said, somewhat superfluously: 'I don't like the look of this one bit.'

Then, above the relentless pounding of the bass drum, there was a knocking. Rimmer had a horrible feeling it was coming from inside the coffin.

There was more knocking, and this time Rimmer saw the coffin lid rattle with each thump. He exchanged looks with the Cat, and then scooted to the front of the procession and held up his arms. 'All right, everyone, just hold it right there.' The band stopped marching and the music wound down discordantly. The undertaker reined in the horses, and the small troop of black-clad mourners stopped weeping.

The quiet that followed was broken by a small, muffled plea from inside the coffin. 'Let me out, please.' Not insistent, just kind of weary and plaintive.

Rimmer looked up at the sallow-faced, frock-coated undertaker with distaste. 'What are you doing, man? This chap's not dead.'

The undertaker looked down at Rimmer from under his top hat, and said, dispassionately, 'That's your opinion, friend. I got orders to bury him, and bury him I will.'

'You can't bury the poor bastard, he's alive.'

'Says you.'

'All right then.' Rimmer leapt up on to the hearse and tapped on the coffin lid. 'Excuse me,' he called, 'Are you alive, or what?'

From inside, the small voice said: 'I surely am. I ain't even sickly.'

Rimmer turned to the undertaker. 'Well, according to him, he's alive.'

The undertaker seemed unimpressed. 'Listen, friend. I ain't no medical expert, you ain't no medical expert and that there corpse ain't no medical expert neither. The doc pronounced the feller dead, and far as I'm concerned, that's plenty good enough for me.'

'Well, without wishing to disparage the undoubtedly magnificent skills of the local quack, I'd say there was sufficient doubt to warrant a second opinion. Might I be so bold as to suggest we sequester the services of another doctor? Possibly one blessed with the gift of eyesight, perhaps?'

'Someone castin' aspersions on my abilities?' A man pushed through the crowd. He swatted at a crowd of insects buzzing away at his head, and grinned a black-toothed leer that sat awkwardly among the angry pustules on his scab-ridden face.

Rimmer cocked an eyebrow. 'Pestilence?'

Pestilence acknowledged his name with a nod. 'Old Doc Diagnostics went down with acute bullet poisonin', rest his soul. Now I'm the medical examiner round these parts.'

'I see.' Rimmer jumped off the hearse. 'Well, let me put it like this: anyone who wishes to bury this gentleman is going to have to come through me. And that includes any pox-rotted retards with terminal syphilis.'

Pestilence's leer broadened. 'Well, I reckon I can accommodate you in that respect.' He turned and strode towards the sidewalk, wrapped his arms around the thick wooden strut that held up the overhang and with a single grunt tugged it free. The roof splintering and collapsing behind him, he turned and brandished the strut, two-handed. 'I'm gonna send your teeth so far south, you're gonna be flossing through your butt-hole.'

Rimmer smiled, easy like, 'Well, my disease-brained friend, that should make it all the more pleasant for you to kiss it. And kiss it you will.' He parted the crowd and crossed over to the horse rail. He spat on his hands, wrapped them round the rail, said, 'Pucker up,' and pulled.

And nothing happened.

Rimmer wrinkled his brow, straightened, flexed his muscles and bent to the rail again. And pulled.

And nothing happened.

Disgorging a primal yell, he redoubled his efforts, straining up and up, his neck bones jutting out like the struts on a whalebone corset. His face reddened, then purpled, then turned marble white. With a final hissing grunt, like a steam train pulling into a station, he flopped limply over the rail, arms dangling, lungs scorched and pumping for air.

The horse rail hadn't budged a single millimetre.

'When you's done with all your squealin' and strainin', friend,' Pestilence grinned, 'I believe I have an open invitation to beat your stinkin' brains out.'

Rimmer looked over to the Cat and rasped, 'What the smeg is going on?'

'Don't look at me, buddy,' he said, delight illuminating his features. 'You're the one who promised to make this handsome dude French kiss your butt-hole.'

Pestilence advanced.

Rimmer backed away. 'For smeg's sake, shoot him,' he squealed.

The Cat took out his harmonica and started to play.

Rimmer's voice hit the falsetto range: 'Shoot the ugly goitre-faced gimboid! Shoot him! Now!'

Reluctantly, the Cat decided Rimmer had suffered enough, and dropped his hand to his pistol, aiming to put six shots through the wooden strut, severing it at just the right angle to collapse back on to Pestilence's head and plant him out cold.

Only it didn't exactly work out like that.

What happened, exactly, was the gun went off while it

was still in its holster, drilling a neat hole through the centre of the Cat's boot. He froze, his eyes wide, staring in disbelief at the street through his foot, then threw his head back and yowled like a B-movie wolfman.

'Oh smeggy pudding,' Rimmer chittered, 'we've lost our special skills.'

The Cat grabbed his wounded foot and started hopping and howling.

Pestilence came on, relentlessly. 'Your compadre don't dance so fancy no more,' he giggled.

Rimmer kept on backing away, holding out the palms of his hands, his eyes flitting from his menacer to the Cat and back again. 'Does it hurt?' he screeched dry-mouthed, hoping against hope that the Cat was wailing because his footwear had been ruined.

'No!' the Cat yelled. 'It's fun! I'm having a good time.' He tumbled on to his back and started thrashing around in the dirt, thick spurts of blood geysering over his hands through the sole of his boot.

Rimmer's brain was screaming. This was an electronic reality. They shouldn't be able to feel pain. What in the name of the merciless nothing that spawned the universe had gone wrong? Then it hit him with a jolt: *the virus had spread to the Artificial Reality unit!*

He glanced behind him: he was fast running out of retreating space. All things considered, now would be a most propitious time to leave. He called out to the struggling Cat. 'Time to go! Clap, clap!' He clapped his hands together.

And absolutely nothing happened.

He clapped again.

And still he was stuck in Kryten's fever nightmare. Still his rot-faced tormentor was bearing down on him with murderous intent. He looked over at the Cat, who had temporarily released his wounded foot and was clapping with the dedicated fury of an audience at a special all-nude version of a Lily Langtree revue.

The virus had sealed them in.

Rimmer had only two options: make a stand and slug it out with this maniacal demon from hell, or plead and beg for mercy like a quivering, spineless jellyfish.

Rimmer daringly plumped for mimicking a marine coelenterate of the class *Schyphozoa*. From deep down inside himself, he dredged up his most winning smile. 'Uh, Mr Pestilence, sir, it would appear that, due to circumstances completely beyond my control, there's been a bit of a cock-up in the bravado department. I may have come across as being slightly more brave than I, in fact, am.'

Pestilence swung the strut. Rimmer leapt backwards, barely getting out of the arc of the swing in time. He staggered, regained his balance and was retreating again before Pestilence had the chance to raise the weapon back to his shoulder.

'Now I may have given the impression that I held you in low esteem, particularly in regard to some rather thought-less remarks I passed in relation to various features of your appearance, which were not only childish and peevish, but also highly inaccurate, and which, on mature reflection, I utterly withdraw. I ask you now, in the spirit of brotherly harmony and world peace . . .'

'Shut your sissy bitchin', you worthless son of a filthy whore,' Pestilence said.

'Fair enough,' Rimmer said, and Pestilence brought the strut swinging down on to his left shoulder.

There was a thump and a sickening snap of bones. Rimmer tried to black out before the pain hit him, but he didn't make it. The faces of the onlookers loomed and waned in his eyes. He sagged to his knees. He twisted his flopping head and drove his blurry vision over to the struggling Cat. Step by satisfied step, Pestilence was advancing on him. Rimmer tried to persuade the screaming in his shoulder to shut the smeg up, but it kept on screeching, and through the throbbing swelling his eyesight had become he watched the huge wooden strut rise up over the struggling Cat and fall, and saw the Cat lay still.

Rimmer pitched head forward into a pile of dung thoughtfully dropped for him by the funeral horses.

Then everything went blissfully black.

TEN

Lister stared at the blood on his hand like it was a Rorschach ink-blot test. Pulsing thickly through the small nick on his palm, it spread slowly, becoming a butterfly, then a bat, then a huge ugly dragon, its head reared, its wings spread.

He slipped a cream kerchief from the breast pocket of his tailored jacket and mopped up the dragon. He was thinking how oddly unfamiliar his hand looked to him, and how strangely inept the expression 'to know something like the back of your hand' was. He doubted he could pick out the back of his hand in a police line-up if it had stolen his cattle and burnt down his ranch.

Lister tugged the kerchief in a tourniquet to stem the blood flow. He shouldn't really have been thinking about hands. What he should have been thinking about was why he'd cut himself at all. He'd been whittling away at a chunk of wood, carving a fairly elaborate rendition of Venus on the half shell, when his knife had slipped and sliced into the soft skin of his palm. And if he'd been thinking what he should have been thinking, he'd have been thinking that shouldn't have happened. In this electronic reality, he was supposed to be perfect with knives. Impeccable.

If he'd been thinking that thought, it could have saved him a lot of pain. A lot of pain.

He flicked his eyes over to Kryten, who was bent over his dove guns, trying to make sense of the senselessness of them.

Outside, the sound of the funeral procession started up again. Lister had no idea why it had stopped in the first place. He'd toyed with the idea of stepping out to investigate, but reasoned that Rimmer and the Cat could probably handle anything that came at them, and he'd decided against leaving Kryten alone.

He set down the unfinished, blood-stained sculpture on the desk and stretched. 'Getting anywhere?' he asked. Kryten didn't even hear him. Good. At least he was concentrating. Lister prodded around the office, in case there was anything, just some small thing, that might help the cause.

He flicked his forefinger abstractedly over the wanted posters on the notice-board, tooting a tuneless song in a kind of quiet half-whistle. Finding nothing of interest, he strolled into the jail cell.

The jail section was about twelve feet square, split by bars, so that the cells took up about two thirds of the room, enough to accommodate a dozen or so desperadoes, so long as nobody cared to lie down. The rest of the room was a corridor. There was an old wooden rocker, a rack of rifles, and something Lister hadn't seen before: a stand-alone closet. Where had it come from? He tried the handle. Locked.

'Have you got a key to this thing?' he called, but if Kryten heard him, he didn't reply. Lister looked around. There was an enormous bunch of keys dangling from a hook on the wall. He took the bunch down, and quickly flipped through the dozens of keys, but couldn't find one that looked as if it might fit.

He shrugged, sighed, raised his spurred boot and kicked through the closet door panel.

A huge shard of freshly bared wood slashed a gully of flesh six inches up his shin. He stared down at the wound in astonished disbelief and saw the whiteness of his exposed shinbone suddenly flush deep red as the pain blossomed to its exquisite fullness; then he launched into the babbled litany of expletives he reserved exclusively for cursing his own clumsiness.

'Stupid smegging farty stupid shitty shit shit smeg fart poo shit . . .'

And again, he failed to make the essential connection: that in this reality, he should not have been able to feel pain.

He hopped to the rocker, carrying his wounded leg stiffly, so that every time he landed it brought a fresh burst of pain, which he accompanied with his mindless cant. He flopped down in the chair and squeezed its arms till his knuckles went white, though how this was supposed to help the pain he had no idea. Eventually, the pain did subside to a pulsing throb, and Lister managed to bring himself to look down at the leg again. His pinstriped trousers were split neatly up his left leg, from the top of his boot to just below the knee. The blood was just beginning to coagulate. With luck, he'd only need four or five stitches. He closed his eyes and clutched his thigh.

Then his eyes blinked open again. On the periphery of his vision, he glimpsed the closet. The shattered door had swung open, and inside was a magnificent suit of clothes. Gleaming, unreal white, it was a fantasy gunslinger's outfit. Dangling from a hook, there was a gun belt, the metal buckle burnished blinding bronze in the shape of a dove.

Lister stood and walked over to the closet, barely noticing his dragging right leg. Kryten stepped into the room. 'Are you OK, friend?'

'What are these threads for, man?'

'Them? Them's my fancy gunslinging duds, partner. Ain't seen 'em in a mule's age.'

'Check out the gun belt.'

Kryten reached in and took out the belt. 'Fine piece of leather work, no question.'

'The bullets! Look at the bullets!'

But before Kryten could comply, they heard the creak of the office doors and a heavy footfall on the naked boards. Kryten turned to the office, but Lister laid a hand on his shoulder and nodded towards the back of the cell corridor. Kryten stepped aside. Lister ran his fingers over his jacket to check his arsenal of throwing knives, and, trying his damnedest to pass his limp off as a macho swagger, he Lee Van Cleefed into the sheriff's office.

It was the fat Apocalypse boy, Famine. He'd parked his double-dirigible-sized ass on the sheriff's chair and slung his tapered legs on the desk. The chair was creaking fit to bust apart.

His greasy fingers were toying with Kryten's shooting irons.

Lister twitched his chin and set his face in a don't-screw-with-me sneer. 'I'm thinking maybe you'd like to put those guns down, friend.'

Famine looked up at him and smiled an oily smile. Dried spittle and chicken fat glistened on the pork of his chin. 'Well, now. If'n I'm figurin' this rightly, you don't got no call barkin' orders at the newly appointed sheriff of this burgh in his own jailhouse.' He wiped a sticky mitt over the badge on his breast, and grinned big enough for Lister to itemize every component of his last four meals from the gristle and gunk lodged between his teeth.

Despite the gnawing in his leg, Lister was actually enjoying this little scenario. 'Is that a fact? Now, tell me. Who in their right mind would appoint an obnoxious tub of stinking lardy effluence as sheriff?'

'I was duly elected, Hopalong, by an overwhelming majority of one. Me.'

'Well, much as I respect the democratic process, flab face, I'm here to tell you: you just got unelected. So why don't you just squelch yourself into a huge ball and roll out of here like the pink, soggy blob you are?'

Famine replied with a huge bellowing fart.

'When you say that . . .' Lister kept his face impassive '. . . smile.'

The fat boy smiled, and ripped off another one.

Lister half-turned his face in disgust, and that was all the leeway Famine needed to make his move. With a speed Lister couldn't have predicted in one so porcine, his chubby fingers dropped to the handle of his gun. With his legs on the desk, he wouldn't even have to clear his holster to squeeze off a shot.

Lister slid his hand inside his jacket to grab a knife and hurl it in the same move, but his movements seemed strangely sluggish and inept. Still, he was obviously faster than the Apocalypse boy, because there was no gunshot before his hand cleared the jacket and he threw.

Something wet and harmless plopped against Famine's forehead, and slid down his face, leaving a thin red trail down his features.

Lister looked at his hand. His right forefinger was missing. He held the hand up, incredulous as it pumped its little bloody geyser spasmodically.

He looked over at Famine, who looked like he was laughing, but Lister must have been in shock, because he heard nothing. Famine dipped into the top of his waistcoat and pulled Lister's finger out of his fatty cleavage. He held it up for Lister to see, then popped it in his mouth. Lister's hearing must have returned, because he could definitely make out the obscene crunch as Famine chewed on his severed digit.

Famine belched and slapped his quintuple-deckered belly with both hands. 'Fine appetizer, friend.' He stood, and the chair splintered and collapsed behind him. 'I'll be coming back later for the main course.'

Still in shock, Lister didn't move as the blancmange mountain wobbled towards him, arms held out as if to hug.

He was suddenly aware of being surrounded by the sweaty stench of Famine's body. He felt his legs leave the floor and then blinding pressure all over his torso as Famine enveloped him and squeezed. He heard sounds like bulbs popping. The fat man crushed him as, one by one, each and every rib in Lister's body cracked. Then he was tumbling to the floor, every part of him bellowing with agony. He hit the floorboard, doubling his pain, and bounced, redoubling it. He looked up to see Famine tip his hat, hitch up his denims and push through the double doors out on to the street.

He must have slid momentarily out of consciousness, because the next thing he knew, Kryten was by his side, examining his injuries. 'Looks like you got banged up pretty good, friend. You got more broke in you than a bankrupt's prison.'

Lister snorted a laugh, and almost killed himself.

'Easy, friend. Yes sir. Good and proper damaged. You ain't gonna be bustin' no broncos in quite an age.'

In fact, there were only three discernible bits of Lister that didn't hurt: his nose, his left leg and his penis.

He was just thanking heaven for small mercies, when there was the tremor of hoof beats, so loud they rattled the floorboards of the jail, each thud squeezing new pain from Lister's racked body. Kryten stood and crossed to the doorway. Before he reached it, the opaque office window shattered, blasting the office with glass and debris, followed immediately by two bodies. The Cat landed on Lister's face, crushing his nose, and Rimmer thumped down on Lister's left leg, snapping it cleanly.

When the Cat rolled off his face, Lister saw, with an almost amused detachment, that a huge shard of glass was jutting out of his pinstriped groin. He thought, 'Well, gambling man, you've got yourself a full house,' and giggled insanely.

The giggle brought the sharp edge of a snapped rib brushing against his lung, and the pain drove him out of consciousness.

ELEVEN

The Cat was staring into a broken hand mirror, barely able to believe what he was seeing. 'Hot damn!' he said, for the eighth or ninth time. His face was flat. His nose had been squashed squat against his cheek, as if someone had swatted a huge ugly death's head moth and left its corpse rotting on his face. He turned the hand mirror over, again, just to check once more that it wasn't some kind of optical illusion trickery, and then flipped it back to study the horror again. 'Hot damn!' he said, for the ninth or tenth time.

'For God's sake!' Rimmer squealed, 'Must you go on and on about it?' He swivelled round, so he faced the Cat. He couldn't move his neck, because it was secured in a plaster cast, along with his shoulder and most of his arm. His head was tilted at an odd angle, so what he saw of the world came at him sideways. 'We've all been injured you know. You don't hear the rest of us bleating about it.'

'I ain't talking about *injured*, buddy. I'm talking about *ugly*. Look at me. At least you have to *turn* to see your profile in a mirror. I can see mine straight on.' The Cat got up and limped to the tiny washroom, to see if the mirror in there gave better results. 'Hot damn!' he said, for the tenth or eleventh time.

Lister lay quietly on the bench as Kryten gingerly bound his ribcage. Lying quietly was about the top of his action potential right now. Even thinking about the slightest movement filled him with dread, and when Kryten's ministrations accidently brought two edges of raw rib bone together, he had to fight back the impulse to wince or scream, either of which would have induced still more agony.

Rimmer stood and hobbled over to the boarded window, his left arm bent in a triangle inside the cast, so he looked as if he was permanently leaning on some invisible bar top. He peered sideways through a knot hole out on to the street's twilight. There was no movement outside. Candlelight flickered through windows over the stores opposite, occasionally silhouetting a watching form. Everybody was waiting for the showdown.

'All right.' Rimmer twisted to face Lister and Kryten. 'It's time for some serious questions to be answered. The virus has spread to the Artificial Reality unit from Kryten. It's robbed us of our special abilities, and rendered us capable of feeling' – Rimmer winced as his collar-bone sent a bolt of agony down his left side – 'pain. Which eventuality, as a matter of interest, I was assured was non-feasible.' He shot a look of pure hate at his prone shipmate.

Lister just moaned, softly.

'Question one: just how serious is this? Can we actually be killed in this reality? Question two: given the demonstrations we've all been kindly given at first hand of the awesome destructive powers of the brothers Apocalypse, does this useless lump of remedial plastic we call "Kryten" stand a Nazi in hell's chance of beating them? Question three: what's to stop the virus spreading to my hologram generation unit and rewriting my personality?' He widened his eyes. 'Anybody? Take your time.'

Lister raised himself painfully on to his elbows. 'OK, Rimmer. I'll give you your answers. Probably, probably not, and nothing.' He eased back down on to the table.

'Oh, good. Sterling. *Excelente*. That's settled then. Marvellous. I suggest we contact old Pete Pessimism down the road and have him knock up four coffins for us, so we can be lying in them conveniently when the Apocalypse bastards ride into town, and save everybody a lot of clearing up.'

The Cat wandered back in from the washroom, with his trousers round his knees. 'Hot damn!' he said. 'Look at this,' he turned and flashed his buttocks. 'My ass is prettier than my face! When we get back, I'm gonna have them surgically swapped.'

Lister said, 'When we get back, we won't be injured. The virus in the AR unit is simulating all this stuff.'

'*If* we get back,' Rimmer corrected.

Lister noticed that Kryten had stopped tending to him, and was staring off, unfocused. 'What is it, Kryten? Are you remembering?'

'Yes,' Kryten said, his Western drawl slipping. 'This . . . badinage. This childish quibbling. It strikes a chord.'

Rimmer was affronted. 'Is he saying we quibble? We don't quibble.'

Lister held up his hand to silence Rimmer. 'Go on, Kryten. Concentrate.'

'I just don't like being accused of quibbling,' Rimmer protested. 'It makes me sound small and petty.'

Lister half-closed his eyes. 'Rimmer, for crying out loud, get a *mind*. Kryten. Think.'

'You,' Kryten focused on Lister. 'Something about you. When I see your face, I get an image of curries and morning breath that could cut through bank vaults.' He turned to Rimmer. 'And you. You seem familiar, too, somehow. I keep getting a name. Smuhhh . . . Smuuh-hehhh . . .?'

'Smeghead? Rimmer offered, tentatively.

'That's it!'

Rimmer beamed. 'He remembers me!'

Kryten turned to the Cat. 'And you. I don't know why, but you make me think of a drive-in wardrobe the size of a warehouse.'

The Cat furrowed his brow. 'Don't know what that

could be.' He snapped his fingers. 'Unless you're thinking of that drive-in wardrobe of mine, which is the size of a warehouse.'

'All right!' Lister twisted his legs and eased himself off the desk top. 'The guns. Do you know how to use them?'

Kryten picked up the chamberless guns and shook his head. 'I know they're important. That's all.'

Lister cringed into the cell room and came back with the gun belt. 'What about this? What about the bullets?'

Kryten took the belt and looked at the dozen bullets. 'I don't understand. They're made of ice. Why don't they melt?'

'Because they're impossible.' Lister was faint from his exertions. 'They can't possibly exist. They must be part of the answer.'

Kryten plucked out one of the bullets and examined it. It was egg-shaped. 'There's some sort of code on them.'

Lister nodded and instantly regretted it. 'Look, whatever part of you is creating the virus antidote has made these guns and these bullets. You have to work out the sequence, I guess.'

'Yes.' Kryten pulled out the bullets and laid them on the desk. He cracked open the cylinder of one of the guns and studied it for a second, and then rifled through the bullets and chose one. 'This, I think, should go here.' He pressed the ice bullet against the smooth metal of the gun cylinder, which yielded magically to allow the bullet inside.

'Brutal,' Lister grinned. 'Can you do the rest?'

'I don't know . . . I think . . . if I had more time . . .'

As he spoke, a clock appeared on the wall behind Kryten's head. There were no figures on it. The hands were set at one minute to twelve. As they watched, the minute hand ticked over, and the clock began to strike.

'High midnight,' Kryten said. His shoulders sagged. 'Too late.'

Rimmer peered out through the knot hole. He could make out the outlines of four horses, lined up at the end of the street. From one side of them, the orange glimmer of the blacksmith's forge illuminated the steam rising from their flanks, cloaking them in an unworldly glow. There was no mistaking the identity of their riders.

'They're here,' he said, softly.

'I've failed.' Kryten shook his head. 'I've failed you all.'

'Not yet.' Lister turned to the Cat. 'Break out the rifles.'

The Cat slipped into the cell room.

Rimmer watched as the four horsemen dismounted and started walking slowly towards the sheriff's office.

The Cat returned with three rifles. Lister took one. 'Kryten, you concentrate on the bullets. We're going to buy you some more time.'

'Excuse me?' Rimmer twisted from his vantage point at the knot hole. '*Pardonnez-moi*? In what way are we buying him time?'

Lister snapped open his Winchester and checked it was loaded. 'We're going to go out and face them.'

'Define "we".'

'We. The three of us. You, me and the Cat.' Lister snapped the rifle closed. 'Have you got a problem with that?'

'Well, now you come to mention it, yes. I do have a minor problemette with that. My head is jammed at an angle of forty-five degrees, my shoulder has a couple of bones jutting out of it, and my right arm is set rigid in plaster of Paris. The Cat has a hole in his foot, and his face is concave. And you, Listy, you don't have two bones in your entire body that are actually connected. One strong gust of wind and you'll come apart like a matchstick model of the Eiffel Tower. How long do you think we'd last against these guys? How long d'you think we'd last against a couple of enthusiastic grannies with Zimmer frames?'

'We just need to distract them for a few minutes.'

'Oh, we'll distract them all right. As soon as they see us

hobble out of the door like refugees from a geriatrics ward, they'll collapse in fits of helpless giggles. Our one hope would be they die laughing. Come on, let's have a sanity check, here. We belong in an intensive care unit, not the OK Corral.'

The Cat thrust a rifle into Rimmer's good hand. 'Let's go, bud.'

'But we could get killed. Forgive me if that's not quite the macho, cowboyistic thing to say, but it's true.'

Lister was buttoning up his shirt. Even that small exertion brought a sheen of sweat to his forehead. 'Look at the alternatives, Rimmer. Unless Kryten can work out the sequence, he's finished, and even if we manage to get back to reality, the ship will be uncontrollable, and we're goners anyway. We've got nothing to lose here. Nothing.' Painfully, he shucked on his jacket. The throwing knives jangled against his chest, and he felt like some demonic surgeon was using his ribcage as a xylophone.

Rimmer raised the rifle so it rested in the crook of his broken arm. 'How about if I cover you through the knot holes?'

The Cat thrust the barrel of his rifle into Rimmer's nostril. 'How about I cover the ceiling with your brains?'

'Just a suggestion. No need to get uppity.'

Lister winced towards the doors. When he reached them, he looked back at Kryten. 'Don't take too long, matey pie,' he said, and pushed through the doors out into the unforgiving gloom of the midnight street.

TWELVE

A small argument later, the Cat prodded Rimmer out on to the sidewalk, thereby rejecting Rimmer's latest plan, which was that they should go out and face the brothers one at a time, with the plan's originator as the last line of defence.

Rimmer's eyes flitted right, which, for him, meant he was looking up. A smoky blue cloud was drifting across the full face of the moon. Someone somewhere was playing a lilting theme on a muted trumpet. War, Pestilence and Famine stood in a line about thirty yards in front of them. Lister stopped. The Cat and Rimmer lined up either side of him.

Famine leered lustily at the sight of Lister. 'You sure you want to do this, boy?' he grinned. 'Because I'm in the mood to suck your liver through a straw.'

'Wait!' A voice like glaciers colliding echoed down the street. A thin, gloved hand laid itself on Famine's chest and effortlessly slapped him aside. From behind the three brothers, the hand's owner stepped forward.

Death Apocalypse was not a handsome fellow. Beneath the black rim of his hat, there was no white in his eyes, just huge, milky grey pupils that stared out of deep sockets, more reptile than human. The pallid, green flesh of his face hung loosely on his skull, as if he was wearing someone else's skin. Below that, there was no colour in his clothing. His black longcoat brushed the ground, the front pushed back over the handles of his guns in their ebony holsters.

He was a good seven feet tall, but there seemed to be nothing but bones under the tight-fitting suit.

'This is a private party,' he rasped. 'You weren't invited.' Even at this distance, Lister swore he could feel the chill of the man's breath.

'Anyone comes down this street has to come through us.' Lister nodded at Rimmer and the Cat, and straight away wished he hadn't. He felt like Bruce Lee had dealt a flurry of rapid blows to his neck with steel nunchakas. He had to concentrate, keep movement to a minimum. The key was delay, delay. Keep the bastard talking.

Death flicked his tongue over his thin lips. There was something obscene about the way he did it. Almost as if the tongue had a life of its own; a slimy, grey snake nestling in his mouth. 'You don't know what you're dealing with, son. Stand aside.'

Lister smiled. 'Don't any of you gutless turdburgers have the *cojones* to take me on? One on one. *Mano a mano?*'

The three brothers all moved forward, but a flick from pappy's eye stopped them dead. 'I'd have thunk you'd had ample demonstration of what my boys can do. But maybe I can spare a couple seconds to punctuate the point.'

On the P of 'point', Death's hand moved. By the time he hit the final consonant, he'd drawn, aimed and fired and the gun was back in its holster.

Lister had no idea where the bullet had gone. He established that it hadn't entered him, and that the other two were still standing. Rimmer was looking puzzled, too. Lister turned and saw the Cat, standing wide-eyed. There was a hole in the middle of his forehead.

'Ouch,' the Cat said, ineffectually, and keeled over backwards.

Death said, 'You catch my drift, now?'

Rimmer knelt beside the Cat and lifted his head. The Cat was still staring, shocked and bewildered. 'Are you all right?' Rimmer asked.

The Cat turned his face to Rimmer's and looked at him, incredulously. 'I've been better,' he said. 'I have a hole clean through the centre of my head, but on the bright side, I now have somewhere to keep a pool cue if both my hands are full.'

Rimmer looked up at Lister. 'He's alive.'

'Then they can't kill us.'

'No,' Rimmer concurred, 'but they can inflict limitless pain on us, which has got to be considered a major negative.'

'It's not real. It's just an illusion.'

'Well,' the Cat chipped in, 'as illusions go, it's a damned good one, bud. I, for one, am totally convinced. I cannot move my body, and I feel like someone's stuffed an umbrella in my brain, opened it up and started twirling it around.'

Lister glanced anxiously at the sheriff's office. No sign of Kryten. Time was the precious commodity here. Whatever the cost, he had to keep them talking. 'We don't need guns,' he said, and threw his rifle down. 'Come on, fat boy. Bare-handed.' He took an unconvincing step forward. He had no doubts that Famine would deal with him swiftly, and extremely painfully but at least it would take the lardy blob *time* to cover the distance between them, and that was all that mattered. 'Come ooooon!' he taunted, palms up, wiggling his fingers. 'Come on, you flab-titted slag.'

Death was looking at him, curious. Famine grunted in anger and hitched back his sleeves, but the thin, gloved hand snaked out and stopped him. Death nodded at War. 'Tommyhawk the son of a bitch.'

War's eyes lit up with delight, and he reached around his back, under his jacket, crouched, and threw.

Lister could see the tomahawk spinning towards him, almost as if it were in slow motion. His brain was telling his body to duck, but his legs weren't keen to bend. He made a half-hearted job of dipping at the waist, but it was too little, too late.

The tomahawk hit him, and suddenly he was spinning over and over, the pale moon orbiting his vision far too quickly to be real.

He hit the floor, dazed. When the dust settled, he looked up. To his astonishment, he was looking up at himself. He could see his body, swaying, his fingers still wiggling. He was thinking '*how could this be happening?*'

The realization swept over him like a tingling wave of static.

The tomahawk had decapitated him.

His headless body turned towards him. He could still control it. Still felt its pain.

Rimmer looked down at his head, horror and disgust and fear jostling his features. 'Lister,' he gasped, 'are you OK?'

'Boy,' the Cat shook his head. 'In the awards for all-time stupid questions, that one takes the Nobel prize.'

Lister's head snarled. 'Come on, you spineless bastards. You're going to have to do better than that.' Through the blur of pain, he turned his body to face them and started advancing, blood gushing generously from his severed neck.

'Wow,' the Cat grinned in admiration. 'Does he have balls of steel, or what?'

Death nodded again, and War reached back, pulled out a bola and hurled it knee-high down the street. The metal balls wrapped around Lister's legs, snapping his knees with a sickening crack, and his poor body pitched forward and lay, wriggling in the dust.

The Cat looked up at Rimmer. 'OK, Flash,' he said. 'You're on. Take 'em.'

Rimmer looked over at the Apocalypse boys. He looked over at the sheriff's office. He looked over at the Apocalypse boys again.

He let the Cat's head down and stood. 'Right,' he said,

rubbing his good hand down the front of his chaps. 'I think I can honestly say I've seen enough to convince me of your awesome awesomeness. As you can see,' he raised his broken arm as far as he could, 'I really am in no condition to offer anything other than the most token resistance, so, under the circumstances I must reluctantly adopt the most prudent course open to me, which is to surrender, totally and unequivocally.' He put his right hand in the air. 'This is me, surrendering. Obviously, we'll have to imagine I've got both hands up. Good enough?'

Pestilence reached down to his belt and pulled his machete out of its sheath. 'I'm gonna carve you up so small, the worms won't even have to chew.'

'Now, now,' Rimmer started to back away from his stricken companions, 'you can't frighten me. I'm a coward – I'm permanently scared.'

Rimmer tried to keep his eyes on Pestilence's crouched advance, but something drew him to look at Death. The lizard eyes were staring at him, strangely. Something about the stare disturbed Rimmer deeply. He slowly became aware of heat in his heels. He looked down.

His boots were smoking.

The heat spread up his feet. He took another step backwards. There was a gruesome squelching sound and the step left him a good inch shorter.

What the smeg was going on now? Sweat drooled down his face in salty panic. He felt as if he was melting from the feet up. Then, the full horror of what was happening slapped him.

He was, in fact, melting from the feet up.

The virus had invaded his hologram generation unit. He looked around for some water, spotted the horse trough and tried to move towards it, but found himself rooted to the spot. Suddenly, his boots gave way and he lost a foot in height. He looked at his arm which was a fizzling, moving mass of seething white boils. He opened his mouth to scream, but only smoke billowed out of his scorched lungs. This was pain beyond pain. An infinity of agonies.

Then he was down to his knees in a puddle of steaming, melted flesh. He tried to will himself unconscious as his thighs gave way and the hellfire reached his reproductive system.

He was aware of the brothers striding past him through his own choking smoke. A stream of sputum from Pestilence's snarled lips hissed as it hit his face and sizzled down his nose.

He was still conscious as his chin slumped to the ground.

Then he was just a pair of eyeballs in a boiling puddle of his own fomenting flesh. And he was still conscious.

On the periphery of his sight, he saw the Cat's eyes flick towards him. 'Hey buddy,' the Cat leered, 'are you all right?'

Lister was trying desperately to swivel his head, but it was no use. The Apocalypse boys were behind him, and he had no way of seeing what was going on. At the very edge of his vision, he spotted the chiselled toe of the Cat's tailored boot. 'Cat!' he yelled, 'can you reach my head with your foot?'

'I can't move, bud,' the Cat yelled back.

'Try! I need you to turn me round.'

The Cat strained, concentrating on his leg muscles. He felt a twitch in his toe. With a supreme effort of will he moved the twitch up his foot to his ankle to his trembling knee, and put everything he had left into one last kick.

He caught Lister's head on the temple, spinning it end over end.

Lister's head landed with a sickening glop in the bubbling gruel that Rimmer had become. He was upside down, his hair glued by the Rimmer mess to the ground, and almost blinded by the throbbing pain from the Cat's kick, but at least he was pointing in the right direction.

The Apocalypse boys were maybe ten steps from the sheriff's office.

Lister yelled out for Kryten, and right on cue, he emerged on to the sidewalk.

The Apocalypse boys stopped.

Kryten had the suit on.

His face was lit by the white gleam of his stetson brim. In the ethereal glow of his perfect white outfit, he looked as if some massive floodlight was trained on him as he clicked a handful of easy steps down on to the street and turned to face his tormentors.

Lister watched the back of Death's head tilt slowly up and down as he took in the view. 'Well, looky here, boys. Ol' Sheriff Carton's got hisself all dudded up to die.'

Pestilence turned and grinned at his father. 'He's gonna look mighty purty once we fit him in his wooden overcoat.'

When Kryten spoke, every twinge of his Western drawl was gone. 'Excuse me, gentlemen, but I don't believe you'll be around to enjoy that particular scenario. Thanks to the courageous sacrifices of my companions, I am of the opinion I am sufficiently empowered to dispose of you on a permanent basis. And so, if you'll forgive the rather confrontational imperative: fill your hands, you scum-sucking molluscs!'

'That right?' Death said, calmly. Lister watched as his hand slipped casually behind his back and tensed. Some hidden mechanism ejected a sawn-off shotgun into the waiting palm.

Lister screamed 'Nowww!' but his shout only served to distract Kryten at the vital moment, and Death's hand whipped round and blasted both barrels at Kryten's chest.

Kryten staggered back as both rounds thumped into him, and in the instant of delay they caused, all the Apocalypse boys had their weapons in their hands and were slapping off shots with a carefree glee of FBI agents at a religious cult's stockade.

Jerking pitifully with each blast, Kryten tottered back, as if some invisible puppeteer were tugging him from behind.

Then silence broke out. Kryten staggered and swayed in the burnt stench of gunsmoke. He seemed, incredibly, to be pretty much intact. Dazed and staggering, but alive.

There was a barrage of metallic clicks as the Apocalypse boys broke open their guns and emptied their spent cases on to the ground.

As they tinked another round of bullets into their smoking chambers, Kryten moved.

Slowly, almost casually, his hands reached down for the black pearl handles of his dove guns.

In an easy, flowing arc, he lifted them clear of the leather, his thumbs cocking back the hammers, and raised them chest high.

His white-gloved fingers squeezed the triggers.

And the guns became birds.

Perfect white doves.

They flew, as if in slow motion, out of Kryten's hands, and as Lister watched, they multiplied, until the air was filled with the beating of wings and a symphony of birdsong.

He felt the pain flooding out of him. His decapitated body kicked off the bolas, stood and picked up his head. He jammed it on to his neck, and looked around.

Where the Apocalypse boys had made their stand, there were just four piles of black ash, slowly being blown away by the wind from the wings.

He turned and looked for his crewmates. The Cat was sitting up, feeling his forehead for holes.

But Rimmer still lay in a molten pool of flesh.

And Kryten was motionless on the ground.

Lister clapped his hands, dreading the reality he might find when he got back there.

THIRTEEN

He slid off the helmet and looked around the ops room. The Cat was beside him, sitting on the deck, struggling with his own helmet. Rimmer's light bee was dangling from the AR unit. Lister picked it up. Melted beyond repair.

He raced over to the medi-bed where Kryten lay. The mechanoid was motionless. Gingerly, Lister peeled back his skull section. Ugly, black smoke wisped up from inside. The circuits were charred and warped.

The Cat peered over his shoulder. 'Bad as it looks?' he asked.

Lister nodded. 'Worse. Kryten and Rimmer are both totalled. Question is: did Kryten cure the virus in time to save the NaviComp?'

The Cat shot out of the room. Lister slipped Kryten's skull piece back reverently, and then bounded down the stairway after him.

When he reached the cockpit, the Cat was already jabbing at the controls. 'He did it! We're in!'

Lister slid into Rimmer's navigation station, trying not to think of the fact that Rimmer was gone, that Kryten had cured the virus and, instead of ridding himself of the infection, had chosen to save the navigation computer. Yet another friend had sacrificed his life for Lister. He'd better make damn sure it wasn't a hollow gesture. He powered up the station. The planet they were hurtling towards filled the screen. 'Less than fifteen minutes to impact. We're too close to steer away. Better slam on the anchors, pronto.'

'Buddy, I am so far ahead of you, you can't see me with an atomic-powered telescope.' The Cat reached out and fired the retros.

They'd been constantly accelerating, now, for several hours, and even with the retros on full power, their forward motion was hardly impeded.

The Cat turned to Lister, flustered. 'What's happening, bud? I'm hitting maximum reverse and it ain't working.'

'It is. We're slowing down.'

The Cat's eyes raced over his read-outs. 'Well, we're not slowing down fast enough to save my boxer shorts from major laundry work.'

'No – it's OK. I think we're going to make it.'

'Think?! Define "think".'

'Well, according to the NaviComp we'll stop completely in . . . just under thirteen minutes. That's so long as the fuel supply holds out.'

The Cat checked the fuel read-out. They were at the bottom of the red. The NaviComp prediction was that, at full thrust, they had just under twelve minutes' fuel. 'Well now, I'm no maths genius, bud, but those numbers don't fill me with good cheer.'

Lister shook his head. 'There's always more left in than the computers reckon.'

'You're sure?'

Lister looked Cat straight in the eyes. 'I'm betting my life on it.'

And there was nothing to do then but wait, and watch the arid face of the oncoming planet slowly reveal its geographical features. Geographical features of which they would become a part if Lister was wrong.

After three years that lasted for ten minutes, the Cat said. 'That's it, bud. We're registering empty.'

But the retros were still firing. Twenty seconds . . . forty seconds . . . and the jets sputtered and died.

Lister stared at the velocity readout. They hadn't stopped.

They'd slowed dramatically, but they were still drifting towards the planet's gravitational field. Once that grabbed them, they'd be accelerating again. To an inevitably lethal collision.

Impact in thirty-three minutes.

'Well,' the Cat flung up his hands, 'that just about rounds off a perfect week.'

'We're not finished yet.'

'Not finished yet? Get out your street map and look up Reality Central. There's no way we're getting out of this in one piece. Or if we are, it's going to be one big, flat piece.'

'There's still . . .' and suddenly, *Starbug* pitched violently to the right.

'Now what?' the Cat yelled in exasperation. 'We're not in enough trouble, the gyroscope has to screw up on us?'

Starbug yawed equally violently to the left.

'It's not the gyro.' Lister lurched to his feet and jammed his hand against the cockpit hatchway, as the ship rocked over again. 'It's *Wildfire*. Come on.'

He staggered into the mid-section and started slipping into his spacesuit. The Cat pitched out after him. Lister yelled, 'Suit up!'

The Cat tottered to the locker and grabbed his suit. 'What's that about *Wildfire*?'

Lister hauled himself into his leggings. 'Ace's ship – it's still tethered outside. When the *Bug* slowed down, *Wildfire* didn't . . .' *Starbug* lurched again. 'It's whirling around up there on the end of its tether, like a conker on a string. And it's dragging us around with it.'

The Cat yanked on his alarmingly light oxygen tank. 'So what's the plan?'

Lister sealed his collar and tugged on his gauntlets. 'We're going to try and shimmy up the tether. If we can make it to

Wildfire, we'll cut ourselves loose, and whammo! We've got ourselves a working ship.'

Lister dug out his oxygen tank. Seven minutes of air. The Cat had nine. Would that be enough? Lister shrugged and clamped the tank. They were fresh out of choices. He sealed up his helmet and stepped into the airlock.

Outside, the face of the planet looked shockingly large. *Widfire One* was indeed whirling overhead like a stone in a sling, but with every revolution *Starbug*'s counterweight was slowing down the spin and the climb didn't look nearly as lethally impossible as Lister had secretly feared.

They scrambled up the roof with magnetic clamps, and scurried over to the point where Commander Rimmer's ship was anchored to *Starbug*.

It would be impossible to jet up to *Wildfire* without risking being sliced in two by the rotating tether. There was nothing for it but to grab the line as it span by and shimmy up.

The Cat went first. Despite his injured leg, he made it look easy, and was halfway up before Lister moved.

Lister didn't find it quite so straightforward.

The line's spin was at its most violent near the bottom, and a couple of times, he was almost yanked loose.

When he finally clambered within grabbing distance of *Wildfire*'s cockpit, he had fifty-one seconds of oxygen left.

He tumbled into the cockpit, and squeezed in, on top of the Cat. His eyes raced across the control fascia. It was all disturbingly unfamiliar. 'Where's the damn cockpit cover control?' He saw the lever by his left hand, and reasoned it controlled either the cockpit cover or the ejector seat. He pulled it, anyway.

The cockpit swung down, squashing him on to the Cat.

Lister's air ran out. He sucked, but nothing came. It occurred to him that the craft might not be fitted with its own oxygen regenerator.

He ran his eyes over the controls again, but he was beginning to feel light-headed and his vision was getting giddy.

He leaned in closer. There was a switch marked 'OR'. It was either 'OR' or 'QP', but Lister had given up caring. He flicked it anyway, and tugged off his helmet.

And breathed.

He spent a few moments making sense of the controls, and when he thought he'd grasped them, he pressed the button that shot loose the tethering line.

The Cat saw that Lister was breathing successfully, and took off his own helmet. 'You reckon you can fly this thing?'

Lister shrugged. 'Looks self-explanatory. Everything's marked up: tertiary, secondary and primary ignition. A lot of it's computer-controlled, anyway.'

'So, we head back for *Red Dwarf*?'

Lister shook his head. 'What's there for us, now?'

'My entire suit collection, for one thing.'

'There's no Holly, no Kryten, no Rimmer . . .'

'True, but on the bright side, there's no Rimmer. Besides, where else can we go?'

'We can go anywhen.'

'Huh?'

'Ace has programmed this little baby for another dimension jump. I reckon we fire her up, and see where she takes us.'

'Where's that gonna be?'

'Dunno. I don't think Ace knew himself. Another place. Another dimension. Somewhere along our own destiny lines where our lives took a different path. You up for it?'

The Cat shrugged. 'I have no particular plans for the rest of this reality.'

'Right then.' Lister leaned forward and flicked on the tertiary ignition. 'Let's see what's out there.'

FOURTEEN

A combination of the intense G force and Lister's generous buttocks crushing him down rendered the Cat blissfully unconscious for the jump between dimensions. When he came to, he was more than happy to be in one piece and, apparently, still breathing. 'Did we make it?

Lister hunched his shoulders. 'As far as I can tell.'

'Where are we?'

Lister looked down at the control panel, but the readouts were blank. 'No idea. The panel's down. Radar's dead.'

'Well, wherever we are, we are getting out of this cockpit, bud. I'm so badly crushed, they're going to have to dig my testicles out of this seat with a pickaxe.'

'Hang on.' The control display flickered. 'Coming back on line. Radar shows something fairly huge close by, about six miles long and three miles across. If it's a ship, it could be . . .'

The computer screen indicated an incoming message. Lister flicked on the comms panel.

'. . . ship. Repeat: calling unidentified ship. Come in, please.'

It was Rimmer's voice.

'This is the mining ship *Red Dwarf*. You have encroached on our airspace without warning, which we must consider an act of aggression. Ergo, we surrender. Totally and unequivocally. Do you copy?'

Lister grinned and switched to 'send'. 'Rimmer, you are such a world–class smeghead.'

'Lister? Switching to visual.'

Rimmer's image appeared on screen. He peered forward, baffled and confused. 'Lister??'

Kryten squeezed in beside him. 'Sir? Is it you?'

'It's me.'

Rimmer said. 'How can we be sure it's you? Tell us something only you could know.'

Lister thought. 'I know gazpacho soup is served cold,' he tried.

Rimmer gritted his teeth and nodded violently. 'It's him all right, the obnoxious little gimboid.'

Kryten looked perplexed. 'I don't understand, sir. You're dead.'

'Dead?'

'We buried you some years ago. You and the Cat. You were both trapped in a lethally addictive game. There was nothing we could do to save you.'

The Cat poked his head over Lister's shoulder. 'Who are you calling dead, dog-chew head?'

'You're both alive? But how?'

'We'll tell you when we get on board. If we don't get out of this ship soon, the Cat's conkers are going to be crushed beyond recognition.'

'Well.' Rimmer's forehead wrinkled. 'You picked a rare old time to show up. We're about to be . . .'

Kryten cut him off. 'There'll be time aplenty for that, sir.' He leaned towards the screen. 'Head for docking bay four seven five, sir. I'll have a vindaloo sauce sandwich waiting for you. Signing off.'

Kryten reached down and ended the transmission.

Lister sighed with his entire body. They'd encountered a dimension where he and the Cat had died playing 'Better Than Life'. Where Rimmer and Kryten had never entered the game to rescue them. It wasn't quite what he'd been hoping for, but it was better than the dimension he'd left behind. At least Kryten, Rimmer and, presumably, Holly were still around.

Lister grabbed the throttle stick and brought *Wildfire* around in a slow, lazy arc. For as long as he could remember, all he'd wanted was to get back home.

He'd always considered that Earth was his home, but as the ugly red brute of a ship loomed into view, he felt a tingling in his stomach, and thought maybe he'd been wrong.

Maybe this was home.

The rear jets flared and *Wildfire* looped gently towards the docking bay.

EPILOGUE

The Difference — 2

Arnold J. Rimmer, aged seven and almost five-sevenths, is crouched at the starting line for the Junior C two-hundred-yards dash.

His sports kit, handed down from his brother, Howard, is two sizes too big. But Arnold has spent the last three evenings sewing, and though his needlework leaves a lot to be desired, his stitches too large and uneven, the shorts and T-shirt hug his body tightly. His spiked running shoes are padded at the back with heel grips he's made himself out of papier mâché, and the fit is snug.

There are seven other boys at the starting line, and there's no doubt in anyone's mind that Rimmer will beat them all.

He has an unfair advantage over them.

While the rest of his class of the previous year have moved up to Junior B, young Arnold Rimmer has been deemed scholastically unsuitable to join them.

He's been Kept Down.

All his mother's entreaties failed to impress the headmaster, and he's spent the last three terms in a class where he's a good foot taller than the rest of the kids.

And to everyone's astonishment, Arnold has started to excel. The arithmetic that had seemed so ungraspable to him a year before has now become a breeze. The second time around, he actually understands his French lessons. He's even begun to develop a knack for the piano.

He looks to his left for the starter to signal marks, and

Bull Heinman winks at him. A year ago, Rimmer had be-longed to the chapped legs and doctor's note brigade when it came to ball games. Nowadays, he's the one who picks the teams. He's one of Bull's blue-eyed boys.

Nowadays, he's a leader.

He made a tough decision when his mother failed to save him. He decided, since he couldn't rely on his parents, he'd better start relying on himself. He could either wallow in shame and self-pity at being Kept Down, or he could roll up his sleeves and get stuck into making something of his life.

He discovered that the twelve inches he had over his classmates didn't single him out for ridicule, it made them look up to him.

And already today, he's won first-place medals for seven events. Winning the two-hundred-yard dash will net him a school record. He will have surpassed all the achievements of all his brothers.

Not that they'll hold it against him. They'll be there at the finish line, cheering him on like blue thunder. Slapping his back when he wins, and carting him off on their shoulders to the winners' podium.

His mother will be there, too, of course. Not cheering. Nothing so undignified. She'll watch him break the black-and-yellow once again, and when he's looking over, she'll favour him with the familiar nod. Then she'll turn and walk to the refreshment tent, and when he's collected his medal, he'll follow her there and she'll have chilled lemonade waiting for him.

And she won't say 'congratulations' or 'well done', but while he's sipping his well-earned drink, she might brush a stray lock of hair from his forehead, and that will be enough.

And suddenly, Rimmer's aware that the boy on his right is mumbling. He turns. It's Bobby Darroch. His eyes are screwed up like a new-born puppy's. Rimmer can't quite make out what the kid's saying, but it sounds as if it could be a whispered prayer.

He's a good sprinter, little Darroch. Rimmer usually picks him first for team games, partly because of his speed, and partly because the boy's parents divorced just before Christmas, and his father leaving home has been pretty tough on him.

The boy opens his eyes and glances nervously across at the spectators. Rimmer follows his glance and sees a man wave in his direction.

Bobby turns back and sets his eyes on the track before him. His teeth are clenched. His knuckles whiten against the red clay.

And the whistle blows, and Rimmer hoists off his front legs instinctively.

Before the slowest starter has left the line, Rimmer is three strides ahead of his nearest rival.

He can hear his brothers' raucous yells as he pounds away at the track, his arms and legs pumping rhythmically in synch, his breathing easy and measured.

And though it's not the thing to do, as he crosses the hundred-yard mark, he chances a look over his shoulder.

Bobby Darroch is right behind him. His face is purple with exertion. His balance is wrong. His arms are wind-milling round. He's not keeping up with good technique, he's keeping up with sheer willpower.

Rimmer looks forward again. He finds another gear and pulls away. And with thirty yards to go, he looks back. Darroch must surely be digging deep into reserves Rimmer didn't know he had. He's two paces behind, running for all he's worth.

And he doesn't stand a chance.

Even if he keeps his mad pace up, there simply isn't enough track left for him to make up the gap.

And suddenly Rimmer understands that Darroch has to win this race. He simply has to.

Falling over and making it appear like an accidental trip is not the easiest thing to do, but Rimmer is determined to make it look good.

He slides his front foot slightly too far over, and manages to catch his heel with the toe of his oncoming shoe.

It is a spectacular enough tumble. He crashes headlong on to the clay just yards from the tape.

And to his horror, his momentum sends him skidding forwards, skinning his knees and propelling him towards the line.

For one awful moment, it looks like he's going to win, anyway, but little Darroch drags some extra effort from some hidden place and breasts the tape just inches before Rimmer's skidding nose.

Darroch collapses, spent, to the ground and Rimmer tumbles into him.

The purple-faced boy opens his eyes and looks into Rimmer's face. He smiles and says, 'Thanks, Ace.'

Rimmer curls his forehead. 'Nonsense, old sport. Fair and square.' He offers his hand and the two boys help each other to their feet.

Rimmer looks down at his raw knees. He tests his weight on his right ankle and winces. He'll be limping for a week.

His brothers crowd around him, offering commiserations and inspecting his injuries. Over their shoulders, he spots his mother.

She is looking at him, puzzled. Her head tilts slightly to one side. She's asking him 'why'?

Rimmer simply smiles and shrugs.

After all, losing isn't nothing.